I0675434

The Adventurous Young Philosopher
THEO HOSHEN
of Toronto

The Adventurous Young Philosopher
THEO HOSHEN
of Toronto

CHARLES BLATTBERG

ANGST PATROL

Published by Angst Patrol Books, 2013
Montreal, QC, Canada

Library and Archives Canada Cataloguing in Publication

Blattberg, Charles
    The adventurous young philosopher Theo Hoshen of Toronto /
Charles Blattberg.

Issued also in an electronic format.
ISBN 978-0-9917926-1-0 (bound).--ISBN 978-0-9917926-0-3 (pbk.)

    I. Title.

PS8603.L384A64 2013   C813'.6   C2012-908225-2

To Mark and Jay

CONTENTS

THEO HOSHEN

CONTENTS

CHAPTER I

In which we are introduced to our hero, Theo Hoshen of Toronto

In a college of the University of Toronto, the name of which I shall always remember, there was a young philosophy student, one of those who carried his books in a backpack, worked on an old computer at home, and used a bike to get around. At this moment we find Theo Hoshen, for that is his name, in Diablo's, the college coffee bar. He has just finished yet another cup – his fourth – but not for the reason that students are ordinarily seen drinking so much coffee there. For he had no exam to study for, nor a paper with some fast approaching deadline to write; indeed, it was only a few weeks into the beginning of term. No, Theo Hoshen wished to stay awake solely that he might continue reading or, rather, devouring the book that he had in his hands: Aristotle's great text, *The Nicomachean Ethics*.

Now it must be said that it was only quite recently that this undergraduate had begun studying works of philosophy written before modern times. In fact it was not until the previous summer had already commenced that he first perused some of the texts listed on the syllabus for his upcoming course in ancient ethics. From that moment on, however, he was unable to stop. Nights and days, and days and nights, passed as if in a blur, Theo Hoshen having become totally absorbed in these old books. And what he encountered there so fascinated, amazed and excited him that when September finally came and the course in question finally began he was astonished to find that the professor said nothing about how wonderful were the texts they would be studying.

Theo Hoshen suspected that he knew the reason why, however. Because where the ancients held that nothing was more important than honour and the common good, we moderns cared instead for dignity, the respect for the individual, as well as for efficiency. *But even these misguided ideals could not exist without honour*, he thought to himself. And then he read some more.

Needless to say, Theo Hoshen looked bad and felt worse. Normally, he was quite a handsome lad, with curly dark brown hair and piercing brown eyes. And though somewhat thin he was far from being *tantum pellis et ossa*; in fact, he had even recently begun to develop muscles. This was, curiously enough, the result of a particularly long night of reading, one which led him to conclude that the longstanding disdain in which he had held the body was a mistake. For Aristotle taught that, in addition to the theoretical reasoning of the philosophers, scientists and mathematicians, there were practical forms of reason, and these required all who would engage in them to remain intimately connected with their feelings and desires and so with their bodies. Hence the body, Theo Hoshen concluded, was not simply a source of irrational passions; it should thus be well tended to. Regular trips to the gym soon followed.

Theo Hoshen still felt somewhat torn, however. Because Aristotle also showed that theoretical reasoning should take precedence over the practical and so that the true philosopher ought to be above concerns with the merely corporeal. This goes some way to explaining why the young man had allowed his eyes to become encircled with the darkest of shadows – so black that some who saw him wondered if he had recently been in a fight. And along with foregoing much sleep, Theo Hoshen also often forgot to eat. There were times when his hunger pangs just could not be ignored, but rather than allow this to distract from his reading he would rush into the kitchen he shared with his two housemates, empty a bag of frozen corn and two scoops of butter into a bowl, and melt the whole for precisely twelve minutes in the microwave – all the while keeping his eyes glued to the pages of the book that he had in his free hand. Theo Hoshen knew that this did not make for the healthiest of diets, but he reassured himself with the thought of the multivitamin pill that he took without fail every single day. Regardless, as his whole way of seeing the world was undergoing a remarkable transformation he was not going to let his stomach interfere with that. And he was right to do so, for though he did not know it at the time, the day would come when his conversion to Aristotelian philosophy would lead him to perform an act of world-historic significance.

Finishing his coffee now, and utterly exhausted, he resolved to return home and continue reading in bed. Once there, however, he fell fast asleep, waking only long enough to inform his housemates that he was feeling rather unwell. In fact, he had developed quite a fever and, in his delirium, he was overheard saying many strange things: about philosophy, about honour, and about Sandy Horne (that alluring bass player from The Spoons of Burlington, Ontario). Needless to say, this worried the others a great deal, and so they retired to the kitchen to discuss what action to take.

"Such a *tit*," announced Simon, who had come all the way from England to study optical physics. "I mean, I told him this'd happen. So what, we ring his parents?"

"He'll be fine," countered Avigail, another philosophy student, albeit one whose brown eyes, matching brown hair, and high cheekbones meant that though, or perhaps because, she cared not a whit for her appearance she was far prettier than Theo Hoshen. She was also much further along academically than he was for she was soon to submit her doctoral thesis whereas he rarely submitted anything. "He does look sick," she allowed, "but that's what comes from reading Aristotle three days straight. I never should've shown him my Iris Murdoch book, the one with *The School of Athens* on the cover – he just kept staring and staring at Aristotle's steady outstretched hand." Avigail then proceeded to inform Simon that Aristotelian philosophy was utterly obsolete, for its epistemology was but a form of mysticism.

"And what's that, then, an epistemology?" inquired Simon, regretting the question the moment he'd posed it. Simon had begun to wonder if his decision to move into a house with two philosophy students had been a mistake. But he had needed a room and the rent was far from steep.

"It's a theory of knowledge," explained Avigail. "It's what every good philosopher needs to have worked out before he or she starts thinking about anything else."

"Right," said Simon, who then quickly changed the subject: "Look, Viggy, what d'you make of the dodgy way Hoshen-boy's been acting of late? I mean, you know him well."

"Not much better than you," she corrected. "I've been way too busy with my thesis to speak with him or anyone else much. Theo always wants to talk shop but there's just not much in it for me. You see, the guy's become totally obsessed with the Greeks – real philosophers gave up on that stuff back in the Enlightenment."

"What, as opposed to fake philosophers? How can you tell?" Avigail did not know how to respond to the question, or even whether it was a real question, and so she allowed Simon to continue: "Alright then," he said, "how about we take the books he's reading right now out of his room? Least that way he won't be able to open them as soon as he gets up. And then we could distract him."

"Distract him? With what?"

"I don't know, philosopher's porn? Got any pictures of naked chicks arguing?"

"And when he flips 'cause his books are missing," objected Avigail, "what'll we say then, that some wizard whooshed in here and took them? Even Theo'd find that hard to believe. *Oh alright*, I guess I could claim that I had to borrow them for some reason and didn't want to bother him. Doubt he'll buy it, though, and anyway he'll just take them back. Hey I know," she said with a giggle, "we could say there's been an accident. You know, like a fire…"

"Don't think so," said Simon with a chuckle of his own. "Still, we'd better come up with something. I'm telling you, Viggy, he's not just knackered. He's on his way to becoming a real nutter."

"Yeah, well, we all have our little idiosyncrasies." Of course Avigail was referring to none other than the Englishman standing before her. Simon had seemed quite ordinary at first: he was of average height and build and, except for the accent, appeared to be little different from the other science students she knew. But then she noticed how, despite his never attending the gym, his meagre diet and innumerable daily push-ups meant that he had virtually no fat on his body, it being covered with what appeared to be hundreds of tiny yet incredibly defined muscles. Simon also sported a crew-cut that he trimmed almost daily with an electric razor, his only appliance, and in the middle of his angular face sat a pair of extremely thin nerdish glasses. As for his wardrobe, it was strictly t-shirts and jeans. Yet despite all of this it was only when Simon politely declined her offer of a houseplant for his completely bare room that Avigail began to suspect there was something peculiar. For its lack of furniture and other accoutrements turned out to be no accident.

"I like to travel light," he explained.

"But the trip's over," she objected. "I mean, your master's going to take, what, at least two years?"

"Probably longer, the way my research's carrying on."

"So you're not really going anywhere."

"Yeah, but I don't see why that means I've got to take on such a responsibility."

"You're kidding."

"Look," said Simon with what appeared to be a straight face, "the thing's got to be watered, right? And doing that well – regularly, not too much and not too little – it'll be a distraction."

"A house-plant distraction?" asked Avigail rhetorically.

"Exactimundo," confirmed Simon. "You Canadians. So casual about the environment."

Returning to our young Aristotelian, Theo Hoshen slept deep into the afternoon of the next day. His books no longer lay on the floor beside his bed but he took no notice of this when he awoke. Emerging from his room now, he encountered Avigail in the hall.

"You're up," she said with a titter. "How're you feeling?"

"Fine, Avigail, just fine. In fact, I am feeling so well that I would like to go dancing."

"Dancing? Really?"

"Yes. This is Friday, right? Reznikoff's will be open tonight."

"Rezzie's? Really?"

"Yes, really. There has been enough reading, Avigail. Let us roll."

CHAPTER II

About some strange goings-on one Friday night at Reznikoff's Pub

And so it was that, late that very evening, our three housemates could be found getting their hands stamped at the entrance to Reznikoff's, the University College student pub. By day, it was no more than a large room that served as a basement cafeteria; by night, with all of its tables and chairs pushed to one side and turntables and speakers set up at the other, it managed to project a certain panache.

Perhaps this had something to do with its name, which paid homage to one Ivan Reznikoff, a ghost that was reputed to haunt the gothic college's halls. As legend had it, Reznikoff was a Russian immigrant who worked as a stone mason when the college was built in the late 1850s. Unfortunately for him, his lady turned out to have an eye for another of the masons, a certain Diablo who hailed from one of the Greek islands. Apparently, among the many gargoyles that Diablo had carved into the side of the building was one that represented Reznikoff and another, directly beside it, Diablo himself laughing behind the cuckolded man's back. Needless to say, when Reznikoff learned of his girlfriend's infidelity he confronted Diablo and the two were soon raining blows down upon each other as they tumbled through the unfinished college's halls and then up its recently completed tower. It was the Russian who fell: he swung a little too enthusiastically on a heavy axe that he had aimed at his adversary's head; it missed and carried him over the edge. Fearing the authorities, Diablo is said to have buried the body in secret on the grounds somewhere, and indeed many years later the great fire that engulfed the college during the Conversazione Dance on Valentine's Day 1890 (someone had tripped and dropped a tray of trimmed oil lamps on the southeast staircase) led to the unearthing of an unidentified man's remains.

Now it must be said that none of our three housemates cared much for this story, indeed for history of any sort – they were students of philosophy and natural science, after all. What drew them to the pub, like most of its other patrons, was the music: tunes replete with synthpop beats, tape loops, and sombre electric guitar chords. There was also the fact that it was so dark that one could drink as much, and dance as oddly, as one wished without drawing much attention.

Once inside, the three made their way to the bar where they purchased beer tickets and promptly traded them in for three cups each. It was not long before Theo Hoshen had consumed all of his, leaving Simon and Avigail to marvel at how little the alcohol seemed to affect him.

"Guess you've got to be sober first," muttered Simon. But Theo Hoshen only ignored the remark.

"And now, if you will excuse me," he announced before heading for the dance floor, whereupon he began the jerky, off-beat movements that constituted his unique interpretation of the music.

"I'm telling you," shouted Simon to Avigail over the din, "there's something really not quite right about this one."

"Well it's not like his dancing's any weirder than the others," countered Avigail. "And he's not feverish anymore. Plus he's taken a break from reading."

"Then what's with the shirt?" objected Simon. "A mite formal for Rezzie's, don't you think? Or haven't you noticed that he's been doing himself up like a dog's dinner of late? And what about his posture? Really, I mean it; just look at him: he's always standing there, and even sitting, straight as a board.

Shit, even his voice is different now, all low. *And* there are the missing contractions."

"The what?"

"Listen to him. He'll say 'he is' instead of 'he's', or 'how are you?' instead of 'how're you?' It's fuckin' weird."

"Get out," protested Avigail.

"I'm not taking the piss. Why would I? The guy's going wacko; why we're partying with him I've no idea. I'm telling you, Viggy, it won't be long before we'll have to find someone else to pay his rent."

"Oh so *that's* what's worrying you."

But Simon did not answer, leaving Avigail to turn and peer through the darkness to the dance floor. Theo Hoshen was no longer there, however. Instead, she noticed him flashing his stamped hand to the bouncer at the entrance; evidently, he was making his way outside to one of the washrooms down the hall. She told herself to remember to check his speech upon his return.

As Theo Hoshen proceeded down the hallway he passed a student with his arm around a young woman, presumably his girlfriend. Yet the young man was staring, and in a very menacing manner, directly at our hero. This reminded Theo Hoshen of something, of a look that he nevertheless could not quite place, and so he began to ponder it as he entered the washroom. Then, overcoming his forgetfulness, that devourer of all things, he recalled that he used to see the very same look quite often during his days as a junior high school student. For Theo Hoshen had attended what was by Toronto standards a problematic institution, located as it was in one of the city's poorest neighbourhoods. At Mapledale Junior High one could expect to witness a fight almost every single day, for the school counted many, many bullies among its student body. They were the ones who would throw Theo Hoshen the kind of look he had just received from the kid in the hall. Its message was a simple one: fight? To direct one's gaze downwards meant that one wished to decline the offer, whereas to meet it and hold the stare, even if only for a moment, was to accept and so declare that one was prepared to duel either in the schoolyard during lunch hour or after school should the lunch period have already passed. Such challenges were usually issued in the mornings, however, since this ensured that, if accepted, the issuer would be guaranteed a good-sized audience of outdoor diners for the bout.

Now Theo Hoshen had been a skinny, nerdish boy. This meant that he had little choice but to master the swift lookdown. In fact, like all of Mapledale's nerds, he found it necessary to develop a series of techniques in order to avoid getting a beating. These were especially useful in the locker room directly after gym class, perhaps the most dangerous of all the school's settings. For it was in that room that one could expect to find oneself undressed and in close proximity to the perhaps two, and sometimes even three, bullies present in every single class. The experienced nerd, or 'browner' as the bullies would call them (for propriety's sake, the reader is invited to look the term up), would thus have so honed his senses that the moment there was a pause in the goings-on in the room he could identify precisely which bully was likely to start up. The next step was to engage him in conversation. "How about Keon's assist last night?" or "Palmateer really sucked, eh?" were often effective openers, since references to the travails of the Toronto Maple Leafs hockey team rarely failed to elicit a response. And once involved in hockey talk, even the meanest of bullies knew that it was bad form to begin pounding on one's interlocutor.

All this Theo Hoshen recalled as he stood in the washroom.

Then, after finishing his business, he stepped outside to find that the young man was still there, still staring his menacing stare. Only now his arm was no longer around his girlfriend but, like the other one, at his side. And both of his fists were clenched.

He certainly wants to fight, thought Theo Hoshen to himself. Yet he could not recall ever having even seen the young man before. And then he realized something surprising: not only were his feelings wholly free of fear, but there was even something that appealed to him about the situation. Partly, of course, this was because he was no longer a skinny little nerd. But mostly it was the fact that here was an opportunity to exchange blows with a drunken man in a pub, and this struck Theo Hoshen as a truly classic instance of the genre. Because if he was finally going to get into a fight, then this, surely, was a most appropriate setting. Moreover, the thought struck him that his challenger may have taken him for an interloper, which is to say for a student from one of the university's other colleges. If this was what had so upset him, that he felt a need to defend his college's honour, well then Theo Hoshen could hardly imagine a more worthy adversary.

Then again, perhaps he should simply correct the young man and explain that he, too, was a member of this college. Yet might doing so not make him appear cowardly? *Better to say nothing*, he thought. This seemed to be his adversary's policy as well, for he did nothing but stare and stare; indeed, the situation was becoming quite awkward. *Perhaps he is waiting for me to do something*, thought Theo Hoshen. And so he said what he assumed was expected of him on such an occasion:

"Would you care to step outside?"

The young man appeared somewhat startled at first. But it

was not long before he announced that this was precisely what he wished to do. And so, with a shrug of his shoulders, Theo Hoshen began to climb the stairs towards the exit. His soon-to-be fighting partner followed closely behind.

This could get messy, thought Theo Hoshen on his way up, and so he removed his shirt – not thinking of how his under-shirt revealed him, good Aristotelian that he was, to be no stranger to the gym (why, to some, he could even have been taken for a giant). And then, when he reached the top, he turned and faced his opponent.

What now? Theo Hoshen wondered. *How do these things actually begin?* Looking about, he noticed a handful of stu-dents mulling around. They, too, were more than a little per-plexed about what was transpiring before them. Yet before he could look back at his adversary, Theo Hoshen received from him such a wallop in the stomach that he immediately keeled over, unable to take another breath. The wind had been knocked right out of him. This meant that he could but lie there in his very sore predicament as the young man standing above him contemplated his next move: was it to be a kick to the side or a kick to the head? In the moment that it took to make the decision, however, the young man heard the voice of his girlfriend:

"Fighting again, eh?" she demanded, although in truth it was more of a hypothetical question. "Well you know what I think about that." And then, without another word, she struck him. The young man tottered there for a moment, whereupon down he went, albeit only to his knees at first and tilting somewhat in Theo Hoshen's direction. Another blow, however, and there he was: lying prostrate directly on top of our hero. "That one's for Laura Secord and Viola Desmond," she announced inexplicably. "They had a reason." And then: "I'm breaking up with you, you know," following which she windmilled her arms and let go with yet another powerful stroke. Satisfied, she simply walked away.

It was Theo Hoshen's fine fortune that there was a good Samaritan in the crowd, one who responded to the opening by reaching over and rolling the now helpless belligerent off of our young philosopher. This allowed the latter to catch his breath. It took no small amount of time for him to do so, and yet when he finally managed to pick himself up he could see that his adversary had chosen to remain lying upon the ground emitting groans.

"I *am* from this college, you know," was all that Theo Hoshen could think to say. And then, with his head held perhaps a bit too high, he left. Back down the stairs he went, through the dark cloud of music and in search of Simon and Avigail.

He found them both on the edge of the dance floor, beer cups in hand. Simon was shouting into Avigail's ear, complaining about the volume of the music:

"Flippin' hell," he cried. "There's just no way to pull with all this row. I mean, how the fuck will the birds hear my accent?"

"Your what?" shouted Avigail.

"Accent! It's the second best part of the Englishman. Hey look, it's Hoshen-boy."

"Theo," exclaimed Avigail, "where were you?"

"It was the strangest thing," came the young philosopher's reply.

"What was?"

"Well, there was this student..." But then he stopped himself. For Theo Hoshen realized that this was not at all the kind of story he cared to relate, so foolish and shameful did the recent event appear to him. Evidently, he was in need of a different, more worthy adversary. "If you will excuse me," he said, making as if he suddenly had somewhere important to be. And then he promptly turned and left.

"See," said Simon. "No contractions."

Back home that evening, the physics student managed to squeeze the story of what had happened out of Theo Hoshen.

"So the wanker offered you out?" inquired Simon with a bemused look upon his face.

"Well, given the way he was staring at me, it seemed appropriate to suggest that we step outside," explained Theo Hoshen.

"Just like that?" Simon chuckled. "Straight away? That's not how you do it, mate; you skipped a bunch of steps. You don't just go right to having arms like that – you've got to exchange some serious words first." This was the voice of experience speaking, for Simon had been involved in more than one scrap back in England. "The guy might've backed down."

"It was my first time," confessed Theo Hoshen. "I should have tried dialogue. It was wrong of me."

"Whoa there," said Simon. "Your timing was off, is all. But where you *really* blew it was when it was supposed to start. I mean, you don't just bloody well stand there and wait for it. You're damn lucky with what you got – if he'd wanted to he could've hoofed you in the bollocks. And that there's rule number one, by the way: *always protect your kit*. Number two is that once it's on then off you go; no jerking around. You hit them with everything you've got: head-buttin', ear-biting, hoof'n'em and the like. Trust me on this one, 'cause it ain't something you're gonna pick up from some book. I don't even read books, did you know that? Not real books, anyhow, which are a load of crap, just maths and physics texts. Wha'ever. You get my point, right, about going all out?"

"I believe so," replied Theo Hoshen.

"'Cause it's the only way to cash in. Really. Either that or you might as well just put together a suicide note right now and stick it in your wallet. Yup, that's the law of the earth: everyone's either a friend or an enemy and if you wait for your enemy to hit first then you're in major pain for sure – *if* you're lucky. No, you got to nuke 'em right off – either that or you're done like dinner. So can you do it, Hoshen-boy, can you let the gang in you out?"

"The *gang* in me? There is no gang in me."

"There'd better be if you're not gonna get pasted. I'm telling ya, when you're in a real fight it's all or nothing. There's just no other way. Remember that."

"Fine," said Theo Hoshen. "I shall. Next time."

CHAPTER III

Concerning an astounding event at Convocation Hall, and how it led Theo Hoshen to a most interesting discussion with members of the Engineering Society's venerable Brute Force Committee

It was not long after Theo Hoshen's great discovery of Aristotelian philosophy that he resolved to audit a course in introductory psychology. Not that he expected to learn much about the Good there; his interest was strictly that of someone who wished to know his enemy better. For Theo Hoshen was aware that, in these calamitous times of ours, it was not philosophers but psychologists who were responsible for the school of thought that served as the chief rival to his own: cognitivism.

At base, cognitivism is a scientific conception of the mind according to which our mental functions consist of information processing. To the cognitivist, in short, the mind is like a computer.

How ridiculous, thought Theo Hoshen, *when so much of our thinking depends on context in a way that does not – and never will – compute. These cognitivists clearly have no soul.* Thus did he resolve to develop a thorough grasp of their utterly wrongheaded theory. *Perhaps one day I shall write a book – a vicious attack on, a stab to the heart of, this cognitivism. But for that I will need to know it much, much better.*

And so it was that, first thing Monday morning, an eager Theo Hoshen could be seen riding his bike to attend what would be his third lecture in Psychology 100. The course was being taught in no ordinary classroom, since its immense enrolment – the largest in the whole university – meant that its lectures had to be delivered in the great auditorium of Convocation Hall (or "Con Hall" as the students referred to it). The building, a brown-bricked, green-domed rotunda with six impressive pillars adorning its entrance, was modeled on the Sorbonne theatre in Paris and it seated an astounding seventeen hundred people. It was already almost full that day, however, which meant that Theo Hoshen had to find himself a place up towards the back of one of its six immense balconies.

Soon the professor, a distinguished scholar approaching retirement, mounted the stage and began his lecture. Many years had passed since he had first taught in that room and he had truly come to master it; indeed, he managed to hold the attention of almost every single student present for each and every lecture's full hour. Of no small assistance in this was the remote microphone that he had tucked into his shirt pocket, for it allowed his voice to be carried over speakers and so into the far corners of the hall. It also freed him to walk about on the stage as he lectured, though given what those lectures contained Theo Hoshen could not help but notice the irony. For it was at the Lyceum in Athens that Aristotle had founded the Peripatetic school of philosophy, whose name derives from the ancient Greek word for walking. And yet this professor was certainly no Aristotelian.

"You will recall from where we left off last week," he began, "that the researcher in abnormal psychology must face many challenges which are often unique to the disorder in question. Consider our subject for today: suicide. Much of what we know about it is based on 'psychological autopsies': interviews with family members, friends, and physicians that are conducted soon after the death. Though they are subject to memory biases, intentional distortions, and many other problems, researchers have no choice but to perform them."

Suddenly, and without the slightest warning, there came a shout from somewhere in the audience:

"Not necessarily!" And before anyone could react, there was another, this time from the opposite side of the hall:

"No, Steve, no! Don't do it!"

"I must," came the reply. "For science!"

And then, to everyone's amazement, two hooded men in dark blue overalls and hardhats appeared and threw what Theo Hoshen immediately perceived to be a stuffed mannequin over the side of one of the balconies. It had a noose around its neck and, after falling for ten feet or so, the rope caught with a loud and violent snap. Needless to say, those students sitting directly below who could see only the soles of the now swinging dummy's shoes were confronted with what they believed was a truly horrific sight. Many began to scream, whereas most of the others in the hall burst out laughing instead.

"God dammit!" shouted the professor. The pranksters took this as their cue to leave. So up they fled, along the rows of their respective balconies and into the back corridor; evidently, they were heading for the stairs. To everyone's surprise, the venerable but enraged professor gave chase. He bounded down one side of the stage and then back into the main perimeter corridor hoping to head them off before they reached one of the exits. Of course this meant that he had little time to disengage his microphone.

"Fuckers!" he yelled, his voice booming out over the speakers. The remote even picked up his footsteps as he ran. "God damn engineers," he muttered, breathing heavily. "This is the last time you interrupt my class!"

By now, everyone in the hall was laughing heartily. Even Steve the hanging dummy turned out to have an enormous smile painted upon his face. But then the laughter died down, there being no sign of the professor. Everyone assumed, and quite rightly it turned out, that the culprits had escaped. And yet the professor did not return. So after a short while, when it became clear that the lecture would not be resumed, they all began slowly filing out of the hall, Theo Hoshen among them.

Given the unexpected free time, our young philosopher decided to make his way to The Hangar, the pub owned and operated by the Students' Administrative Council, or SAC, the union which represented the university's thirty thousand full-time undergraduates. They were not the only ones who frequented The Hangar, however, for the varieties of beer it served were both plentiful and cheap. And although it was still relatively early in the afternoon, Theo Hoshen decided that it was indeed a draft that he desired. So he made his way directly to the bar.

"Alright!" declared a student to two others. "That was great. Just great." Theo Hoshen suspected that he knew what the young man was referring to and so he turned to him and said:

"Are you Steve?"

"Shit! Who're you?" came the response.

"I was there just now – at Convocation Hall."

"Oh. Skule rules, eh?" said the young man with a grin.

"School?" inquired Theo Hoshen.

"No, man, S-k-u-l-e – it's the metric spelling of 'school'. We're the Engineering Students' Society, right?"

"Ah, that explains the overalls and hardhats."

"*Blue* hardhats. BFC," he said proudly.

"BFC?"

The student stared at Theo Hoshen with a look of disdain.

"Artsie, eh?" he inquired.

"I study philosophy, if that is what you mean," said Theo Hoshen.

"Thought so," said the engineer. "That's why you know nothing. Blue means that we're in Skule's Brute Force Committee. Not that it exists."

"I see," said Theo Hoshen without much enthusiasm.

"You artsies, you really don't give a shit, eh? No spirit at all. Still, at least the philosophers aren't as bad as the psycho-ologists."

"What do you mean?"

"Well, *you* know you're just making shit up. *They* think that they're doing real science, like us. But really they're just artsies in disguise."

"True," agreed Theo Hoshen. "They fail to recognize the methodological distinction between the natural and the human sciences, which corresponds to Aristotle's great division between the theoretical and the non-theoretical forms of reason."

"What the fuck?" exclaimed the engineer, looking at his partners.

"Just what you said," said Theo Hoshen.

"Whatever. The point is, we nailed 'em."

"You did indeed," said Theo Hoshen. "How about if I buy you gentlemen a drink?"

"Alright!" came their reply. And so Theo Hoshen ordered a round of beers for them all.

"So where do you come from, then?" asked one of the engineers.

"What do you mean?" wondered Theo Hoshen. "From here, Toronto, of course."

"Oh, I thought you were an exchange student or something."

There was an awkward pause. Then the first engineer turned to the others and said: "That was a beauty number five, eh?"

"Number five?" inquired Theo Hoshen.

"The BFC – even though we don't exist – performs five types of pranks. Today's was from category five: Theatrics."

"Ah, I see. And the other four?"

"Well," began the engineer, clearly relishing the opportunity to enumerate them, "there's Campus Beautification, like when we paint over the SAC dome. Last year we did it as a baseball. The stitches are mine," he added proudly. The SAC offices were located in the old Stewart's Observatory Building, which had a dome atop its three-story tower. So every year the engineers spent a night braving the campus police in order to repaint it with some mocking design.

"There's How'd They Do That?, like when we took apart that university administrator's car and reassembled it on the roof of a building." The other two engineers nodded approvingly.

"There's Shits and Giggles, which is just minor stuff, like when we fill hardhats up with concrete and stick long metal poles into them before they harden. Then we shove them into the ground and watch the pathetic artsie frosh try and take 'em.

"And then there's Property Liberation, like when we stole Queen's' grease pole. Every year their engineers plant this greased pole into a pit of muck and garbage and make their frosh climb it to get a hat nailed to the top. It's pretty cool 'cause while they're climbing other engineers throw rotten fruit and shit at them. Anyhow, one day when they weren't looking we took the pole and gave it back only after auctioning off a piece – you know, to cover the gas for the truck."

"I see," said Theo Hoshen. "I wonder why have I not heard of these before."

"That's 'cause *The Varshitty*," which is how all engineering students referred to *The Varsity*, the main campus student newspaper, "never reports 'em. They used to but they take themselves way too seriously now. Whatever, guy, this's been fun and all but we've got to go. So thanks for the beers. *Disrupto ergo sum.*"

"What?"

"It's our motto – I thought you said you were into philosophy."

CHAPTER IV

Wherein Theo Hoshen comes up with a most interesting idea and begins to research how he might best carry it out

Theo Hoshen was left more than a little astonished by his meeting with the three members of the Brute Force Committee. Here were some students, indeed a whole faculty, which had a genuine sense of honour; more than that, they even appeared to appreciate Aristotle's great lesson about the difference between the human and the natural sciences. So Aristotle still lives, and right here in the engineering school of the University of Toronto! Moreover, as the attack on Psychology 100 demonstrated, the engineers did not merely defend the methodological distinction in theory, putting it in books that few would read; no, they did so in practice. How Theo Hoshen admired them!

And yet, he corrected himself, when all is said and done they were still more foe than friend. For they did not merely recognize the distinction; they also worked to dishonour one side. After all, what was their "artsie" if not a term of abuse? Evidently, they viewed the human sciences, not to mention the humanities, as a matter of – how had he put it? – "just making shit up." Suddenly, Theo Hoshen felt himself becoming enraged. "Those ignorant whitecoats," he declared aloud and with fury. "*Philosophy* is the master science. How dare they?"

That was the precise moment, Theo Hoshen would later realize, when he found his worthy adversary. Because the matter had to do with more than mere methodological differences; Theo Hoshen believed that, ultimately, nothing less than the whole world was at stake. Technology without a theoretically grounded conception of the Good to guide it – what was this if not a supreme danger, one that, sooner or later, would lead to the veneration of mere life and, following this, to the end of us all? Yet despite – or perhaps because of – this most worrying prospect, Theo Hoshen's heart then began to fill with joy. For no longer were there cowardly, drunken undergraduates at Reznikoff's to concern himself with, nor errant and soulless cognitive psychologists; no, here was a whole faculty, one with many years of tradition behind it (why, some of them even wore uniforms) that was in dire need of having its methodological prejudices set aright. Even better, these people did not have to be convinced of the importance of honour before they could be properly dishonoured; on the contrary, they would appreciate what hit them, and it would serve to teach a most important lesson, namely, that the greater spirit is, and always will be, with the "artsie."

There is much work to do, thought Theo Hoshen. *I must learn more about this "Skule."* And so the very next day he rose early and set out in haste for Robarts Library, the largest in the university, indeed the country. Its books were housed in a brutalist, peacock-shaped concrete building, considered the safest place to take shelter should a nuclear bomb ever strike the city. Theo Hoshen made his way directly to the "head" as he knew that this was where he would find the Thomas Fisher Rare Book Collection, which contained all of the old documents relating to the university's history including, of course, that of the engineering faculty. It was not long before he was opening the first of the many boxes that the librarian placed before him. This is what he learned:

The University of Toronto Engineering Society was established in 1885. From the start, its founders put great stock in Skule spirit. They did so because they believed that engineering was by necessity an honourable profession. Their reasoning was simple. It began with the recognition that, like medicine but unlike law, engineering projects were often a matter of life and death. Should a bridge collapse, a dam burst, or a vehicle be unsafe, then innocent people could end up paying with their lives. Yet academic work alone was far from sufficient for producing professionals with the requisite sense of duty. This was especially the case given the many challenges and temptations they would face while practicing their craft in the business world. So in order to ensure that engineering graduates were mindful not only of how to operate slide rules but also of their responsibilities towards the community, a number of Skule traditions were established, the hope being that those who participated in them would develop a sense of identification with the engineering ethos. These traditions included rich and spirited initiation rites; the selection of special colours (blue and gold) to represent the school; the publication of a humorous newspaper, *The Toike Oike*; the performance, since 1921, of an annual theatre revue; and the inauguration of a school yell, first heard the previous year. The yell goes like this:

> Toike Oike, Toike Oike,
> Ollum te cholum te chay.
> School of Science, School of Science,
> Hurray, Hurray, Hurray.
> We are (we are),
> We are (we are),
> We are the Engineers.
> We can (we can),
> We can (we can),
> Demolish forty beers.
> Drink rum (straight),

Drink rum (straight),
And come along with us,
For we don't give a damn
For any damn man
Who don't give a damn for us!

Years later, an optional female chorus was added:

We are (we are),
We are (we are),
The female Engineers.
We can (we can),
We can (we can),
Drink as many beers.
Drink rum (drink rum),
Drink rum (drink rum),
And come along with us,
For we don't give a damn
For any damn man
Who can't get it up for us!

Now to this day no one is quite sure what "Toike Oike" means, though some have attributed its origins to an Irish caretaker who used to toil in the School of Practical Science back in the 1920s. It seems that whenever he came upon students who had chosen to remain in the building late into the night to study, he would shout at them to "take a hike," only his accent ensured that it came out as "toike oike."

Three Skule traditions towered above all the rest. Perhaps the oldest was the Lady Godiva Memorial Band, whose membership consists of whoever happens to show up at an event with an instrument. Practice is, of course, strictly forbidden, and yet the LGMB has managed to develop an impressive repertoire. Among the most elaborate of its compositions is the Engineering Hymn, which begins with the story of Lady Godiva's naked ride through Coventry. To the engineers, Godiva is the greatest symbol of dedication to the community and so they decided to make her their patron saint. According to legend, Godiva's husband, a nobleman who controlled the town's finances, challenged her to ride through it in the nude – if she did so, he swore, he would lower the peasantry's tax burden. To his great surprise, she agreed. It is said that, out of respect for her, all of the townsfolk made sure to avert their gaze as she rode by (except for one, of course, a certain Peeping Tom).

All this is recounted in the Engineering Hymn. Indeed the score goes on for over one hundred lines, moving from Godiva's tale to stanzas that glorify the drinking and sexual exploits of engineers, degrade those of artsies, and generally regale the enormous challenge that is engineering studies. Other LGMB songs are far less elaborate, such as the somewhat repetitive More Beer. It goes like this:

> More beer.
> More beer.
> More beer.
> More beer.
>
> More beer.
> More beer.
> More beer (more beer).
> More beer.
> More beer.

More beer.
More beer.
More beer.
More beer.
More beer (just one more beer).

The second great Skule tradition is that of the infamous Brute Force Committee, the acquaintance of certain members of which Theo Hoshen had made the previous day. The BFC has come to be fronted by Mario's Bakery, which promotes itself as providing fine catering services for the university community. In reality, its Beverage and Food Committee is none other than the BFC, whose declared mission is the "upholding of Skule spirit by performing pranks of the highest order." Led by Da Chief and his number two, Da Chief's Ass, the BFC counts at any given time up to twenty volunteers, each of whom is designated a Minister of one sort or another.

However Theo Hoshen's eyes truly began to widen only when he came upon documents that referred to the third, and surely the greatest, Skule tradition, that of Ye Olde Mighty Skule Cannon. The Cannon was the symbol of the Society, its mascot. It was on November 2, 1905 that some sort of small gun, shrouded in mystery, was first reported to have been fired during a Skule event, producing an enormously loud boom. Then came the even louder Cannon Mark I, built in 1936 by a machinist from the civil engineering shop. Forged from axle stock, it had a ten-inch barrel with a six-inch bore and an eight-inch-by-four-inch-by-one-inch base made from a cast iron pillow block. The Mark I was also a matter of great secrecy, since concerns about safety had already led the authorities to try – though always fail – to track down its predecessor.

Theo Hoshen read on. November 23rd, 1944 was considered one of the darkest days in Skule history. Skule had been competing with University College in the Mulock Cup football final. It lost not only the game, but also its dear Cannon, which had been brought along for firing at what was believed to be a certain victory. A dastardly group of University College students managed to snatch the mighty mascot. Stunned and desperate, the Engineering Society took out a small advertisement in *The Varsity*:

LOST, STOLEN OR STRAYED: One Skule Cannon. Finder please return to Miss O'Toole. This ad will guarantee safe passage to finder.

Alas, the next issue contained the following response:

Borrower of Skule Cannon desires to know amount of powder required to load same.

"Serves us right for appealing to an artsman's honour," Bill Tamblyn, the then Skule president, was overheard complaining. Yet a few days later University College announced that it indeed had the Cannon and that it was willing to return it during a ceremony at the upcoming annual UC Arts Ball. The engineers had merely to send their Society's foreign secretary to receive it. Aghast at the humiliation of it all, Skule plotted to steal back their precious jewel, which they indeed managed to do just as it was being brought into the ball. As *The Varsity* reported:

Six frustrated Schoolmen succeeded in capturing the famed School Cannon before the formal presentation at the Arts Ball last night. In a concerted and strategically timed rush they overpowered the cannon bearers and vanished.

The following day, the engineers fired it off during a meeting of the UC Literary and Athletic Society held in the college's Junior Common Room, an event which was promptly followed by a massive exchange of snowballs outside. The hostilities only escalated, and on February 15th, 1945, it came to pass that the UC Lit declared war on Skule; Skule followed suit with its own Declaration of Hostilities a few days later. And so it was that, though he had initially opposed their own declaration, President Tamblyn became caught up in the general thirst for vengeance sparked by the Cannon's theft and was led to announce the following in a most eloquent speech delivered before the Engineering Society assembly:

> Gentlemen, this was surely one of the most infamous and treacherous acts of aggression ever perpetuated against a peace-loving faculty. For fully three months our Cannon was hidden by one of the cabinet members of this treacherous people. Not once was it used according to our custom, for the pleasure and general welfare of humanity. Perhaps the mechanism of our proud symbol was too elaborate for the citizens of University College to comprehend.

Soon after, the engineers published detailed plans for the destruction of the UC building. Cooler heads prevailed, however, allowing for the animosities to be channelled instead into the version of warfare known as "democracy," which in this case took the form of that year's elections to Hart House, the university's student centre.

Yet a terrible precedent had been set. Theo Hoshen read that, four years later, immediately after the Cannon had been fired to mark the start of the Annual Chariot Race's second heat, and directly in front of the more than three thousand students in attendance, a lone medical student made a mad grab for the gun. A huge brawl ensued for, according to *The Varsity*, he was quickly joined by several hundred fellow medical students, all of whom found it necessary to "punch, kick, and fight their way through a mass of engineers." Of course other faculties soon entered the fray, each hoping to acquire the Cannon for themselves. It was nevertheless the medsmen who managed to convey it to their school's building. But just before entering, a single brave engineer succeeded in grabbing it. In a flash he had tucked it under his arm and raced back to the engineering building. The recovery was only temporary, however, as Theo Hoshen learned from *The Varsity*'s account of what happened next:

> Just as he got inside the door two unknown meds-
> men patted the gallant engineer on the back and
> shouted "Good boy! Give it to us." Heaving a sigh of
> relief the unsuspecting engineer passed the Cannon
> to the willing helpers who raced down the corridor,
> out the side door, and across the road to the medical
> building.

In this way, a dastardly group of medsmen – they called themselves The Femury Gang – had managed to procure the Cannon for the glory of their faculty. In a fit of rage, a mass of engineers laid siege upon the medical school building. Though they ended up doing no small amount of damage, they were unable to locate their cherished tool. In consequence, they decided to abduct the Medical Society's vice-president. So at seven o'clock that evening four engineers visited Bob Hetherington's fraternity house and asked for an audience with the young man. The moment he came out they threw a fishnet over him, whisked him away into a waiting truck, and drove off to a place unknown. Hetherington was held over the entire weekend, during which he managed to make but a single, though valiant, escape attempt (he lunged for a window yet was quickly hauled back). And so it was that, as he passed the time playing bridge with his guards, Skule representatives managed to negotiate an exchange: the vice-president for the Cannon. The trade was soon made and the mighty symbol was home again — albeit marred by a short message that had been engraved on its barrel: "Captured by Meds 5T2 3 Feb. 1949."

In order to prevent such a disgraceful deed from ever being perpetrated again, the Ancient and Honourable Society of Skule Cannoneers (later simply The Cannon Guard) was founded. Its members were charged with escorting the Cannon during public events, thus ensuring its security. A fearsome band of nine strapping Skulemen, they came to wear uniforms that consisted of black coveralls, hoods and hardhats. Their leader, usually the largest amongst them, goes by the title of Chief Attiliator and it is his duty to carry the Cannon as well as to set it down and fire it with the light from the butt of a burning cigarette. As for the other eight guards, all of whom carry billy clubs, four are literally chained to the gun by long shackles that extend from its base and are wrapped around their waists like belts, while the others form an outer perimeter square, their eyes ever vigilant for potential ne'er-do-wells.

Alas for the Guard, it was caught wholly by surprise that very same year during the infamous Cannon Steal of 1949. At least its members could avail themselves of the excuse that it all happened while most of them were off duty, for the Cannon had been taken out to what was to be a less-than-public event. Once again, it was the scoundrels from University College's doing. The Cannon had been brought, in secrecy and so relatively unguarded, to *The Varsity* offices in order to be photographed. Yet before a single picture could be taken a group of UC students who had been lying in wait (a spy had informed them of the upcoming photo shoot) snatched the treasure and swiftly made off with it in a car. In response, a mass of engineers demonstrated in front of the college. But this was just a diversion since, as they did so, a small group of engineers disguised as construction workers stole into the building from the back and, after setting up appropriate con-struction barricades, carefully removed the famous wooden dragon from the newel post of the east wing stairway. And soon after a group of Skulemen kidnapped a UC cheerleader, one Miss Joan Ellis. So it was that, once again, a trade had to be negotiated. This time the result was a noon hour ceremony before the wrought-iron gates on UC's front steps, whereupon the dragon and the cheerleader were exchanged for the cher-ished gun.

All of these skirmishes had begun to take their toll, which is to say that the Mighty Skule Cannon was no longer in fine form. That is why, during the winter of 1950, the Mark II was built. It had wheels on its base and a bronze alloy barrel that was two inches in diameter, eleven and a half inches long, and with a three-quarter inch bore. The whole was electroplated with nickel and chromium and was, Theo Hoshen read, a truly awe-inspiring sight. Yet it, too, had to be replaced only a few years later, for it was decided that the symbol of Skule's honour must always shine bright.

Of course, the Cannon's glimmer also served as a beacon of temptation, which is why in the ensuing years there were many further attempts at its theft. In 1951, for example, some students from Western University in London, Ontario, tried to take it by posing as journalists and then simply asking to see it; they were quickly shown the door. The following year, some University of Toronto Victoria College students attacked the engineering homecoming float, but the Cannon Guard managed to fight them off. The Meds then attempted the same deed in 1955, also to no avail. And in 1958, Vic students tried again, this time by stealing the safe from the Engineering Society offices; alas, there was only money inside. However the next year, the Meds, now in league with *The Varsity*, managed a successful strike. Yet it only led to more kidnappings and other hijinks, and ended with another negotiated exchange.

Skule will, however, surely never live down the notorious Incident of 1967. It saw two traitorous engineering graduate students take advantage of a lapse in security to snatch the brass jewel. In their treachery, they carried the Cannon away with them all the way to England. Six Skulemen were promptly dispatched to retrieve it, which they indeed managed to do, locating it in a room that had been rented by one of the thieves. Needless to say, during the return voyage a side trip was made to Coventry in order to pay homage to Lady Godiva with a firing of the mighty relic; her statue was also left covered with a University of Toronto engineering jacket. Nevertheless, to this day the whole sorry tale is recounted in hushed tones.

On it went, the storied history of the Mighty Skule Cannon. Theo Hoshen read of a few more attempts at its theft, of the odd defacing incident, and even of forgeries having been built. Yet spirit at the university had clearly begun to wane. For as he well knew it had come to pass that the average student today cared for little other than obtaining his or her diploma and entering the job market as quickly as possible. And it goes without saying that there is not much room for honourable hijinks when all one has on one's mind is money, money, money. Thus it was that few outside of the engineering faculty were now even aware of the Cannon's existence, much less of the venerable tradition of purloining it. This, surely, explains why there had not been a single successful Cannon caper since that shameful day back in 1967.

It was now October 1989. *That makes twenty-two years*, thought Theo Hoshen to himself. *A long time. A very long time.* He left the library.

CHAPTER V

In which Theo Hoshen endeavours to convince his housemates to assist him in stealing the Mighty Skule Cannon

"I knew it," said Simon, "he's gone daft as a brush."

"We can at least hear him out," objected Avigail, though she was suppressing a smile.

"It is a truly wonderful prize," urged Theo Hoshen. "Definitely worth having."

"What are you talking about?" exclaimed Simon. "What would we do with it?"

"Think of the honour it would bring," said Theo Hoshen.

"The *honour*? Listen, you wazzock, if they ever found out who took it what it'd bring is us honourably beaten to a pulp. I've seen some of those engineering nerds – they're ginormous!"

"Well *I* am not afraid," said Theo Hoshen.

"Don't even try that shite on me, mate. You do know that Avigail and I are *graduate* students, right? This is kids' stuff. And getting caught could get us expelled *as well as* beaten up. Oh man, I can't even think about this right now, what with everything going all weird and wonky down at the lab. Still, there's no way I'm going to blow it just because my housemate's a nutter. Jeez, Avigail, he doesn't even *talk* normal anymore. I mean, Theo, what time is it?"

"It is six o'clock," answered Theo Hoshen after glancing at his watch.

"*It is* six o'clock? Did you hear that, Viggy? *It is* six o'clock. Who on earth says that?"

"What, it is not six o'clock?" wondered Theo Hoshen.

"There's just no way, *no bloody way* that I'm getting mixed up in some crazy stunt with this git. I'll bet you don't even know where the thing is, do you Hoshen-boy?"

"Well, that is not exactly true. After I left the library, I managed to get my hands on one of this year's Engineering Society datebooks. And look here." Theo Hoshen withdrew a copy from his backpack and opened it to a page at the back which contained a map as well as an excellent description of the Engineering Society offices. "Notice how they give a detailed account of each and every room: what is inside, who normally works there, and so on. Yet listen to what they have to say about this little windowless office, the third from the entrance: 'Nothing to see here, folks. Nothing at all. So just move along'. Now I ask you, is that not engineering code for something important? It is surely very strange that they would suddenly be so secretive about this one little room. I believe I know why that is. Moreover, it having been over twenty years since the Cannon was last stolen, it only stands to reason that they would no longer go to elaborate lengths to secure it. They shan't have done much more to protect it than simply putting it in that little room."

"*Shan't? Shan't?* We *Brits* don't even say that anymore! Did you hear that, Viggy?" Simon was becoming quite excited.

At least it's a contraction, thought Avigail to herself.

"Listen, Theo," she said turning to the young philosopher, "what do you plan to do, just break in there?"

"Precisely. It would be much more effective than taking the Cannon Guard on directly."

"You don't say," said Simon with a scowl.

"But Theo, you've got to admit that Simon's made some good points. I mean, we are a bit old for this sort of thing. And none of us has any experience robbing places."

"Speak for yourself," interjected Simon. "But at least I had a good reason; I needed the beer tokens. This is just wacky."

"Yes, well," Avigail continued, "the point is that it *is* risky. Sure it might be fun to try but I've got say, Theo, while your idealism's admirable it's kind of misplaced. Frankly, the whole thing just doesn't seem worth it."

"Alas, Avigail," sighed Theo Hoshen, "that is because honour is one of the many things in heaven and earth forgotten by your philosophy. I see now that it was foolish of me to try and tempt you with the call of this ancient ideal. How sad that you do not hear it as loudly as I do. Still, it only stands to reason. I allow myself to say this because I am able to report that, of late, my studies have attained an extremely high level; it all makes sense now, you see. Regardless, it is evident that I am left with nothing more at this time than to thank you both for your patience." And with that Theo Hoshen fell silent, rose with a most solemn demeanour, and exited the room.

CHAPTER VI

Wherein Theo Hoshen meets Carl Landsberg, the handsome young president of the Students' Administrative Council, and the two begin a most interesting discussion

It was soon Friday again and the three housemates found themselves walking together on the way to spend another evening at Reznikoff's Pub. Though Theo Hoshen had passed the week assiduously attending his classes, he had also made the odd sojourn for reconnaissance purposes to the exterior of the Engineering Society offices. Once he even ventured inside, doing his best to commit to memory everything that he saw there, especially the particulars of the door to the little room that he believed contained the Cannon. He also made sure to take note of any other detail that he thought might be worthy of notice. Of course while there he was careful to say nothing to anyone and, in order not to draw attention to himself, he quickly left.

Reznikoff's was its usual dark and perspiring self. The three arrived early so as to pay the cheaper one-dollar cover charge. The only others in attendance were a group of mods, about fifteen in number, all dressed in their uniform black. Most had already taken to the dance floor and were moving, beer cups in hands, in time to the dulcet tones of an Art Bergmann composition. Theo Hoshen could not help but notice that one of them stood out somewhat from the rest, for he wore a t-shirt of dark grey rather than black. He also looked familiar, though the young philosopher could not quite place him.

"Do you recognize that one?" he asked Avigail, pointing discretely.

She peered into the darkness. "I think that's Carl Landsberg, the SAC prez. Cute, but does he ever dance funny – then again, I guess you all do." Evidently, Avigail was new to the alternative music scene.

In time, the room filled up. Theo Hoshen, Avigail and Simon repeatedly wandered on and off the dance floor, although they made sure to leave it the moment a hard song with a thrashing beat began. For they knew what that meant: in an instant the mods would be replaced by slam dancers who, heads bowed and arms stuck out protectively in front, would bounce violently up and down and run madly in all directions until they collided into one another. From time to time, two or more slammers would meet in a full-on collision and great splashes of sweat would be brought forth, flying off of their bodies and spraying everyone in the vicinity. Occasionally, someone would even be knocked down, only to get up again as if nothing had happened.

Theo Hoshen noticed that Landsberg was among the few who remained on the floor when the slammers took to it; indeed, he had not stopped dancing once in all of the time that they had been at the pub. And now there he was slamming away with a reckless abandon equal to that of the rest of them. Of course Theo Hoshen did not approve of this sort of dancing; not at all. He believed that people should "dance seriously," by which he meant that they should strive to move in harmony with the music, as if they were trying to reach a sort of understanding with it. Slam dancing was far too violent and irrational an affair; at best, slammers were like negotiators who, when they managed to collide without falling, could be said to have struck a balance or accommodation between them. But accommodations are compromises, not expressions of verity, which is precisely why people view them as temporary lodgings rather than genuine homes.

Evidently, President Landsberg did not share this opinion; he was quite clearly exhilarated by each and every slam. Through the dark, Theo Hoshen could just make out the large smile that he had on his face. And sometimes, abandoning all caution, he would even run, eyes closed and like a superman, directly into a group of slammers. Moreover, when not in the midst of it all he could be seen hopping up and down in time to some hidden, internal rhythm, for his jumps in no way matched the beat of the music (making them somehow all the more beautiful for that). On occasion, his body would even burst into wild convulsions, as if its owner had suddenly been injected with an energy that he could not contain. Then would he shudder, flail and spin wildly about, now falling to the floor, now bouncing off one of the walls. Theo Hoshen found it all quite bewildering. *People actually voted for this man?* he wondered.

"He's a better speaker than dancer," said Avigail, as if she had been reading Theo Hoshen's mind. "I remember the first time I saw him. It was during last year's election campaign, at Trinity College's all-candidates debate. Quite boring for the most part, except for the end when they asked the candidates to tell a joke. Now *that* was interesting."

"What happened?" inquired Theo Hoshen.

"Well, it was pretty obvious that none of them saw it coming, even though it's an old Trinity tradition. And I don't know about you, Theo, but if I were standing in front of a hundred or so people and someone asked me to come up with a joke, well my mind would just go blank."

"Mine too."

"Still, it wasn't a problem for the first candidate, Gillian Lawmore of the Socialist Action ticket. Her joke was even pretty good, if I remember right. But the next guy, Bill Greene, the right-wing candidate and Landsberg's chief rival, well he was obviously in major trouble. He's this big chubby guy, and by the time the moderator turned to him he was already sweating profusely, all bright red and embarrassed. He didn't have a joke, so he asked for some more time to think of one. Was that ever a mistake, 'cause the moderator just agreed. 'Alright,' she said, 'thirty seconds.' So now you've got everyone in the room waiting, staring at Greene. Imagine the pressure! You know how when you're watching a play and an actor's forgotten his lines? Well this was worse – we all just sat there, shifting and squirming in our seats; man, you just felt so bad for the guy. And then when his time was up he *still* didn't have a joke! 'I…I just can't,' he said, and that was that; I'm sure he lost whatever votes he might have had left in the room right there. The worst part is that the moderator then said that she'd come back to him.

"So next it's Landsberg's turn and his joke, given all of the Trinity-types in the room (you know, those elitist, pseudo-intellectuals), was perfect: a little pretentious, but not too much. It was actually a philosophy joke, a play on Descartes' cogito."

"I would love to hear it."

"Alright. So René Descartes walks into a restaurant and orders some French onion soup. The waiter returns with a bowl, puts it down in front of him, and says: 'Perhaps Monsieur Descartes voold care for zum crackers vith ees zoup?' Descartes pauses for a moment and says: 'No, I zink not.' And then he disappears."

"A fine joke," declared Theo Hoshen, "despite the unconvincing French accent. Still, very humorous."

"Yeah, I can see it really cracked you up," teased Avigail. "You know, Theo, sometimes I wonder what that would take. Anyhow, next it's the fourth and final candidate's turn and he makes this weak but acceptable effort. But then it's back to Greene – and the guy *still* hasn't come up with a joke! So we get some more agonizing moments as we all wait. And then, to everyone's surprise, Lawmore the socialist offers to help him out. 'Alright,' she says, 'I've got a joke for you.' What a relief; she'd give him a joke, he'd repeat it, and then we could all go home. 'Okay,' he says, all breathless. So she goes 'Say "knock knock".' And he says 'knock, knock.' 'Who's there?' she replies, and Greene's stuck staring back at her; he's got no idea what to say. 'Uh…' finally comes out. 'Who's *there*?' she repeats. God was it ever pathetic. Everyone in the room broke out laughing. Those socialists sure can be vicious, eh? Anyhow, that was it; the meeting was adjourned. I'm sure it wasn't enough to cost Greene the election, but the fact is, he came in second."

"Democracy cannot do without winners and losers," declared Theo Hoshen. "Of course, if citizens fulfilled their responsibilities instead of electing representatives, then the common good would be realized and everyone would win."

"I don't know about that," replied Avigail, "but then I'm just an epistemologist." Theo Hoshen could not tell if she meant this ironically or not, and he dearly wished to find out and then convince her of the truth of his proposition, but the many beers he had imbibed meant that he had a pressing need to use the facilities. And so he excused himself and made his way out of the room. Then it was down the hall and into the men's washroom.

"Jew, eh?" said a voice from the urinal next to his. Theo Hoshen turned and was surprised to find that it was none other than Carl Landsberg.

"What?" he stammered in reply.

"Thought so," said the student politician, evidently a little drunk. "When I was a kid I used to have this Sephardic friend, Alex Perez. You look just like him – same nose and everything. Where're you from?"

"I was born here, in Toronto," answered Theo Hoshen.

"Well where's your family from then?"

"Morocco, but –"

"Knew it!" said Carl with a satisfied look on his face. "Man, could I ever go in for some *matbookha* right about now. You know, that oily tomato spread, served cool but tastes spicy hot. Alex's mom used to make it."

"Yes...well."

"I'm an agnostic myself," continued Carl. "You know, a Woody Allen Jew."

"I see," said Theo Hoshen, turning to wash his hands. "I too have no time for the rabbis. I study philosophy, you see. Athens, not Jerusalem."

"Uh huh," said Carl. "I took a philosophy course once, but I'm a poli. sci. major."

"And the student council president."

"Oh, so you know. Did ya vote for me?"

"Uh," stammered Theo Hoshen. "Actually, I did not vote."

"Just kidding," said Carl. "I'm a bit tipsy, you see. Rezzie's my break. And man do I need it."

"Why do you say that?"

"Long story, so don't get me started. Anyhow, I need some air. You want to step outside?" And so out they went. Then it was up the stairs and, because Carl said nothing more, Theo Hoshen felt obliged to follow him as he began to walk. It was only when they were some distance from the building that the student union president spoke again:

"Ah, quiet. Sometimes I need a break even from my break." And then, despite his inebriation, Carl managed to explain how Reznikoff's had come to serve him as a form of oasis, as an island amidst the turbulent waters that had become his life as a student politician. Its low lighting, he explained, hid spaces in which he could abandon all decorum, free of the fear that a photographer from one of the campus newspapers would try to take his picture. Yes, in Reznikoff's he was just another student. In fact, that very night he had noticed one of his political enemies, a prominent member of the university's International Socialists club, dancing right there beside him. "I mean, the guy didn't even give me one of those dirty self-righteous looks they love to throw my way."

"And why do they do that?" inquired Theo Hoshen.

"I guess you haven't been reading the campus papers."

"True."

"It's just as well."

"And?" urged Theo Hoshen.

"What's your name?" asked Carl, evidently attempting to change the subject.

"Theo Hoshen."

"And you're from Morocco?"

"Toronto."

"Right. Whatever, Theo, you came here to dance, right?"

"There are many forms of dance. And I would very much enjoy hearing about this issue you are involved in."

43

"More 'embroiled' than 'involved'," corrected Carl. "But listen, Theo, it's really damn complicated; there's no point in getting anyone else as confused about it as I am."

"Perhaps I can see its point. I am a philosophy student, after all – including political philosophy."

"Yeah, but this is no thought experiment, right? What I've been through is real."

"And philosophy is not?" challenged Theo Hoshen with what was clearly a look of disappointment on his face.

"Sorry, I didn't mean it like that. It's just that it's such a long, long story. And anyway, Theo, I'm starved; I really need to eat."

"Well then I will buy you a meal and you will tell me the long story," proposed Theo Hoshen. It seemed the young philosopher had something to prove; he needed to be taken seriously for once.

"Jeez, you're as pushy as Alex Perez was." Then Carl paused to reflect. Finally, he spoke again: "Still, if you're half as smart as him, then it might actually be worth it. Alright then, burgers on you at Room 338." Carl was referring to a local diner that was popular with the students. It was a five-minute walk away.

"Excellent!"

The two exchanged nothing but pleasantries until they arrived, whereupon each approached the counter and selected the large hamburger and fries combination. From the menu on the wall, Theo Hoshen could see that this was no ordinary burger, for it had an eponym: "The Carl Landsburger." Apparently, it was the custom at Room 338 to name their largest burger after the current year's SAC president. So it was that, when the man behind the counter finished dressing Carl's with the various condiments that he had requested, it was handed over to him with a wink and an "Enjoy yourself."

44

"Yeah, yeah," said Carl with a wry smile.

Then the two took their seats at a booth in one of the corners at the back of the restaurant. And Carl, in a calm and pleasant voice, began to tell his tale. This is what he said.

CHAPTER VII

In which Carl Landsberg recounts how he found himself at the centre of an astounding political adventure

"First off," said Carl, "I should say that I know how naïve I'm going to sound in all this. But I knew I was naïve going in; in fact, that was kind of the point. You see, I went into the SAC presidency thing as kind of an experiment. Ever since I was a kid, I'd thought of becoming a politician. But whenever I told people this, they'd always say something about how self-serving and unprincipled all politicians were. It has to be that way, they said, 'cause you can't do politics without getting your hands dirty. Well I wasn't convinced, though I've got to say that four years of poli. sci. sure didn't help one way or the other. All we ever studied was whether this or that correlation of poll data was statistically significant, whether this or that party system was efficient, whether this or that war could've been predicted, and so on. Except for the theory courses, no one ever asked about what made for *good* politics; you know, about what justice was and all that. And yet the theory courses were just that: theoretical, in the clouds kind of stuff. No offence to philosophy, Theo, but I was looking for something much more down to earth; you know, like what justice should mean for us Canadians here and now. Plato, Rawls and all those guys – well they just don't seem to help very much with that."

"But –" interrupted Theo Hoshen, though he was himself interrupted in turn:

"But nothing," said Carl. "Let me just tell you what happened, okay? Then you can take it from there."

"Agreed."

"So, as I said, I'd figured it was time to try the real thing and run for SAC. I told myself that, if I won, I could do a test to see if politics really had to be dirty. I'd be a politician who acted in a wholly principled way; no compromising, no taking the easy way out, and so on – I was going to be one hundred percent fair, always, no matter what."

"But did you ever think," interrupted Theo Hoshen again, "that perhaps politics is not a domain well-suited to experimentation?"

"Theo," said Carl in a scolding tone.

"I shall not interrupt again."

"Good. So, it's just the second day into my presidency and this guy shows up at SAC. He says he's the head of the U of T Vietnamese Students' Society and that he wants to talk to me about getting some office space for his group. Seems SAC has control over a number of buildings on campus so it was up to us who could stay in them. And his club has over three hundred members and it's become really hard for them without an office. They've no place to store their things, hang out together, receive their mail, that sort of stuff. So he wants to know if I'd help, if I'd give them some space. I said that I'd see what I could do.

"But before I could even start, I get this letter from another guy looking for space. He used to run this little publishing house called The T.O. Press, right, and SAC had been real kind in the past by allowing them to have a little room in the building behind the university's admissions office – the one that mainly houses the Sex Ed Centre. The Press'd been successful there for a couple of decades and now, though they'd been inactive for a few years, he wants to start it up again. But it seems that during the hiatus their little room had been taken over by another group, GLAUT, the Gays and Lesbians at U of T. The guy had apparently tried, but failed, to reach last year's SAC prez to get him to kick GLAUT out so the T.O. Press could move back into its old office. And that's why he was writing me: he wanted to know if I'd do it.

"Well I'd never heard of the T.O. Press, the Sex Ed Centre, or GLAUT. I didn't even know that SAC, thanks to some agreement between us and the university administration, had control over all these buildings on campus. It turned out there were four of 'em: the little one that housed the Sex Ed Centre and GLAUT; a big white house on St. George Street where the radio station and Downtown Legal Services were based; another house just down the street which contained *The Varsity* and the African Caribbean Students Association; and our own SAC offices in the Stewart's Observatory Building. But I couldn't find a SAC policy for how the space was allocated; it seemed to be all a matter of who had the best connections with the SAC executive committee, which basically meant, you know, who was friends with the prez."

"So the situation was corrupt," declared Theo Hoshen.

"I don't know, that's a little strong, don't you think? It's just that there was no written policy or anything."

"I see. Please continue – I shall not say another word."

"Okay, so then I get a visit from two people who say

they're the heads of The Volunteer Centre, this new organization that they were starting up. It was going to provide students with advice about where they might volunteer some of
their time. Seems the previous year's SAC prez had actually
promised them some office space, which they said they desperately needed to hold interviews with prospective volunteers.

"So I checked with Dr. Tealands, the administration's Assistant Vice-Prez of Student Affairs, and he tells me that, though
they were happy to continue our agreement regarding the four
buildings, they wanted me to know that they weren't keen on
our having given offices to GLAUT and ACSA, the gays and
the African Caribbean students. Seems it violated the university's space allocation policy, which forbids granting space to
any and all student clubs – what they called 'informal student
organizations'. And it does so for what looked to me like a
really good reason: given the over one hundred and seventy
student clubs, there just wasn't enough space for them all.

"Anyhow, Tealands said that the administration was willing
to let the matter with GLAUT and ACSA stand. Apparently, a
few years back, SAC had actually tried to evict ACSA but this
led to threats of a race riot as well the then ACSA prez chain-
ing himself to a desk in their office and daring SAC to get him
out of there by force. So SAC backed down.

"But I got to thinking: wasn't it time that we had our own
space allocation policy? I mean, at the very least it'd put an end
to the practice of handing space out on the basis of who knew
who. 'Cause if space was this scarce and valued commodity,
then it was only right that SAC had a policy which gave it out
in a fair manner. So I set about figuring out what such a policy
should look like. I decided that, given that there were so many
student groups – over a hundred and seventy, remember –
we'd have to categorize them in some way. Those like the

Camping and the Chess Clubs I designated 'sports or gaming organizations'; those like the Young Conservatives and the Marxist-Leninists I called 'political organizations'; those like the Vietnamese Student's Society and ACSA 'ethnic or cultural organizations'; those like the Campus Crusade for Christ and the U of T Buddhists 'religious organizations'; and, finally, those like *The Varsity*, the radio station, the Downtown Legal Services, and the Sex Ed Centre I called 'service organizations'. That last category was the key. I based it on the idea that these were groups that provided students – *all* students – with services: *The Varsity* was a free bi-weekly newspaper; CIUT-FM put out radio shows and acted as an informal school of broadcasting; the DLS offered free legal aid from U of T law students; and the Sex Ed Centre provided counselling about sex."

"That seems like a sensible category," confirmed Theo Hoshen.

"Yeah, but here's the crux: the policy meant that only the service organizations would be eligible for space – you know, at least until we could get our hands on more of it. Because only the service organizations could be said to provide genuine services that were geared towards *all* undergraduates. The other groups, while technically open to everyone, have a much narrower focus, given that they appeal only to those who are into this or that particular sport or game, this or that culture, ideology, or religion. The way I figured it, we at SAC shouldn't be in the grubby business of judging between these groups; it's not our place to say that the Chinese students were better and so more worthy of space than the Italians, or the Jews the Christians, or the Greens the Young Liberals, and so on. No, we're supposed to represent *all* undergraduates, so we've got to be neutral towards such groups. But when it comes to the service organizations, well then it *is* right for us to ask which ones best serve the undergrad population as a whole. For example, say one day U of T students lost all interest in sex – 'course this is what you philosophers call a 'hypothetical'."

"Of course," confirmed Theo Hoshen.

"So let's say that happened, that sex became passé and so students now had a bunch more free time and they wanted to spend at least some of it volunteering for various worthy causes. Well then we at SAC might decide to replace the Sex Ed Centre with the Volunteer Centre. What'd be wrong is if we tried to make this kind of judgment regarding the various cultural, ideological, or religious groups, 'cause that's just not our place.

"Anyhow," Carl continued, "you've probably guessed that this new policy of mine meant that ACSA and GLAUT, given that they went under the category of ethnic or cultural organizations, had to go. I figured they wouldn't be happy about it, but I thought, hey, if that's what justice demands, that's what justice demands – I had to be true to my little experiment, after all. And anyway, despite all the protests in the past, I figured that the vast majority of people in the university community would back my policy. 'Cause it was completely colour- and sexual-orientation-blind.

"Yes," concurred Theo Hoshen, "I can certainly see the blindness there."

"*C'mon* Theo, you said you wouldn't interrupt," complained Carl.

"You are right. Not another word. I promise."

"Until the next one, eh? *Alright*," said Carl with a huff. "Now the fact is that, when I brought my policy forward for approval to the next SAC board meeting (which is attended by over seventy elected student reps), it passed *unanimously* – and that, I can tell you, doesn't happen every day. So next I tried to set up meetings with GLAUT and ACSA. But given that it was the middle of summer, it was really hard to reach them. Finally, I got a hold of the GLAUT prez. We met and I explained the new policy to him and pointed out that it meant his group would have to go. And guess what? He agreed right off! He'd never been comfortable with the way they got their office in the first place, he said, and he very much appreciated that we at SAC were now explicitly treating gays and lesbians as equal to all of the other campus ethnic or cultural groups. And so that was that for GLAUT; out they went. The prez even offered to write a letter to *The Varsity* praising me and my policy!

"Another week and I finally managed to get a hold of the president of ACSA – Ogunsheye Agyei's his name. Rumour has it that it used to be much less exotic but that he changed it after he took this trip to the Caribbean and came back a radical, Afro-Caribbean nationalist. Anyhow, Ogunsheye's this tall, thin, soft-spoken guy and he was real calm as he took in the news about our new policy. He'd just one question: could ACSA still keep its office? I said no, of course. And anyway, I added, given that ACSA already had its space for some time, didn't he think it was another group's turn? He said nothing to this and just asked me if we could meet again, after he'd had a chance to consult with his group. I agreed and so we met a week later. Then he said that he thought my policy was fair but that my way of implementing it was wrong – 'cause ACSA, you see, *is* a service organization: it provides 'the service of fighting racism on campus.' It's also geared towards the participation of all undergraduates since everyone could – indeed should – be joining in its struggle.

"I just stared at him real hard, trying to figure out if he was being serious. It turned out he was, so I just said that I disagreed.

"'Fine,' he replied, 'but you must admit that it was unfair of your board to pass your policy without giving us some warning first. We never had an opportunity to respond.'

"'Respond how?' I countered. 'This is the only logical policy. The fact is that there're over one hundred and seventy clubs and we at SAC can't favour some ethnic groups over others, just as we can't favour any of the religious groups, or the sports groups, or the political groups, over others. And anyway, what about the other African groups? I mean, why should ACSA get priority over, say, the Afro-Students Association, or the anti-apartheid Friends of South Africa, or the Afropan Community Campus Group? What do you say to that?' Not much, it turned out. 'Alright,' I said, 'if you want to make an appeal to the SAC board, well I guess that's your right. And if the board agrees that you should stay, well then I'll of course go along. But I've got to say that I really don't see that happening; I mean, as I said, the policy passed unanimously.'

"So next it's a few days before the appeal and ACSA announces that they were going to hold a protest on the lawn in front of SAC. And the day before it, Ogunsheye wants to meet with me again. Now he says that he not only agrees with the policy but also with how I was implementing it. His problem is really only with the timing: if we could just give them some more time – say a year – to find another office, well then they'd agree to go and there'd be no need for the appeal. I protested that a year was way too long as it'd mean forcing the issue on the future SAC prez (something that my experiment ruled out). I suggested that, instead, they take until the month before my term ended in the spring. Surprisingly, he agreed. I was ecstatic and offered to do my best to help them find an alternative space – as long, I pointed out again, as it wasn't SAC space. He seemed real pleased with this and said that now they could cancel their protest. He even asked how he could get involved in SAC himself since he wanted us to deal with the question of the undergraduate curriculum, of why it was that there were so few works written by blacks in its cannon of texts.

"'I don't know anything about that,' I said, 'but it certainly sounds like something worth considering. So welcome aboard!' I was really, really happy.

"But the next morning, given that there hadn't been enough time to contact everyone, a handful of ACSA members showed up for the protest. Beaming, I handed them – and anyone else who would take one – copies of a press release announcing that SAC and ACSA had reached an historic agreement, that the space issue between us had finally been solved. This turned out to be a great disappointment to the editor of *The Varsity*, who complained that she'd reserved the whole of their next issue's front page for pictures of the protest. 'Well now you can put *this* on the front page,' I told her. 'Why not report some good news for a change?'

"'Course that wasn't gonna happen. Plus, the protesters had come in the mood for a protest, not for some historic reconciliation. So, right there on the SAC lawn, they started this big argument with Ogunsheye. I started getting nervous, so I invited Ogunsheye and a couple of the loudest arguers into my office. And what did they say in there? That they wanted me to *guarantee* that I'd find them an alternative space. But that wasn't what Ogunsheye and I'd agreed, I objected. And anyway, there was just no way I could make such a guarantee.

"'Well then,' said an unblinking Ogunsheye, 'we're just going to have to continue with the appeal to the board.'

"'Fine,' I said.

"So now it's the day of the appeal, and the whole thing's over real quick. The board agreed with almost nothing that Ogunsheye had to say and all but six members voted against him (with two abstentions). The message to the SAC executive committee was clear: we were to continue implementing the policy as we had been up till then. Given this, I approached the ACSA members present and suggested that they go with the agreement that Ogunsheye and I'd reached beforehand. 'Course they refused, and from that moment on, well, I guess you could say that that's when things *really* started to get interesting."

CHAPTER VIII

Wherein Carl Landsberg continues to recount the story of his struggle with the African Caribbean Students' Association

"The next day, I had the lock on ACSA's office door changed and their stuff moved to a locker on King Street. SAC's lawyers told us to post a notice on the door informing ACSA that they could arrange to pick up their stuff. I'd never done anything like that before and, well, I got a bit of a charge out of it."

At this Theo Hoshen furrowed his brow.

"Oh don't give me that. Look, Theo, the bottom line is that I believed I was doing the right thing. Needless to say, ACSA didn't agree.

"So September came, classes began, and the students found the campus papers filled with articles, letters, and opinion pieces about the issue. Almost every one of them supported ACSA and were critical of SAC; obviously, ACSA'd been doing some serious organizing. Their members also protested for three days straight: a group of about sixty of them, along with some International Socialists, roamed about the downtown campus shouting slogans and waving placards. And for the most part, I was their target: they called me a liar, a racist, a dictator – one even pointed out that I had a bad haircut (which was true – the whole thing'd shook me up so much that I kept forgetting to go to the barber). Anyhow, I was also really amazed by how little support I got from the university community. The general reaction was either silence from most or complaints from the odd columnist about the 'heavy-handed' way in which we at SAC had treated ACSA. Remember, I'd thought that my policy was unquestionably just – so how anyone not in some way connected to ACSA could possibly disagree with it really threw me. And given the apathy shown by everyone else, I figured that issues like this one probably tended to get decided on the basis of which group, you know, shouted the loudest, protested the most, and so on. Well there was no way I was going to let that happen on my watch. So the less support I got, the more resolved I became to stick to my position. I was just not going to allow SAC space to be distributed in anything but a totally fair and neutral manner.

"I should say that while all this was going on, two possible alternative spaces for ACSA opened up. One was this little office in the Sidney Smith Building that was being used by the Friends of South Africa. You see, earlier, I had worked so SAC would have an anti-apartheid policy which called on the university to refuse donations from companies that had investments in South

Africa. This had put me on very good terms with the head of the Friends of South Africa and when he heard about my fight with ACSA he told me that he was going to contact Ogunsheye and offer to share his group's space with them. And around the same time, this SAC board member, a rep from New College, says that he was on the verge of getting his college to offer ACSA an office that would be associated with the African Studies Department that was based there. In fact, the college's space committee had already voted to award ACSA the space and so now it was just a matter of getting the full council to rubber stamp it.

"But Ogunsheye turned down the offer from the Friends of South Africa; he said their office was too small. And as for New College – which, by the way, was a large office, much bigger than the one I'd evicted ACSA from – I learned from the flustered SAC rep that Ogunsheye and others had actually secretly lobbied *against* ACSA getting the office. That's when it began to dawn on me that this whole issue wasn't really about space but something much bigger.

"Next came an announcement from ACSA that they planned to occupy the SAC offices. Now I'd never had offices before, much less had 'em occupied, so I had no idea what to do. And then, on top of everything, the day before the occupation, the engineers' Brute Force Committee stole our War Room door."

At this mention of the engineers, Theo Hoshen was visibly discomfited.

"What," inquired Carl, "you know about the BFC?"

"I have heard of them."

"Then you'll know that they just love making trouble. A psychology prof actually retired mid-semester because of them. One of his grad students told me that he'd had enough after they'd yet again pranked his class; putting up with them was like living with a bad cold that just never went away. Anyhow, this time their target was our door, which opens to this room where the SAC executive committee used to meet. A long time ago, someone painted a knight on it and the words 'THE WAR ROOM'. Since then every few years or so this supposedly secret group of engineers breaks into SAC, steals it and fires their Cannon into it. So now there's this large black crater burnt into its unpainted side and 'Stolen by Skule' is engraved above a list of the years they've taken it. Pretty funny, eh? I didn't think so either. Anyhow, normally there's supposed to be negotiations over a ransom, but I didn't have time for that since there's some really expensive computer equipment in the room and I just couldn't leave it unprotected from the protesters. So I called the BFC's Chief and explained the situation. He was real nice about it – being an engineer, he said, he was particularly touched by the threat to the computers – and so he not only agreed to return the door right away but even offered to have the Cannon Guard come and protect SAC during the occupation. Needless to say, I didn't think that would be such a good idea and so I said no thanks.

"I was still really worried about how to handle the protest. Everything was upside-down. I mean, wasn't *I* supposed to be leading students in office occupations? What should I do? Should I tell my staff to just ignore the protesters, or should we talk with them? Should we try to do our work as usual, or should we leave? And what if at five o'clock when the office was supposed to close down they just stayed? It's not like I could call the cops and have 'em thrown out; someone could get hurt, and it sure wouldn't look good on TV.

"Then I vaguely remembered seeing this clip on the local news about a protest at Queen's Park. Some construction workers were angry about a government bill and so over a hundred of 'em marched right into the building and were making their way to the debating chamber to do a little re-verse-renovating. Suddenly, there was Lisa Bay, the leader of the official opposition, wading into the group and speaking Italian to their leader. Somehow, she managed to talk them out of their deconstruction project and got 'em to leave peacefully. *Why not give her a call?* I thought. *She used to be a SAC-hack herself, way back. Maybe she'd have some good advice.* So I did.

"'What can I do for you?' she said. I explained the situation. She asked what the protesters were protesting and so I told her that they were a campus club and that I'd evicted them from their office because of our new space allocation policy. Then I gave her a quick run-down on the principles of the policy.

"'That sounds like a fair policy,' she said. 'And what's the name of this group?'

"'The African Caribbean Students' Association.'

"'Oh,' she said. There was a pause. And then: 'Carl, are they calling you a racist?'

"'Why yes, yes they are.'

"'Then give in.'

"'What?'

"'Give in.'

"'But what about all the other clubs? I mean, you said it was a fair policy.'

"'Look, Carl, this is politics not logic. There are things you want to do during your year at SAC, right? Well you've got to be around to do them. And there's just no way you can win this one. So give in.'

"'But that's not fair.'

"'Carl,' she repeated, 'this is politics.'

"'Course she knew nothing about my little experiment and I wasn't about to go into it. So I just said that there was no way

58

I'd be giving in. She didn't skip a beat and replied that in that case I should tell my staff to act as naturally as possible, to be polite with the protesters at all times and, if they didn't leave by five, to just let 'em stay. Oh, and I should have coffee and donuts ready for them when they arrived.

"They got there first thing the next day and, I got to say, the coffee and donuts really threw 'em. Then, after a half hour or so, I left – something I should've done right away – and they started to get really bored. So it wasn't long before they just got up and left themselves, just like that, and headed off for another round of waving placards about the campus. And that was it; end of office occupation.

"But then we had this really big board meeting coming up. The SAC constitution requires us to pass our operating budget for the year at that meeting. So, after hearing rumours that ACSA planned to disrupt it, I called Ogunsheye. And what did he say? He demanded that we put ACSA on the meeting's agenda so they could have *another* appeal. Either that 'or there will be no meeting'. I thought of hanging up right there, but then I remembered the budget and so I explained to him that, though the agenda had already been approved by the executive committee and distributed to the board, I'd be willing to move a motion to grant him speaking rights under the Other Business section at the end. I'd still be voting against any appeal, I said, but I wasn't in principle opposed to ACSA having another one. He seemed satisfied with this and hung up.

"Right. So it's the day before the meeting, a Sunday, and I get this phone call at home. Now I gotta say, Theo, I'm not an especially intuitive kind of guy, but somehow, the moment that phone rang, I just knew I was in trouble. It was like I'd connected with the phone or the phone line or something without even having picked it up. Anyhow, I answered.

"'Mr. Carl Landsberg?' said this man's voice, real stern, real scary. Right off, I knew it had something to do with ACSA.

"'Yes?' I said.

"'Well, Mr. Landsberg, I would appreciate a meeting with you in order to discuss certain ramifications of your space allocation policy – ramifications, I might add, of which I am certain you are quite unaware.'

"'Uh-huh,' I said.

"'And I strongly suggest that we have this meeting as soon as possible,' he went on.

"'Uh-huh.'

"'In order to discuss the matter.'

"*Who was this guy?* I wondered. I mean, he sure didn't sound like he was from on campus. I guessed that he came from the 'real' world.

"'Well, what exactly do you mean by "ramifications"?'

"'It would be preferable if I explained it all in person, Mr. Landsberg.' The guy was really starting to freak me out. I figured that he was some kind of anti-racist vigilante fanatic who'd read about me somewhere and had decided to find me and kill me.

"'As soon as possible, eh?' I said. I was going to have to meet with him at some point, I thought; after all, I was an elected politician and he was a 'concerned' member of the public. But I'd already hardly been sleeping and I was sure that meeting him later rather than sooner would only mean more sleepless nights. The image flashed of me tossing and turning for hours wondering if now my space allocation policy was going to get me killed. But then I thought: *fine.* This was a matter of principle and there was just no way I was going to give in, no matter what. Even if it killed me.

"I guess that's when I realized just how important my experiment was to me. I wanted to know – no, I *needed* to know – that it really was possible for a purely just policy to be applied in the world, you know, for a politician, at least when it mattered, to govern for the sake of justice and nothing else.

"And so, wanting to get it over with as soon as possible, I told him that I'd meet him in my office at SAC in a few hours. But then I thought: wait a minute, just 'cause I'm being principled doesn't mean I've got to be suicidal. No way am I going to meet with this guy until he tells me exactly who he is and what he wants – even then I'm not going to do it on a Sunday when nobody's around. So I demanded to know what was up. He was reluctant to say anything, but I told him that unless he did there simply wasn't going to be a meeting. Finally, he piped up.

"His name, he said, is Boyd Terry and he's a lawyer who works for, of all things, the Olympics – or, rather, the Toronto Olympic Committee. Seems Toronto was making a bid to have the 1996 Games come to the city and up until then it was considered a frontrunner along with Athens. But that very week – in Puerto Rico, if you can believe it – there was this meeting of the International Olympic Committee in which the five African delegates, each of whom had a vote on the final decision over which city would get the Games, stood up and started asking all these angry questions. What's this, they wanted to know, about some black group in Toronto being evicted? Don't they like black people in Toronto? And so on and so on.

"'Course it all came as a big surprise to the Toronto Olympic Committee. So given that Terry, who was black, had been given special responsibility for the city's black community, they sent him in to find out what the hell was going on. And that's how he learned about this crazy kid student union president and his space allocation policy.

"'Mr. Landsberg,' he said to me, 'would you be willing to be a little more accommodating on this issue? I wonder if you are aware of just how important the Games are to this city. It would do so much good in so many ways. Why, even just economically speaking, it's estimated that the Games would bring in literally hundreds of millions of dollars. Hundreds of millions, Mr. Landsberg. You wouldn't want to put all that in jeopardy, would you?'

"Without flinching I launched into my by-then standard spiel about the lack of space on campus and about how important it was that we at SAC distributed what little space we controlled in a completely fair manner. He was surprised and admitted that, after having read the city's black community newspapers, he'd took me for a bigot. But now he knew otherwise, and he asked if I had Ogunsheye's number so he could speak with him. I was sceptical about his getting very far, and told him so, but I gave him the number anyway. Then he said he'd talk with some of the leaders of the black community and explain what was going on; they might be able to do something about getting the papers to change their coverage. There was certainly no objection from me there.

"I saw the guy for the first time at the board meeting the next day. He'd found a seat in the back of this packed room in Hart House. ACSA members, along with about fifty or so International Socialists, had already started demonstrating outside. I was hoping that they'd just stay there but no chance, of course. A few minutes after the meeting began they slowly filed into the room. I could see my vice-prez, who'd already started her speech introducing the budget, get all antsy as they came in. The room was really small, you see, which meant that they had to move in a single file and then stand right behind the SAC directors who were seated around the board table; they were literally breathing down their necks. At first they were pretty quiet, but then they started chanting: 'Give the space back! Give the space back!' louder and louder. The speaker called for order but they just kept on going. ACSA was now in charge of the meeting.

"First, they barred both doors to the room shut. Then, still chanting, those with the protest signs took their placards off, turning the posts into clubs that they shook in time to the chanting, just above and behind the heads of the directors. This went on for a bit until Ogunsheye finally shouted for quiet. Then he turned to the speaker and me and asked if now we were willing to hear ACSA's appeal. The speaker started explaining that we were already in the middle of an item on the agenda but the protesters interrupted him and started chanting again, this time with a much angrier tone. And with a fire in his eyes like I'd never seen before, Ogunsheye joined in: he started smashing his hand on the table right in front of my poor VP. At the same time, some of the protestors pointed and shouted at one of my board's black members to stop appeasing 'them'. And then they turned on me.

"'Racist!' screamed one.

"'Fascist! Dictator!' shouted another.

"I sat there as deadpan as I could – though inside, I can tell you, I felt a mix of fear and fear. I looked around. Some of the board members had begun crying. All I needed, I thought, was to say or do something stupid and that'd be it: the room would be set off for sure; there'd be a riot and some people – not least me – would get hurt and it'd be all my fault. I can't say, now, whether I was more worried about my safety or about what'd happen to my reputation if I screwed-up. So what to do? Or what not to do? Because doing nothing – you know, ignoring what was happening and just following the agenda – well it also meant doing something; it seemed that there was no way to be neutral. In the end, I decided to follow the agenda. 'Cause as I saw it the agenda stood for democracy and I wasn't about to let it be hijacked by some mob. So I just sat there, as crazy as it sounds, and waited for my turn to speak to the motion.

"But the situation was building to a fever pitch. I felt sure the room was about to blow. Yet then, suddenly, amidst all the noise and the screaming, one of the protesters pointed at me and shouted: 'You – you're just like Hitler!' At this everyone froze; a hush actually fell on the room.

"Still I did nothing. I was more comfortable with the fiction that I was simply waiting for my turn to speak. I was going to follow the rules no matter what."

"Nothing?" said Theo Hoshen. "You really did nothing at all?"

"That's right."

"But *what an insult.* You should not have stood for it."

"Well, maybe not. But the weird thing is, that's what saved us. 'Cause everyone knew I was Jewish and the Hitler line went a bit far even for the protesters. One of them actually shouted 'He's not *that* bad,' and they all burst out laughing. After a minute or so they went back to chanting, but now much less intensely than before; in fact, from that point on it seemed that there was no more risk of a riot breaking out.

"Then a couple of campus cops finally showed up and pushed their way into the room. They went directly to the speaker and told him that he had to adjourn the meeting. He looked at me, saw that I didn't agree, but adjourned it anyway. And so that was it. No budget – but no appeal either.

"The next day I saw Boyd Terry again. 'Those people,' he said, 'why they're nothing but a bunch of fascists. You simply cannot give in to them.'

"'But what about the Games?' I wondered. 'The hundreds of millions of dollars?'

"'Yes, well, sometimes it's the principle of the thing.'

"'Exactly,' I said.

"Still, principle or no principle, we didn't pass our budget and it didn't seem like we'd be able to anytime soon. This was a big problem 'cause it meant that the executive wouldn't be able to spend any money on SAC's programs and events. So our whole year was in jeopardy.

"Then I get this call from the university ombudsperson. She'd read about the near-riot at the board meeting and offered to mediate between SAC and ACSA. I had nothing else, so I took her up on it. And after only a few meetings, attended by myself and a few ACSA people (though not Ogunsheye, for some reason), we made some real progress: I agreed to let ACSA make another appeal to the board before we dealt with our budget and they agreed that they'd accept the result peacefully, however it turned out. So it was time for another meeting.

"Just in case, I arranged for it to take place at Simcoe Hall, which is where the Governing Council of the whole university meets. It's got this really big room and I figured that, even if ACSA kept their word about being peaceful, they couldn't speak for the International Socialists who had a reputation for being anything but. The room also made getaways possible. There were two exits: a main one and a relatively hidden one in a back corner. Since it was the executive committee who would be in the most danger if the protesters turned violent, I figured we should sit at the end of the table closest to this hidden exit. There'd also be a number of undercover campus cops present (uniformed ones, we were told, would only provoke), two of which would guard the executive should we need to make that quick exit, while the others would protect the board members. A squad of Metro Toronto police would also be standing by.

"So the day came and the meeting began. It was seven in the evening and the room was totally packed. The agenda got adopted with little fuss and we moved right to Approval of Minutes from Previous Meetings. This always includes minutes from all of the recent meetings of the various SAC commissions and committees. If they're adopted, it means that any motions they contain are approved by the full board and so they become official SAC policy. Usually, however, a significant motion gets 'externalized', brought up for discussion by the full board. And this was what was done to the motion that I'd passed at our University Affairs commission, the one which called on the U of T to refuse donations from companies with ties to South Africa. As the mover of the motion, I was expected to speak to it, you know, to explain its rationale. But even though I knew that this would help my image with the people in the room – or rather *because* I knew that – I said nothing. It's not as if the policy was in any danger of being rejected, and I decided that my speaking up for it would amount to a cheap rhetorical move – something that my little experiment, which required that I be concerned only with substance and never with image, ruled out. And so I was quiet.

"With the minutes approved, it was on to the first item of business: ACSA's second appeal. It'd been agreed that Ogunsheye would speak first, then answer questions from the board, and then it'd be my turn.

"He began with his usual argument about how ACSA *really was* a service organization geared towards all students, thus making it eligible for space under the policy. Other groups, he noted, might meet the policy's criteria as well, and he did not contest this, but 'it was up to them to argue their own case.' What we needed to appreciate was how SAC's labelling ACSA as 'narrow' just because it was an ethnic group was racist. More than that, he declared, pausing to stare directly at me, what some obviously failed to grasp was how 'rolling back anti-racist gains' was also racist. Of course, as you might expect, that word came up a lot in his speech, and every time he used it I could feel a shudder run down the backs of the board members.

"In implementing our policy the way we did, he went on, the SAC executive had essentially put ACSA on trial, forcing them to justify their very existence. And that, too, was racist. So we had wronged them, just as whites had wronged blacks throughout the history of the world. The question, then, was not whether they should be apologizing for their treatment of the board during the last meeting, but rather why we at SAC had forced them to go to the lengths that they did. Who did we think we were? Had we no shame? Because *everyone* knew that racism was wrong, that it was one of the world's great evils – how, then, had this managed to escape the SAC board? Finally, our evicting ACSA amounted to no more than students doing the administration's dirty work: it solved nothing and it distracted all of us from the need to fight the administration for more space.

"Throughout his speech, there was this elderly black woman seated in the back who from time to time would cry out with this gospel-like 'Oh yes, Lord!' and once even with a 'Hallelujah!' I got to say, it was powerful stuff.

"Next came the questions from the board. At first, it seemed that most of the board members had rejected Ogunsheye's arguments. One even asked him whether SAC should be deciding who deserves space on the basis of who protests the loudest. But then, as the questions continued, I got the sense that the board – this very same board which had originally passed my policy unanimously and had then voted overwhelming against ACSA's first appeal – was beginning to waver. As one member put it: 'Carl should be fighting for more space instead of taking away what has already been successfully fought for.'

"Then it was my turn and, I got to admit, my speech was weak. That all the arguments I'd been making till then had failed to convince, well, I was really at a loss. But what else could I do? So I just made 'em again. And again. Still, I'm sure the audience could detect the doubt in my voice; in any case, it was no match for the power of Ogunsheye's self-righteous tone. I went on to say that while I'd already begun to work for more space and would continue to do so, the reality was that there was a shortage *right now* and that we all had to deal with that. And what was the point of us students *fighting* against the administration; I mean, isn't the whole problem with the weak fighting the strong that the weak, being weak, are bound to lose? So there's got to be a better way: we should be working together to *convince* the administration to provide us with more space. I then admitted that I was wrong not to have told ACSA about the new policy before first presenting it to the board, but I pointed out that ACSA no longer seemed to be contesting the policy and, anyway, they were granted an appeal. Also, the fact was that the policy was just: SAC simply shouldn't be favouring some ethnic or cultural groups over others; doing *that* would be racist. I concluded with a paraphrase of Martin Luther King: did we really want to be part of a university in which student groups were judged by the colour of their skin rather than by their service to the student body? The answer, I declared, was no.

"But the speech fell flat. Everyone could tell that my heart just wasn't in it and this only contributed to a growing support among the board members for ACSA. So what I had once thought impossible seemed to be happening: they were changing their minds. I even got a few notes from members usually loyal to me apologizing because they were going to vote in ACSA's favour. 'At least this'll all finally be over,' my vice-president whispered in my ear after she'd read one of the notes.

"Then the question was called; the votes were counted; and the result was in: 34-31 against. ACSA's second appeal was denied.

"Everyone went quiet. We all looked to see how ACSA and their supporters would react. Quietly, they got up, gathered their coats and things, and made their way towards the door. They were respecting our agreement and leaving peacefully. Only the International Socialists bent the rule a little by chanting – the *Internationale*, of course. Still, out they went as well, fists clenched with universal love. You could hear 'em even after they'd gone down the stairs: 'So comrades, come rally / And the last fight let us face...'

"From that day on, ACSA and its allies totally forgot about SAC and directed their energies to fighting the administration. And *that* sure didn't take long. One protest in front of the university prez's house, which got coverage in the *Toronto Star*, and the administration was ready to violate its own space allocation policy and give ACSA an office. I was told that the president was going to make the announcement during a press conference. And the day before it, I got this call from one of the vice-prezs. Apparently, ACSA had – surprise, surprise – told them that they preferred holding on to their old office, and so he wanted to know if I'd be willing to transfer it over to the administration's jurisdiction in exchange for a much bigger office that we could use as we saw fit.

"'No shell games for me,' I said. And that was that."

CHAPTER IX

Concerning the momentous discussion that passed between Carl Landsberg and Theo Hoshen, and how it led the former to make a surprising decision

"An impressive story," declared Theo Hoshen. "And very well told."

"Yeah, well, before you give me your take, Theo, I should say that while that was the end of the political battle, another one, right up your alley, had just begun. 'Cause I'd started to wonder if my policy really was just after all. It was all thanks to this tiny doubt planted in my head by a side argument buried in one of ACSA's first letters to me. It went like this: yes, Downtown Legal Services provides a service to all undergrads, but not all undergrads can participate in it fully since only law students can provide the legal aid. So if ACSA wasn't eligible for space because it wasn't geared towards the full participation of all undergraduates, well then DLS shouldn't be eligible either.

"At first, this struck me as just a silly technicality. I mean, anyone who needed DLS's services could get them. Yet I found myself coming back to the idea again and again. Because it *was* true that DLS wasn't *completely* open to all undergraduates –

you did have to be a law student to get involved with them. And yet the whole point of my policy was to make groups like the DLS eligible. This led me to wonder about the other groups I'd labelled service organizations: were they really as open as I'd thought? Take *The Varsity*. Sure, anyone can volunteer to write for it, but would anyone want to? I mean, it's got this particular, left-wing slant; what if that just wasn't your politics? And what about CIUT-FM? As a campus-community station, it puts out anything but mainstream radio. So what if you just weren't into spoken word or alternative music? Well then you probably wouldn't want to listen to the station, much less be a DJ there.

"And so on and so on. The more I thought about it, the more I began to doubt that my service organizations category really was neutral after all. And this led me to wonder: if I couldn't even come up with a neutral category of student clubs, well then maybe neutrality just wasn't an option in politics. Because after all, isn't *every* group geared to some people and not others? Heck, isn't that what the definition of a group is? A specific bunch of people as distinct from everyone?

"So my doubts only grew. They were already pretty big by the time of ACSA's second appeal – which as I said was one reason why I gave such a shitty speech. And since then, well, I've got to say that I've become even more confused. In fact I'll admit that, right now, I've no idea what a just space allocation policy – hell, what *any* just policy – should look like. I guess I've become what you philosophy-types call a sceptic. And you know what, Theo? I don't like it, not one bit. 'Cause if there's no justice, well then what the hell's the point of it all?"

"A truly unnecessary question," declared Theo Hoshen. "Of course there is justice. One only needs to conceive of it properly."

"And?"

"And, Carl, this means, among other things, that it must not be equated with neutrality. Allow me to explain. Neutrality is fine for hockey referees, but politics is no game; it cannot be governed by a rulebook, by some overarching, systematic set of laws, since it is by nature too messy for that. We must approach it with a different spirit: instead of disengaged neutrality we need to remain engaged and sensitive to the context. Only that way can we bring happiness to everyone, to each according to his function as a member of the human species. And as Aristotle tells us, this means striving, above all, to treat people *honourably*."

"Honourably? Sounds nice. Means nothing."

"I am not surprised at your scepticism, Carl. But I can guarantee that, if you carefully follow my every step, you will see that what I have to say is right. Moreover, I am not claiming that what you did was wrong; in fact I think that, for the most part, you did the right thing. Only by neglecting honour you did it for the wrong reasons."

"Go on."

"Let me begin by stating that 'anti-racism' is not at all the appropriate way of thinking about how to do justice to an issue such as campus space allocation. And I mean this as regards both the neutral kind of anti-racism that you yourself could be said to have defended as well as that which your adversary, Ogunsheye, spoke for. Let us begin with your own.

"Now your policy, as you pointed out, was blind to such things as sexual orientation or skin colour, which is why you felt you had to treat GLAUT and ACSA exactly as you did all of the other ethnic or cultural groups. Neutrality, you believed, put you above the fray, so to speak, rather than dropping you in with all of the messy, partisan politics of *hoi polloi*. To be neutral is to be as pure as the whitecoated natural scientist in his laboratory. Recall your talk about SAC's need to avoid the 'grubby business' of judging between all of the ethnic, political, sports or religious groups; evidently, you had the sense that a just policy must transcend them all if it is to be clean. Or consider your refusal to engage in anything that smacked of rhetoric, as when you kept your opposition to South African apartheid to yourself. What is that if not also revealing of a desire to be 'above it all'? But as I will demonstrate, Carl, purity has no place in politics. Not because politics is necessarily dirty and unjust, but because justice requires that we always be true to the messy particulars of a given context.

"Before I show this, however, I want to point out that neutrality is not merely undesirable, it is also impossible, as you learned when your service organizations category collapsed and you became as you are now, mired in scepticism. Even if you had not come to this realization and so continued to believe in the policy's neutrality, you must nevertheless accept that your willingness to find ACSA space outside of SAC's jurisdiction was itself non-neutral – the neutrality being restricted to that jurisdiction, just like a game which stands apart from practical life. Regardless, you now consider the view that one position is as good as any other to be inescapable, hence that there is no reasonable way of deciding which groups merit space and which do not. But notice something that both neutrality and scepticism have in common: they eschew discriminating judgment. The neutralist refuses to discriminate because, as you tried to do with your service organizations category, he aims to be above it all, while the sceptic refuses to because he thinks that nothing is justifiably better than anything else. In consequence, both these ways of thinking not only undermine racism, sexism and homophobia, the unholy trinity of our day, but also all other discriminations. And this is grave, Carl, because discriminating – affirming that some things matter, that some are good and others are bad – is essential to all judgment. Indeed, it is only because we discriminate that we have reason to get up in the morning, and the very society we get up into exists because of the discriminations that its members share, since these support the virtues and taboos that keep them from falling into barbarism. And yet the popularity of neutralist and sceptical approaches has resulted in a widespread discrimination against discriminating. This has led, as if by default, to a reverence for equality in its most impoverished form, which is to say equality as uniformity. Indeed, as Alexis de Tocqueville once pointed out, our passion for it has become virtually invincible: we desire it in freedom but, if we cannot have it that way, then we will take it in slavery.

"Yet there is another way, Carl, one which fights racism by striving for a richer form of equality than that favoured by those who go no further than being 'anti-'. You see, anti-racists do no more than demand that people eliminate their racially-based discriminations; they have nothing to say about the non-racial discriminations that we should be affirming in their stead. And faced with this emptiness, the result more often than not is resentment, backlash, or worse – the urge by some to become racists as a means of rebellion. I am thinking of the most alienated among us, Carl, of those utter failures who are desperate to take revenge on society for neglecting to recognize them. They turn to racism not, at least at first, because of any genuinely racist sentiments, but because they sense that it is something so reviled that they will be guaranteed to give offence and in this way receive the attention they so crave.

"I am sure you find it strange that anyone would seek such attention, but that is because you have never tasted their desolation. You see, Carl, these poor individuals have come to feel virtually nonexistent, and in a way that is possible only within modern society, the society of misters. In the premodern world, which asserted a fixed social hierarchy instead of the equal opportunity of today, the worst place one could find oneself was – not nowhere – but on the bottom rung, which is to say within the lowest class. So even the lowest of the low had their place, their minimum of honour; they were still on the ladder, still with a recognized role to play. But today's failures are often so hidden, so ignored, that they prefer infamy over invisibility. Thus do they seek out contemporary society's ideals in order to attack them and thereby gain attention for themselves. And one such ideal, Carl, is none other than anti-racism. Are you following me?"

Carl was so entranced by the flow of Theo Hoshen's words that he could only manage a weak reply:

"Um, yeah, I guess so."

"Excellent," said Theo Hoshen. "So as you can see, anti-racism can actually feed racism. Yet it does so not only by providing some with a means of gaining attention. Because in the case of the other racists – the genuine, despicable article – it discourages them from changing. The reason is that these people will abandon their reprehensible discriminations only when they have been convinced to adopt alternative ones; for, as I have said, we all need to discriminate in order to make sense of our lives. You see, the only way to get people to give up one sort of discrimination is to show them that another is superior. Think, for example, of what would happen the moment Martians appeared and attacked the Earth: there would be no need to demand that people abandon their racially-based discriminations because there would be an obvious reason to affirm an alternative, namely, one between the human species and Martians. Discriminating on the basis of race would simply lose its point.

"This need to persuade people to favour alternative, non-racial discriminations is, I say again, something completely ignored by anti-racists. Indeed their impoverished, levelling mode of egalitarianism has no room for the basic claim that I have been leading up to here, which is that the very act of being 'anti-' is, while occasionally useful for standing up to injustice, utterly powerless when it comes to encouraging people to undertake the positive journey *towards* justice. That is why we should try never merely to stand *against* something in politics, Carl, to slam doors in the faces of those walking through them; we must also open other doors and show people why going through *them* is best. And to do that, to discriminate properly between doors – or student groups – we need an engaged kind of judgment, one very different from that of the neutral referee. Taken too far and neutrality closes all doors by leading, as it appears to have done in your case, to the nihilistic conclusion that no group meets its criteria of justice. Now engaged judgment is different in that it requires discriminating among all of the messy particulars of a given context. Yet though it calls for different things in different situations, it is not relativist since one can carry it out properly only by being *true* to the well-being of all, and this requires a correct theory of how we human beings function and flourish in society. Fortunately, Carl, we have that theory, for it is none other than Aristotle's, the greatest of all philosophers.

"Shall we turn, now, to your friend Ogunsheye's form of anti-racism? Are you still with me?"

"Uh, yeah," replied Carl.

"Very good. Now Ogunsheye's approach is very different from yours, as far from affirming a neutral point of view as

Malcolm X was from Martin Luther King. And although it may seem to you that all Ogunsheye cares about is his own group's self-interest, I can assure you that he is indeed striving to fulfil a genuine form of equality, albeit one that is unlike yours since it cannot be reduced to uniformity. Rather, it is much closer to Aristotle's, for whom equality consists of treating likes the same and unlikes differently. Because what Ogunsheye wants – even though he never said so in these terms – is for his group to be recognized for its specificity within the university community. And he is right to do so, Carl; right to oppose those who, in a neutral spirit, suggest that his group is just like any other. But he is wrong in chasing recognition by clinging to this one office at all costs, and not only because it would be unfair to all of the other student groups, including the other black student groups. By associating recognition with a material thing like an office, he is only reifying it. He is changing it into a commodity, something which represents a gain for some and, necessarily, a loss for others. But at its best, recognition is like love. It differs from gold and clay, for to divide is not to take away. Shelley."

"What?"

"And this desire to be properly recognized, what is it if not a concern with being treated honourably? You see, Ogunsheye has essentially been struggling on behalf of his group's reputation, its place in the university community. He never used the word 'honour', I suggest, partly because the language of redress for oppression or discrimination has so much more power today, and partly because calling on others to recognize one's worth puts one in a vulnerable position – and there is little room for vulnerability within the battles that go by the name of politics. Regardless, Carl, what I am saying is that rather than fighting for special treatment over office space, ACSA should have focused on issues like the one Ogunsheye raised about the lack of texts by blacks in the curriculum. For that is a much more effective, not to mention suitable, way of obtaining the honour that his group deserves.

"All of which is to say that you were right not to make an exception of ACSA while applying your space allocation policy. Not for reasons of neutrality, however, nor because 'anything goes'; no, you were right to do so since one must always strive to give everyone, and so every student group, their due. The just student council president, in other words, is someone who always acts magnanimously, nobly – in short, honourably. This means not only doing but also being good, by which I mean virtuous, since honour is but the reward of virtue. It is honour, Carl, that you should always strive to put at the centre of your concerns, and this means that when you do good you must do it, and be seen to do it, well. So you were indeed wrong not to have consulted with all of the groups concerned before passing your policy at the SAC board, as you were when you failed to speak up on behalf of your anti-apartheid motion during the meeting, even if it was going to pass anyway. For it would have revealed that you do not, in fact, wish to treat ACSA the same as all of the other groups since, of all of the possible motions that you could have introduced, you chose to put your energies behind one which happens to be of particular concern to them. In so doing, Carl, you would indeed have been magnanimous, a result of having engaged in the proper judgment of particulars rather than of being neutral. And that is precisely what acting justly, honourably, is all about."

Carl was most astonished at this speech of Theo Hoshen's. For a time he found himself unable to do anything more than stare silently back at its speaker. And then, when he finally found his tongue, this is what he said:

"You know, Theo, you actually make sense. I really hadn't thought of it that way before. Which is good 'cause I sure can't go back to shooting for neutrality. Still, I got to say, all this honour-talk – it's a bit old fashioned, don't you think? I mean, who even uses the word nowadays?"

"It is no more old fashioned than justice," objected Theo Hoshen.

"Yeah, well, it's not that I think you're wrong, it's just that, well...You know, Theo, I'm not really sure what to say."

"That is fine," said Theo Hoshen. "So then, Carl, how might we go about finding that protestor, the one of the Hitler insult?"

"What? What do you mean?"

"Why, to get him to retract and apologize for his abominable affront."

"Retract and apologize? You can't be serious. Look, Theo, I'm a politician, right? I can't go chasing after everyone who throws an insult my way. I mean, for one thing, there's not enough time."

"But Carl," protested Theo Hoshen, "he said you were *like Hitler*. Surely you cannot let such an attack on your honour stand."

"You're kidding, right? There is such a thing as free speech in this country, you know. I mean jeez, Theo, get with the program."

"Ah, yes, 'the program'." Theo Hoshen then fell silent.

"In fact, you know what," continued Carl, "I think that this points to a hole in your whole theory. Sure you may be on to something with all the neglect of honour stuff, and I can see how it points to the need to recognize people's uniqueness in the community, but *everything* can't be a matter of honour, can it? I mean, sometimes we've got to do things that aren't particularly honourable, right? And then what?"

"I cannot imagine a single such time," challenged Theo Hoshen.

"Listen, all I'm saying is that if there's one thing I've learned from this whole space allocation mess it's that there can be issues – like the conflict between honour and free speech, for example – which just can't be reasoned through. I'm not just talking about neutral reasoning; even your sensitive-to-the-particulars, discriminating kind of reason isn't all-powerful. And when it fails, Theo, well then I think we've got to accept that the best we can do is try and reach some sort of compromise."

"Now, Carl, you are speaking of a politics that is not only messy, but dirty," protested Theo Hoshen.

"Maybe," replied Carl. "But I really think that, sometimes, that's as good as it gets. I'm not going back on what I said before; I still think you've got a point. It's just that, you know, you may be taking the argument a bit far. Still, I'm really grateful, Theo. Really. Your honour idea has helped me figure some of this stuff out. Now I wonder how one would go about being honourable with the engineers."

"The engineers?" came Theo Hoshen's startled reply. "Why do you mention them?"

"'Cause remember how I told you about their stealing and giving back our War Room Door? Well they took it again – just last night, in fact. And this time the nerdy bastards sent a ransom note. Here, take a look." Carl then reached into his back pocket, pulled out his wallet and removed a blue piece of paper that he then handed to Theo Hoshen. This is what he read:

BRUTE FORCE COMMITTEE

Being a totally fictitious and imaginary organization which does
not exist, has never existed, and never will exist

Ransom Note

Dear SAC (Stupid Asshole Committee),

First off, we do not, never have, and never will
   have da door. But if we did, diss is what wee
   would want:

25 O'Keef's Extra Old Stock

41 Oz Cockspur Rum

30 Oz of Skreef

400 gummy bears with da heds bitten offa dem

1 29" pizza with hot peepers and ground beef

14 donut holes (with the original donuts)

1 vice-president for one afternoon's use – some
   nurse (Samantha) says she will oblige Carly for
   the same afternoon in case he's jealous

2 working Skydomes

3 Japanese sooper cooshun toilet seets

35 B25 Stealth Bombers with air and CD, sunroof
   – some fuzzy dice and a radar detecter would also
   be nice

1kg (2.2lb) kryptonite

1 Superman to use it on

16 cybernetic pogo sticks from Sears

Still owing from da last time:

2 Romulan cloaking devices

10 steam tunnels to SAC Dome

1 ladder up to it

3 escape slides down it
1 emergency button to send da mice – dat's da U of
   T police – away
1 Equality for ~~women~~ sexes (we mean it man)
2 Shrubbbbbrey

Some more stuff we just thought of:

3 machines that go 'ping'
10 queen size water beds with rum in them
1 gangbang with all SAC Directors with sweet in
   sour sauce
1 case of Dom Perigon
2 Peewee Hermans
donate to Shinerama 0.99^n (get a mathie to work this
   out)

But seriously (hah! Everything is serious space in
SAC, eh?), we don't have your door nor do we know
who took it. But if supplied with ~~some of~~ these
demands we could be persuaded to seek out these
individuals, acquire da door, and return it without
too much damage (well, it will still work).

Da Chief

"Well, well," said Theo Hoshen. "So they have struck again."

"Yeah," said Carl. "But you know, given what I've been
through lately, this stuff comes as kind of a relief. Still, I got to
say, we SAC-hacks are getting real tired of getting yanked
around by these guys all the time. But a few bottles of rum'll
do the trick and we'll get our door back."

"Is that all that you wish to have returned?" challenged
Theo Hoshen.

"I knew you'd say something like that. What, we've got to get our *honour* back, is that it? And how would we do that?"

"What I have in mind would certainly bring the required recompense. But I fear it may be a little much for you."

"Try me."

"Well, how did you say they made that black crater in your War Room Door?"

"By firing their Cannon into it."

"Precisely."

"What, we should fire a cannon into one of their doors?"

"No," said Theo Hoshen. "*The* Cannon. You should take it."

"Take it?" exclaimed Carl. "How? The thing's guarded, you know; it's their mascot."

"Yes, the symbol of their honour."

"Oh come on, Theo. Taking it's just not an option. They've these guys, right, really big guys. With clubs. And they're literally chained to the thing."

"I know. I also know that 'magnanimous' is a synonym for 'big'. So the question is: who is the more magnanimous?"

"Oh that's the question, is it?"

"Yes. Because recognition – honour – can also come from defeating an adversary. Yet notice, Carl, that I am not saying you must take the Cannon directly out of the Cannon Guard's hands. For you see, I know where they have it hidden."

"The Cannon? How could you know that?"

"Let us just say that I have being doing some research."

"What? On the Cannon? Are you serious? I thought you were a philosophy student."

"And what do you mean by that?"

"I don't know. Just that you'd be into deeper stuff – trees falling in forests and the like. Not school mascots."

"What is so deep about a tree falling in a forest?"

"You know, if it doesn't make a sound."

"That does sound deep. But then there *was* a sound."

"What?"

"Precisely."

There was a pause, following which the two shared a hearty laugh. Finally, Theo Hoshen spoke again:

"What I am 'into', Carl, as I have told you, is honour. And I believe that taking the Cannon would be a truly honourable thing to do; indeed, it would serve to remind the whole university community of how honour is the prize of all virtue – a prize, moreover, that had you striven for it from the beginning would have led you to handle your space allocation issue much better than you did."

"Listen," said Carl, "I already admitted you had a point there. But come on, Theo, the Cannon? I can't remember when was the last time someone managed to steal it. It was a long time ago, I can tell you that."

"Twenty-two years."

"Really? Twenty-two?"

"Really."

There was a pause, following which Carl said: "And you're saying that you think you know where it is?"

"I am."

Yet another a pause. Finally, Carl spoke again:

"You know, this *is* SAC's seventy-fifth birthday; I've been telling everyone that we should do something special. But man, if they ever found out, they'd just tear us apart! Still, nothing worth doing comes without some kind of risk, eh?" Theo Hoshen nodded. And then Carl said: "Alright, I'm in."

"You are?"

"Yes. But listen, Theo, *under no circumstances* can we get caught. I mean it. I'm the president for God's sake!"

"I assure you," said Theo Hoshen, his heart filling with joy, "God shall have nothing to do with it."

"He'd better not," said Carl.

CHAPTER X

Wherein preparations are made for the theft of the Mighty Skule Cannon

It being well known that *non est ad astra mollis e terris via*, Carl was far from convinced by Theo Hoshen's account of how he had determined the Cannon's location. And so he had the young philosopher agree to let him manage a reconnaissance mission of his own.

Carl's first idea was to see if he might arrange for some kind of double-agent, since that would surely be the most efficient as well as the safest way of getting the information they required. At once he thought of a certain SAC volunteer, one Larry Corretti who had been a long-time active Skuleman as well as a not-so-secret member of the Brute Force Committee. Weak grades had meant that he had to transfer out of engineering studies and into a major in history, however. In consequence, Carl decided that it would be a good idea to, very delicately, prod his sense of Skule loyalty.

"So now that you're taking courses at UC," he asked Corretti the next day, "I guess that makes you an artsie like the rest of us?"

"I'll never be an artsie," replied Corretti, not bothering to lift his eyes from the screen of the computer he was working on.

"But you're not taking engineering courses anymore," objected Carl.

"Yeah, but I still hang around EngSoc a lot."

"You really go for all that Skule stuff, eh Larry?"

"Always," came the reply. Clearly, the man was not for turning.

The double-agent route seemingly blocked, Carl's next thought was to visit the Engineering Society's offices himself, just to see what he could see. So the next day, when his External Affairs commissioner (who had developed close relations with Skule; indeed, she was having a romantic affair with a Skuleman) announced that she was off to pay the Engineering Society a visit, Carl offered to join her. The commissioner was somewhat taken aback by this, since it was not every day that the SAC president set foot in that place. Carl began to worry that she had somehow become suspicious. Yet he quickly dismissed this as paranoia.

When they arrived, everyone was surprised by the sudden high-level visit. They soon took it in their stride, however, and Carl was offered a tour. He accepted, of course, and was introduced to the head secretary, who cheerfully escorted him from office to office. Somehow, however, she managed to pass over the one room that formed the centre of his and Theo Hoshen's interests. Sounding as nonchalant as possible, Carl inquired as to what was behind its door.

"Oh nothing," said his guide evasively. Then Carl noticed her exchange a furtive glance with the two Skulemen present. So Theo Hoshen had been right after all; the Cannon really was in that room. Carl casually changed the subject and, after a few minutes, the tour having been completed, he graciously offered the head secretary his gratitude. Vigorous handshakes were exchanged between all present and it wasn't long before Carl was outside the main door.

"It's there alright," he said to Theo Hoshen that evening. They were meeting in the kitchen of the latter's house.

"Indeed," replied Theo Hoshen.

"Indeed-dee-do," piped in Simon who, along with Avigail, was also present. "Now you guys just got to break in and enter. Forgive a foreigner's ignorance, but exactly what's the penalty for pulling a job in this country? I mean, in your Criminal Code – is it two to five or five to ten years?"

"Oh come on, Simon," said Avigail. "It's just a college prank. No one'd get arrested, much less have charges pressed against them by the engineers."

"We're dead certain of that, are we?" retorted Simon. "I'd think twice, mates; she might be having the painters in. Look, sure everyone used to nick the Cannon once, but that's long past. So when you try it and get caught, they might just throw the book at you."

"But Simon," interjected Theo Hoshen, "we shall be very careful; there is no reason to assume we shall be captured."

"Uh oh," said Carl in a humorous tone, "Theo's reasoning again. Still, getting caught *is* out of the question. And I'm not just talking about the cops. I mean, can you imagine the press coverage? The campus papers would go totally nuts. They've already pegged me as an enemy of the people just 'cause I got myself elected. No, we absolutely can't get caught; no way."

"So it is decided," announced Theo Hoshen with a smile. "Now, what of the plan? It strikes me that we have two questions to confront. First, how do we get into the Engineering Society offices? And second, how, once inside, do we get through the door to the room that is our objective?"

"Why not use glass cutters on the office windows and then pick the lock of the door when you're in?" suggested Avigail.

"Excellent," declared Theo Hoshen.

"Alright," said Simon. "I can see where this is heading. Tell me, gents, do either of you know how to pick a lock? Thought not. And it'll be a serious yonks before you figure out how to use glass cutters. Right then, to the tool shop."

Surprised, everyone stared at Simon.

"Don't go losing it on me," he chided. "I'm not joining you silly buggers. I'm just making sure you've got the right equipment."

So the four climbed into the van that Carl had driven from SAC and made their way to the nearest Canadian Tire outlet. Inside, Simon, followed by the other three, went directly to a salesman standing in the tools department.

"I'm looking for a light but schtum drill," he announced.

"What do you want to drill into?" inquired the salesman.

"Oh, a hunk of wood about this thick," said Simon as he held out his thumb and forefinger.

"Like a door," added Carl with a chuckle.

"And you might throw in an acetylene torch," contributed Avigail, also laughing softly.

"Zip it, gits," ordered Simon, "or I'm going home." And so Carl and Avigail struggled to suppress their mirth. Simon then turned to the salesman: "Cancel the torch, mate," he said. "But we'll be needing a good nick handsaw."

"What if it's in a safe?" whispered Avigail into Simon's ear.

"Then they'll just have to bring the whole thing back, won't they? And they'll have to use their own loaves to figure out how to open it − 'cause I've no idea."

"Right," replied Avigail. Turning to the salesman, she then

said: "Where are the glass cutters?" She had to bite her lip to keep from laughing.

"Won't work," said Simon. "Trust me."

"What, we're just going to smash the window?" said Carl a bit too loudly. Realising that he may have just let slip something incriminating, all four of them immediately shot worried looks at the salesman. But to their amazement, he simply ignored the remark.

"The glass cutters are down that aisle," he said matter-of-factly.

"Well then, sir," said Carl, "could you also tell us where we might locate some plastic explosives and an electric timer?" At this both Carl and Avigail – though not, of course, Simon or Theo Hoshen – burst into hysterical laughter.

"Sorry, mate," Simon said to the salesman, "they're just a bit wellied – laagered up, if you know wha' I mean; don't pay them no mind. C'mon, nippers, it's time to go home." But as Simon marched towards the exit Carl retrieved the drill, Theo Hoshen the handsaw, and Avigail the glass cutters. So Simon found himself having to wait outside in the van while the others stood in line at the checkout. Carl paid using the SAC credit card.

"Official business," he said to them with a wink.

Whereupon they returned to their house in order to begin work on the rest of the plan. Simon explained that, since picking the lock was out of the question, there was really only one way to get through the door and that was *around* the lock. The drill, he said in a serious tone, could be used to make a circle of holes around the door handle and lock. Then, with the saw, someone could "connect the dots," so to speak. When the job was done, it should be possible to push the door open while the part with the handle and lock remained in place.

Carl then raised the question of what they should do if they actually managed to get inside the room and seize their prize.

"Because if we get to it," he continued, "then we've got to take it in style."

"In what way?" asked Avigail.

"Well, you guys may have noticed that *The Varsity* building's been without its sign for some time now. A little bird told me that the Brute Force Committee, pissed off at all the Varg's politically correct criticisms of the engineers, took it one night in retaliation."

"'A little bird told you'?" echoed Simon. "Well la-di-da."

"Yes, well," continued Carl, "here's what I say. Thanks to some fancy photocopying, I've managed to make some Varsity letterhead. So why don't we leave a sheet behind – you know, with writing on it demanding the return of the sign in exchange for the Cannon? What do you think?"

"A red rose left atop the note would serve as a nice touch," said Theo Hoshen.

"It would indeed, my wisdom-loving friend," said Carl. "And what about the Cannon itself? I mean, we've absolutely got to engrave something on it. How about 'Stolen by SAC 1989–90'? Though if and when we gave it back it'd mean that SAC's toast. Maybe something in code?"

"Boys," interjected Simon, "you haven't got the thing yet. Yer – you'll fancy this, Carl – counting chickens before they've hatched."

"Yes, but the early bird catches the worm," Carl objected.

"Not always," countered Simon.

"Friends," chided Theo Hoshen, "it is unbecoming for young men to utter maxims. Aristotle once said so."

"Oh he did, did he?" said Simon. "Well what was that just then?"

"What was what?"

"That, young man. Wasn't it a maxim?"

"I guess it was," admitted Theo Hoshen. "But then can you blame me? After all, birds of a feather."

"There he goes again," said Simon.

"That time I was attempting to be funny," remarked Theo Hoshen.

"Oh God," said Simon.

"In any case," Theo Hoshen continued, "I believe the moment has arrived for me to issue the early-bird with an invitation: Mr. President, would you happen to be free tomorrow morning, say at around three?"

"Why yes, my good man, I believe that I am available at that time," replied Carl.

"Excellent," said Theo Hoshen. "You may pick me up at two forty-five."

"Isn't this great?" said Carl to Simon and Avigail. "My first date with an Aristotelian!"

CHAPTER XI

*In which the wise Theo Hoshen and the brave Carl
Landsberg set forth on their stupendous attempt to
steal the Mighty Skule Cannon*

The rest of the evening passed somewhat less light-heartedly as Carl and Theo Hoshen endeavoured, with a series of entreaties, to convince Avigail and Simon to assist them with the theft of the Cannon. In authoritative voices the would-be thieves explained how, throughout the night, they could expect to face a patrol of campus police (or "mice," as they called them, following the custom of the engineers). If they were to avoid capture then there would have to be lookouts who could warn them of an approaching patrol car. Carl had brought along four two-way radios (normally used by SAC volunteers during orientation festivities) and he and Theo Hoshen wished only that Avigail and Simon would each agree to take one and post themselves where they could keep watch on one of the entrances to the alleyway that ran along the Sandford Fleming building's south side. For that was where the Engineering Society offices were to be found and it was through one of the windows facing the alley that Carl and Theo Hoshen would attempt to enter. Either Avigail or Simon, it was hoped, would keep an eye on the relevant part of King's College Road, which ran along the building's west side, whereas the other would surveil St. George Street, which ran along its east.

"Coax me, cajole me," said Avigail with a twinkle in her eye. Surprisingly, it did not take much of either for her to agree. Unsurprisingly, Simon was far more difficult. But Avigail's acquiescence had made it seem churlish for him to decline, as did Theo Hoshen's grand declaration – upon his "word of honour" – that he and Carl would never, ever, reveal Simon's identity to anyone. Simon knew that if he refused under those circumstances Theo Hoshen would consider it a great insult, so great that Simon would probably find himself short one rent-paying housemate. And as it was already fall, he knew how difficult it would be to find a replacement.

It could cost me a bomb, he worried to himself. *'Sides, I'm covered. And it might even make for a bit of fun.* Fun was something that Simon was in particular need of at this time, for things had been going mysteriously wrong in his laboratory; so much so that he was beginning to be concerned about the fate of his master's thesis. He agreed to take one of the radios.

It was decided that Simon would be the one, accompanied initially by Carl and Theo Hoshen, to man the St. George Street post. It would be his job to spot any patrol car coming south down that street, the assumption being that it would then turn left onto College Street whereupon Avigail could then catch sight of it. She was to follow it with her eyes and determine if it then turned north up King's College Road towards the Sandford Fleming building. Should it do so, she would immediately use her radio to warn Carl and Theo Hoshen, who would then have just enough time to conceal themselves in the alleyway.

It was a little after three in the morning, on what was a moonless, extraordinarily cold and crisp October weeknight, when they all reached their posts. Simon was already complaining about their tardiness, a result of Theo Hoshen's by now infamous inability, whenever some fresh philosophical idea came to him, to keep from scribbling it down into the little notebook that he carried with him at all times. This is precisely what happened at two o'clock that morning, with the inevitable result of delaying them all.

But now there they were at last, in place and all prepared. Even though it had been below zero for the past week, the roads were mostly free of snow and it took only a few minutes before the three young men spotted their first patrol car. Just as they had expected, it proceeded south down St. George Street and then turned left onto College Street.

"Mouse in view," announced Simon into his radio.

"Got it," replied Avigail over hers. And then: "It's coming. Now it's turning north," she said, which meant that it was proceeding up King's College Road. "It's three o'six. B-base clear."

"Right. Three o'six," confirmed Simon.

"You should say 'over' now," instructed Theo Hoshen.

"What?"

"One always says 'over' at the end of a broadcast."

"Why?"

"That is just the way it is done. It confirms that you have completed your transmission."

"She bloody-well knows it's complete, mate, 'cause I'm not saying anymore."

"But how does she know that you do not plan to say anything more?" objected Theo Hoshen.

"And why does she have to know that, you tosser?"

"I am just telling you how it is done."

"Fine," said Simon. And so he said "over" into his radio.

"Over what?" came Avigail's response.

"Fuckin' hell!" exclaimed Simon. "Over nothing," he said into his radio. "Forget it. Over."

"Okay. Over," said Avigail.

"You see," said a satisfied Theo Hoshen. But Simon only glared at him.

Eighteen more minutes passed before they saw the patrol car once again.

"Let's time another one, just to make sure," said Carl to the other two.

"Fine," said Simon. And then: "Mates, I need to take a leak. Be right back." Following which he wandered down along the hidden side of *The Varsity* building to do what he alone could do for himself.

"Simon seems annoyed," remarked Carl.

"Pay him no mind," said Theo Hoshen. "He is always like that."

"Avigail's sure into it, though. She's pretty cool, eh? Not to mention hot."

"Yes," confirmed Theo Hoshen.

"You know, Theo, there's something I wanted to ask you about that."

"Which is?"

"Well, not about Avigail specifically. More about your favourite philosopher, Aristotle. Now correct me if I'm wrong but, from what I remember from my political theory class, he wasn't too keen on women. I mean, he thought they should just stay home all the time and work with the slaves, right? Because only a male elite could be citizens and rule."

"That is correct," said Theo Hoshen.

"So, what, you agree with that?"

"In spirit – yes, of course."

"Really?" said Carl aghast. "And about slavery too?"

"I agree that some people are, by nature, unfit for freedom," replied Theo Hoshen. "This can be seen the moment real liberty is thrust upon them, for it makes them deeply unhappy."

Carl was stunned. And he was no less so when Theo Hoshen, wearing what appeared to be a straight face, added:

"In fact, Carl, I am quite certain that you, too, endorse the institution of slavery. Only you do not know it."

"Oh come on, Theo. You're kidding, right?"

"Certainly not."

"Alright then, let's hear it."

"Well to begin," said Theo Hoshen, mustering himself with relish for what was sure to be yet another speech of no small dimensions, "one must be aware of an important distinction that runs through the heart of Aristotle's moral philosophy, namely, that between 'life', on the one hand, and 'the good life', on the other. By 'life' Aristotle means all of those things that we humans share with the animals, which is to say all that we as a species must do in order to live as well as to enjoy living. And today, in this demotic age, life consists of such activities as holding down a job or a career as well as having a family and access to items such as washing machines, cars, electric can openers, CD players and television sets. Of course enjoying life's small pleasures also means being a sports fan and a moviegoer, indeed a consumer of many, many sorts of entertainment (as distinct from art). And it requires good health thanks to low cholesterol and dental insurance, not to mention all of the benefits that come from having friends (who are not, of course, too close), hobbies, and knowledge of the best cooking recipes. To which we must not fail to add all of the talk, talk, and more talk about what one has eaten, is eating, and will eat. For it cannot be denied that, today, those who enjoy life love nothing more than to recount their meals and to do so while making ample use of adjectives such as 'fabulous', 'amazing' and 'wonderful'. You know, as in: 'That was a truly fabulous beef stroganoff!' or 'What a simply amazing soup!' or 'This cake – my God, how wonderful!' Not that we should neglect drink, of course, for life today also consists of knowing the difference between a Merlot and a Cabernet, as well as of smelling and tasting whatever the waiter has poured into one's wineglass on the pretence that one might very well order the bottle's return should it fail to meet one's approval. Yes these are the pleasures of life, Carl. But do not get me wrong: each and every one of us must live – all must eat, even if it is only the flowers from the field. We simply have no choice in this, none at all; only a foolish drug-addict would claim otherwise.

"But – and this is a most important conjunction – some of us are also free to choose more. And when we make that choice, Carl, what we choose is 'the good life'. It is important to appreciate that what Aristotle meant by this is certainly not, as many think today, but an intensification of the pleasures of life – that which may come from, say, having access to a great deal of money. No, the good life is a qualitatively different kind of thing; it is that which transpires *above*, which is to say *on top of*, life. For it consists of the higher activities, those in which only a certain few, thanks to their special capacities, can participate. Because while there are animals, including the human animal, that can reason technically and so make and use tools to help them live, only certain people can also reason both metaphysically and prudentially, which is to say in ways that strive for truth and honour. And it is upon these that philosophy and politics are based – as well, you shall be pleased to hear, as activities like that in which we are participating tonight. They are what make for the good life.

"Now in the wonder that was ancient Greece," Theo Hoshen continued, "it was held that those who were capable of living life and only life should work to support those who could also live the good life – for in that way everyone would be happiest. In fact, it was nothing other than everyone's manifest happiness that was considered the chief sign of the justness of the whole arrangement. All were happy since none were forced to play a role that did not suit them."

"Oh come on, Theo," objected Carl, "you're telling me that if you asked the slaves back then they would've said that they were *happy* being slaves?"

"Well, why not look to today's slaves for the answer?" replied the young philosopher. "I am referring, of course, to all of the doctors and repairmen, the bus drivers and centrefolds –

all those whose job it is to provide us with services, who offer themselves up as tools, as mere objects, for the realization of the ends of life. To be sure, they may vote every four years or so, but none of them believes that his vote – one of millions – is meaningful, and he is quite right about that. The fact is, Carl, that for all intents and purposes the average person today is without political power and so, in that sense, he is unfree. And yet if you told him that he had to quit his job tomorrow and become a cabinet minister, that he could, as our parliamentary tradition has it, attach the appellation 'honourable' to his name, what do you think he would say? Would he be happy at the prospect? Or would he not rather complain that politics was an onerous business, one that he wanted no part of? Or say you impelled him to become a philosopher. Would he not protest that the material was all so very dry and abstract, that he could make no sense of it, and that he would rather think about almost anything else? Of course he would! And the reason, Carl, is simple: such men are just too busy living their lives, for they are not suited to the good life."

"And women?" challenged Carl. "What about women, *all* women?"

"Ah yes, women," said Theo Hoshen. But at just that moment, Simon returned:

"Guys, guys, what's going on? Have you been watching the road?"

"Uh..." said Carl.

"Jesus!" said Simon. "Stop pulling your puds and keep an eye out for the mice!" And indeed, just then, the patrol car drove by. "See, *there*," said Simon. He reached for his radio: "Mouse in view. Over."

"Okay," responded Avigail. And then a few seconds later: "Got it. It's three thirty-five. I'm making the call." It had been decided that Avigail would use the payphone nearby to telephone the Engineering Society office in order to ensure that no one was present. After about twenty seconds, she returned to the radio:

"All clear. Over."

"Right. Over," said Simon. "Well that's it, mates. If you leave now you'll have about fifteen minutes to get inside before the next patrol. It should be enough."

Both Theo Hoshen and Carl, their hearts suddenly pounding, stared back at Simon. Then they stared at each other.

"Okay?" asked Theo Hoshen.

"Okay," said Carl.

"Let us go then," said Theo Hoshen, "and make our visit." So he reached into his pocket, pulled out a black balaclava (which, given the cold weather, did not appear too out of place) and covered his head, adjusting it so that his eyes and mouth matched up with its three holes.

"Okay," repeated a resigned Carl, who then reached into his pocket, pulled out one of his own, and donned it.

"So?" said Simon. "Off you go then."

"Right," concurred Carl and Theo Hoshen in unison. There was a pause, however, after which they finally began marching towards the street. Yet they had not gone twenty steps when, suddenly, Carl felt as if the sidewalk were being pulled out from under him. He was slipping on a patch of black ice.

Down he went, directly onto his behind, although he did have the presence of mind to jut his right arm sharply upwards so as to keep the radio in his hand from smashing on the pavement. Yet this meant that both he and Carl could not avoid hearing Simon's voice emanating from it:

"The prez is down! The prez is down!" he said uproariously.

"I'm okay," said Carl into his radio the moment he got up.

He then promptly turned down the volume on Simon's laughter.

"Thank goodness I take no stock in omens," said Theo Hoshen gravely.

Briskly, and without saying another word, the two made their way to the alley and then down it to their objective. Of the windows that opened into the Engineering Society offices they chose the one farthest west, as it was a little more distant from King's College Road. With Theo Hoshen keeping watch on the alley, Carl reached into his backpack, pulled out the glass cutters and set to work. But as Simon had predicted, the tool failed to fulfill its function. Indeed, it barely scratched the surface of the glass.

"It's not working. It's not working," said Carl. Suddenly, there was a noise. Both of them froze. It had come from a large enclosed dumpster that was attached to the side of the building, not five metres along the alleyway to the west. Some fool was throwing out the garbage at a quarter to four in the morning! But then they realized that it must be the night shift of the cleaning staff. At first, Theo Hoshen thought that they would have to abandon their undertaking for the night, yet he then perceived that the noise might actually work in their favour. For it could mask what would have to be Carl's unavoidably noisy attempt to break open the window.

"Just smash it," ordered Theo Hoshen. "I will go near the bin and listen for how bad it sounds."

"B-base clear. B-base clear," announced Carl's radio. It was Avigail reporting in. There was no response from Simon, however. What had happened to him? Then they heard:

"A-base cl...gbzexrbablelizt...A-base...gbzexrbablelizt."

"Great," said a dismayed Carl. "Something's wrong with Simon's radio."

"He sounds calm enough," remarked Theo Hoshen. "I believe everything is fine."

"Okay," said Carl.

So Theo Hoshen marched up to the dumpster. He could hear that more garbage was about to be cast inside and so he turned and gave his partner the thumbs-up sign.

SMASH! CRASH! Carl punched his gloved hand directly into the window. *Man*, he thought, *it's so loud!*

Both held still to see what they could hear. Thankfully, the garbage dumping continued unabated.

"Okay!" announced Theo Hoshen in what was at once a shout and a whisper.

Carl continued. *SMASH! CRASH! SMASH! CRASH!* It seemed to be taking forever. But as the garbage was still being dumped, Theo Hoshen maintained his thumbs-up sign. *SMASH! CRASH!* went Carl.

"Hurry up!" said Theo Hoshen, who then trundled over to inspect the window. "How are you progressing?" Like Carl, his heart was pounding so much that he could feel it urging the blood through his veins. Both of them felt very much alive.

"Look," replied Carl, pointing. "There's a second layer of glass."

"Damn!" exclaimed Theo Hoshen. "Smash it!" he ordered. Carl hesitated for a moment, staring directly at the intact sheet. Then: *SMASH!* He put his hand right through it.

Theo Hoshen returned to the dumpster.

"B-base clear...B-base clear," came out over Carl's radio. Following which, as expected, Simon replied:

"Gberxbablelizt...gberxbablelizt."

Carl continued his work with the window: *SMASH! CRASH! SMASH! CRASH!* And then, finally, he announced:

"Theo! It's done!"

Theo Hoshen flew back from the dumpster. It was indeed done. There Carl stood, a small pool of broken glass lying on the ground beside him. Both layers of window pane had been completely removed and the result was a space just large enough for each of them to crawl through.

"Excellent," declared Theo Hoshen. "Let us go."

"All clear," whispered Carl into his radio. "All lines clear," he repeated. "We're going in." Carl found that he had some trouble digesting his own words. "It's funny," he remarked to Theo Hoshen, "I'm sure I'd never do this if I were older. And yet there's less to lose when you're closer to the end."

"Do not you start," rebuked Theo Hoshen. "We must get inside."

And so in they went. Theo Hoshen was first and, once within, he turned to receive Carl's backpack and then made way so that his partner could follow. Carl did so and, after having entered, he reached into the pack and pulled out a flashlight which he shone into the dark. They could see that they were in a small office and that they were standing upon a couch just under the window.

"We're in," whispered Carl. "We're in." They removed their balaclavas.

Approaching the door, Theo Hoshen listened to determine if anyone was on the other side. Then he opened it – just a crack – to see what he could see. The lobby was fully lit yet there was not a soul present. Squinting his eyes against the light, Theo Hoshen entered and went directly to the main entrance door. For some reason, it was unlocked; worse, without a key there appeared to be no way to lock it, even from the inside. It seemed that he would have to stay and keep watch. So he peeked outside to ensure that there was no one around and then turned to Carl, who had been watching him anxiously, and said:

"All clear. To work." Both then went to the centre of the lobby, still blinking as they strove to accustom themselves to the room's bright florescent lighting. Carl reached into his backpack and pulled out the electric drill. He looked about. There being no socket nearby, he reached in again and withdrew an extension cord. One end he plugged into the drill and the other into the outlet in the wall on the opposite side of the lobby. Then he returned to the door to begin his work.

Holes first, he thought, recalling Simon's instructions, *and then connect the dots.* He was aware that he was struggling to remain calm. His mouth was very dry. Was his partner's the same?

"Theo, is your mouth dry?"

But Theo Hoshen simply ignored the question: "Try the door first," he said. "Just in case."

"Right," said Carl. He tried it, but it was locked. "No go," he reported.

"To it, then," commanded Theo Hoshen, who then returned to the lobby door.

So Carl began to drill. It was a relatively quiet machine but by no means silent and the noise terrified them both. Theo Hoshen knew that a member of the cleaning staff could easily be lurking about in the halls just outside and so he lay himself down: by stretching out on the floor he found that he could just see through the line of light under the door. Thankfully, there was no one. Then he looked back at Carl and quickly surveyed the lobby. He noted the following items: a couch, two seats, and a table, on top of which could be found a portable stereo, two hardhats, some empty cans of beer, coffee spoons and teacups. Theo Hoshen had an idea.

"Carl, take this," he said as he handed over one of the hard-hats. Carl accepted it and immediately placed it in his back-pack. "No," said Theo Hoshen. "Put it *on*." Theo Hoshen then donned the other one and turned on the stereo. "If someone comes," he said, "they will assume we are engineers who have decided to take apart our office."

"Right," said Carl breathlessly. Then he went back to drilling. Theo Hoshen returned to the crack under the entrance door.

Carl was making excellent progress with the drill; the holes were surprisingly easy to bore. So it was not long before he was able to move on to the handsaw. He sawed away furiously while Theo Hoshen maintained his post. But since no one seemed to be coming, the latter scuttled across the floor to see if there was some way he could help his partner.

"How is it going?" he asked.

"Almost there."

"Let me try something," said Theo Hoshen. He motioned for Carl to stand back. Then he gave the door two hard kicks with the base of his foot. Though the holes were almost all connected, a small piece of wood still held the door to the lock. And so Carl had to take up the saw once again, bracing his foot against the door as he did so.

As both would later recount, then came the moment of crisis. For Theo Hoshen had made a big mistake. When Carl had resumed sawing, the young philosopher, instead of returning to watch the crack under the lobby door, chose to remain by his partner's side. They were so close that he felt quite impelled to stay and ready himself for a few more kicks. Suddenly, however, the lobby door swung open and in poked a man's head. It was looking directly at them.

CHAPTER XI

Carl and Theo Hoshen froze, the former in the middle of a saw stroke, the latter with his hand on his chin, bent over and staring intensely at the cut. They turned their heads towards the man.

And then, in a flash, he was gone.

"What?" exclaimed a breathless Carl.

"Keep going!" came Theo Hoshen's reply. "We're so close!" And indeed Carl had but an inch or two left to cut before he would be all the way through. So back to work he went. Moments later, however, Theo Hoshen stopped him:

"Carl!" he yelled.

"Yeah?"

"That guy!"

"Yeah?"

"He just saw us!"

"Yeah?"

"He's going to call the cops!"

"Yeah!"

"We've got to get out of here!"

"Shit!" And with that the two scrambled to get all of their equipment back into Carl's backpack. To save time, Carl wrapped the extension cord in a loop and hooked it around his shoulder.

"That everything?" demanded Theo Hoshen.

"I think so."

"The hats!" said Theo Hoshen, and they threw them both to the floor. "That's it. Let's go!"

In a flash they were out the lobby door. Down the hallway they ran, towards the north-east exit. But who did they see on their way if not the very man who had stuck his head into the lobby and spotted them? Evidently, he had taken them for engineers instead of the thieves that they were and so he had simply returned to his task of mopping up the floor. Seeing them now in their fleeing, terrified state quickly disabused him of that notion, however.

Shit! thought Carl and Theo Hoshen in unison.

The two virtually flew past the man. Up the stairs they went, then out the door and into the night. They headed west on Galbraith Road, then north and then west again onto Russell Street, panting heavily all the way.

"We had better slow down," said Theo Hoshen. "It looks less suspicious."

"Okay," said Carl. As they did so, he reached into his backpack and pulled out his radio. "It's over," he said into it. "Back to home base."

It was only when they reached Spadina Avenue that the extent of their failure began to take hold.

"We blew it," said Carl. "We really blew it." Theo Hoshen said nothing.

On they walked, sullenly and in silence, for another ten minutes or so. Each looked about suspiciously as he went.

"You know," said Carl, breaking the quiet, "you never did finish your shtick about Aristotle on women. So what, they're supposed to stay home all the time?"

"You amaze me," said Theo Hoshen.

"I'm just curious. I mean, if Avigail'd stayed home we would've been short a person for the watch. And as it happens, she did a good job; *you* were the one who screwed up."

Theo Hoshen glared at Carl. "I never said that women should stay home."

"But Aristotle did, right?"

"Look, I shall only say this once and then there is to be no more discussion of the subject. Is that understood?"

"Fine," said Carl.

"It is true that Aristotle believed women were naturally suited for the home. They were to run the household, or *oikos*, which is where our word 'economics' comes from."

"So?"

"So, the science of *oikos* has since shifted its focus, for with modernity the economy has moved from the private sphere to civil society. And for some time now, we have accepted that the state has a role to play in guiding that economy. Ergo, in the modern world, economic questions are now not only public but also political. One thus ought to conclude that today – and this is fully in keeping with the spirit of Aristotle's argument – there are women who can, indeed must, become true citizens, by which I mean politicians."

"Ah," said Carl, "so you admit that they're equal to men."

"Most gladly," replied Theo Hoshen. "But to say that they are equal is not to say that they are the same. For anyone who wishes to honour them will accept that they are different and should be treated accordingly."

"And how's that?"

"I shall give you but one example. Call a man a 'slut' or a woman a 'wimp' and you will not get much of a reaction. But do the reverse and I am certain that you will learn to never again treat the two uniformly."

There was a pause, and then Carl said:

"You've an answer for everything, eh Theo?

"Perhaps not I," answered Theo Hoshen, "but Aristotle, yes. Now let us get home."

CHAPTER XII

*Wherein the events of this chapter – not
particularly exciting but nevertheless still worthy
of mention – take place*

And so it was that Carl and Theo Hoshen, as well as Simon
and Avigail, spent the next few days with a sense of impending
doom. Were the police investigating the break-in? Did that
cleaner recognize Carl? Or perhaps he could describe him well
enough such that someone else might do so? Every knock on
the door and ring of the telephone brought with it such terrifying thoughts. Mercifully, however, not a word was heard from
the authorities. Indeed, there was not even anything of note
emanating from the engineers, although it was to be expected
that they would try to keep the incident quiet so as to discour-
age copy-cats. Still, there had been one sign. Almost two
weeks following the break-in, Carl was seated in his office at
SAC perusing a copy of the latest issue of *The Toike Oike*
newspaper when he noticed a column that listed the names of
the masthead alongside those of a number of individuals who
were thanked for their assistance. Near the bottom of that list –
which, for whatever reason, included "Don Cherry" and "the
ghost of Elvis" – he saw "the burglars." And just below it, in
slightly smaller font, was printed "We don't know who they
are, but boy are they stupid."

Unable to resist, Carl marched out of his office to see if
Larry Corretti, the former engineering student, was about. He
was indeed and so, attempting once again to portray himself as
nonchalant as possible, Carl raised the subject:

"Larry, what's this in *The Toike* about burglars? And why
are they so stupid?"

"Oh that. Can you believe it? Some goofballs actually tried

to steal the Cannon. 'Course they blew it. But they sure hacked-up one of the doors at EngSoc."

Carl wished desperately to inquire further, but he feared appearing overly interested. And so he said nothing. Larry, however, was happy to elaborate:

"They've lost their chance now," he said. "Because we've moved it."

"Oh," replied Carl, doing his best to feign disinterest. Then he quickly changed the subject and asked if Larry would be participating as an engineer during the university's Homecoming ceremonies, which were only two weeks away.

"Yeah, I'll be there," he said. "Once a Skuleman, always a Skuleman."

"Good for you," said Carl, wincing somewhat for not having thought of something more appropriate to say. Then, feeling a little flushed, he returned to his office.

On the way home that evening, Carl dropped by Theo Hoshen's place to see if he was in. It was Simon who answered the door:

"Hoshen-boy's nipped out for a bit, but he should be back soon. You can come in if you like. Fancy a lager?" Carl nodded and the two made their way to the kitchen. "So it's been, what, a fortnight since the big heist?" said Simon, pulling open the tabs on two cans of beer.

"You mean two weeks? Yeah," said Carl in a discomfited tone.

"Man, have you ever got a face like a slapped arse. Don't get down about it, mate; you gave it your best shot. I didn't think you'd get as far as you did."

"Well it wasn't far enough."

"Yer partner's not narked at all, you know. He'd give it another go."

"Yeah. Theo says we've just got to be more careful. Better prepared, with a foolproof plan."

"Always handy, those."

"Uh-huh." There was a pause. And then Simon spoke again: "You know he's a mite tapped, eh? Bit of a space cadet?"

"Oh come on, Simon. So he's a little different."

"Different?" said Simon, wondering if Carl was being serious.

"Yeah," insisted Carl. "He's really not so bad. And anyway you've got to be bad if you're going to be great, right? I've always been attracted to people like that; you know, creative types, on the edge, a little less together than the rest of us. Guess that's why my friendships never last. Sooner or later, they fall apart."

Whoa, thought Simon to himself, *guys over here really let it out.* "Man," he said, "you sound like a girl with a thing for bad boys."

"That's ridiculous," declared Carl. "And anyway that's only a myth. Girls want to be treated well like anyone else."

"Uh-huh," said an obviously sceptical Simon. "Like Avigail," he added.

"What?"

"Viggy. You like her, don't you?"

"What? I don't know."

"Yeah right," said Simon. "Wha'ever. My point is, if she's going for anyone it'll be Hoshen-boy. You can bank on that. So don't even bother; that's all I'm saying."

Fortunately, a sound at the door released Carl from having to come up with a reply. Theo Hoshen had returned.

"Theo," said Carl. "I've got some news."

"About the Tomato?" inquired the young philosopher. They

had all agreed to use the term as a code-name for the Cannon, in case they were ever overheard.

"Yup," said Carl. "So here's the thing. I was at SAC today and I came across this in *The Toike*." He handed Theo Hoshen the newspaper and pointed to the item. "So I asked that former Skuleman, Larry Corretti, about it – don't worry, I was discreet – and he said that it'd been there but that now they've taken it somewhere else. I'm guessing off-campus; probably to one of the Guard's homes. I bet it's the Chief's."

"Hmm," said Theo Hoshen. "If only we knew who the members of the Tomato Guard were. Evidently, they are masked for a good purpose."

"You know what we could do? If we looked closely the next time they fire the Tomato we could take note of their watches and then see who wore them when unmasked. That way we could identify them."

"Excellent," said Theo Hoshen. "We would only really need to discover the identity of the Chief, for you are almost certainly correct that the Tomato is hidden in his home. Then, just before it is to be fired next, we could wait outside and surprise him as he brought it out. Or we might choose to break into his place beforehand."

"But what if it's off-campus?" objected Carl. "I don't like the idea of trying something like that there."

"I knew you would say that," chided Theo Hoshen. "But let us see where it is first and then, if need be, we can discuss the matter."

"Fair enough. We'll have a good chance to check out the Guard this Thursday. The engineers have invited me to make a little speech during some kind of pre-Homecoming ceremony they're having. It's in Con Hall and I bet they wrap it up by firing off the Tomato. You guys can come and sit in the audience. Whatever we learn could be useful."

"Whoa there, mate," said Simon. "'That was serious fun the other night but I've my research to do. I'm sure you and the sand-monkey here can handle things on your own just fine."

"Sand-monkey?" said Carl, looking nervously in Theo Hoshen's direction. "What's that supposed to mean?"

"Now don't go getting your bollocks in a knot," cautioned Simon. "Where I come from it just means 'Arab'. But it's not meant in a bad way or anything. Really."

"The word 'really'," declared a stern and sceptical Theo Hoshen, "is meant to emphasize a relation to reality. Regardless, I am not an Arab."

"Oh?" replied Simon. "I thought you said your family was from Morocco."

"Yes, but we are Jews not Arabs."

"Well what's their first language? Ain't it Arabic?"

"Yes, but —"

"So they're Arabs. Jewish Arabs. Ergo: sand-monkeys," said Simon with a satisfied grin.

This was more than enough for Theo Hoshen. With a shout of "Sand-monkeys unite!" he leapt from his seat and lunged at Simon. A fierce scuffle ensued and it took Carl no small amount of effort to separate the two before they were able to cause any real damage. Needless to say, it was agreed that Carl and Theo Hoshen would be doing without Simon's services at Convocation Hall.

CHAPTER XIII

In which Theo Hoshen and Carl Landsberg attend the engineers' pre-Homecoming ceremony in the hope of gathering whatever information they may gather

The days passed uneventfully. Carl continued to perform his various duties as the fine SAC president that he was, while Simon, Avigail and Theo Hoshen carried on with their studies. Then came the Thursday morning of what promised to be a bright and sunny November day. Theo Hoshen approached Convocation Hall just as two hundred or so chanting engineering frosh, all sporting red hardhats and t-shirts with large 'F!'s emblazoned upon them, were being marched inside. They were in groups of forty or so, each led by a more senior engineering student carrying a megaphone. Theo Hoshen followed them inside and found a place among the many upper-year students. He wisely chose a front row seat so as to ensure himself the best possible view. Carl was already there, seated in a chair on the stage beside another chair in which could be found the head of the Engineering Society, one Peter Certaine, and another which supported Dr. Tealands of Student Affairs.

It was not long before the Lady Godiva Memorial Band, consisting on this occasion of a cohort of fifteen or so, began marching up and down the centre aisle, performing the Engineering Hymn to the accompaniment of claps and cheers from the audience. The atmosphere was most festive, and Carl could not help but remark that few, if any, of the other colleges or faculties could come close to matching this one for spirit.

After a time the band stopped, which meant that the moment for Certaine to mount the podium had arrived. He said a few rousing words about Skule, in particular, about how wonderful was its soon-to-be-completed float for the Home-coming parade. This, of course, brought forth hearty applause from the crowd. Certaine then graciously thanked Dr. Tealands and Carl for having accepted his invitation to join them that morning, and he announced that each would now say a few words to the gathering. He called upon the assistant vice-president of Student Affairs to speak first. As usual, he went on for a short while saying nothing worthy of mention. But then it was Carl's turn. He mounted the podium with an enormous smile and, after a pause for effect, spoke the following words into the microphone:

"Thank you," he began, "I want –"

But just then, at the sound of a cymbal smashing, the Lady Godiva Memorial Band broke into raucous song. This turned out to be the cue for five members of the Brute Force Commit-tee to appear and launch themselves onto the stage, whereupon they tackled Carl to the floor, forced him into a wheelchair they had brought with them, and tied him fast to it with a rope, wrapping it around a dozen times or so. Then they gagged him and topped the whole exercise off by placing an engineering hardhat on his head. All of this delighted the audience to no end, as was evident from the many cheers and howls of laughter. It goes without saying that Theo Hoshen was not among the celebrants. Indeed, his first impulse was to charge to Carl's rescue, but realising that this would be worse than useless he managed to hold himself back, looking about with concern to see if anyone had noticed him flinch. All eyes had remained fixed on the stage, however, whereupon Peter Certaine spoke again:

"Oh dear," he said. "It seems as if President Landsberg would prefer to sit back and wear one of our hardhats rather than make a speech. Guess we can't blame him for that now, can we?"

"Nooooooo," replied the audience in mocking unison.

"Well then," continued Certaine, "perhaps we could ask him to move to the side a little to make room for a very special event. Would that be okay, Mr. President?"

"Mmmff," answered Carl through the gag.

"I think we can take that as a 'yes'," said a smiling Certaine. He then motioned for the members of the Brute Force Committee to wheel Carl away from the centre of the stage. They did so and then turned him around so that he had no choice but to witness what would happen next. Two trumpeters from the Lady Godiva Memorial Band then broke into some rousing fanfare and the audience began to cheer and applaud with even more gusto than before.

It was coming.

The next thing everyone saw was the nine members of the Cannon Guard marching onto the stage. Led by a flag bearer, whose helmet and overalls were as black as those of the Guardsmen, he used both of his arms to hold aloft a pole on the end of which hung a large flag, also black but with a golden border and the Skule insignia at its centre. The Guard moved in what was its standard formation: four constituted a menacing outer perimeter square, tapping their billy clubs in unison on the palms of their free hands as they marched, and four others an inner square, each masked and with his club in one hand and a chain in the other – the latter being wrapped around his waist and then extending out to the centre, to the base of the precious object that they were all there to protect. This, of course, was none other than the Cannon, which entered the hall cradled in the arms of the Chief Attiliator, its brass skin gleaming ever so bright under the stage lights.

Once the Cannon Guard reached centre stage they stopped and turned to face the audience. Then the band began to play, accompanied by yet more rousing cheers. This continued for a good while until a nod came from the Chief Attiliator, whereupon everyone fell quiet. The drummer began a drum roll. The Chief knelt down and placed the Cannon squarely on the stage. The four Guardsmen of the inner square then pulled their chains taut, thus ensuring that the Cannon was held in place. Some loud but indecipherable shouts from the Chief then followed, each of which was echoed back by the Guardsmen. The drum roll became louder, and the Chief removed the lit cigarette from his mouth. Slowly, he lowered the butt towards the fuse at the rear of the Cannon's barrel, whereupon a great *BOOM!* resounded throughout the hall, accompanied by a large plume of smoke which burst forth from the gun's turret. The crowd went wild, its members cheering with great passion and jumping violently up and down in front of their chairs. At this, the Lady Godiva Memorial Band broke into its special Cannon Song, whose beat was assiduously kept with clapping from the many engineers present. Great fun was being had by all.

Or almost all. For Carl and Theo Hoshen were, of course, preoccupied with the serious task they had set for themselves: both were straining to gather as many details as they could about the members of the Cannon Guard, especially the Chief Attiliator. Though Carl was unable to move because of the rope, he nevertheless had an unobstructed view of the young man, including his watch, which he studied as closely as possible. Then the Chief knelt to pick up the Cannon and, cradling it in his arms once again, rose and yelled something, whereupon the other Guardsmen immediately snapped to attention. Another order was barked out and, in perfect unison, the nine of them turned rightwards and, accompanied by deafening cheers from the crowd, they began to march off-stage.

Certaine returned to the microphone and spoke a few rousing words about Skule's participation in Homecoming. Then he thanked everyone for having attended, especially the administrator and the still-immobilized student union president. Further activities just outside of the building required the participation of the frosh, he explained, following which he wished one and all good luck as he waved a hand in salutation. Everyone then began to file outside, the groups of forty or so frosh collecting into larger parties depending on the type of engineering science that they would be studying. All sang along with the band as they went.

Theo Hoshen looked at Carl, motioning his eyes in the direction that the Cannon Guard had just taken. Carl managed to nod his head only a moment before his three Brute Force Committee guards whisked him off of the stage.

"It's time to go home to SAC, Mr. Prez," declared one as the others giggled mischievously.

Theo Hoshen quickly took his leave, exiting through one of Convocation Hall's many side doors. He was grateful beyond words for his luck, for he caught a glimpse of the Cannon Guard as they marched their precious jewel towards the Sir Sandford Fleming building. Cautiously, he followed them. He was just the right distance when they entered the building and made their way down the hallway – the very same that he and Carl had, in a panic, run through in the opposite direction not a few weeks ago. Then they went into the Engineering Society offices. Theo Hoshen dared not follow them inside, of course, and so he simply stopped and took up a post just far enough from the entrance that he would not draw attention to himself.

He was close enough, however, that he could observe all who entered or exited. Not that he had much idea about what, specifically, he was looking for, but he wisely judged that any information he might glean could come in useful.

It was only a short while later when he saw a woman exit the offices. She was much older than the average student so Theo Hoshen guessed that she was the Engineering Society's secretary. She appeared to be looking about rather nervously and – even more worthy of note – her hands were tightly clasped to her handbag. Quickly, she turned and walked determinedly down the hallway to the west. Could she have the Tomato in that bag, he wondered. He felt his heart beat as he began to follow. She certainly did seem to have a suspicious attitude, for she continued to look furtively about as she walked. And yet she failed to notice the adventurous young philosopher just behind her. Nevertheless, he soon judged that her bag was both too small and too light to contain the item that interested him. So he swung about and returned to his post.

Another twenty minutes passed before Theo Hoshen found himself confronted with an even more intriguing sight: four strapping young men, two of whom were carrying large hockey bags, emerged from the offices and made their way hurriedly down the hallway right past him. As they did so he immediately began an intense study of the floor in front of him. Then, the moment there was enough space between them, he turned and followed. Out the building's front entrance they went, with an increasingly excited Theo Hoshen only a few steps behind. Once outside, he spied them making their way briskly across King's College Road. Then, having reached the other side, they entered the narrow parking lot that was situated between the two buildings there. Theo Hoshen also could not help but notice the many engineering frosh seated along the middle of the road; they were organized into rows of two and were singing or chanting according to the instructions of their respective group leaders. Yet none seemed to take any notice of the four men nor of the young philosophy student who then crossed the street after them. Once on the other side, Theo Hoshen waited behind a tree that stood between him and the lot, for it did a fine job of hiding him as well as of allowing him to observe all he wished to observe through its many leaves and branches. What he saw left him truly amazed.

The four had marched directly to a rather decrepit car, an old blue sedan, that was parked in the lot, and while one kept watch the others opened the trunk and put the two bags they had been carrying inside. The trunk was then slammed shut and, without saying the slightest word, the four turned and proceeded straight back to the Sandford Fleming building. Theo Hoshen could only stare in wonder at it all.

My God, he marvelled, *the Cannon is right here, right now, in an unguarded car. I must reach Carl immediately.* So, briskly but orderly, he made his way down the road and past all of the engineering frosh seated there. Then, once he reached the grass of King's College Circle, he began to run. For there was no time to lose.

It was not more than a half a minute later that, breathing heavily, he arrived at the front door of SAC. He went directly inside, not even remarking upon the three members of the Brute Force Committee who, having escorted Carl there, were now pushing an empty wheelchair out.

Once in the main office, his eyes fell directly upon Carl, who was busy conversing with one of his secretaries. Carl looked up and shot Theo Hoshen a worried glance. But Theo Hoshen simply turned and walked out. In no time, as he knew he would, Carl had joined him.

"What? What is it?" demanded the student union president. "You know you shouldn't come in here. But listen," he added excitedly, "I got a real good look at the Chief's watch." Yet Carl could tell from his friend's demeanour that this piece of information was somehow of no interest to him. Theo Hoshen simply looked around to see if anyone was nearby and, satisfied that they were alone, he turned to Carl, seized him by the arm, and spoke the following words in a quiet but steady voice:

"Carl, we must go. Now." And then, with no small emotion, he recounted all that he had just seen in the parking lot off of King's College Road.

Carl was speechless.

"Yes," said Theo Hoshen. "My sentiments exactly. We shall surely never get another opportunity such as this. So here is how we must proceed. I will return to the site and keep watch. You must obtain a car, go directly to Canadian Tire for a crowbar, and then bring it and the car immediately to the site. Understood?"

"Yeah," replied Carl breathlessly.

"Good," said Theo Hoshen. "And Carl, we have no time to waste." Then he turned and walked briskly in the direction whence he had come. Carl went back into the SAC building and, after about a minute or so, emerged with the keys to the SAC accountant's car. A short while later, he was turning it into the parking lot of the nearest Canadian Tire.

CHAPTER XIV

*Wherein Theo Hoshen and Carl Landsberg make
their second attempt at stealing the Mighty Skule
Cannon*

Soon after, Carl, sporting a baseball cap and sunglasses, was driving up King's College Road. The crowbar he had purchased was heavier than he expected, but then he had never wielded one before. He spied Theo Hoshen standing across the street from the Sandford Fleming building and so he went to pick him up.

The young philosopher entered the car. "We must go around King's College Circle and then make our way back," he instructed. "I checked and the only way into the parking lot by car is through Taddle Creek Road, which is to the west a little off of College Street. Here is the plan: the lot is deserted most of the time, but since the car with the Cannon is parked on the King's College Road side we will need to block it from anyone who might be able to see from the road so that we may work on the trunk. That is where this car comes in."

"You're sure no one'll be able to see?" asked a slightly panicked Carl.

"No, Carl, I am not. But sure is dead, is it not?"

"I thought we said we'd have a fool-proof plan this time."

"Carl," came Theo Hoshen's reply, "*I* thought we agreed that this was the rarest of golden opportunities. We simply cannot let it pass without making an attempt. Now watch where you are going; as you can see, there are a number of engineering frosh about."

"Holy shit! What the hell are they doing here?"

"Control yourself," chided Theo Hoshen. "If you bothered to look you would see that they are busy being hazed." As indeed they were: after having certain unspeakables done to them earlier that day they were now all quite drunk and lining up on the street to have their arms dipped to just above the elbows in barrels of dark purple dye. Their skin would remain that colour for at least a week.

"Again with the hazing?" complained Carl. "Wasn't orientation week enough? Goofballs!"

"Carl, this works to our benefit; they shall be distracted. And regardless, this car will hide us; they also have no inkling that their cherished Tomato is in the other car's trunk. So there is no reason they should spot us. If anything, I am more concerned about people coming into the lot from the other side. Here, turn left onto College Street."

Carl did so. He had begun to feel as if they had entered a dream. His heart began to pound and his dry mouth returned with a fury.

"Oh man," he said.

"Take a left here," directed Theo Hoshen. "This is Taddle Creek Road. Now go up to the end and then left again. That will take us to the lot."

"Man oh man," repeated Carl as he drove.

"Carl!" said Theo Hoshen sternly.

"Okay, okay. I just can't believe we're going to try this now, here, in broad daylight."

"There is the car," said Theo Hoshen, pointing to the blue sedan. "Put us in line with it, but on the other side of the lot. We will have to back up and then stop between it and the road when the time is ripe."

So Carl parked the car on the north side of the lot.

"The crowbar. Do you have it?" asked Theo Hoshen.

"There," said Carl, pointing to a plastic bag on the back seat.

"Excellent. Now we must see if anyone is coming." And indeed someone was, walking leisurely across the lot towards King's College Road. This meant that there was nothing for them to do but wait.

"Have you another pair of sun glasses?" asked Theo Hoshen. "The sun is very strong." For though buildings bordered the north and south sides of the lot, the fact that it was noontime meant that the sun's rays were unobstructed and so everything was brightly lit.

"Sorry. These are the only ones I've got."

"Then give them here."

"No way," protested Carl. "I'm the one with the famous campus face."

"True," said Theo Hoshen. "Point taken." So, squinting as he stuck his head out of the car window, he took another look around to ensure that the coast was clear. It was. "Okay!" he announced. So Carl shifted the car in reverse and drove slowly backwards until it was parallel with the blue sedan. "I shall be just a moment," said Theo Hoshen as he reached back and grabbed the crowbar. Holding it tightly to his body, he went outside into the sunlight. "Keep watch," he ordered.

Moments later, Carl could discern the torturous sound of metal against metal; Theo Hoshen was attempting to pry open the trunk. Also discernible was the chanting of the many engineering frosh sitting on the road not a few yards away. "Perfect," said Carl sarcastically. And then, upon looking over to his right, he noticed the form of a man coming onto the lot from the other end.

"Theo!" he shouted through the open car window.

Whereupon the young philosopher promptly stopped what he was doing and made his way around the car and back into the passenger seat.

"Go!" he said breathlessly. So Carl drove the car back to the other side of the lot. "This is going to take some doing," declared Theo Hoshen. "But I think we shall manage it."

Indeed the task was not an easy one. Three times they drove the car back and forth from the side of the sedan to the side of the lot, where each time they were forced to wait impatiently for some pedestrian to go by. Perhaps twenty minutes of this had passed and yet the trunk, though heavily damaged, still refused to open. And then, while waiting to make their fourth attempt, they saw a most frightful sight.

It was the four young men who had earlier placed the bags in the trunk. They were crossing the street, making their way towards the lot.

"Down?" urged Carl. He was asking if they should duck and so hide themselves as best they could behind the dashboard.

"Freeze," came his partner's reply, for Theo Hoshen did not want movement in their car to draw any attention to them. This was a great gamble, of course, because it meant that they would be visible to the four. And so did the two remain absolutely frozen in place, neither breathing nor blinking. Only the angel of death could have brought greater stillness.

The four approached.

Miraculously, however, they just continued on, walking directly past the front of their sedan and so without detecting the damage that had been done to its trunk. Nor did they notice the two covetous young men sitting motionless in the car on the other side of the lot.

With this particular danger past, Carl and Theo Hoshen were able to exhale.

"So close," was all that Carl could manage to say. He found

himself reclining into his seat, head tilted upwards and eyes closed.

"Indeed," confirmed Theo Hoshen, no less assuaged. "They passed over us. Like a gift." And with that he ordered Carl to drive the car over to the other side of the lot so that he could make yet another attempt on the trunk.

This time it was not long before Carl heard a sublime *POP!* as its lock finally surrendered to Theo Hoshen's exertions and released its hold. Up flew the hatch, following which Carl could see Theo Hoshen quickly reach inside. This was Carl's cue to exit their car and open its truck. Despite quivering hands, he managed to fit the key into the lock on the very first try. And then, looking over to his right, he saw his friend unzip one of the bags in the trunk of the sedan and peer inside.

"Well?" demanded Carl.

"Yes!" came Theo Hoshen's reply. Hastily, he then zipped up the bag, grabbed it and, with one swift movement, thrust it into their car's trunk. Carl was about to close its hatch when his partner yelled for him to stop. For he wished to claim the other bag as well.

"Both?" exclaimed an astonished Carl. But Theo Hoshen said not a word, leaving Carl with nothing to do but wait as the other bag was secured in the trunk. Then he closed it and pulled the key from the lock. And with that, they were done.

"May I drive?" requested Theo Hoshen.

"Sure," replied Carl, glad to be relieved of the duty. So Carl took the passenger seat and Theo Hoshen slid into the driver's. He started up the car and began to direct it across the lot. Carl looked back. They had forgotten to close the trunk of the sedan! No matter, he thought to himself as he spied the many engineering frosh who were now marching up and down along the road, for it was evident that they were utterly oblivious to what had just happened. A feeling of elation began to dawn upon him, one such as he had experienced only once before: the night when he learned that he had won the election for the SAC presidency. Yet, somehow, this time was sweeter.

Looking over at his friend now, he saw Theo Hoshen concentrating deeply on the road ahead. But then Carl's heart stopped. For suddenly, right before them, was a sea of engineering frosh: a large group in red t-shirts were blocking their way out of the lot.

Yet as their car approached Carl noticed that the frosh were all looking in the other direction. It still made for a most terrifying sight. Once the car reached them, however, Theo Hoshen simply rolled down his window, stuck his head out and, stretching a hand over them all, waved it as he uttered the following words in an annoyed tone of voice:

"Ladies. Gentlemen. *Please.*" The frosh turned to face the car, whereupon the adventurous young philosopher added: "Would you mind?"

"C'mon, c'mon," shouted the group leader into his megaphone. And so, as if pushed by a strong wind, the frosh divided, allowing Carl and Theo Hoshen to go directly into the midst, a wall of red on their right hand, and on their left. Forward they went, ever so slowly, until they were able to just drive on by. "My God," said Carl. "If they only knew what we have in the trunk."

But they did not, of course, and moments later all of the frosh had been left behind. Theo Hoshen then drove the car along Taddle Creek Road and, speeding up, he took a left onto College Street. They were away.

*Which contains much revelry, as well as a drunken
yet profound debate about the nature of
multinational states*

"What? What is it?" demanded Simon. It was late in the afternoon and he and Avigail, each weighted down with plastic bags filled with groceries from the local supermarket, had just entered the house to find a beaming Theo Hoshen seated comfortably at the dining room table. "I can tell by that look in your eye, Hoshen-boy, that something's up. What, you've figured out the meaning of life? God is head, right? Knew it!" It was evident by Simon's frivolous tone that he was making an effort to forget his recent contretemps with the young philosopher.

"Yet more confirmation," Theo Hoshen said with a smile, "of how natural scientists are good on the universe, but utterly miss the world."

"Oh here we go," declared Simon. "Viggy, you deal with him. I'll put the shoppings away." And with that he took her bags along with his own and went into the kitchen.

"I advise you not to take too long," Theo Hoshen called out after him in a teasing tone.

"You're in a good mood," remarked Avigail.

"He's not alone in that," shouted Carl from upstairs.

"Oh, the prez's here?" said Avigail as she entered the living room, her curiosity growing.

"Yes, the prez is here," confirmed Carl as he came down the stairs. "And he's got something to show you."

"What is it?"

"Not until Simon returns," cautioned Theo Hoshen.

"Simon!" shouted Avigail. And moments later, the science student appeared.

"So what's up?" he said, though a glance in Carl and Theo Hoshen's direction made him add: "Man, do you gits ever look happy as pigs in shit. Alright then, let's have it. No wait, I got it: you've a foolproof plan for nickin' the Tomato, right?"

"In a sense he is quite correct," said Theo Hoshen to Carl. "For the plan's perfection is beyond all possible doubt."

"Oh yeah?" challenged Simon. "Bet ya a fiver I can poke a hole in it."

"A fiver?" said Carl with a big smile on his face. "Why not something much more valuable? You know, something like this." And with that he walked daintily around to the back of the couch and dragged the two recently captured hockey bags out into the middle of the room.

"What're those?" wondered Simon.

"Take a look," replied Carl. "I'd start with the one on the left."

And so Simon, with a quizzical glance at Avigail, approached the bag on the left and unzipped it. Then he peered inside.

"Fanfuckingtastic!" he exclaimed.

"What? What is it?" implored Avigail.

"Check. It. Out," said Simon, moving aside so that Avigail could see into the bag. When she did so she was struck by the flash of something brass.

"My God. That's it, isn't it?" she said. "The Tomato!"

"It is indeed," said Theo Hoshen proudly.

"Too much!" declared Simon. "And what's all this other stuff? Ace! You got their uniforms *and* their hardhats!"

"Yup," confirmed Carl. "And you'll find the chains and their clubs in the other bag."

"Get out!" said an astounded Avigail. "*All* their stuff? You got it all? Amazing! How?"

"Let me just say," declared Theo Hoshen, "that Carl here is a truly wonderful man. He has talents of which *The Varsity* has never – and we may hope will never – know. I cannot praise him enough."

"Good on you, mate!" announced Simon as he slapped Carl on the back. "Okay then, details. Tell us everything."

And so, in an excited tone, Carl recounted all that he and Theo Hoshen had done earlier that day.

"Wow," said Avigail, whereupon she got up and gave each an enormous kiss on the cheek. Simon was satisfied with vigorously shaking their hands.

"The poor frosh," said Avigail. "Right under their noses. And while they're being hazed, of all things. How pathetic."

"I take it you do not approve of hazing," said Theo Hoshen.

"What's to approve?"

"Why, everything. It is not for nothing that ancient Spartan boys would undergo *diamastigosis*, a contest designed to determine who could endure the severest flogging. For it was only by participating in such an ordeal that each came to feel truly a part of the group; indeed, it made for a unit with the strongest possible bonds between its members. And this is precisely what hazing accomplishes today: individuals who are prepared to put their common good ahead of their personal interests. That is why the engineers are such formidable adversaries, and why we must never underestimate them."

"Yeah, yeah," said Avigail. But she had no wish to enter into a debate at this time and so she said nothing more. Instead, given that a great celebration was clearly in order, she invited Simon to go out with her again so that they could obtain the requisite quantities of snacks and drink. Simon happily accepted.

Upon their return they found Carl and Theo Hoshen dancing madly on the living room floor. Ever foresightful, Carl had brought a selection of records from his collection, and The Parachute Club's "Rise Up" was now blaring from the stereo. Simon and Avigail joined in at once. There was much merriment.

Soon, Avigail retrieved her camera from her room. Then the four, dressed in full Cannon Guard garb, began swinging their new billy clubs wildly about. Turns were taken posing both alone and alongside others with the mighty gun. For one photo, Carl and Theo Hoshen stood upon an Olympic gold medal podium, beaming as they held their prize aloft. For another, Simon used his mouth to mimic an unmentionable with the gun, which he had fitted with a prophylactic taken from his wallet. Their elation knew no bounds; indeed, they all found it quite impossible to stop laughing. Of course, three of them were already quite drunk; only Theo Hoshen maintained his sobriety despite imbibing as much, and perhaps even more, than the others. Yet all four had become one in jubilation.

It was time once again for dancing. Carl put The Tragically Hip's "Three Pistols" on the stereo. There was little he, always the natural leader, loved more than introducing others to his preferred music. However this song was one that they all knew well – all except Simon, of course, who had never even heard of the celebrated band from Kingston, Ontario. Not that this prevented him from joining the others when they took madly to the floor. And as they danced the three Canadians sang along in unison:

Alright
Well Tom Thomson came paddling past
I'm pretty sure it was him
And he spoke so softly in accordance to the
Growing of the dim
He said, "Bring on a brand new Renaissance
'Cause I think I'm ready
I've been shaking all night long
But my hands are steady."

And so on. More loud music and dancing of the most rambunctious kind followed. A good time was being had by all. Carl put on many other records: Chalk Circle, 54-50, Art Bergmann, and the like. At one point he turned to Theo Hoshen and shouted in his ear:

"Isn't this great?" he slurred. "All of us here together, singing and dancing to the best Canadian music?"

"*English* Canadian," corrected an equally besotted Avigail at the top of her lungs.

"What?" yelled Carl.

"It's not Canadian music, *mon ami*," shouted Avigail. "There's no such thing."

"Now what does *that* mean?" said Carl.

Avigail raised the bottle of beer that she had in her hand and, perhaps because she was unaware that *absentem laedit cum ebrio qui litigat*, she motioned in the direction of the kitchen. Carl accepted the invitation and so they both made their way inside and sat down at the table. Avigail took another gulp of beer before she began:

"Those songs you were playing, they were all in English right?"

"Yeah."

"So the best Canadian music – it's all English?"

"Well," said Carl defensively, "I dunno."

"You don't know because you don't know any French Canadian music, right?"

"Guess so."

"So you don't know *any* of our music and yet you think you're qualified to judge the best music in the whole country."

"What? You're French? But you've no accent."

"I'm not only francophone, *mon cher*, I'm a *Québécoise –*
that's my nation." She paused to take another swig from her bottle. "As for my missing *maudit tabarnac* accent, well I went to an anglo summer camp as a girl. I just figured that it'd be fun to see what English Canada was like if no one knew I was from Quebec."

"But you do have an accent," objected Simon as he and Theo Hoshen joined them at the table. "The lot of you do."

"Buddy," retorted Carl, "here *you've* the accent."

"Hey don't change the subject," said Avigail. "The fact is that Carl the English Canadian here thinks he knows the best Canadian music even though he's totally ignorant of non-anglo music." Avigail then began to lean somewhat too heavily to one side, whereupon Theo Hoshen moved over and gave her a gentle push, righting her. "It's typical," she continued, "just like all those books on so-called 'Can Lit', not one which – *not a single one, osti* – mentions a work written in a language other than English. Or what about *The Globe & Mail*, 'Canada's *National* Newspaper'? How can it call itself that when it's written in only one of the country's official languages?" It was evident from Avigail's voice that she was becoming quite upset. "Well I've discovered how. It's that you people are closed – not cold, but closed, because remote. If something's not quite in, then it's out, definitely out. Somehow, you think you protect yourselves that way. Why you feel you need to – I don't know. But it lets you dominate the rest of us, dominate, and with this maddening civility. And so you fool yourselves into believing you're inclusive while sending us francophones the message that we're not really 'Canadian'. Well most other Quebecers have given up the word, but I say: *va chier* to that!"

"C'mon Avigail," objected Carl, "you know that's not right."

"Give me one counter example," she challenged.

"Okay," said Carl, pausing before he continued. "No one knows this, right, but on the night of the Montreal massacre, I called the student union at the University of Montreal. The moment I'd heard about that madman killing all those women students, I called. I figured: I'm a Canadian student union prez, so I should be expressing our condolences to their prez. I wouldn't have done it if they'd been in the States, for example."

"What did they say?" pressed Avigail.

"Their prez was really upset, as you can imagine. He thanked me and said that I was the first to call and that it meant a lot to him that it was coming from English Canada. And then he said: 'It's so lonely here.' I didn't know what to say. And then he goes: 'He fired holes everywhere, you know. Then he shoved the girls right in those holes. Do you see what I'm saying?' I said that I didn't really (I figured he was having trouble speaking in English) but that I was listening. Then I told him I was sorry that I couldn't speak French. 'It's okay, *mon ami*,' he said.

With tears in her eyes, Avigail embraced Carl.

"Oh jeez," said Simon. Theo Hoshen said nothing.

"I know your heart's in the right place," said Avigail to Carl in a quivering voice, "but you just don't get it." And then, turning to Simon and Theo Hoshen, she added: "They really don't, you know. They have no idea how they make us feel." Neither Carl, Simon, nor Theo Hoshen had ever seen Avigail that way before. It pulled at their hearts – except for Simon's, that is:

"So you're getting a bit of the elbow," he objected. "Why give a duck?"

"Oh shut up," snapped Avigail. "I care because it's my country and these guys run it as if my nation didn't exist. All day every day they say 'Canada' when they should say 'English Canada'. I mean, even you Brits figured out that Britain and England aren't the same."

"She's got a point, gents," said Simon grinning.

"Sure I do. Because Britain and Canada are *multi*national countries. You've got the English, Scottish, Welsh and Irish; we've got the aboriginal nations, Quebec, and *maudit* English Canada – oh and maybe the Acadians. That's why, Carl, when you talk about 'Canadian' culture when you should say 'English Canadian' you leave no room for the minority nations. And you wonder why so many Quebecers are separatists or so many aboriginals are pissed off all the time. Well we loser *Québécois* will probably keep taking it but I'll bet that, one day, the natives'll have enough. And then you'll see."

"Nah, that's not it," interjected Simon. "You wanna know why all the frogs and snow-monkeys have such a big bag on? It's 'cause the whole country's so fucking twee!"

"Twee?" said Carl.

"Twee, mate: tame, lame, nice, no spice; you know, milque-toast. Really, who'd want to live here? You're beyond being Americans without guns; you're so nice that you bore even yourselves. I'm telling you, this is one country of sad arses. The Yanks – now they know how to kick ass."

"Ah," interjected Theo Hoshen, "the United States of America. An exciting place, to be sure, but not very interesting."

At this the others shouted at him in unison to be silent. And for once, Theo Hoshen did so.

"At least he cares about doing the right thing," commented Avigail. "But you, Simon, you just don't give a damn."

"Look," said Simon, "the great thing about being a techie is that you can forget all of that ethics stuff. So maybe I'm not Mr. Justice, but I know when a place is fucking boring. I mean, I've listened to the CBC."

"And what's wrong with the CBC?" demanded Carl.

"Everything, mate. It's all so goddamn *pleasant*. There's nothing there; no risk, no edge, nothing. Take that Lindsey Osbourne bird – you ever heard her do an interview? It's just one bootlicking question after another. I mean, she bends over backwards so much it's a wonder she hasn't stuck her nose in her own arshole!"

"It is a point worth considering," said Theo Hoshen, which caused the Englishman, always on the lookout for a good pun, to burst into uproarious laughter. "What?" said the still-sober Theo Hoshen. But Simon had gone into hysterics and the three had to wait some time before he was able to continue:

"Here's another one. What about this so-called CFL football? I mean, I've seen you watch it, Carl, so tell me: why even bother when you've got the NFL?"

"Because the CFL's better, that's why. For one thing, the Grey Cup Final's always a better game than the Super Bowl."

"Oh yer just pretending to like it better 'cause you're a wacko Canadian nationalist."

"*English* Canadian nationalist," corrected Avigail.

"If he's an *English* Canadian," rejoined Simon, "then what

would I be if I were daft enough to immigrate here? I mean, I'm from England, and I'd be a Canadian, so that'd make me an 'English Canadian' right?"

"Well," replied Avigail, concentrating hard, "there's the English Canadian *ethnic* group, made up of people like you would be, and there's the English Canadian *nation*, which has no direct connection to England – if you speak English and identify with English Canadian culture then that's enough to make you a part of it."

"Perhaps 'Canuck nation' would be a simpler and so more effective term," offered Theo Hoshen.

"Or perhaps," added Simon, "all these labels are just a big fucking waste of time. Everyone's different, everyone's separate, so what we really need is just for Carl here to admit that the NFL's got the better players. Which makes sense 'cause that's where the money is. Shit, the CFL's so poor all their teams can't even afford their own names. Did you know that two of them are called 'Roughriders'? I mean, what *the fuck* is up with that? There are only eight teams in the whole damn league! What happens when those two play each other? Bet ya the Roughriders win every time!"

"Well, actually," objected Carl, "it's the 'Saskatchewan Roughriders' and the 'Ottawa Rough Riders'. It's two separate words for the Ottawa team."

"Oooh," replied Simon, "I stand corrected then. And another thing," he continued after gulping down yet more beer, "what country's got buildings where the ground floor's the first floor and then, right next door, the first floor's one up? Or supermarkets where the veggies and stuff are in either metric or imperial but you can never guess which? I mean, it's a bloody miracle you all agreed to drive on the wrong side of the road!

"And what's with the ice hockey fights?" Simon continued. "You guys go around the world pretending to be peacekeeping do-gooders and apologizing whenever someone bumps into you and then you cheer like crazy when your hockey players go at it on the ice. 'Glorious and free' eh? More like 'fucked-up and free'."

"Once again," said Theo Hoshen, "there is something to what Simon says," which only started the latter laughing again. But Theo Hoshen ignored him and continued: "For the citizenry here has indeed become complacent, pusillanimous, given over to decadent pastimes such as horseplay and making money. Dull and virtually allergic to ideas, all that Canadians seem to care about is shirking challenges in the misguided belief that it will somehow protect their easy comforts. Evidently, they have chosen peace and order over good government."

"Theo," said Carl, "when you talk like that you sound like a guy without a country."

"I suppose it is true, *de facto*," confirmed Theo Hoshen. "Nor am I part of what Avigail would call a nation, for I do not identify with the Canucks."

"So what?" countered Avigail. "That's true of about half of anglophones. But the other half *do* form a nation because they care about its culture. And it sure works for them, since it lets them rule the country without having to admit it. It's always in the interests of the majority nation to pretend that it doesn't exist; that way it gets to label as irrational everyone in the minority nations who claim to be distinct. It's like that all over the world, which has maybe thousands of nations but less than two hundred states."

"In Quebec too, right?" challenged Carl.

"What?" said Avigail.

"Well," said Carl, "if I'm following your logic then just as I should be distinguishing between the Canuck nation of English-speakers and Canada, you should be distinguishing between the *Franco-Québécois* nation and *le Québec*. Because if Canada's multinational then Quebec is too, right? Otherwise it's just Trudeau all over again."

"Um," was all that Avigail could say.

"Friends," interjected Theo Hoshen. "Really, what is to be gained from trading in all these ethnicities?"

"Not ethnic," corrected Avigail, "national."

"Regardless," objected Theo Hoshen, "both are the stuff of barbarians. For they serve only to divide us, to make us strangers to each other when what we need to see instead is that we are all friends of a civic sort, members of a citizenry who share a good in common. That is why, instead of celebrating Canuck national culture, Carl should be putting the political culture of all of Canada first, just as Avigail ought to give up her own people's sense of victimhood. It is true you were conquered once, but that was a long time ago; instead of nursing your resentments you should be celebrating the common good that, today, you share with all other Canadians. How strange is this upside-down modern ethic whereby, in order to obtain some recognition, people embrace their status as victims. There was a time, you know, when only heroes deserved glory."

"Inside-out," corrected Simon.

"What?" said Theo Hoshen.

"Well," said Simon, "it's not upside-down if there are still heroes getting glorified, inn'it?"

"I do not follow."

"It's like this: you got the Don in cricket or the Great One in ice hockey, right? So guys are still getting the glory, *alongside* the losers. That means the modern world's an inside-out premodern one, not upside-down. And another thing," he added turning to Avigail, "you frogs weren't conquered. In Billie Shakespeare Land, where we actually learn history, we know that the 1763 Treaty o' Paris was just an exchange between colonial powers. The Frenchies were fed-up with the New Frenchies and so they traded you to us for some Caribbean beaches. A real bargain, if you ask me."

"History," said Theo Hoshen with disdain. "There is no way to dwell upon it without making this the country of our defeat."

"Guys, guys, I've no idea what he just said," interjected Carl, "but I do know that we've got more important stuff to deal with right now than going on and on about Canadian politics. C'mon, how about it?"

"He's right," said Avigail, relieved along with everyone except Theo Hoshen at the prospect of a change of subject.

"Sure is," confirmed Simon. "So how about this," he said, raising his bottle in a toast: "To the Tomato – and the brilliant tossers who stole it!"

"The Tomato!" declared the others in unison. Then each took a drink and pondered what was to come. For it was time to decide upon their next move.

CHAPTER XVI

*Wherein the famous yet secret society, Fahrenheit
1710, is founded and its first communiqué issued*

"Alright then, my friends," announced Theo Hoshen in a strong
and authoritative voice, "let us to it. I believe we ought to begin by
taking up a suggestion that Carl made to me not long ago, namely,
that our first step should consist of sending the engineers a ransom
note."

"It'd really throw them," enthused Carl.

"What would we demand?" wondered Avigail.

"I dunno," said Carl. "Something to annoy them."

"And who would sign it?" asked Simon.

"An excellent question," declared Theo Hoshen. "For we
cannot use our real names."

"This one's really bright, for a philosopher," commented
Simon. But before Theo Hoshen could respond, Carl spoke:

"C'mon, guys. We're making campus history here."

"Got it!" announced Simon. "Hang about – be right back!"
He left the room and returned not half a minute later leafing
through a science text. "Now where is it...where is it...here!
The Tomato's made of brass, right? So how about this: you call
yourselves 'Fahrenheit 1710'. It's the melting point of brass."

"Perfect!" said Carl. "But what do you mean 'you'? You and
Avigail are in on this with us, right?"

"But you already did the hard part," objected Avigail. "I'm
not sure it'd be fair."

"Nonsense," retorted Theo Hoshen. "We had, all four of us,
already formed a genuine partnership from the first attempt.
Even Simon the whitecoat fulfilled his role. Had there

been the opportunity, I am sure you would have supported us again the second time around."

"So it's decided," announced Carl. "Now, what about the ransom note?"

Another round of beers was then distributed (Theo Hoshen was handed two bottles), and the four seated themselves to begin composing. When they were finished, Avigail brought out her calligraphy set and some fine paper, later to be aged by blotting it with wet teabags. This is what she wrote:

October 26th, 1989

Peter Certaine, Esquire
President
University of Toronto
Engineering Society

Dear Mister Certaine,

We wish to express our sympathy to you and your unfortunate colleagues at Skule™ in this your darkest hour. Enclosed you shall find compensation for $250 in damages sustained by a certain decrepit Pontiac Grand Prix, licence number 865-HYK. We hope you spend this money wisely.

As for the other matter, further communication shall be forthcoming. For the present, however, and as a gesture of good will on your part, we suggest that you perform the following ceremony. At high noon during Homecoming this Saturday, just before the parade, the entire Cannon Guard shall appear on King's College Circle. Dressed in nothing more than workboots, jock straps, and engineering hardhats, and accompanied by the mellifluous sounds of the Lady Godiva Memorial Band, they shall proceed to march, in single file, not less than one time around the full perimeter of the Circle. While doing so, moreover, they shall bear aloft a banner of not less than twelve feet in length and three feet in width and upon which shall be *boldly emblazoned (in Skule™ colours, of course) the following words: "Artsies Rule!"*

Should this observance be performed according to instruction, and in a proper spirit of solemn humility, then the return of your trinket shall remain a possibility.

With warmest regards,

Fahrenheit 1710

There had been no small amount of disagreement over the proper figure for the money order. Theo Hoshen argued strenuously for a much larger figure than two hundred and fifty, and he even offered to pay the difference from his own pocket, but the others complained that the engineers deserved much less lest they come to profit from their loss. Theo Hoshen scoffed at this, of course, but in the end he acquiesced to the above sum, one that Carl declared represented a fair compromise. Avigail then sealed the letter in an envelope with some red wax that she had melted over a candle's flame and, just before it hardened, she impressed the number 1710 upon it with a rubber date stamp. It was decided that, the very next day, the missive would be taped to the bottom of a chair in a classroom in Sidney Smith Hall, whereupon a telephone call would be made to the Engineering Society offices informing them of its location.

In the meantime, there was more celebrating to do. And so the revelry, with impressive gusto, began anew and continued on until the early hours of the next morning.

It was well into that day's afternoon when Theo Hoshen finally awoke Carl, who had fallen asleep on the couch in the living room. The president was rather late for work at SAC, of course, though it must be said that this was already no rare occurrence ("one of the luxuries of being in charge," he once explained). And so off he went, having arranged to meet Theo Hoshen again later that evening – after the latter had placed the ransom note in the location that they had decided.

Arriving at SAC, Carl was deeply disquieted to learn from one of his secretaries that two officers from the campus police force had visited earlier that morning. They had already met with his vice-president and so he quickly entered her office to inquire about what had happened. She told him that, as the police had informed her, the engineers' Cannon had been stolen the previous day. Carl feigned shock. She then re-counted that the engineers had somehow got it into their heads that a group of students from University College were respon-sible. That is why, at about two o'clock that morning, over one hundred engineering students raided the UC student residences in search of their mascot. They began by strewing innumerable rolls of toilet paper about the halls, making a great racket as they did so in order to rouse everyone from their slumber. Yet the sleepy-eyed UC students who emerged from their dorm rooms seemed to have no idea what was bothering the engi-neers. The moment some of them grasped what it was, how-ever, they made the mistake of taking responsibility for the deed. As one of the officers read from his notebook:

"'We've got your [explitive] Cannon,' yelled one of the students, 'and there's no [expletive] way we're going to give it back.'"

Of course, the officer reported, this served only to throw the engineers into an even greater rage. A number of scuffles ensued; fortunately no one was hurt. And after a short while the engineers became convinced that they had been mistaken about UC's involvement. Apparently, they now suspect a group of Victoria College students instead. The police were worried that, as a consequence, there would soon be a similar incident at that college and that the whole matter would only escalate further from there. They were visiting SAC, they explained, simply to inform them about what had happened and to ask that they report back should they learn anything of relevance to the case. And that, Carl's worthy vice-president said, was that.

Carl suppressed a smile as he made some derisive comment about the immaturity of the engineers. Then he left and entered his own office, whereupon he closed the door and released that smile into the world.

It was six o'clock that evening when he arrived at the northwest corner of Bathurst and Bloor Streets. As usual, the area was all lit up by virtue of the thousands of light bulbs that constituted the spectacular sign in front of Honest Ed's department store situated right across the street. And there, bathed in the light, stood Theo Hoshen.

"It is done," he informed Carl. As they had agreed, the young philosopher had taped the envelope with the ransom note to the bottom of a chair in the southeast corner of room 2101 in Sidney Smith Hall.

"Great!" replied Carl. "Can I make the call now?"

"You can indeed."

"Alright!" said Carl, pleased to no end. Together, the two of them made their way towards the entrance of the Bathurst Street subway station, where they knew a bank of public telephones stood. They had decided to dial from there out of a concern that the engineers, given all their technical know-how, might have some way of tracing the call. Carl was a little nervous as he reached into his pocket and pulled out a quarter along with a piece of paper upon which the number of the Engineering Society offices was written.

"You know, I've always wanted to do something like this," he said to Theo Hoshen with a smile. "Okay, here goes." And then he picked up the receiver, covered it with his scarf, and dialled the number. There were two rings before a woman answered.

"Engineering Society." Carl guessed that it was the very sec-retary who had, not long ago, given him the tour of the Engi-neering Society offices (the same woman that Theo Hoshen had followed for a short while on the day of the successful heist).

"Hehwoe," said Carl, who had further masked his voice with a powerful lisp that he produced by holding his tongue fast to the roof of his mouth. "Eye wood yike to speake to Mistuhr Pee'er Surtayne peaz."

"You sound ridiculous," remarked Theo Hoshen in the background.

"And who may I say is calling?" inquired the secretary. Thus arrived the moment that Carl had been waiting for, the one where he could say:

"It's duh keednahppers!"

There was a gasp at the other end. Some muffled sounds ensued whereupon, after a few moments, a man's voice came on:

"This is Peter Certaine. What do you want?"

"Peecisely duh quesdyon eyou shuld be asking, Mistuhr Surtayne. And for duh answer, you should doo duh fal-wohwing. Send an underling Skuleman – or a perty Skule-woman eef one kan be found – to woom number 2101 of Sidney Smith Haul. Dere, undeur duh chair in duh south east korner of da woom, dey weel find sumting adwessed toeyou. I suggest dat eyou wead it vehwee vehwee kerhfuhwee."

"Oh yeah?" replied Certaine angrily. "Well –"

But Carl had hung up.

CHAPTER XVII

About what transpired during Homecoming, as well as the plans for Fahrenheit 1710's next move, as fitting as they are ingenious

It was just before noon on the day of the university's Home-coming ceremonies that the four members of Fahrenheit 1710 could be found peering anxiously down through one of the windows of the large examination room on the second floor of University College. Their object of interest was, of course, none other than King's College Circle.

"I'm telling you," said Simon, "they're going to pull a no-show."

"Just wait," countered Theo Hoshen. "It is not yet twelve."

"I wouldn't say that," said Simon.

"No?" said a somewhat perplexed Theo Hoshen.

"No one would."

Theo Hoshen simply ignored this, and so the four contin-ued with their peering. However as Simon had predicted, noon came and went and there was nothing to see but the large and empty field encircled by King's College Road.

"The fools," muttered Theo Hoshen.

"You'd think they'd at least do *something*," said Carl, echoing his friend's frustration. "Oh well, guess the next move's ours. But right now I gotta go and prepare for the parade."

"And I've got to get some books from Robarts," said Avigail. "See you guys at home tonight? We'll have to put together another ransom note."

"It appears so," said a mightily disappointed Theo Hoshen. "Eight o'clock?"

"I'll be there," said Carl, and off he went. With nothing else to do, Theo Hoshen and Simon walked home together.

"So strange that they did nothing," said Theo Hoshen. "Their faculty's honour is at stake."

"C'mon, Hoshen-boy, you really thought they'd march? You don't reckon they take that honour shite seriously, do you? Even they know the Tomato's just laddish undergrad bullocks, somewhere to put all their nerd energy, which comes from their having famously small wangers."

Theo Hoshen just stared at Simon.

"Well that's why *I'm* here," said Simon with a wink. "You know, just relivin' my childhood. It's actually kinda fun – and real welcome, what with everything that's going on down at the lab."

"And what is that?"

"Real rum shite, is what. But it'd be a pig of a job for me to explain, what with you not being a 'whitecoat' and all. Not that I've sussed it out myself; in fact, I've no idea what's going on. Not a good sign for the thesis, eh? But then that's science: you never know what you'll find, or what you won't find. It's no life of Riley, I can tell you that."

"You know, Simon, sometimes you have a very colourful way with words."

"Ta!"

"Still, I cannot help but wonder if your speech is not a means of compensating for your bleached out, scientific world view. Regardless, words have meaning – they are not just sounds."

"Oi Theo," called Simon, his attention suddenly elsewhere, "check out that one over there."

"What one? Who?"

"The tall skinny bird with the long brown hair. Right there, walking just in front of us. Now that, I tell you, is a perfect ass. See the subtle curves and how there's not an ounce of extra fat? Gorgeous."

"Simon, that is a man."

"Fuck off! Bet ya a fiver right now she's not."

"Come," said Theo Hoshen, and he picked up his walking pace. Moments later, the two of them passed what was definitely a long-haired young man.

"Shite," said Simon. "Look, I'm no beaver-leaver, right? Still, it's a bit of a relief, if you know wha' I mean."

"Well no, Simon, I do not."

"It means I don't have to feel I missed out by not making a go of it."

"I am afraid I still do not follow."

"What, you don't feel a bit of regret each time you see some gorgeous bird that, for whatever reason, you can't put it in?"

"You cannot be serious."

"Ah don't play the nit with me, Hoshen-boy. Now that you're working out at the gym I figured you'd given up pretending you don't think with your knob like the rest of us."

"Think with my knob."

"Yeah, the thing you pull on every night. Oh right, you don't got a bird but I'm supposed to believe you're not wanking away with madam palm and her five daughters? Well here's some news for you, mate: after a while it starts to defeat the purpose. Really. That's why I keep my baby batter inside, ready for the real thing. 'Cause you know what they say: abstinence makes the cock grow harder."

As he had done so many times before, Theo Hoshen found that he could only stare back at Simon in disbelief.

So let us leave the two young men, engrossed as they were in their profound conversation, and join Carl who at this very moment was being handed a bundle of blue and white balloons (the university's colours) as he joined the twenty or so other SAC representatives in the Homecoming parade. It was just about ready to depart from the corner of College and St. George Streets but, as usual, they all had to wait for the Lady Godiva Memorial Band to make its appearance. Its tardiness was intentional, since it ensured a grand entrance. And indeed, moments later, everyone began to hear the semi-melodious sounds of the band marching towards them. They were leading a small contingent of engineering students that would also join the parade. Then, once they were in place, which just happened to be directly behind the group from SAC, the parade finally began its advance.

Surveying the crowd on the sidewalks lining the street, Carl noticed an inordinate number of engineers, easily identifiable given their hardhats of various colours. They appeared to be looking for something and Carl immediately guessed what it was. *Idiots*, he thought. And then, glancing behind, he could see that the engineers in the parade had unfurled a banner that they held proudly aloft. On it, in big bold letters, was painted the following:

1710 AIN'T HOT ENOUGH !

Carl could not hold back a smile. He slowed his pace until he was walking alongside one of the members of the band, a trumpeter. At the first sign of a break in their playing, Carl asked him about the banner.

"Oh that," came the reply. "It's just a song we sing."

"Uh-huh," said Carl, who then promptly made his way back to the head of his group.

"At least that is something," remarked a still disappointed Theo Hoshen later that evening. "Right then," he announced, "to work." And so the four opened their bottles of beer to mark the start of another meeting, the second, of Fahrenheit 1710. The sole item on the agenda: the composition of another ransom note. And this, dear reader, is what they came up with:

October 28th, 1989

Peter Certaine, Esquire
President
University of Toronto
Engineering Society

Dear Mr. Certaine,

It has been some time now since our last correspondence. How are you? We are fine.

It must be a source of great embarrassment,

both to you and your unfortunate colleagues at Skule™, to know that in failing to comply with our very reasonable request as outlined in our previous dispatch you have prevented the return of your trinket for a perhaps immeasurable length a time. As for us, well, we are left with naught but questions: Has the skill and vigour of Skule™ evaporated in this generation? Have Skule™ men and women become so bereft of spirit that they could not bring themselves to perform a simple yet all-important ceremony? And this despite the great stakes involved? Or was it, perhaps, a failure to maintain a trim physique that kept embarrassed members of the Cannon Guard from displaying their wares on that fine day last Saturday? Sadly, we expect never to learn the answers to these queries. No matter;

whatever the motive, your grievous failure to follow our simple instructions shall, we can assure you, only prolong your suffering.

Now, although your Cannon Guard drag has provided us with hours of stimulation and entertainment, we have grown weary of these baubles. In consequence, as you shall discover should you make use of the enclosed key, we have decided to return them to you. Not so the bijou, however. For that, we fear, you must meet another challenge.

But the charge is not yet forthcoming. Instead, alas, the time has come for you to face the disgrace that rightly comes with dishonour ...

With warmest regards,

Fahrenheit 1710

P.S. It is hot enough.

It was decided that the missive was to be affixed, along with the key it mentions (which could be used to open a locker in Union Station downtown), to the genitals of the horse part of the equestrian statue of King Edward VII located in the middle of Queen's Park, itself situated in the centre of the downtown campus. Another phone call from "duh keed-nahppers" was then made to the Engineering Society offices informing them of its whereabouts, following which work began on the next stage of the plan.

Theo Hoshen insisted that they simply must exact a suitable revenge for the engineers' failure to meet their first demand. And the best way to do that, all agreed, was to publicize the Cannon's theft and so put to shame all who were responsible for its loss. As Carl informed them, however, the secret was sure to get out soon anyway, since the Engineering Society's annual CannonBall, which usually saw many engineering alumni in attendance, was fast approaching. In fact, it was scheduled for the Saturday evening of the very next week, and as it was another event in which the firing of the Cannon was customary, the mighty gun's absence would be impossible to miss. In order to underline this, it was decided that Fahrenheit 1710 should send a singing telegram to all those attending the ball. Moreover, to ensure that word of the theft reached beyond the engineering community, at the very same time a press release would be conveyed to the media throughout the university and the city. Carl would accomplish this task by using SAC's fax machine, being careful to delete the machine's identification code. The new plan was exceedingly satisfying to all the members of the group, and so they finished their beers and allowed themselves to go merrily about their business.

CHAPTER XVIII

*In which Skule learns of the dishonour that comes
from daring to defy Fahrenheit 1710*

The week passed terribly slowly for the four members of
Fahrenheit 1710, as tends to be the case whenever one feels
a sense of great expectation. For a time, they questioned
whether it would be safe for any of them to be close to the
ball when the singing telegram was delivered. But Theo
Hoshen refused even to consider being absent; and Avigail
admitted that she, too, could not keep herself away. They
simply had to see the look on the engineers' faces.

Now Carl had learned that the guests, before retiring to
dine in Hart House's Great Hall, would first attend a cocktail
reception in the Debates Room. So it was decided that this was
where the telegram would be delivered. A bout of reconnaissance led a delighted Theo Hoshen to announce the discovery
of a small room the size of a broom closet (for that is what it
was) situated directly adjacent to the Debates Room's east side.
And most conveniently, there was a small hole in the wall
between the two rooms. Anyone who chose to peer through it
would thus be granted a sublime view of whatever transpired
on the other side. Needless to say, it was both Avigail and
Theo Hoshen's intention to so choose.

Arrangements were then made over the phone with a
woman named Betty who worked at Top Hat & Tails Singing
Telegrams. It remained for a stranger to be asked to leave an
envelope for her at the Hart House porter's desk; it would
contain her payment of eighty dollars and twenty-five cents in
cash along with one hundred song sheets, each folded closed.
Upon them were printed the lyrics that she was to sing to the
tune of God Save the Queen. Betty was instructed to retrieve

155

the envelope at precisely seven o'clock that Saturday evening and then to distribute the song sheets to everyone at the reception just before she began to sing. Her audience was to be informed that, the moment she commenced, they were welcome to unfold the sheets and read – or even, should they so wish, sing – along. She was warned that there was little chance of their doing so, however.

It was six o'clock on Saturday evening in a Hart House hallway when Avigail and Theo Hoshen, pretending to be in a hurry, approached a young man walking in the direction of the porter's desk and requested that he accept a large envelope to leave with the porter. He agreed and they spied on him until he reached the desk and did as they had asked. Then they went directly into the comforting darkness of the aforementioned broom closet.

"God, Theo, this is so exciting. It sure beats working on the thesis."

"Indeed. But I have been meaning to ask you: how is it progressing? You are close to finishing, are you not?"

"No. Well, yes. I mean, I should be but writing up this last bit has turned out to be really hard. I don't know, Theo, I guess I've run into some writer's block. Except that I know what I'm supposed to say; I'm just wondering about the point of saying it."

"Why to conclude the argument, surely."

"Yeah, to conclude. Thing is, I'm starting to have a problem with the whole notion of bringing the thing to a close. You know, of making a totality of it."

"What do you mean?

At that very moment, however, they heard some chatter in the hallway outside. The staff was preparing for the arrival of the guests by readying the coat check at the end of the hall, which was only a few paces from the broom closet. Theo Hoshen peered through the hole in the wall and saw that the Debates Room, while still empty of people, contained a series of tables lined up along one side. Upon them stood numerous bottles of wine, rows of empty glasses and plates, and platters of hors d'oeuvres covered with transparent plastic sheets. Then he noticed that the three members of a jazz band had entered and were setting up in the far corner beside a piano.

"They are getting ready," he whispered to Avigail. "It shall not be long now. But forgive me, you were saying..."

"Oh I don't know. I've just been reading a lot of Levinas lately. You know, the Jewish philosopher."

"What, you mean he is a philosopher who happens to be Jewish, or that he is someone who does philosophy in a specifically Jewish way? Regarding the latter, I must admit I am rather sceptical."

"Well it's both, actually; his philosophy's grounded in Judaism, especially the Talmud."

"I am afraid I am not familiar with that text."

"Set of texts," she corrected. "But I thought you were Jewish?"

"So is William Shatner."

"Point taken. Anyhow, Theo, the thing is that I came across this book of his, *Totalité et infini*. Just picked it up by chance, actually, but it's led me to take a look at some other Jewish writings, real old stuff. And man is it ever weird! I can't say I understand much of it, but there's definitely something going on there. And whatever it is, it's been making me wonder about my own work."

"In what way?"

"Well –"

At just that moment, however, someone turned the handle on the door to the broom closet. In a flash Avigail reached over, pulled Theo Hoshen to her and kissed him most vigorously. So when the door opened and light streamed in from the hallway, whoever it was could be heard emitting a short gasp. Then, as quickly as it was opened, the door was closed again; evidently, the genteel stranger had judged it unwise to interrupt.

Yet Avigail and Theo Hoshen continued kissing. Indeed, it wasn't long before Theo Hoshen found himself hesitantly pulling her even closer to him. There being no argument forthcoming from her, the two soon became so enflamed that there was no longer any place for hesitation.

Modesty compels us to leave our young philosophers to love wisdom as they have seen fit, so let us join instead Betty of Top Hat & Tails, who at that very moment was entering the building. She did so on two long, black nylon-clad legs, each of which jutted ever so elegantly from a tuxedo jacket, while on her head sat an extremely tall top hat. Approaching the porter's desk, she asked if there was an envelope for her and was told that there was. She opened it and soon inquired about the location of the Debates Room. Not more than ten minutes after that, she was marching inside.

By that time it contained almost one hundred formally dressed partygoers, all busy making merry and enjoying the wine, hors d'oeuvres and jazz music – exactly as one is supposed to do at a ball. Without so much as a sideways glance, Betty strode up to the band's guitarist and introduced herself with a deft tip of her hat. She explained that she had an urgent singing telegram to deliver.

"Cool!" replied the musician, who motioned to his band mates to stop playing. Once they did so, Betty handed out bundles of the folded song sheets to everyone standing nearby and, with great courtesy, she asked each to take one and pass the others along. Then, in a strong and clear voice, and holding her top hat in front of her with both hands, she made the following announcement:

"Ladies and gentlemen," she began. "Ladies and gentlemen. My name is Betty and I'm from Top Hat & Tails Singing Telegrams." A hush fell upon the room as everyone turned to look at her. "As you can see, I am handing around some song sheets. Please be so kind as to take one, though I humbly request that you not open it until I begin singing. Then, should you wish, you are more than welcome to join me in what I am sure you'll find is a lovely piece. I ought to add that we shall be singing to the tune of God Save the Queen." Smiles and sporadic applause erupted from members of the audience. There were even a few whoops and whistles, for Betty was as handsome as she was eloquent.

"Does everyone have a song sheet?" Many heads nodded. "Excellent." Then she gave her top hat a little spin and, with a most graceful gesture, placed it back upon her head. "And now, if I may?" she said, looking over first at the pianist and then at a specific location on top of his piano. He promptly rose and brought his two arms forward, offering, in this way, to support her as she climbed up. She smiled, reached out for him and, with one swift motion, was aloft. Then she stood straight up, glided a hand into the breast pocket of her tuxedo, and carefully removed one of the song sheets. Unfolding it, she turned to face the crowd and, after tastefully clearing her throat, made the following declaration: "This is called We've Got Your Gun." And then, in an utterly endearing, dulcet tone, she began to sing:

Where did your Cannon go?
Perhaps you'll never know
We've got your gun

Stolen in broad daylight
Taken without a fight
With countless frosh in sight
We've got your gun

Seventeen-ten is hot
Your Cannon Guard is not
We've got your gun

Artsies victorious!
Skule's shame notorious!
You're going to crawl for us
We've got your gun

And then, still reading from the sheet in front of her, she announced: "This message has been brought to you, with warmest regards, from the members of Fahrenheit 1710."

Two things happened before Betty managed to complete her singing; she was quite unaware of one, but she had more than a little trouble ignoring the other. The first consisted of Avigail and Theo Hoshen managing to tear themselves away from each other just long enough to take a turn spying on the proceedings through the hole in the wall. Then, after each took a good look, they returned to their previous business. The second involved some of the engineering students present who, once they grasped what Betty was singing about, promptly broke into a song of their own in order to drown her out. It was too late for this, however, since the message had reached all of the alumni in attendance: somehow, that year's engineering class had managed to lose Skule's precious Cannon and, to make the matter worse, it appears to be in the hands of artsies! So when Betty dismounted, took a most graceful bow, and began to leave, those who had tried to sing over her divided: some followed her outside, pleading for information about the Cannon's whereabouts and, in particular, about who had taken it ("Oh I know where your Cannon is, all right," was Betty's audacious reply, "but I'm not telling!") while others turned to the alumni and began desperately offering excuses and explanations. Yet nothing they said could cover the shameful fact that the Mighty Skule Cannon was missing. And lest any of the alumni who failed to attend the ball be allowed to remain ignorant of this, Carl was at that very moment busily faxing press releases to various media. The secret was well and truly out.

CHAPTER XIX

In which are related the events that transpire after
Chapter XVIII and before Chapter XX

The next morning, Avigail awoke to find Theo Hoshen, who had passed the night with her in amorous bliss, beside her bed and recording something in his notebook.

"What're you writing?" she asked.

"Nothing."

"Is it, by chance, a love poem?"

"I am no poet, Avigail. I am a philosopher."

"So it's philosophy then?"

"Really, it is nothing," repeated Theo Hoshen.

"Let's see." And in a flash, Avigail had swung over and snatched the book from Theo Hoshen's hands. He made no move to interfere, allowing her to pass her eyes over the most recent item:

"'The transcendental unity of apperception...'" she read. "Kant? My guy? Alright, that's it! That's it! Get out!"

Theo Hoshen shot her a wounded look.

"No, no. I'm only kidding. Jeez, Theo, lighten up."

The next days passed much like this, which is to say relatively uneventfully. Theo Hoshen resumed his classes as well as his intensive reading of the ancients; Carl attended to his various duties as SAC president; Simon returned to attempting to determine what was going wrong in his laboratory; and Avigail once again took up the arduous task of avoiding the completion of her thesis. As for what had passed between the two philosophy students, let us say that their discretion knew no bounds. For neither mentioned anything to anyone, including to each other, regarding what had happened that evening in the broom closet or later between Avigail's sheets. Not that Simon could avoid detecting that there was something different between the two, for they rarely failed to say or do something peculiar when they were in each other's company. Often, this consisted of no more than Theo Hoshen becoming curiously inarticulate, whereas Avigail would from time to time take up his role of lecturing on some subject or other. Indeed, the first of these was given over breakfast not two days after the singing telegram had been delivered. It began with Simon witnessing a curious exchange between the two philosophy students over bowls of cereal at the kitchen table:

"Theo, have you ever wondered about different cultures' attitudes to sex and how they're expressed in body language?"

"No."

"I haven't given much thought to this sort of circumstantial, heteronymous stuff before myself, but it's really interesting," said Avigail. "Of course, you still don't want to let your prejudices interfere with your perception, especially if you're dealing with someone from a different culture."

"Um-hm." Evidently, Theo Hoshen was holding his tongue.

"Here's what I mean," continued Avigail. "You know I grew up in Montreal, then did high school in Toronto, McGill for my undergrad, London for an M.Phil, and the Sorbonne in Paris for another masters. So I bet you're wondering: which city's sexier? It's Montreal, actually, especially during spring. That's when everyone comes out of their cocoons and the girls rip off their sleeves and turn on all of the beautiful losers. Everyone really checks everyone out there. It was only after I'd lived in England that I figured out why. London, you see, is basically Toronto squared: no one really looks at anyone because, though they're incredibly multicultural, they've still got this anglo, post-Protestant thing going, and in that culture the body's something separate from the self; it's considered superficial, not part of the 'real' person. That's also why we Kantians are so screwed-up about sex. But Catholics or post-Catholics, like in Montreal, well they see the body and self as intimately connected: the believers consider it a source of potential sin while the secular have the opposite take but it's equally strong.

"That," Avigail continued, "is why people from Latin cultures, both male and female, are much more sensual. So the cashiers in France will always put your change down in front of you instead of dropping it into your hand and risking touching you, while in England most of the men's washrooms, at least, don't even have mirrors."

"She's right about that," confirmed Simon.

"And in the rare case that there *is* a mirror in an English men's loo," Avigail added, "when this Canadian friend of mine was spotted actually looking into one – you know, to fix his hair or whatever – he found that the others there, total strangers, actually made fun of him: 'You're *real* pretty' and all that. Obviously, they felt weird about a man unafraid to show that he cared about his looks.

"You see the same difference in the streets. In Montreal, the women'll actually look at whoever they're attracted to, unlike the Torontonians. Oh they'll want to look, sure, but if they do it'll be with stolen glances. I remember this one time when my cousin from Argentina was visiting me in Montreal after having first gone to Toronto. She's this respected and attractive Buenos Aires lawyer and she said something that you'd never hear from a *Torontoise*: 'What's wrong with Canadian men?' She was complaining that when she walked around in Toronto she felt invisible because none of the men looked at her. It was better in Montreal, but still. I told her that it's 'cause they didn't want to objectify her but she thought I was nuts.

"The funny thing is," Avigail went on, "this difference between Montreal and Toronto really came out when I was in Europe. I'd figured that, if London was Toronto squared, since it's the old colonial metropole, then Paris'd be Montreal squared and so even sexier. But I was wrong."

"How come?" inquired an obviously intrigued Simon.

"Because of the men, both the macho native Frenchmen and the immigrants, especially the Algerians. They're very aggressive, you see. The moment a woman so much as glances in their direction they take it as an invitation to *drague* her, to try and pick her up. So the women there have got to be real careful. But in Montreal the *Québécois* are, given the Anglo influence, much less macho and so the women feel more secure flaunting their sexuality; they'll even go after men that they're attracted to in a way you'd rarely see in Toronto – unless there's some obvious pretence for stealing a kiss, that is," she added with a glance in Theo Hoshen's direction.

"What?" wondered Simon.

"Nothing," replied Avigail, which led Simon himself to look over at Theo Hoshen. But the young philosopher was studiously contemplating the cereal box in front of him. "And that," concluded Avigail, "is my anthropology lesson for the day. Theo?"

Unable to remain silent now, Theo Hoshen's gave a response that had a predictably Aristotelian provenance:

"To conceive of the good and happiness as pleasure," he declared, "is to be like a grazing animal, enslaved to the life of gratification – an inevitability when only respect motivates morality." Avigail did not know what to say to this. Simon, however, responded with the following remark:

"His nibs makes a good point about a major screw-up in modern moral philosophy."

"You really think so?" said a surprised Theo Hoshen.

"'Course not!" declared Simon. "You are *such* a tosser."

Time passed. Over the next few days, Carl began to receive reports at SAC about a vandalism incident that had been discovered in a washroom of the Sandford Fleming building – the very same, the reader will no doubt recall, that houses the Engineering Society offices. It seems that the facilities were, as the saying goes, "trashed": the mirrors were broken; the doors to the stalls were unhinged and left lying about; toilet paper was strewn everywhere; the faucets were left running and the drains plugged so the room contained no small amount of water; and "Fahrenheit 1710" was spray-painted in dark red all over the walls. In fact, similar spray-paintings began to appear throughout the campus: on the sides of buildings, on the fronts and backs of university signs, and even on the sidewalks. After consulting with the three other members of the organization, Carl took it upon himself to once again disguise his voice and telephone the Engineering Society, this time to deny that the real Fahrenheit 1710 was in any way responsible for these incidents. When he reached the secretary to convey the message, he was surprised to learn that there was a message waiting for him: Peter Certaine, she informed him, wished to meet with representatives of their group in order to engage in good faith negotiations for the return of the Cannon. It went without saying, although it was nevertheless said, that no harm would come to the negotiators in any way. Carl replied that they would consider the offer and respond in due course.

"What the hell is that?" demanded Simon, pointing to Carl's t-shirt as the latter entered the kitchen in which the other members of Fahrenheit 1710 had been waiting for him. His shirt was all white except for the words "Canuck Canadian" imprinted in small red letters above the heart.

"What? You don't like?" said Carl with a grin and a glance in Avigail's direction.

"I think it's lovely," she said.

"Yeah, well so's me arse," remarked Simon. "Wha'ever. Look here, I've just one thing to say to you nobs tonight and it's this: there's no bloody way you should go and meet with the engineers. Do it and you're ballsed-up for sure."

"But that is the tradition," objected Theo Hoshen. "There must be a meeting. Moreover, the time has come for us to receive the recognition that is our due. And it is not as if we were planning to keep the Tomato in our possession forever."

"Yeah," concurred Carl. "Also, I'm ready to move on. Things are starting to pile up at SAC and we've made our point. The singing telegram nailed it and we can't even come up with any more demands for a new ransom note. So I'd say that, as long as they promise publicly not to take any kind of revenge, we engrave a little something on the Tomato and give it back. Frankly, just getting the word out that SAC was involved is good enough for me. Maybe we could make them take out some kind of humiliating ad in *The Varsity*. What do you say?"

"Even that shall not be necessary," commented Theo Hoshen. "The moment it is revealed that the SAC president was in possession of the Tomato the rumour mill will effectively spread the news. And regardless, there is sure to be coverage in the campus papers."

"I'm with Simon on this one," interjected Avigail. "At the very least, couldn't you guys just negotiate over the phone? You know, to see what they have to say and then decide?"

"But the point, my dear," said Theo Hoshen, "is that there is no longer any need for negotiations."

"My dear?" repeated Avigail.

"Sorry," said Theo Hoshen.

"No, it's okay," she said with a smile. At this, Simon and Carl could not help but exchange glances.

"What I mean," continued Theo Hoshen, "is that it is not as if we are criminals who must hide ourselves. We ought to be proud of what we have done and so we should act accordingly. That means showing ourselves. And why not return the Cannon when we do so? This way we get the recognition we deserve and they get their mascot back. It is not like we have any use for it anyway; in fact, its only value to us is in its being returned. So there is no need for a drawn out session of give and take since our returning the Tomato would be to everybody's benefit; it would realize rather than compromise the

167

common good. Everyone is always so quick to negotiate when they often have only to sit down together and reconcile their differences with conversation. So that is what I propose we do. Then, once we have reached an understanding, we can return the Tomato."

"What an excellent plan!" declared Simon. "And they say philosophers are impractical. Still, you tossers'll keep Viggy and me out of it, right?"

"As you wish. Your names shall not be mentioned."

"Oh we so wish," said Simon, with Avigail nodding in approval.

"So it's decided," said Carl. "I'll tell them we're ready to meet. I can't wait to see the look on Certaine's face when he sees me!"

"Nor can I," said Theo Hoshen.

And so Carl made the telephone call, his voice disguised somewhat less than before. A rendezvous was quickly agreed upon; it would take place in the diner, Room 338, beginning at eight o'clock the very next evening.

As they had planned, Carl and Theo Hoshen arrived a few minutes late. The diner was relatively empty, but there, seated at a corner booth, was Peter Certaine alongside a rather surly looking well-built young man who Theo Hoshen surmised was the Chief Attiliator.

"Hi Peter," said Carl as he approached the booth. "How's it going?"

"Okay," replied Certaine, though it was plain to see that he was more than a little ill at ease. "Look, Carl, we're expecting some people here for an important meeting; sorry, but I can't ask you to stay."

"Really?" said Carl. "What's the meeting?"

"Long story."

"About this long?" Carl held his hands apart in front of him with the precise length of the Cannon between them. At once Certaine turned as white as the freshest Ontario snow.

"You?" he stuttered. "You took it?" his voice fading to naught.

"SAC," grumbled the Chief Attiliator under his breath.

"Not only SAC," said Theo Hoshen. "For if I may be permitted to make proper introductions, I am Fahrenheit," he said pointing at himself, "and this fine student union president here is 1710." Certaine and the Chief Attiliator could only stare back at them in disbelief. Beaming, Theo Hoshen and Carl sat themselves down in the booth.

There were a few moments of silence as the parties sized each other up. At last Certaine spoke:

"Do you know how serious this is?" he began sternly. "You put the whole Cannon Guard's careers in jeopardy. You shouldn't have told the alumni."

"Yes, well what could you expect?" said Theo Hoshen with a smirk. "We are artsies, after all."

"You just don't get it, do you?"

"Perhaps it is you that does not get it," said Theo Hoshen. "But now that we are here we can discuss the matter. So please, let us begin."

"Oh we'll begin the begin alright, you asshole," said Certaine. "But it's not us you'll be talking to." And with that he and his companion looked up and behind Carl and Theo Hoshen, prompting the latter two to turn around. Now it was their turn to become white, for what they saw was the dismaying sight of two campus police officers marching directly towards them.

"These the guys?" said one to Certaine.

"Yeah."

Betrayed, both Carl and Theo Hoshen were speechless. At length, Carl recovered his voice:

"You called the mice. *You*, the EngSoc president. I can't believe it."

"Believe it, sir," said the other officer. Then it was the first's turn to speak again:

"We have some questions for the both of you. First, do you admit to having taken the Cannon? And second, are you prepared to return it? I have been made to understand that, if so, the Engineering Society is willing to let the matter drop, as are we. But if not, then I must tell you that things could go extremely badly. Theft from a motor vehicle is a serious offence."

"I really can't believe this," was all that Carl managed to say. Theo Hoshen, despite his mounting anger, was much more articulate:

"With respect to your first question, constable, the answer, I am proud to say, is yes. As for the second, in regards to which I am also very proud, the answer is no."

"Now hold on there," said Carl.

"What?" demanded Theo Hoshen, a growing fury in his eyes. Never before had Carl seen him in such a state.

Carl paused. He glanced over across the table to see Certaine's face staring back at him as grimly as ever, while that of the Chief Attiliator's projected the wide, sickening grin of the genuine rogue. Then Carl looked up at the two officers, both of whom were expressionless.

"Sir," said one of them sternly, "I suggest you answer our questions. Now."

"My answers are the same as my partner's."

"So we call Metro," said the officer.

"What?" exclaimed Carl. "You mean the Toronto police?"

"I said it'd get serious."

"Whoa, hold on a sec," objected Carl. "That's a bit much for a college prank, don't you think? Alright, let me talk to my partner."

"Go ahead," said the officer. At this, Certaine and the Chief rose and, with the two officers in tow, crossed over to the other side of the room. It was quite clear from how the officers were directing their eyes at them that Carl and Theo Hoshen were not to leave the booth.

"C'mon Theo. We were going to give it back anyway."

"Yes, but not like this."

"But we could get into real trouble."

"No. If they go through with it, it shows that they are the ones in trouble."

"Theo, this is serious."

"Carl, if you wish to you may tell them that you would return the Cannon if you could but that I have it in my possession and I am refusing to cooperate. In fact," he said with disdain, "this may even be the truth."

"But I know where it is. It's in your room, right?"

"Wrong."

"What? You moved it?"

"Yes. Not that I imagined anything like this would happen. It was just in case the Guard ever discovered us."

"Well they discovered us."

"Indeed."

"So that's it? You're not giving it up?"

"I am not giving it up."

"Alright," said Carl, sensing that he felt the pain of their misfortune more keenly than his partner. Yet he had no choice but to call the others back. "Listen," he said to them, "I'm willing to return it, but it's up to my partner here, since only he knows where it is. And he says no."

"Then I'm calling Metro," said the officer.

"You do know who I am?" said Carl.

"It doesn't matter who you are," replied the campus policeman as he reached for his two-way radio. Then, after pronouncing some inaudible things into it, he looked up. "It'll be just a little while," he informed them.

CHAPTER XX

Wherein Theo Hoshen and Carl Landsberg make the acquaintance of Officers Martin and Smith of the Metropolitan Toronto Police Force

It was far more than a little while before anyone came. Not a word was exchanged between those in wait, even though it was evident to all that Carl and Theo Hoshen were becoming increasingly perturbed, each for his own reasons. Then one of the campus policemen asked to speak to Peter Certaine alone, and so the two made their way to the other side of the room.

"So who is he, exactly?" asked the officer.

"You mean Landsberg?" replied Certaine. "He's the SAC prez."

"Really? The president?"

"Yup."

"Why didn't you say anything?"

"You never asked."

"Great," said the officer. And then, once they had rejoined

the others, he turned to Carl and, in a somewhat sheepish tone of voice, said: "I like your burgers." Needless to say, Carl did not respond.

At last, two Metro Toronto police officers appeared. They wore the dark blue uniforms of the force, with single red stripes down the sides of the trousers and red bands encircling their smart caps, and they were impeccably groomed. Not without enthusiasm, which is to say with a smile and a wave, one of the campus policemen left the group and approached them.

"Hi fellas," he said. "I called you in. But look, it seems we may have been a bit premature on this one. Why don't you let me handle it from here?"

"It's no problem," replied the city officer, "we wanted to get something to eat anyway. So we might as well see what you've got. What's up?"

Unable to dissuade them, the campus policeman offered what little information he had.

"This could be fun," remarked the city officer. "Larry," he said to his partner, "how about getting us a couple of burgers while I chat with the victims?"

"Oh," came the obviously offended reply, "*I'm* to get the burgers."

"Come on, Larry." And then, after a pause, he whispered: "You're still mad 'cause I shot that guy, is that it?"

His partner only sighed heavily and went to get their meal.

And so, as one officer presented himself before the counter to order, the other approached the booth within which could be found Certaine, the Chief Attiliator, Carl and Theo Hoshen.

"I'm Officer Rick Smith from 52 Division," he began, "and that's my partner over there, Officer Larry Martin. Now, I've just been informed that two of you have allegedly had something stolen by the others. It sounds like a bit of a lark, so let's see if we can just work it out. I'll have a short talk with the victims first and then with the others. So, which ones are the victims?"

At once Certaine, the Chief Attiliator, and Theo Hoshen raised their hands. "Funny," said the officer, but it was evident that he was far from amused. "Okay, who're the engineers?" Certaine and the Chief Attiliator nodded, whereupon the officer asked them to join him for a few words at the other side of the room.

"Now," he said to them, "I've been given a brief outline of what's happened. I understand that it's just a prank but I need to hear from you exactly what's up. So what can you tell me?"

Certaine explained everything.

"Right then," said Officer Smith. "So what do you want done about it? You want us to take further action?"

"We were told," Certaine replied, "that either we'd get our Cannon back or they'd be arrested."

"Okay, so if I had a word with them and got it back we can just give 'em a warning and square the whole thing away, right?"

"Sure," said Certaine.

So the officer walked over and seated himself in the booth across from Carl and Theo Hoshen. This was also the moment when his partner arrived with their food. He took a place in the booth as well, whereupon the two policemen removed their caps and set to work on their burgers.

"You'll have to excuse us," said Officer Martin. "We haven't eaten all day."

"Now," said Officer Smith, his mouth full, "I'm told you've taken some sort of cannon-thing from the engineers. Will you give it back?" Of course, it was Theo Hoshen who spoke first:

"No, we shall not."

"How come?"

"Because, officer, at this moment it belongs to us."

"How's that?"

"Because it would be wrong for us to return it," came Theo Hoshen's reply.

"Oh it would, would it? And why's that?"

"Because of the situation."

"And by 'situation' I take it you mean that you've been caught, is that it? Well that's what can happen when you take something that doesn't belong to you. So my suggestion is that you apologize to those two gentlemen over there and promptly return their property."

"Well my suggestion is that they apologize to us," retorted Theo Hoshen.

"Look, we're not social workers okay? Either you return the thing or you'll be arrested; it's as simple as that." At this the officer placed his burger down upon his platter and then swung around to put it on the table of the empty booth behind him. His partner did the same. Then they both turned back, carefully placed their caps on their heads, and adjusted them. Officer Smith then said the following to Carl:

"And you? Are you with your buddy on this one?"

"He's not my buddy," came Carl's exacting reply.

"Whatever," sighed the policeman. "I'm asking if you also think you deserve an apology."

"From him, yes," replied Carl, pointing his finger at Theo Hoshen.

"And the cannon-thing?"

"It's not up to me," said Carl.

"And why not?"

"Because he's hidden it somewhere."

"Oh I'm sure he has," said Officer Smith sceptically.

"Uh-oh," muttered Carl to himself, for as he had by then learned to expect, Theo Hoshen now had something to say:

"Sir," said the adventurous young philosopher sternly, "are you aware that to accuse someone of lying in front of an honourable man is a great affront to the latter?"

"What?" said the startled officer. "What're you talking about?" The question was posed in earnest but Theo Hoshen took it as yet another affront, leading him to stand straight up and shoot an angry look directly at the policeman. At this both officers also got up but, before anyone could say a word, Carl rose and, placing his hands on Theo Hoshen's shoulders, gently pushed down to direct him back to his seat. Carl followed him down as he did so and, smiling sheepishly, he said the following:

"You know, this reminds me of a story. I once knew a guy who wanted to become a cop. But they suspected he was a bit of a druggy so they were reluctant to let him into the academy. He assured them he'd never done anything, however, and he even agreed to take a lie detector test to prove it. So he took the test – twice in fact – and because he was stoned he passed with flying colours. Apparently, he's now a great cop. Ironic, eh?"

"Alright," announced Officer Smith, "you two are really starting to annoy me. I'll say this one last time: return the cannon-thing or you're under arrest."

"But I said I can't," protested Carl. That was enough for Officer Smith. He walked over to Carl and Theo Hoshen's side of the booth.

"You're both under arrest for theft from a motor vehicle," he said. In the background could be heard a rapturous "Yes!" from both Certaine and the Chief Attiliator.

"Let's go fellas. Up." Carl and Theo Hoshen rose and each was taken in hand by one of the policemen. "It's my duty to inform you," said Officer Smith, "that you have the right to retain and instruct counsel without delay. You may call any lawyer you want or a legal aid duty lawyer will be available to provide legal advice without charge and explain the legal aid plan to you. You are not obliged to say anything unless you wish to do so but anything you do say may be given in evidence. This statement includes the rights at the time of arrest as outlined in the Charter of Rights and Freedoms as well as safeguards such as the right to a legal aid duty lawyer. Do you understand?"

"No," answered Theo Hoshen.

"Okay," said Officer Smith. "It means that you can get a lawyer and that you don't have to answer any of my questions but if you do say anything it could be used at your trial. Also, all your rights under the Charter will be respected."

"No, no," objected Theo Hoshen. "What I do not understand is why you are so quick to invoke our rights. I mean, why do you get to do your duty while we must already fall back upon rights? Surely we should have the opportunity to be arrested as dutiful citizens first." Of course at this both officers could only give Theo Hoshen a quizzical look.

"It'll all be explained to you later," said Officer Smith. And with that Carl and Theo Hoshen were escorted out of the diner while Officer Martin informed the campus policemen and engineers that he would be returning momentarily to obtain more details. Outside, it was Officer Smith who spoke:

"Before we put you in the car we're going to have to search you. Do you have anything you shouldn't have?"

"No," said Carl.

"What do you mean?" inquired Theo Hoshen.

"Drugs, guns, knives...anything dangerous."

"Ideas?" said Theo Hoshen. This the policemen promptly ignored and, after performing quick body searches on their suspects, placed them both in the back seat of the squad car. Then, while his partner returned to the diner, an irritated Officer Smith sat himself down in the front passenger seat.

"We're going to take you down to the station," he explained. "I'm asking you not to speak to each other on the way." And not a few minutes later, Officer Martin returned. So the four began their journey to the headquarters of 52 Division.

CHAPTER XXI

In which Carl Landsberg meets his very own defence attorney, one Mr. Samuel Henna

Upon reaching the station, both Carl and Theo Hoshen were directed to a room in which a man behind a desk asked them a number of questions so that he could fill out a form on their behalf. Then each was placed in a separate cell. Let us first join Carl in his.

It was a small, windowless room, containing nothing more than a toilet and a single wooden bench attached to the wall. On it could be found a woeful mattress and an even less tempting pillow and nothing more. The door was both very solid and very shut.

Sitting on the bench, Carl closed his eyes tightly and leaned his back against the wall. After a short time, he opened those eyes to confirm that, yes, he was indeed confined to a jail cell.

He began to moan quietly and closed his eyes again. He tried to decide who deserved his anger more: the engineers for double-crossing them, Theo Hoshen for having got them into this situation, or himself for having followed the adventurous young philosopher in the first place. He chose Theo Hoshen. What a fool! And his obsession with reputation, indeed his whole honour-ethic spiel, what insanity! Not that these sentiments gave Carl any peace; nor, of course, did the realization that he was most probably the first SAC president ever to have been arrested. And for what? A college prank?

Two hours passed in which these and similar thoughts raced around in Carl's mind. He felt an emptiness deep in his stomach. To distract himself, he began to think about what it would take to escape from that place. Not that he would ever attempt such a thing, of course; still, he wondered how one would go about it. But there really seemed to be no way. *Only an invisible man could manage to get out of here, and even he would have to wait until someone opened the door.* There was a clanking of keys; an officer opened the door and informed Carl that his lawyer was waiting for him in the interview room.

My lawyer? Carl wondered, until he realized that SAC must have sent him. Carl was led to the interview room and into a chair that faced another in which sat a balding man with a slightly bent nose and an ill-fitting suit. This was Carl's attorney, one Mr. Samuel Henna.

After introducing himself, the man explained that they had to get right down to business since directly following their meeting Carl was to be interviewed by an inspector from the burglary squad.

"The burglary squad?" exclaimed Carl. "What, for taking a school mascot from a car?"

"Well, it appears there was a case of breaking and entering

before the theft from the automobile for which you were arrested. They suspect that you and your partner were involved in that too."

"Oh shit. Shit, shit, shit. I can't believe this is happening."

"Yes, the whole thing strikes me as strange as well. Not as strange as the cab driver I defended yesterday, but that's another story. Anyhow, it seems that your partner really annoyed one of the arresting officers, who's got some friends in the burglary squad *and* the Crown's office. So we've no choice but to go through with this. Here's how we'll proceed: I'll explain things a bit at first and then you tell me what you want to do. But remember, my job is to help you so feel free to stop me with any questions you might have. We've got to work on this thing together, okay?"

"Okay," said Carl, running his hand nervously through his hair.

"Good." The lawyer then brought out a small notebook. "So here's what they've told me. A few weeks ago there was a break-in at the U of T's Engineering Society offices. A party, or parties, attempted to enter a room that contained the engineers' Cannon, which, if I'm not mistaken, is the very same item that you and your partner, one Theodore Hoshen of Toronto, are said to have in your possession. The accusation is that you stole it from an automobile just a few days ago. Apparently, you've both admitted to being members of an organization, Fahrenheit 1710, which has claimed responsibility for the theft."

"Yes, but –"

"No 'buts' until I've gone through the whole thing, okay? Because as you'll see it gets a bit tricky. So, regarding the attempted burglary, it seems that, one, they have no witnesses as of yet; two, nothing was taken; and three, all of the evidence – a smashed window pane and a damaged door – is now gone, both having been replaced. The police nevertheless claim, understandably, that they have good reason to suspect that you two are responsible. Yet the whole thing's very unorthodox since, even though they've nothing to go on, they want to bring you both up on the burglary charge. I asked a contact who works here and he said that the guys in the burglary squad agreed to do it as a favour to one of the arresting officers, a Detective Smith. Apparently, as I told you, your partner managed to really upset him. What'd he do, exactly?"

"Oh he was just being himself."

"I see. Well it doesn't seem fair to me; not at all. Either way, you should know that burglary's a much more serious offence than theft from a motor vehicle. You ought to keep that in mind as you consider what I'm about to say. So here's the situation. They want confessions, and whoever confesses can expect to get off with a caution and a few months of community service. However, if Mr. Hoshen confesses and you say nothing, *and* they come up with some corroborating evidence, say another witness, then things could become very serious for you. Because burglary, you see, depending on the value of what was taken, is a crime punishable by up to fourteen years in jail. Of course it would be similarly serious for Mr. Hoshen if you confessed and he said nothing. But here's the thing: if neither of you confess then they'll probably have to drop the burglary charges altogether and you'll both get off with just the theft from a motor vehicle. The problem, of course, is that we don't know what Mr. Hoshen'll do. That's why I am recommending that, if you did do it, you confess. I know it's a tough dilemma, Carl, but that's what I'd do if I were in your shoes. It's the only rational move."

"Dilemma? What do you mean?" asked Carl weakly.

"Well, between taking the very risky option of saying

nothing, which could mean either a serious punishment or getting off lightly for the burglary, or taking the much safer route of confessing, since it'll mean a relatively light punishment for both the burglary and the theft from the car."

"No," objected Carl, "it's not like that at all."

"What, you mean you can be sure that Mr. Hoshen won't confess?"

"No, I can be sure that he will. But not because he wants to get the lightest possible sentence – whether for him or for me. No, what Theo wants is one thing and one thing only, and that's revenge – on both the engineers and the police; in fact, I'd bet on the whole damn justice system."

"Well that's just crazy. I'm sure his lawyer will talk him out of doing anything so rash."

"Well I'm sure he didn't ask for a lawyer."

"Oh yes, you're right. They said that."

"Yeah, Theo'll confess, both because it's the truth and, even more important, because he's proud of having done it, the bastard."

"I take it, then, that you're confessing as well?"

"Yeah, I'm confessing. I'm confessing to a college prank that everyone is taking way too seriously. Jesus, wait till *The Varsity* finds out."

"You've made the right decision, Carl. I'll tell them you're ready for the interview."

CHAPTER XXII

*In which Theo Hoshen of Toronto is interviewed
by Detective Hurdles of 52 Division, Toronto*

As Carl was exchanging these words with his lawyer, Theo
Hoshen found himself escorted into his own interview room
and asked to sit down in front of a small table. After a short
while, long enough to wonder how one's path in life could
have led to such a place, but not so long as to allow for an
answer, a detective entered the room. He was a middle-aged
man who had about him that rumpled look which one expects
from someone in his position if one has followed enough film
or television. He took a chair opposite Theo Hoshen and this is
what he said:

"Hello Mr..." (he paused in order to peruse the clipboard in
front of him) "...Hoshen. I'm Detective Hurdles of 52 Division.
We're going to do a taped interview now. These things here
are the mikes and you're to talk into yours. 'Course it makes no
sense to wave your hands and the like because that won't be
picked up by the recorder; so please remember that. Also, be
sure to speak clearly and slowly, and feel free to ask me any
questions you might have. I'm going to put the tape into the
machine now and then we'll get started." He did so, pressed
the record button on the device, and then read aloud from a
piece of paper fastened to the surface of the table in front of
him. It contained numerous technical points of law. Once
finished, he looked up at Theo Hoshen and said the following:
"I understand you've chosen not to have a lawyer present. So I
should ask if you've reconsidered. Would you like to have a
lawyer present?"

"No thank you."

"Fine. May I ask why?"

"Why? Why would I want to have a stranger speak on my behalf, someone who does so because he is paid rather than because he truly believes in my cause? I would think that the answer is obvious. Regardless, I can fight my own battles."

"I see," said the detective, though in truth he did so about as much as if Theo Hoshen had spoken in ancient Greek. The detective continued on nevertheless: "Now..." (he paused to look down at his clipboard again) "...Theodore, I have here some notes from the arresting officers." He proceeded to read from them, relating the details of all that had transpired in the diner earlier that day. He concluded with an account of Carl and Theo Hoshen's arrest for theft from a motor vehicle. And then he asked: "Is this correct?"

"Yes."

"And, if you may confirm it once again for me, you and your partner have admitted to stealing this Cannon."

"Yes."

"Fine. Now I'd like you to describe to me just how you did that."

"Certainly," said Theo Hoshen, who then proceeded to relate how, with great efficiency, they had broken open the trunk of the car, seized the two hockey bags inside, and then driven off.

"Fine. Now am I to understand that, at the diner earlier today, you refused to return this Cannon even though Officer Smith informed you that, if you did so, he wouldn't proceed with the matter any further?"

"That is correct."

"May I ask why?"

"Because it would have been wrong to return it."

"In what way 'wrong'?"

"Well, you see, we had gone there in good faith, in response to an invitation from the engineers to negotiate. This was in keeping with venerable tradition. But instead of negotiations we were confronted with the police and threatened with arrest. A serious betrayal."

"Yeah, well, betrayal is one thing, Theodore, and theft is another."

"But let me ask you, detective...I am sorry, I do not recall your name."

"Hurdles."

"No, sir, your given name." There was a pause.

"Thomas."

"Thank you, Thomas. Now, what I wanted to ask was: there is no law against betrayal, correct?"

"Correct."

"Even when it is as treacherous as this?"

"That's right."

"But then tell me, would you not agree that, morally speaking, such perfidy is much worse than the theft of a student association's mascot – a theft, I might add, which is itself fully in keeping with many years of hallowed campus tradition?"

"Well, maybe morally speaking, but the fact is that theft is a crime while betraying someone isn't."

"Are you saying that you consider our laws amoral?"

"No, of course not."

"Well what then?"

"I'm not saying anything, Theodore. We've got this interview to finish, okay? I'm just doing my job."

"I can see that," said Theo Hoshen with a markedly critical tone.

"Look," said the detective, "if you'd like we could talk about all this stuff later. But for now I'm the one with the questions, right?"

"Of course."

"So what I want to know is: are you prepared to return the Cannon?"

"No."

"Even though, by not doing so, you could be convicted of a crime?"

"I can assure you that will not happen, Thomas."

"How can you be so sure?"

"No jury – and I am guaranteed a jury trial if I request one, correct?"

"I don't know. I guess so."

"Well, no jury with common sense shall ever convict someone for committing such a so-called crime."

"I see," said the detective. "If you're so sure," he said in a sceptical tone.

"Have you any other questions for me?"

"In fact I do. Where were you on the night of October the tenth?"

"I do not know. When was that?"

"It was a Tuesday night/Wednesday morning about a month ago."

"Oh, you are asking about the burglary."

"Burglary? I didn't say anything about a burglary. Can you explain what you're referring to?"

"The break in at the Engineering Society offices."

"Go on."

"Well what exactly would you like to know?"

"For one thing, I want to know if you and Carl were in any way involved."

"Of course we were."

"So you're admitting that you broke into the engineering offices that night?"

"Yes."

"Well then, would you please describe to me what happened."

"Certainly." Theo Hoshen then proceeded to recount all of the not so glorious events of that night.

"Very good. Now, can you tell me if anyone else was involved, other than you and Carl?"

"No, it was just the two of us."

"Fine. You do understand that burglary is a very serious offence? It's possible that you could spend time in jail for a crime like the one you just described to me."

"I doubt that."

"Well you shouldn't. Which is why I'm asking you again: will you return the Cannon?"

"Would you?"

"I think that I would do so, yes. Given the circumstances."

"But, given the circumstances, what kind of message would you be sending? That it pays to act dishonourably?"

"Maybe, but it would keep me out of jail. Surely that's the important thing here."

"But how could you live with yourself?"

"C'mon, Theodore, be reasonable."

"That, Thomas, is exactly what I am being. I am only sorry that you do not see it the same way."

"Well I don't. I don't. What I see is a college prank that's gotten way out of hand and could end up landing two kids in some very big trouble."

Theo Hoshen fell silent. He was beginning to feel quite dismayed. Because although his mind was busy answering the detective's questions, it had also been occupied with a different task, that of determining precisely who had most disappointed him: the engineers for their treachery, Carl for his willingness to return the Cannon, or himself for having allowed the both of them to be captured in the first place. He settled on the engineers. Still, the detective's latest words called for another response, and so this is what he said:

"I can assure you, Thomas, what we did was no prank. For it was not at all a frivolous act. I fear I am going to have to teach you and the whole criminal justice system that."

"I don't think that would be wise."

"That is always the question, is it not: what would be wise?"

"If you say so," replied the detective. "If you say so."

CHAPTER XXIII

Wherein Carl Landsberg and Theo Hoshen
exchange words, followed by a visit from some
kindly representatives of the environmental lobby

It was a sombre Theo Hoshen and an even gloomier Carl Landsberg who, having been charged with breaking and entering in addition to theft from a motor vehicle, and having promised to appear for arraignment in a week's time as well as to avoid any and all contact with the engineers, went their separate ways home. When each arrived he learned that, during his detainment at the police station, his domicile had been searched. This was too much for Carl, and so he made his way directly to Theo Hoshen's place with the intention of affording the young philosopher a piece of his mind. And who greeted Carl at the door but Simon, clearly relishing the upcoming confrontation. And so, with a grace for which he was not at all known, the young scientist led Carl into the living room where he found Theo Hoshen, despite showing little emotion, being comforted by Avigail.

"Really, I am in no need of consolation," he was protesting.

"We'll see about that," announced Carl as he made his determined entrance. Theo Hoshen looked up at his partner in crime and smiled. "I don't know what you've got to smile about," rebuked Carl. "I can't believe you. Why d'you do it, Theo? Why?"

"Do what?"

"Oh come off it. You could've just given the Tomato – the Cannon – back as we'd planned. But *no*, you had to go and get all high and mighty because of the moronic engineers. So they double-crossed us. You still had no right to get all offended on my behalf. How come I didn't get a say?"

"There is no need to invoke rights," said Theo Hoshen. "For we are friends, are we not? Nor is this a simple matter of taking offence. As you should know, Carl, once the lowly engineers called the police then it was our *obligation* not to cooperate. For when we offered to ransom the Cannon we were being gracious in victory by exercising mercy; in betraying us, they were being devious, dishonourable. And that one simply cannot, should not, abide. Why just think of the damage that would have been done to your reputation if we had acted otherwise. Regardless, Carl, it is not as if we are in any real trouble; I assure you our trial will conclude with a finding of innocent."

"Our trial? You want to go to trial? I knew it, I knew you were going to plead innocent. You think you'll be able to shame the engineers – that's it, right? Incredible. Theo, we could *go to jail*."

"What would be incredible, my friend, is entering a plea of guilty when we did nothing wrong. Our actions were wholly honourable."

"*Your* actions, you honourable piece of shit. *Yours*, not mine!"

"Please, Carl, I am certain that once you have had the time to think it over you will see that we took the right path, as will the jury. And I have been assured that we can have a jury trial if we wish."

"I can't believe you. Listen, Theo, jury or no jury my lawyer says that if there's a trial we're toast."

"A bit of marmite on that and you're good to go," interjected Simon.

"You shut it!" shouted Carl, who was becoming quite enraged.

"Sorry," said a chastened Simon. He then turned to Theo Hoshen and said: "You know, even for a philosopher you're not being very bright."

"Why do you say that?"

"Well if Carl's lawyer says plead guilty, then I'd plead guilty. *He's* the expert."

"But this is no technical matter, Simon; it is not one for legal expertise. It is a question of justice."

"There's no justice," declared Simon. "There's just us."

"You really must think I'm an idiot," inveighed Carl.

"To the ancient Greeks," Theo Hoshen countered, "an 'idiot' was someone who took no interest in public affairs. So as the student union president, it is obvious that you are no idiot."

"Godammit, Theo, just listen to me for a second. You've admitted to taking the Cannon. You can't then go and plead innocent – it makes no sense! That's it, that's it, I'm leaving." And Carl began to make his exit.

"Please wait," entreated Avigail. "Let's try and work this out, okay?" Then she reached over, took Carl's hand and gently guided him to a seat. "Now," she continued in a soothing voice, "tell us what happened at the station. What exactly did your lawyer say?"

So Carl recounted his tribulations at 52 Division, answering, as best he could, the numerous questions that both Avigail and Simon had for him. Theo Hoshen, however, did nothing to hide his lack of interest. So it was that, when the doorbell rang, he was the first to rise and answer it. Simon followed him with his eyes as he did so and, upon glimpsing the two persons standing in the doorway, he could not help but utter a hushed "uh oh."

"What?" said Carl.

"The door," came Simon's whispered reply. "I think it's Greenpeace."

"Oh no," said Avigail.

"I don't understand," said Carl.

"Wait," said Simon, still in a whisper. "If it's anything like the last time with that geezer from Amnesty International, then we're in for a show."

So the three of them turned to look. And this is what happened next:

"But I disapprove of Greenpeace," protested Theo Hoshen to the man on the left who had just invited him, accompanied by nodding and smiling from the woman on the right, to make a financial contribution.

"Disapprove?" said the man, who had obviously never heard of something so preposterous. "Why?"

"It is political," explained Theo Hoshen.

"Political?" repeated the man. "But we're apolitical."

"Precisely the problem," replied Theo Hoshen. "And what is

worse, that you cannot imagine someone opposing your organization strikes me as dangerously *anti*political."

"I'm not sure what you mean." The woman beside him was no less bewildered.

"I do not doubt it," said Theo Hoshen. "Let me put it this way. Greenpeace is an interest group, is it not?"

"Well," said the man, "we see ourselves as an 'independent campaigning organization'. We use non-violent, creative confrontation to expose global environmental problems." At this his partner took to nodding and smiling.

"I see," said Theo Hoshen. "And by 'non-violent' I take it you mean 'without aggression', correct?"

"Yes."

"But – and I am asking this out of a genuine curiosity, I assure you – is it not an aggressive act, your coming to my home and interrupting me living my life simply to collect money for your cause?"

"No," said the man, startled. Evidently, this too was not something he had heard before.

"You do not agree that there is violence in your decision to violate my privacy?"

"No," repeated the man, who was now beginning to feel rather anxious.

"I suppose I should be thankful that you did not use the telephone," Theo Hoshen went on, "that you are willing to show your faces. But I still discern no hint of shame."

"Shame?"

"Yes, for should not shame come to those who commit an immoral act? Yet I fear that you see the matter differently, am I right?"

"Well I certainly don't accept that what we're doing here is immoral," replied the man, who was nevertheless now quite at sea.

"Then let us investigate the matter together. You say that you are from an 'independent' organization. Do you not see how corrupting that is?"

"Corrupting? Our independence is essential to our integrity."

"Ah yes, integrity," said Theo Hoshen. "And one would certainly expect integrity from an organization which professes a concern for the environment. For it is central to green ideology that everything in nature is integrated, part of a whole, is it not?"

"Yes."

"And yet if justice requires integrity, does this not suggest that there is something wrong with an organization that would stand apart, independent from the whole?"

"I'm not sure what you mean."

"Simply that, as you yourself said, Greenpeace is an independent organization – independent even though, as you should know, everything is dependent upon everything else. Do you not see the contradiction?"

"No. Not really," sputtered the man.

"Between advocating the holism of ecology, on the one hand, and campaigning on behalf of a narrowly-focused, single-issue, independent interest group, on the other? It is a wonder that you can miss it. Let me illustrate: what is your organization's position on abortion?"

"Abortion?"

"Yes, abortion. Do not look so surprised. Surely you would agree that abortion is one of the most controversial issues of our day."

"Maybe, but I fail –"

"And surely you would accept that it has relevance to the environment. After all, abortion is at least partly about a woman's control over her body, is it not?"

"Yes." This time it was the woman who answered.

"And bodies are part of the natural world, are they not?"

"Yes," she said again.

"Then it is surely relevant whether one thinks that a foetus should be considered a human life, since life is a category central to ecology. Is that not so?"

"Yes, I guess it is," she said.

"So the question of abortion is indeed intimately related to that of environmental justice. And this only stands to reason since the whole, as any good ecologist will tell you, is prior to, indeed present within, each and every part. Is that not correct?"

"Uh," they said in unison.

"Oh come on. Surely you would agree that there can be no social justice without a proper management of the economy, no healthy economy without roads, running water, and education, no education without health, and no health without a clean environment, and so on and so on. *That* is why it is perfectly natural for me to ask you about a matter such as Greenpeace's position on abortion."

"Well we don't have a position," said the man.

"No, you do not," confirmed Theo Hoshen. "For you have chosen to place a single, isolated matter, the good of the environment, ahead of all others. Now I hope you can see how utterly distorting this is, how it does damage to values that are both directly and indirectly environmental. Because even though all values are related, you persist in thinking narrowly when you should think wide, in giving priority to the interests of a single faction over the common good of the whole polity.

This is the thinking of those for whom it is appropriate to 'just do one's job', that is, to focus closely on a single isolated set of interests without any regard for the big picture. But surely that is not how a human being concerned with justice should act; rather, it is the way of horses with their blinders on, and it is one that can only produce collisions with other, similarly blinkered animals. At best, it brings the corruption that comes from compromise, from the balanced accommodation of colliding interests, rather than justice as truth, which can only come from fidelity to the whole of goods. At worst, well you must admit that even those accommodations tend to be far from balanced since the interest group politics driving them tends to award greater attention to those who manage to be, not the truest, but the loudest. And the squeaky wheel is, of course, not always the one most deserving of the grease. Yet thanks to an apathetic majority we have today a tyranny of squeaky wheels, of the loudest factions, among which, sir, must surely be counted your own, the environmental lobby. So that is why in asking me to support your independent cause you are committing an injustice. Because what is it to place the interests of a part ahead of those of the whole if not the very definition of corruption?"

"Well...I..." stammered the man.

"Yes, corruption," continued Theo Hoshen, "and right here, in my very own home! You come here, asking me to help you put pressure on the state when the truth is, or should be, that *we* are the state, that all of us, together, make up the *polis*. To pressure the state on behalf of some narrow, blinkered interest, well that is only to pressure ourselves, to divide us and so foment strife and disunion. My God, man, why on earth would I want to do such a thing?"

Now it hardly needs saying that, long before Theo Hoshen

had reached this point in the argument, the two Greenpeace volunteers had given up trying to follow the words he was directing at them. So now that they were finally offered the chance to say something, the man replied:

"Look, if you don't want to help –"

"Help? Help? Of course I want to help. I want to save you – from yourselves!"

"Okay," said the man. "I think we'll just be going." And with that the two of them took one, and then two, steps back.

"What?" retorted Theo Hoshen. "To continue your dirty work, spreading your green corruption throughout the neighbourhood? I will not stand for it!" And then, to the two fundraisers' horror, he began to follow them out. Needless to say, this led them to do the next logical thing, which was to turn and run. Theo Hoshen gave chase.

"Theo!" shouted Avigail. It only took a moment for her, Simon and Carl to reach the doorway, from where they could see the young philosopher pursuing the two hapless Green-peacers down the street and around the corner.

"I've said it before," declared Simon. "The man's a tit."

CHAPTER XXIV

About the important conversation that took place between Carl Landsberg and Theo Hoshen, and their arraignment before the judge

"I'm going after him," announced Carl. And off he went in pursuit. "Theo! Theo!" he cried, but his quarry took no notice. When Carl finally managed to reach him he seized the young philosopher by the arm and forcibly turned him around. "Theo!" he shouted. "What the hell do you think you're doing?"

"One would think that is obvious," came the reply. "I am chasing a corrupting influence out of the neighbourhood."

"Greenpeace? Are you serious?"

"Of course. If only you had followed our discussion you would understand."

"Discussion? You call that a discussion?"

"Certainly. We were engaged in dialectic."

"God dammit, Theo! After everything that's happened do you really think it's a good idea to go chasing after two Greenpeace reps? You could get into even more trouble than you're already in, and it's all bound to ricochet onto me. Don't you care, Theo? Don't you give a damn at all?"

"Of course I do, Carl. I am surprised to hear you say that."

"Listen, we really need to talk. Okay?"

"Certainly."

"Then let's go."

The two walked together in silence along Bloor Street. In time, they reached an eatery, one of Carl's favourites.

"Ah, the Blue Cellar Room," remarked Theo Hoshen. "This is where you used to hold your campaign meetings, is it not? The world's darkest Hungarian restaurant. I hope you have not chosen it because you are ashamed to be seen with me."

"Oh come off it, Theo. Let's go."

They entered and made their way down the long, blue corridor to the cavernous dining room inside. It was indeed extremely dark in there and so it took a while for their eyes to adjust. Carl led Theo Hoshen to his preferred table, which was located right beside a softly burning fireplace that projected flickering shadows on the room's walls. It was not long before the waiter arrived and they both ordered the goulash. Then, once the friends were alone, Carl began to speak in earnest. This is what he said:

"So we're going to have a real talk about everything, right?"

"Yes."

"I mean it, Theo. You've really got to listen this time."

"Of course."

"Not debate, dialectic, but real discussion."

"Dialectic is not debate," corrected Theo Hoshen. "You have read Plato's dialogue, the *Republic?*"

"Yeah," replied Carl, quickly becoming frustrated. "In my theory class."

"Well what Socrates was doing there – *that* is dialectic."

"And *that's* precisely the problem. Listen, Theo, I'm no Plato expert, but don't you think there's something wrong with calling his stuff 'dialogues'? I mean, they only ever go in one direction. Is there even one time when Socrates says something like 'Hey, I've never thought of that before' or 'You know, I really learned something here,' or even 'Point taken'?

"I do not believe so."

"And do you know why? 'Cause the guy never listens, that's why. All he cares about is tearing into whoever he's talking to, showing them up for ignoramuses. And since he's *the hero* of philosophy, it figures that all you macho philosophers are always trying to do the same with whoever disagrees with you."

"He is not *my* hero," objected Theo Hoshen. "As you know, I follow Aristotle."

"And why's that? What's he got over Plato?" challenged Carl.

"Well if you must know, as Aristotle explains in his *Metaphysics*, Plato has it all backwards. He believes that the Forms are pure essences, that they exist in a non-physical realm and that the concrete particulars of this world only 'imitate' or 'participate' in them. But reality, as all but dreamers are aware, is right down here. Moreover, as we are shown early on in Aristotle's *Nicomachean Ethics*, Plato was utterly misguided in his assumption that the Good is some universal element common to all good things. Because though the virtues certainly fit together, they are often quite different from one another."

"Oh they are, are they?" challenged Carl. "And I'd bet anyone who disagrees is 'backwards' or 'utterly misguided'? Isn't that always the way with you philosophers: every previous thinker got everything totally wrong? Sounds like you're suffering from a bad case of the anxiety of influence, if you ask me. 'Cause if you're so reasonable, how come you're so violent with your opponents? How come you're so quick to fight for what you believe in?"

"Because, Carl, the truth can only be revealed by the force of the better argument."

"Yeah, well, whatever. All I know is that my prof said that people hated Socrates because he showed them that they didn't know anything. But what if, instead, it was because they were trying to talk with him but the asshole never listened?"

At this a grave look came over Theo Hoshen's face. Carl feared that he may have been overly severe with his friend. "Listen, Theo, I don't mean to be harsh. But please, let's have a real talk for once. This is important to me."

"Agreed," replied a chastened Theo Hoshen.

And so the two of them conversed long into the night. Carl explained why he felt Theo Hoshen had been wrong to refuse to return the Cannon immediately, and Theo Hoshen responded with a long disquisition about why it would have been dishonourable to have done anything else. Carl repeated his wish that they both plead guilty in the case, but Theo Hoshen argued that it would be improper to do so since they were both innocent of any crime. And regardless, it would be cowardly to run from the legal battle. Still, if Carl wished to, well that was his decision and no matter how unwise it might be Theo Hoshen would respect it. And regardless, given that Carl was ignorant of the Cannon's current whereabouts, any condemnation would surely fall upon Theo Hoshen's head and no one else's. Thus it was that the two came to an agreement: Theo Hoshen would stand trial on his own.

This also happened to be the decision of the court upon their arraignment a week later. Not that either the judge or the Crown were at all happy with Theo Hoshen's demand to have his case "go upstairs," which is to say be dealt with by a superior rather than provincial court. But given that the charge of burglary is an indictable offence, they ultimately had no choice but to grant him his wish – and this despite the great expense in both time and money that it entailed since his fate would indeed be decided by a jury of his peers. Nor could the judge or the Crown do anything to persuade Theo Hoshen to relinquish his decision to represent himself instead of making use of one of the defence attorneys available to him. Needless to say, they were both most displeased.

Theo Hoshen, however, mistakenly put this down to his refusal to do as he was instructed and address the judge as "your Worship." As he explained to the court, he believed that there was something idolatrous about the expression.

"Whatever," said the judge. "You are aware, Mr. Hoshen, that your trial judge – who, thank God, won't be me – is to be called 'your Honour'?"

"No, I was not. I have no difficulty with that."

"Wonderful."

"Nevertheless," continued Theo Hoshen, "as you may have noticed I am unable to bow down when entering or exiting courtrooms."

The judge simply ignored this and, hoping to get the young man out of his courtroom as quickly as possible, said:

"Alright then, Mr. Hoshen, you understand that you are to appear on Wednesday, not of next week but the week after, at nine a.m. in room 223, which, from here, is upstairs and to the left. As for you, Mr. Landsberg, your sentencing will await the results of Mr. Hoshen's trial, which I expect you to attend when you are called upon, as I expect you will be, to serve as a witness. Do you both understand?"

"Yes," said the two in unison.

"Fine," said the judge. "Goodbye. Next!"

CHAPTER XXV

Wherein Carl Landsberg and Theo Hoshen engage in yet another argument, following which the latter promptly returns to his research in preparation for his trial, only to be interrupted by Simon, who has some strange news about some research of his own

"I didn't think of that," said a worried Carl to Theo Hoshen, the two of them once again seated at the latter's kitchen table.

"So you will testify," said Theo Hoshen matter-of-factly. "I fail to see the problem."

"Well what if they ask about Simon and Avigail?"

"They shall not ask about them," replied Theo Hoshen sternly, "for they do not know about them – unless, of course, some fool tells them."

"But I'll be under oath," complained Carl. "I don't know the penalty for perjury but I'm sure it's high. I can't just ignore that."

"You can and you will," declared Theo Hoshen. "Nothing could be more dishonourable than to inform upon them. Carl, where is your sense of loyalty? Are you not aware of the honour code to which you must adhere?"

"Code?" retorted Carl. "What code? Who wrote it? I've never seen it."

"Oh come on," objected Theo Hoshen. "You do not need to be aware of its details, only to uphold the spirit underlying it, which is something that cannot be codified anyways. And you shall uphold it, Carl, for we gave our word."

"But taking an oath is also giving your word," countered Carl.

"Carl, do you not see –"

"No," interrupted Carl, "I don't. Listen, Theo, I'm not just thinking of myself here. There's also the justice system, which is there to respect people's rights. And perjury undermines the integrity of the whole process. Surely you can understand that."

"I understand only that you are afraid to do what morality requires. To inform on our colleagues, why, there can be no greater betrayal. Only a dog would do such a thing."

"You see everything so clearly," said Carl, who was beginning to boil with rage. "It shows just how deaf to reality you are. But then I've told myself this a thousand times and yet every time there's more proof I'm somehow surprised. You and that cold war you call philosophy; if you haven't noticed,

Theo, walls are coming down and yet you stay the hardliner. But then I guess you haven't noticed, 'cause you're not really down here with the rest of us. Well I've had enough, Theo. Enough." And with that an obviously furious Carl took his leave.

After a time, Theo Hoshen turned to survey the many books on the table in front of him. And then, with his usual relish, he once again took up the task of preparing for his upcoming legal battle. To a selection of relevant philosophical texts – not the least of which was, of course, Aristotle's *Rhetoric* – Theo Hoshen had added a small tower of legal ones. Up until then Carl had done his best to help, though on more than one occasion he could not stop himself from advising his friend to reconsider his decision to represent himself. Of course Theo Hoshen dismissed the idea. To properly convince a jury, he explained, one must have acquired a deep understanding of Aristotle's treatise on the art of persuasion, yet he felt sure that the book was totally unknown to today's hired legal guns. Show him an advocate who had read Aristotle and he would seriously consider taking him on.

It was perhaps an hour later, as Theo Hoshen's head was buried deep within one of the books in front of him, that he was startled by the sound of Simon's sudden entrance into the kitchen. So deep had been the young philosopher's concentration that he had not even heard the Englishman enter the house. Simon was returning from a late session at the laboratory and he nodded quietly in Theo Hoshen's direction as he made his way directly to the refrigerator to gather the materials for a sandwich.

Now Theo Hoshen, who had by then become accustomed to Simon's habit of directing a mocking comment his way whenever the two encountered one another, found it hard to ignore the latter's silence. And so he promptly stopped his work.

"Simon?" he said.

"Yeah?"

"Oh nothing."

So Simon continued preparing his sandwich. Once finished, he poured himself a glass of skim milk, sat himself down at the kitchen table's far end and, without saying a word, began to eat.

Alas for Theo Hoshen, though Simon was usually a fastidious sort, he was also not one to masticate with his mouth closed, and so the sound of his chewing and swallowing produced no small distraction; try as he might, Theo Hoshen could not concentrate on his work. Yet an oblivious Simon continued to sit there and eat, his mind far from that place.

Once he had finally finished, he rose, gathered his tableware and put it all in the sink, whereupon he promptly began washing. Then he returned to the refrigerator, this time for a tub of chocolate ice cream. He transferred a single scoop into a bowl, sat himself down again and began to eat. Theo Hoshen observed the primitive, four-fingered way in which Simon clasped his hand around the spoon as he did so. This was simply too much to let pass without a remark.

"Simon, do you always hold your spoon like that? I do not believe I noticed it before."

"Like this?"

"Yes. Normally, it is held between the thumb and two forefingers, correct?"

"Guess so. But the ice cream's hard as fuck, so it's easier this way."

"I see. Then let me ask you another question. I noticed – and this is something I have seen before – that you do the dishes immediately after each course. Would it not be easier, indeed much more efficient, to wait until you have finished the whole meal?"

"Guess I'm just into keeping things tidy," replied Simon. "But you're bang on."

"Evidently, you favour aesthetics over instrumental rationality. I would wager that, like so many others, you are quite unaware of this fact. Both lead nowhere, you know." But Simon did not respond, inducing Theo Hoshen to ask: "Simon, is anything the matter?"

"The matter? Why?"

"Let us just say that you are not your usual self."

"Yeah?"

"Where have you come from just now?"

"The lab."

"And is all well at the lab?"

"Guess so."

"You are not sure?"

"Yeah – I mean no. Oh, I dunno. Just ran into another weird hitch, is all. It'll get sorted."

"A problem with the thesis?"

"No way what happened tonight is going into the thesis."

"And what is that?"

"It's hard as fuck to describe; it's all very technical."

"Enlighten me, oh modern scientist." But Simon was oblivious to Theo Hoshen's teasing tone and replied:

"Not sure if I should say. But I reckon it's okay to tell a muffin like you."

"Tell me what?"

"Well, for a while there tonight I lost one of my specimens, or rather a bit of it, after I'd put it under the microscope."

"Why is that so odd?"

"Because there was nowhere for it to go. It was in a vac-uum-sealed column when it got hidden."

"Hidden 'disguised' or hidden 'concealed'?"

"Hidden 'your ass'. Hoshen-boy, I've no idea what you're on about."

"Well, if you can sense something but cannot perceive its true nature, then it is disguised. But if you cannot sense some-thing that is nevertheless present, then it is concealed."

"Then it was concealed. I think. Jesus!"

"So what you are saying is that it became invisible," said Theo Hoshen fatefully.

"Invisible?" Simon paused. "Yeah, I guess so." But he said this in a way that showed him to be far from convinced.

"Simon, please explain exactly what happened."

"Alright. But if I tip you off you say nothing to no one, right?"

"I give you my word."

"Okay. So I'm in the lab and I got a bug under the micro-scope. I study bugs, or rather the eyes of certain kinds of bugs – fruit flies and moths – since they could turn out to be rad models for a new kind of camera lens. That's what my thesis is about. Anyhow, I use a scanning electron microscope, which works like this: I coat the bug with a thin layer of gold to make it conductive so it shows up when I fire electrons at it under the microscope. But the thing is, this scope's a bit freaky, right? Sometimes it just goes on the blink and none of the lads down at the lab have a clue why. It's gonna get fixed at the end of the semester but, till then, we're stuck with it. And tonight it was acting *real* rum: its power levels were so off that I had to check if it was plugged into the wall okay.

"So," Simon continued, "I'm scanning the bug and then – *bam* – in the middle of the scan the scope starts vibrating and making these weird noises with a higher and higher pitch – it sounded like the thing was gonna blow or at least short out or something. So I hit the power-off button and, get this, nothing happens! I had to go and yank the plug right out of the wall.

"Now I'm worried that my specimen's been buggered and, sure enough, when I go over to check it's been knocked about inside the vacuum column. Plus it was mad hot – you could feel the heat through the glass. So I opened the thing up and poured some water in, you know, to cool her down. There was a lot of steam and boiling at first; still, it worked. But when I looked, half of the specimen was missing! And no matter how much I searched about in the column I couldn't find the missing bit. That just makes no sense – it had to be there; there's no way it coulda got out. So I took some tweezers and tried to pick up the half that was left – and that's when things got really weird. 'Cause it wasn't blown in half; somehow, the missing bit was still there only I couldn't see it. I knew 'cause when I moved the whole thing with the tweezers the hidden half just showed up – it's like it'd been covered up somehow, only you couldn't see by what. Sounds mad as a box of frogs, I know, but there's no other way to explain it."

"How can such a thing be possible?" pressed Theo Hoshen.

"Don't know. Can't really."

"This suggests that it did not, in fact, happen the way you describe. You must have made an error of some sort."

"I know. But what? Wha'ever, Hoshen-boy; I'll go back and suss it out tomorrow. It sure seemed real, though; I mean, I even tested it a bit. I moved the specimen around and it really looked like I could hide more of it away if I stuck it deeper into, well, wherever it went when I couldn't see it anymore. It's like there was a hole in the air — 'cause whenever I pulled the bloody thing out, there she was."

"Of course you know, Simon, that what seems to be the case and what actually is are not always one and the same."

"Yeah, yeah. Still right weird, though."

"I notice that you are not wearing your glasses. Perhaps that is behind it?"

"Nah," replied Simon. "I got contacts now. Viggy's idea. She said I'd go for them and man was she right. I can't believe I waited this long. At first I thought they'd be a hassle, but they're *better* than specs: nothing's hanging on my face and I can even see clearer."

"Perhaps not always."

"Yeah. Right then, I'm off to get some peeps." And with that he rose, washed his bowl and spoon, and made his way out.

"Good night, Simon."

"Night."

CHAPTER XXVI

Which finds Theo Hoshen acting as his own
defence attorney during his trial for burglary and
theft from a motor vehicle

"So this is wonderland, eh?" muttered Carl as he and Theo Hoshen, followed by Simon and Avigail, entered courtroom 223 of Toronto's romanesque Old City Hall building. Theo Hoshen took a seat behind the table that was obviously meant for the defence, whereas the others chose the row directly behind him. For once the young philosopher's formal style of dress, with a tie added for the occasion, did not seem out of place.

Just across the way sat the Crown attorney, the very same blonde, blue-suited, bow-tied, thinning-haired gentleman who had participated in Carl and Theo Hoshen's arraignment two weeks before. Since then, the Crown and the defence had managed to have their share of contretemps over the selection of the twelve members of the jury. As Theo Hoshen had pointed out to Carl, his adversary was a man of formidable intellect, not to mention someone thoroughly versed in all of the ins and outs of his profession. But the young philosopher assured his friend that he was up to the challenge.

Jury selection had been an ordeal mainly because of the large number of questions that Theo Hoshen posed to each and every potential juror. This had the effect of thoroughly annoying both the Crown and the judge, one Madame Justice Lucy Thomas. When the defence explained to her that he was simply following Aristotle's instructions in the *Rhetoric*, those that outlined the importance of discerning "the mood" of each and every candidate, it of course served only to irritate her further. And so it was that, despite her ample urgings and cautions, the jury selection process took up two whole days instead of the customary one in such cases.

Justice Thomas entered the courtroom that day wearing her standard flowing black robe and red sash. A middle-aged, African-Canadian woman of no small distinction, she had by then served on the bench for almost fifteen years. Needless to say, she far from relished the prospect of such out-of-the-ordinary cases as this one promised to be.

Once seated, she waited for everyone else to do the same and then, with an only partly suppressed look of distaste on her face, addressed Theo Hoshen directly:

"Mr. Hoshen, I'd like to take this opportunity, at the very beginning of this trial, to once again encourage you to reconsider your decision to represent yourself. I can assure you that having a trained lawyer working on your behalf will only serve your interests, not to mention those of the other members of this court."

"Thank you, your Honour, but as I said before I have far too much trust in the wisdom of this jury. Of course I accept that a professional may be more efficient when it comes to court procedures; still, I believe that no one but myself is more qualified to convince the jury of the justness of my actions. The ends of just persuasion, a *technê*, can only be supplied by the prudential reasoning of the *phronimos*, whose own ends are, of course, disclosed by theoretical reason. Regrettably, there is every reason to doubt that a state-provided attorney would be capable of supplying those ends in this case."

"Let the record show," announced Justice Thomas, "that I have no idea what he just said. Alright then, let's get started. Mr. Kay," she said addressing the Crown, "what do you have for us?" The Crown rose and marched directly in front of the jury, whereupon he stopped, turned to face them, and began to speak. This is what he said:

"In this, the case of Ontario v. Hoshen, the Crown will show that Mr. Theodore Hoshen of Toronto is guilty of one count of breaking and entering and one count of theft from a motor vehicle of an item valued under one thousand dollars. The item in question is known as 'the Cannon', which is the mascot of the Student Society of the School of Engineering at the University of Toronto. Believing it to be hidden in one of the Society's offices, the defendant, along with one Mr. Carl Landsberg – who, I see, is seated right over there – broke into those offices under cover of darkness early in the morning of October 11th. Along with destroying a double paned window in order to enter those offices, the two, employing power tools that they had brought with them, did irreparable damage to a locked door inside. They believed it to be the door to a room that contained the item that they intended to steal. They had to abandon their effort, however, because they were spotted by a member of the building's cleaning staff, following which they fled the scene. Obviously feeling no contrition whatsoever for their act, a little over two weeks later they attempted to steal the Cannon again, this time successfully. Using a crow bar or some other such blunt instrument, they tore open the trunk of a parked car within which the item had been carefully placed.

"Once it was in their possession, the accused and his partner then began sending threatening letters to the victims in this case, letters which were addressed to Mr. Peter Certaine, the president of the Engineering Students' Society. Already greatly distressed at the loss of his school's symbol, one that repre- sented many, many years of tradition, Mr. Certaine was forced to deal with negative publicity surrounding the theft thanks to press releases that the accused and his partner sent out as well as to a mocking singing telegram that they arranged to have delivered before an unknowing gathering of important school alumni. Your Honour, ladies and gentlemen of the jury, as I will show these acts amount to much more than what you might consider a mere college prank. For one thing, the nine student members of the Society's 'Cannon Guard' – which is responsible for keeping the item secure – have suffered grievous damage to their future careers in the engineering profession. The fact is that their employment prospects in this province, indeed perhaps even in the whole country, have been significantly impaired. For another, the loss has caused great disruption to their personal lives, not to mention their studies.

"All this could have been mitigated, however, if the item in question, currently in the possession of the defendant, was simply returned to its rightful owners. But as you will learn, the defendant has repeatedly refused to do so – and this even though he and his partner were informed by their arresting officers that they had only to agree to give it back to avoid being arrested in the first place. In choosing otherwise, the defendant has committed a grievous violation of the property laws of this province, not to mention disrespecting our justice system as a whole. For the fact is, ladies and gentlemen, none of us would have to be here today – which I don't have to tell you comes at great expense in both time and money – if Mr. Hoshen did not so cavalierly refuse to return what he had stolen. Is this how the precious resources of our justice system should be spent? Of course not. That is why the defendant's callousness should be considered an offence not only to the immediate victims of this apparently frivolous yet in reality serious crime but also to all the members of this court, not to mention the taxpayers of this province."

"You're going a bit far with that last bit, aren't you Mr. Kay?" remarked Justice Thomas. "After all, we also wouldn't be here today if you hadn't yourself chosen to pursue the case."

"But your Honour, as I see it this matter has to do with nothing less than respect for the rule of law. Regardless, surely the question is one for the good members of the jury to decide."

"It is now, Mr. Kay. Alright then, Mr. Hoshen, you may present us with the defence's opening remarks."

"Thank you, your Honour." With a flourish an eager Theo Hoshen jumped to his feet and made his way around the table in front of him. He paused, looked down and took a breath. Then he looked up again and addressed not only the jury but also the judge, the Crown, and the dozen or so people sitting in the audience, among whom could be counted reporters from *The Varsity*, *The Toike Oike*, and *The Gargoyle*, the student paper of Carl and Theo Hoshen's University College. Carl, it is worth noting, already knew the journalist representing *The Gargoyle*. He was a chemistry student by the name of Griffin who had written a number of articles about SAC and its president that Carl, at least, felt were deeply unfair. Indeed ever since he first confronted Griffin about one of them, Carl had actually become somewhat frightened of the young man. Because the more Carl spoke, the more he sensed that every one of his words was disappearing down a black hole located where the reporter's heart was supposed to be. The man, Carl judged, seemed bent on destruction. Every moment in his vicinity felt dangerous, since who knew what he might twist for use in his next story? Carl consoled himself with the thought that at least Griffin had no greater weapon at his disposal than his pen. Yet the student union president did not leave it there, for all of Theo Hoshen's talk about the impor-tance of reputation had led him to complain to *The Gargoyle's* editors. It was to no avail, however, for Carl soon learned that campus newspaper editors took complaints from student politi-cians as a sign that their reporters were performing their jobs properly.

But let us return to Theo Hoshen and his opening remarks:

"Your Honour, members of the jury, guests of the court, I do not know what effect the Crown has had upon you, but he spoke so convincingly that I almost forgot who I was. And yet what he said was all quite false. Before I explain why, I must point out that, as the accused, I feel quite oppressed here, slandered even. For I find the charges against me unintelligible, the surroundings abstract and impersonal, and my very being isolated; moreover, I am certain that the so-called victims in this case feel quite the same. Because instead of having to face these proceedings we should, all of us, have been given the opportunity to sit down and converse together –"

"Hold it," interrupted Justice Thomas. "Where are you're going with this? You're not here to question the rules of the game, Mr. Hoshen, only to play it."

"But your Honour, it is my life that is at 'play' in this 'game', as you put it."

"Yes, well, perhaps that was an unfortunate choice of words. Still, I'm giving you fifteen minutes, Mr. Hoshen, no more. So go ahead and say what you want but, when your time's up, that's it."

"Thank you, your Honour." And so, after a pause, Theo Ho-shen continued: "Ladies and gentlemen of the jury, what I want to say is actually quite simple. You have before you a story of two students who have taken something from some other students. Your duty is straightforward: determine the story's meaning, decide whether what we did is justifiable, whether it contravenes the law or not and, if not, then what punishment, if any, it merits.

"You should consider this a great privilege. For today more and more such cases are being 'professionalized', decided by lawyers and judges alone. In so doing they may be said to 'steal' conflicts from us, the citizenry. Of course this is a new, strange form of larceny, but that *is* what it is, for it amounts to taking from us the opportunity to consider the issues, the stories, that are fundamental to our lives. It makes learning from those stories, and so about ourselves, impossible.

"Yet the procedures of this court require that, though you are the ones who will ultimately decide, you must for the time being do no more than sit there quietly and watch as the spectacle of clashing advocates plays out before you. I am certain that you would do more if you could, that there will be occasions when you will wish to speak out, perhaps to pose a question to a witness, perhaps even to make a submission of your own for consideration. And you are right to want to do so. Indeed, I am quite sure that it would raise the quality of the proceedings, making them more in tune with the needs of human functioning. Alas, you cannot; the system does not allow it. I want you to keep that in mind when you render your verdict.

"I say again: this is a conflict. The Crown and I do not agree about the meaning of the events before you. And the system requires us to *fight* our cases, to act as if we were not opponents concerned with the common good, with the truth of the matter, but adversaries who can win only if the other loses. I am surely saying nothing new when I point out that lawyers tend to use words as weapons, as instruments for achieving victory rather than for carrying meaning as part of a search for truth. Imagine, for a moment, that you had come across this story in a novel. Would it not be strange if, hoping to understand it better, you went and hired two literary critics and instructed them to advance diametrically opposed views, leaving you to try and determine the truth as if it were some middle path between their exaggerated and distorted accounts? Surely it would be better to have them say what they truly believed instead, to agree when they agreed and to disagree when they honestly felt they could do no other. That way you could, together, develop the best possible interpretation of the story, the one that made the most sense. There is no doubt that this, and not some trial by verbal combat, is the best means to truth.

"Alas the Crown, as is clear from Mr. Kay's opening remarks, has chosen to take on the adversarial stance typical of his profession. This forces me to defend myself as well. Yet I assure you, dear members of the jury, that I will do my utmost to speak only the truth as I see it and never to skew matters, even in the interests of balance, and even though the Crown's exaggerations and distortions will surely cry out for it. For against the scales of injustice, ladies and gentlemen, I uphold the hope that the day will come when justice is something worth *not* fighting for.

"Justice. More and more today, this word brings to mind courts and the police. But not all conflicts should be dealt with by the judiciary. Only the uncontroversial ones belong here, which is to say those that arise from the fact that someone has done something which we all know is clearly wrong (assaulting an innocent, for example). Such cases confront us with relatively simple questions: 'Did he do it?', 'If so what, if any, punishment does he deserve?', and so on. But when the matter is more contentious, then it is politics and not law that needs to be called in. For we must decide not how to apply a statute but how to make one, and this requires engaging in a dialogue about how to fulfil the common good. Only that way can we develop laws which all of us genuinely *want* to follow – not, that is, because they are backed up by the police. This, then, is our greatest challenge, since today far too many of our laws are but regulations that stand apart from us, reified instruments separate from, hence imposed upon, the political community.

"Can it not be otherwise? Must we rely upon force rather than (ethical) power for the strength of law? I say no, and I say it for the same reason that the career of letters is superior to that of arms. Oh I am not claiming that the pen is mightier than the sword, for the pen's power and the sword's are incomparable – each is mighty in its own way. What I am saying is that, even if we accept that the purpose of war is peace, and that without peace the confusion and hardship that attend war would ensure that there could be no letters, no dialogue about the common good, the fact remains that arms must ultimately be sustained by that dialogue. Because even war must be subject to laws, and what, if not dialogue, could determine them? There is a circle here, I admit, but this does not pose a problem for the argument since our challenge is simply to proceed around it in the proper direction, which is to say to make it a virtuous rather than vicious circle. The fact is that, in a world where the definition of the state as monopolizing the use of force has been revealed as fiction, where swarms of bees with access to the most diabolical technologies increasingly violate the laws, both domestic and of war, the answer to our problems cannot be more enforced laws. For this only encourages more bees, more alienated, invisible, revenge-hungry failures, and the more of them there are then the greater the likelihood that one, perhaps even two, will break through our defences. And when that happens – well, ladies and gentlemen, you do not need me to tell you that we cannot afford even a single such time. People are sometimes terrible, it is true, but there exists no mechanism to ensure their behaviour that does not ultimately rely upon them. So we have no choice but to try and make them better. And that is why I say again that the laws must be empowered rather than enforced.

"Such laws are *honourable* laws. For it is nothing but honour expressed by the laws of the community that can keep the Good in citizens' hearts. You see, honourable laws are those that we follow even if they are no longer on the books, in fact even if there no longer are any books, since it is their spirit and not their letter that motivates us to uphold them. So no, in asking you to find me innocent even though I admit to having done the deeds I am accused of I am not making some absurd call for the legalization of crime, only for fidelity to the law's spirit. You see, where the Crown speaks of the importance of *respect* for authority and the rule of law, I favour *honouring* these things instead. By doing so we actually do more for their respect than if we followed the Crown and upheld the law's letter alone.

"Ladies and gentlemen of the jury, if there is one thing I hope you will come to see as this trial progresses, it is that the Crown is right: this case is indeed about much more than a mere college prank. The Crown nevertheless fails to appreciate the most important thing, which is that Mr. Landsberg and I did what we did in order to uphold a vital university tradition, one which stands for nothing other than honour and justice."

Thus did Theo Hoshen bring to an end the first of his exhortations to the court. As he surveyed the courtroom, however, he could not help but notice that his speech was met with a most uncomfortable silence, one that seemed to last a century.

Even Simon, Carl and Avigail could do no more than sit and contribute to the quiet, although the former, to his credit, did manage a loud clearing of his throat. At once, Theo Hoshen realized which part of Aristotle's *Rhetoric* he had failed to implement properly: he had argued too much and this had interfered with establishing his character as trustworthy. In this way, he convinced himself that his next address was sure to meet with greater success; in fact, he was looking forward to it with relish.

CHAPTER XXVII

In which the witnesses are examined

"Alright then," said Justice Thomas, having just managed to keep a straight face, "examinations. Mr. Kay?"

"Yes, your Honour," said the attorney as he stood up. "The Crown has just two witnesses. I would first like to call Mr. Peter Certaine to the stand." Within moments, the president of the Engineering Society was seated on the witness stand and sworn in. "Please identify yourself for us, sir."

"I'm the president of Skule, the U of T's Engineering Students' Society."

"Your association is called School?"

"Yes, but it's spelled S-k-u-l-e. It's a tradition."

"I see. And would you say, Mr. Certaine, that tradition is important to you?"

"Oh yes. To all engineers."

"And which would be the most important engineering tradition?"

"Our school spirit, I guess, which is symbolized by our Cannon."

"Describe this Cannon to us please."

"It's about so big, it's made of brass, and it's got wheels on the bottom. It really works and we fire it off at our most important ceremonies. We've been doing this for a long time – the first Cannon was built back in 1929."

"You say the 'first' Cannon – there have been others?"

"Yeah. After a few years they can get real worn and so we replace them and give the older one to an important faculty member, you know, as a retirement gift."

"I see. Has Skule ever lost one of these Cannons?"

"Well, a long time ago they used to get stolen by other students. That's why we established the Cannon Guard, which is basically a bunch of guys who protect it. But they're just ceremonial now, since the Cannon hasn't been stolen for a long time."

"How long?"

"I'd say over twenty years, at least."

"I see. So would you say that stealing the Cannon is no longer a university tradition?"

"That's right," replied Certaine. "Like everyone else, we've had to modernize. That's why we've done our bit to get racism, sexism, and homophobia out of engineering, for example."

"Of course. So tell me, Mr. Certaine, how then did Skule recently come to lose its Cannon?"

"It was stolen by those two guys over there." He pointed at Carl and Theo Hoshen.

"Let the record show that the witness indicated the defendant, Mr. Hoshen, as well as Mr. Carl Landsberg. Now how is it, Mr. Certaine, that you are so sure these two are responsible?"

"Well, first they broke into our offices one night, wrecked a door, but they got nothing. Then they came back and, after spying on the Cannon Guard, broke into the Chief's car and took the Cannon and some other stuff from his trunk. I know it was them because they sent ransom notes afterwards and, when we arranged to meet, they showed up and admitted to doing the deed. So I called the police."

"The officers, Constables Martin and Smith of 52 Division, who then arrested the two defendants as they were attempting to extort you?"

"Objection!" exclaimed Theo Hoshen as he shot up from his seat.

"Yes?" inquired Justice Thomas.

"Yes what?" replied Theo Hoshen.

"Well, what are the grounds of your objection?"

"But surely they are obvious."

"Maybe to you, Mr. Hoshen."

"I see. The grounds," Theo Hoshen muttered to himself as he began rifling through the papers on the table in front of him. "Ah, here it is: 'argumentative'. The Crown's question contains an unsubstantiated implication."

"And what might that be?" inquired the judge.

"That we were arrested while attempting to extort Mr. Certaine. Now that is simply not true. We never had time to issue our demands – the police showed up beforehand."

"I see. Mr. Hoshen, while your objection is technically correct, and so hereby sustained, I hope you realize that the way you've advanced it – suggesting that you would have indeed issued extortionate demands if you could – well, it is rather counter-productive to your case."

"You make an excellent point, your Honour."

"Glad to hear it. Alright then, Mr. Kay, please continue."

"Thank you, your Honour," said the Crown with a smirk. "I would now like to enter the following items into evidence. First, photos of the damage committed to the Engineering Society's offices and to the car in question, along with the corresponding police reports. Total estimated damages: one thousand five hundred dollars. Then, the ransom notes received by Mr. Certaine." All these the Crown handed to the judge, who passed them on to the clerk. "Now then, Mr. Certaine," continued the Crown, "regarding the arrest –"

"If I can just say," interrupted the Engineering Society president, "I never called the Toronto cops, only the campus police. *They* called in Metro, I guess because of the way Carl and Theo were acting."

"Objection!" declared Theo Hoshen again, rising. "That is speculation. The witness cannot assume he knows the reason the campus police called the Toronto police."

"That's right, Mr. Hoshen. Objection sustained. Mr. Certaine, please refrain from such speculations."

"Yes, your Honour."

Theo Hoshen sat down with a look of satisfaction on his face.

"Okay then," continued the Crown. "Now can you tell me: how did you come to meet with Misters Hoshen and Landsberg?"

"They called us and asked to get together. So I agreed. I figured we had no choice."

"And why's that?"

"Because of all that had happened. And because, on top of everything, they'd started vandalizing stuff all over the campus."

"Objection!" shot up Theo Hoshen yet again. "He has no proof that we did any such thing – and I can assure the court that we most certainly did not!"

"Alright Mr. Hoshen, take it easy," said Justice Thomas. "Mr. Certaine, what exactly is the vandalism that you're referring to, and why do you think Misters Hoshen and Landsberg are responsible?"

"It's true that I've no proof, your Honour. But someone was spray-painting 'Fahrenheit 1710' all over campus and that's exactly what they called themselves in their ransom notes. They put it on the walls of a washroom (which was also to-talled, by the way) in the Sir Sandford Fleming building, on the outside of buildings around campus, on sidewalks, and even in a classroom. The campus police told me."

"Your Honour," announced the Crown as he handed over some papers, "here are the relevant police reports on the vandalism incidents, of which total damages come out to just over four thousand dollars. A great deal of money. Can you tell us, Mr. Certaine, were any other damages suffered by you or your school during this whole affair?"

"For sure. I know it's not the kind of thing you can put a dollar sign on but, you see, what those guys did, well, they really hurt our reputations. Especially the Cannon Guard and myself. I didn't mention it before but they'd sent this singing telegram to our CannonBall, which is attended by alumni who come from all over the country. I'm sure they thought it was funny but I can tell you that it wasn't. We're all hoping to get jobs when we graduate, right – that's why we're studying so hard – but by making fun of us in front of the alumni, going on and on about how we lost the Cannon and everything, well it really hurts our future careers. I know it might sound silly but it's true, believe me."

"It doesn't sound silly at all, Mr. Certaine. Anything else?"

"Yeah. What they did, along with all the threats with the ransom notes and stuff – it was really, really upsetting. I bombed an exam because of it and I know that the guys on the Cannon Guard also had problems. We came to the U of T to work hard so we could get good jobs, but now all that's in danger of getting lost."

"I see," said the Crown. "So I take it, given all of these damages, that you would say that what happened was certainly no harmless prank."

"That's for sure," confirmed Certaine.

"I've no further questions for this witness, your Honour."

"Thank you, Mr. Kay," said the judge. "Mr. Hoshen?"

"Here I am, your Honour," said Theo Hoshen as he rose and approached the witness box. "First, let us dispense with the monetary damages."

"What?" said Certaine.

"My first question, Mr. Certaine: did you receive the money order for two hundred and fifty dollars that we sent you to cover the damages to the car?"

"Yeah."

"And did you cash it?"

"Yeah, we gave it to the Chief – it was his car."

"Excellent. So tell me, does it make sense to you that we would send money to cover such damages and yet be so reckless as to vandalise campus property?"

"But you didn't send any money for what you did to our offices, did you?"

"Alas, Mr. Certaine, apparently only I am allowed to pose the questions here. But since you ask, it is only right that Skule should pay for those damages. After all, it is SAC, the undergraduate student union, and not Skule that covers whatever repairs are necessary after a BFC strike. We sent money for the car only because we feared that anger directed at your Cannon Guard due to its incompetence might result in the car's owner, who we assumed was the Chief Attiliator, not receiving financial compensation from Skule.

"BFC?"

"Do not pretend you are unaware of the Engineering Society's Brute Force Committee. May I remind you, sir, that you are under oath."

"But they don't exist; I mean, they're not an official organization."

"And that makes all of the difference, does it?"

"Yeah. We at Skule aren't responsible for them."

"I see. Once something has the status of fiction, then there is no place for ascribing responsibility. Anything goes, is that it Mr. Certaine?"

"I don't get what you mean."

"My meaning is that, just like our synecdochic friend the Crown here, you suffer from a failure to connect letter and spirit. The BFC may be unofficial, but it is surely no less Skule's responsibility for that. You do not agree?"

"No."

"Am I to presume, then, that as a responsible university citizen you could be expected to inform on the BFC to the authorities if you came across them performing a damaging prank such as vandalising the SAC dome with paint?"

"I had nothing to do with that."

"That was not my question, Mr. Certaine. It seems evasiveness is a symptom of the condition of hypocrisy." Regarding this proposition the Engineering Society president appeared to have nothing to say. "Perhaps," continued Theo Hoshen, "it would be best if we left the matter for the jury to contemplate, for I would now like to change the subject, if only slightly. Tell me, President Certaine, you claimed that the tradition of stealing the Cannon is no longer with us. How do you know that?"

"Like I said, it's been over twenty years since it was last taken."

"I see. So we are to understand that there is a statute of limitations of sorts on Skule traditions?"

"You could say that."

"And where is this statute recorded? Is it an official policy of Skule?"

"No, 'course not. You don't pass policies like that. It's just something that no one does anymore."

"So it is the *spirit* that has changed, not the letter of any explicit rule."

"Okay."

"And we can tell this because of a change in behaviour, in practices, correct?"

"Okay."

"But then tell me, Mr. Certaine, twenty years ago may have been the last time the Cannon was *successfully* stolen, but it was not the last time that an attempt was made to steal it, am I right?"

"Guess so."

"And when was that last time?"

"I dunno."

"I accept that you do not. Let me assure you that it was more recent than you think. Which is why you must agree that the tradition of stealing, or at least of attempting to steal, the Cannon has not expired after all. Correct?"

"Guess so."

"The frequency of attempts may have declined – a worrying development, I might add – but the tradition is still alive."

"I said okay."

"And this still living tradition is still living precisely because the Cannon is so important. You would agree with my statement that the Cannon is important, would you not?"

"Yeah, obviously."

"More important than, say, the damage that could be done to the future careers of the students responsible for guarding it? I am tempted to point out that one should attend university to study, not to train for a career, but this would mean entertaining the prospect of removing the professional faculties, an intriguing notion that would, alas, take us too far afield from our purposes today. So let me ask you this: do you believe that the members of the Cannon Guard should favour their careers over Skule?"

"Not if you put it like that. But that's not how I would put it."

"And how would you put it?"

"All I'd say is that if an engineer's paid his tuition, followed the rules, studied hard, *and* given some of his time to extracurricular activities, well then I don't see why his career should suffer because of it."

"It sounds to me, Mr. Certaine, that your own contributions as Skule president were done purely in the service of your CV, am I right?"

"No. Well, yeah, but I care about my CV *and* Skule spirit. I care about both."

"I'm sure you do," concurred Theo Hoshen. "I am also sure which takes priority when the two conflict. And speaking of dualities, I wonder: how would you define the verb 'to double-cross'?"

"What?"

"Objection!" exclaimed the Crown. "The defence is attempting to lead the witness somewhere he doesn't have to be."

"Sustained," said Justice Thomas. "Mr. Hoshen?"

"I am sorry, your Honour. I shall rephrase the question. But first, may I ask you one?"

"You may," replied the judge.

"When you say 'sustained' – how does that work, exactly?"

"How does what work?"

"Well, with all due respect, I am wondering what it means. Are the members of the jury supposed to think 'Ah, the wise blackcoated woman over there has just declared that one of the lawyer's objections is correct'? For in what sense correct? It cannot be true simply because you say so, as that would be a case of *argumentum ad verecundiam*, the logical fallacy of appeal to authority."

"Mr. Hoshen?"

"Yes, your Honour?"

"Do you have any more questions for this witness?"

"Yes I do."

"Then pose them."

"Yes, your Honour." And so Theo Hoshen continued: "Now then, Mr. Certaine, correct me if I am wrong but you have expressed a concern that these events have done damage to your and your associates' reputations, right?"

"Right."

"Well let us see now. The Cannon Guard are charged with protecting the Cannon, and yet they lost it."

"So?"

"So it is only right that their reputations suffer accordingly, no?"

"No."

"And as for yourself, have you ever heard of a Skule president calling the campus police – those whom you, in keeping with tradition, disdainfully refer to as 'the mice' – on someone before?"

"But this was serious."

"Indeed it was, Mr. Certaine. And when things get serious, it seems, it is acceptable to violate Skule traditions – even though, as you just told the Crown, tradition is important to you, indeed to all engineers."

"Objection!" announced the Crown again. "The defence is actually accusing the witness of calling the authorities. Incredible!"

"It may be incredible, Mr. Kay," replied the judge "but it's not an objection. Please continue, Mr. Hoshen, though I must say that I'm beginning to wonder where you're going with all this. You are going somewhere, right?"

"Ineluctably, your Honour."

"You may continue then."

"Thank you," said Theo Hoshen with a self-satisfied glance in the direction of the Crown. Turning back to his witness, he was about to ask him another question when he suddenly stopped and said "Yes ma'am?" instead. No one knew to whom, exactly, this was directed, since he appeared to be looking towards the jury rather than the judge.

"Mr. Hoshen," said Justice Thomas, "who are you talking to?"

"Why, to that lady over there," he replied, gesturing to a woman sitting in the front row of the jury.

"And *why* are you doing that?"

"Because as anyone can see from the look on her face, she has a question. I thought I might be of assistance."

"Of *assistance*?" echoed the judge.

"Of course," replied Theo Hoshen. "Perhaps, madam," he said addressing the juror, "you would like to ask the witness something?"

"Mr. Hoshen! Jurors do not ask questions!"

"But surely they, of all people, should be encouraged to do so."

"No they should not!" insisted the judge. "I've had about enough nonsense from you, Mr. Hoshen. Either ask your witness your question or sit down and be quiet!"

"Very well. Alright then, Mr. Certaine, my question for you is the following: we have learned that, when things get serious, you are willing to abandon tradition. What about honouring your word? Do you abandon that too?"

"No. But," he added defensively, "I never said anything about not calling anyone when we set up our meeting."

"Of course, Mr. Certaine, you said nothing. But I fear that, like the Crown, you have chosen to hide from the spirit of the Good by standing in the shadow of its letter. Do you expect this court to believe that it was not part of the spirit of our meeting, not to mention in keeping with venerable tradition, that the authorities were not to be contacted?"

"Objection!" announced the Crown again. "Lying's no crime – not that I'm saying Mr. Certaine lied – especially when it's done under duress. And I remind the court that Mr. Certaine was being threatened with extortion."

"Extortion?" said Theo Hoshen, "Your Honour, if we are accused of committing extortion, why were we not charged with it?"

"Good question," said the judge. "Mr. Kay?"

"We felt the filed charges were sufficient."

"I'm sure you did, Mr. Kay," said the judge with a sceptical tone.

"But your Honour," objected the Crown, "the fact is that Mr. Certaine had something stolen from him and he called the police. It's as simple as that."

"Only," countered Theo Hoshen, "if you separate the legal from the wider issue."

"Well I'm sorry, Mr. Hoshen," said the judge, "but that's precisely what we're here to do. So, do you have any questions for the witness that relate to the *legal* matter at hand?"

"I would have, your Honour. But after the witness's last answer, in which he basically admitted to being true to the letter but not the spirit of his word, I fear – and I suspect the members of the jury agree with me – that there is no point in asking him any more questions. Which is too bad, as I would have liked to hear whether he feels any shame for what he has done."

"I take it, then, that you have no more questions," said the judge. She turned to the witness. "Thank you, Mr. Certaine. You may go now. Mr. Kay?"

The Crown then called his next witness, who was none other than Carl Landsberg.

It was a clearly nervous Carl who found his way into the witness box, whereupon he was sworn in with one hand on a Hebrew Bible.

"Now, Mr. Landsberg, I'd like to begin with a simple question: Did you do it? Did you take the Cannon?"

"Yes sir."

"You and Mr. Hoshen?"

"Yes."

"The both of you calling yourselves Fahrenheit 1710?"

"Yes."

"And why, may I ask, did you call yourselves by that name?"

"It's the melting point of brass. It was a joke."

"The humour deriving from the fact that the Cannon is made of brass, is that it?"

"Yes sir."

"Well I can certainly see how you might find that funny. But I wonder about the members of Skule. I mean, imagine receiving a series of ransom notes signed with that name. They would appear rather threatening, no?"

"Well no, not really. As I said, it was just for fun."

"Just for fun," repeated the Crown. "You send these ransom notes with demands that, you say, will get them their Cannon back if they're fulfilled. But the notes are signed in a way which suggests that the whole point of your group – its very raison d'être, Mr. Landsberg – is the Cannon's destruction. Can you not see how that might put your good faith in question?"

"I –"

"And this makes it rather hypocritical for someone such as Mr. Hoshen here to become all self-righteous and refuse to cooperate when the engineers, in desperation, report the theft to the authorities. Wouldn't you agree?"

"No. We were there in good-faith; there was no need to call the cops."

"Of course *you* felt there was no need, but then you weren't negotiating with a group calling itself 'Death to Carl and Theo', were you?"

"Objection!" announced Theo Hoshen. "The Crown is reading far too much into what is but a humorous moniker."

"Ah," objected the Crown, "you mean I'm putting too much store in its spirit over its letter?"

"Alright, enough," interrupted Justice Thomas. "Mr. Kay, your question about Mr. Hoshen's alleged hypocrisy does indeed constitute a leading and inappropriate exaggeration. The jurors will disregard it," she said matter-of-factly. And then, turning to the clerk, she declared: "I order it struck from the record."

"Your Honour?" said Theo Hoshen.

"Yes?" came the judge's irritated reply.

"If I may, I am wondering how that works, exactly. I mean, you do not really believe that, by ordering the comment struck from the record, it will be erased from the jurors' minds? After all, that is not how meaning works; one cannot just chop it up and throw a bit away."

"Next question, Mr. Kay," said the judge.

"Certainly, your Honour," said the Crown. "Now then, Mr. Landsberg, I would like you to tell us again how many members you said were in your group – what is it called again?"

"Fahrenheit 1710."

"Right," confirmed the Crown. "And how many?"

"Just Theo and I," replied Carl who, from the corner of his eye, could see Theo Hoshen staring directly at him.

"So that makes two, correct?"

"Yes," replied Carl. And after the most miniscule of pauses, he added: "Two."

"Then let me ask you this, Mr. Landsberg: when you hear the word 'group', how many people normally come to mind?"

"That depends."

"I'm sure it does, Mr. Landsberg. And may I remind you that a lot depends on your answer, for you are under oath."

"Objection!" shouted Theo Hoshen. "The Crown is obviously threatening the witness."

"That is not a valid objection, Mr. Hoshen," said the judge. "Please sit down. Continue, Mr. Kay."

"The word 'group', Mr. Landsberg."

"We were a group of two," said Carl.

"So we are to take it that you did not involve anyone else in your plans in any way?"

"Other than the woman who delivered the singing telegram for us? Because she had no idea."

"Other than the woman," confirmed the Crown.

"No."

"No one else?"

Carl stared straight ahead. "No one else."

"Thank you, Mr. Landsberg. Your Honour, I notice from the witness list that the defence intends to put himself on the stand. May I ask if he is still planning to do so?"

"Mr. Hoshen?" said the judge.

"Yes I am, your Honour."

"In that case," said the Crown, "I have no further questions for this witness."

"Really?" said the judge, somewhat astonished. "That's it?"

"Yes, ma'am. All my arrows have been fired."

"Okay then," she said. "Mr. Hoshen?"

"I have no questions for this witness," came his reply.

"Well then," said the judge, quite pleased. "That went quicker than I thought. Time for the witnesses for the defence. Mr. Hoshen."

"As stated, your Honour, I have just the one. The defence would like to call Mr. Theodore Hoshen to the stand."

"Very funny, Mr. Hoshen. Alright then, come on up here and let's see what you have to say." So Theo Hoshen entered the witness stand. And after being sworn in, this is what he said:

"Now then —"

"That won't be necessary," interrupted the judge.

"But I must be directly examined, no?" protested Theo Hoshen.

"Yes, but how about if you just let me ask the questions?"

"But I have only one – okay two – queries that I wish to raise at this time."

"Oh alright. What are they?"

"The first is this: I would like to ask myself if I believe I was right to take the Cannon."

"And?" said the judge.

"And," replied Theo Hoshen, "my answer is that I do more than believe it, I am certain of it. I add this because, as the saying goes, faith without doubt is dead faith."

"Whatever, Mr. Hoshen," said the judge. "And your second question?"

"Is it not true that I really called myself up as a witness only so that I could go head to head with the Crown?"

"Very funny, Mr. Hoshen," said the judge. "Fine. You shall have your wish. Your witness, Mr. Kay."

The Crown had been leaning back in his chair and tapping his pen on the side of his hand. Now he smiled and said:

"You think you're pretty smart, eh Mr. Hoshen?"

"Yes," came the reply. "Apologies for the lack of modesty, but I am under oath."

"You are indeed, Mr. Hoshen. You're a philosophy student, right?"

"Yes."

"And philosophy is?"

"The love of wisdom, of course."

"Of course. And would you say, Mr. Hoshen, that taking the Cannon was wise?"

"Yes I would."

"As well as, how would you put it, honourable?"

"Certainly."

"You say that as if the two always go together."

"What do you mean?"

"Well how come we don't see other philosophy students going around stealing cannons?"

"An excellent question."

"And if I suggested that you were just an overenthusiastic undergraduate who's gotten himself in way over his head? Would you consider that an excellent question too?"

"You mean," replied Theo Hoshen, "better than one about whether you are just a cog in a system that has gone way too far?"

"That's enough, gentlemen," declared the judge. "No more games and ad hominem. I mean it. I want straight questions and answers and nothing else. Is that understood?"

"Of course, your Honour," said the Crown. "So here's a straight question: Fahrenheit 1710, this *group* – you and Mr. Landsberg are the only members, right?"

"Correct."

"Then I'd like you to do something for me."

"Which is?"

"May I have one of the ransom notes, please?" requested the Crown. Then, once he had one in his hands, he said: "I must say, this is quite a beautiful note – I mean the way it's written. I take it that you appreciate calligraphy as well, Mr. Hoshen?"

"Yes I do."

"I wonder. And Mr. Landsberg here, does he also do so? Because I must admit, neither of you strike me as the calligraphy type."

"And I must admit," said Theo Hoshen, "that you *do* strike me as the lawyer type."

"What did I just say?" exclaimed Justice Thomas. "One more such comment, Mr. Hoshen, and I'll find you in contempt."

"I am sorry, your Honour."

"Continue Mr. Kay," said the judge.

"Well, I was wondering what Mr. Landsberg would say if I asked him to come back up here and write us a little something with *this*." And with a flourish he reached into his pocket and pulled out a calligraphy pen. Beside her in the audience, Avigail could just hear Simon mutter a "shite" under his breath.

"I think he would tell you that he did not know how to use that pen," said Theo Hoshen.

"Oh he would, would he? So I guess that means it was *you* who wrote out the ransom notes, correct?"

"Correct." This took the Crown somewhat by surprise. He remained undeterred, however, and said:

"Well then, Mr. Hoshen, here's the pen – and here," he reached into his pocket, "is some ink."

"Paper?" said Theo Hoshen. The clerk passed him a sheet. "Shall I write anything in particular?"

"Whatever you wish," replied the Crown testily.

"Hmmm. Well let me see." Theo Hoshen paused. Then he paused again.

"Mr. Hoshen, please," begged Justice Thomas, "let's get on with it." And so Theo Hoshen, as he tended to do whenever he put great effort into something he was writing, bit down lightly on his tongue and stuck a part of it out through the left corner of his mouth. Then, when he had completed his task, he handed the sheet over to the judge. And here, in an impressively fine hand, is what she saw:

The Crown is dead. Long live the citizenry.

We are hot, you are not,

Fahrenheit 1710

"May I see one of the ransom notes?" requested the judge. Then, after comparing the two documents, she said: "Looks the same to me. Any more stunts, Mr. Kay?"

"Uh, no your Honour."

"Well then, have you any more questions for this witness?"

"No ma'am."

"Alright then, Mr. Hoshen, you may return to your seat. I suggest that we all take a ten minute break before we hear the closing arguments. Is that okay with the Crown and the defence?" There being no objections, Justice Thomas banged her gavel to announce the recess and, in this way, provided everyone with a few moments to prepare themselves for the upcoming finale.

CHAPTER XXVIII

Wherein the trial of Theo Hoshen is brought to a close

Carl and Simon followed Theo Hoshen outside, all of them making their way to the men's washroom. Legal battles and other such intellectual struggles are one thing; nature's call is, many believe, something else altogether. Once there, the three stood side by side in front of the urinals and, as they did their business, they exchanged the following words:

"I would say that it is going quite well," opined Theo Hoshen.

"I don't know," said a somewhat dejected Carl. "Simon?"

"Don't ask me." And then, after a pause, he added: "Mates, I know we're in the middle of a slash and all, but I wanted to say thanks."

"No need," said Theo Hoshen. "We gave you our word."

"Yeah, but still," insisted Simon. This was followed by some more silence as the three washed their hands. And then, Carl having left, Simon turned to Theo Hoshen and asked: "You learned calligraphy just for this?"

"Well, I suspected the matter might come up. Of course Avigail and I had only so much time; I cannot write much more than those words there."

"But what if he'd asked for something else?"

"I would have belittled his choice and written what I wished instead."

"Good plan," said Simon sarcastically. "Still, Hoshen-boy, I've got to say: I'm impressed. I used to think you were just a silly tosser off of his box. But I was wrong; you're not silly after all."

"Thank you," said Theo Hoshen.

"So go back in there and kick 'em in the bollocks," encouraged Simon.

A short while later and everyone had retrieved their places in the courtroom. The time had come for Theo Hoshen to make his closing argument. This is what he said:

"Ladies and gentlemen of the jury, Mr. Kay of the Crown, honoured guests of the court, Justice Thomas. Could it be that that which is among the things most important to you is nevertheless hidden from you? Ask yourself: when are you angriest? When can you just not get something out of your head? I suggest that, more often than not, it is when you have felt slighted by someone, treated with contempt or even just discourtesy. And you feel this way, I want to inform you, because it is none other than your honour that is at stake. Oh I know that this sounds old fashioned, but there is a reason the offended person's memory is stronger even than the lender's. Because honour is in fact *more* important today than ever before. In the pre-modern world it was, of course, largely a matter of keeping everyone in their place, which is precisely why most people did not concern themselves with it very much. They lived their lives within a fixed hierarchy, you see, whereas today everyone finds himself constantly competing with everyone else for status or recognition, which are but forms, albeit often degraded, of honour. And so nowadays we worry about it almost all of the time.

"I shall be making only two points in my defence today, both of which concern honour. The first is relatively simple and I hope that it shall be enough to win my case, even though it is ultimately only part of the truth. The second is more challenging and may very well not help my case, even though it is closer to the truth as a whole. But then I trust the members of the jury to meet their charge, to face all of the reality that is set before them.

"To begin, then, let me say that it is beyond the deepest in-sincerity for the engineers to have arranged for Carl and I to be charged with the crime of stealing their Cannon. Because this is precisely the kind of thing they do to others all the time. In turning to the authorities to protect them – what is that if not the deepest hypocrisy? Let me remind you of some examples of their handiwork, acts which they do not hide but publicize as triumphs. My first encounter with them was as a student in a psychology class that they had repeatedly pranked, indeed so often that the professor was driven into retirement. Then there are their many thefts, whether of the engineers' grease pole at Queen's University or of one of our own university administrator's cars, which they promptly disassembled and reassembled on the roof of a campus building. I could go on.

"But what do the engineers do when a comparable trick, the theft of their Cannon, is played upon them? Do they seek to recover their mascot by honourable means, say by negotiating its release in good faith? No, they call upon the authorities, the very same who have overlooked their hijinks a hundred times over. And the authorities have done so, ladies and gentlemen, for the good reason that those acts were not at all criminal. It is for the same reason that you should dismiss the charges against me with the contempt they so rightly deserve.

"I suppose this is where I should stop; unfortunately, I cannot. For there is a part of me – yes, the philosophy student part – that cannot avoid posing challenging questions. They lead me to try and advance a second point, one that, I fear, will serve only to complicate the first.

"For is there not a deeper truth here? Would it not be wrong to claim that the engineers are mere hypocrites? You see, I have no wish to win this case on the grounds that, while my side may be bad, theirs is worse and so they deserved what they got. Because the engineers have been dishonourable in a way that goes far beyond the application of a double standard: they have forsaken the very idea of honour. Worse, it seems that they are not alone in having done so.

"What I mean is the following. The difference between humans and animals is that we have a moral capacity, the ability to uphold honour and the common good, and they do not.

And it is most suitable that we sometimes choose objects to symbolize these things, to remind ourselves of what one might call simply 'the Good'. These symbols express the best in us, what is most precious. So to occasionally kidnap them, and to challenge others to recover them, well what is that if not a way of reminding everyone of their value, of what makes us human? This, I suggest, is what the Brute Force Committee at its best is doing with its so-called pranks. And it is what Mr. Landsberg and I did.

"The tragic irony, however, is that the engineers no longer see it. They have indeed become witless college pranksters, adolescents amusing themselves to death with empty theatrical performances. Which is why, when we offered them the gift of a challenge to their honour, a chance to ennoble themselves by rising to it, they declined and, worse, betrayed us.

"Truly, this is everyone's tragedy. For it means that one of the last vestiges of genuine honour in this world is but a sham. You, however, can partly right the wrong that has been committed. No, not by acquitting me because my little college prank pales beside my accusers' hypocrisy; rather, you must find me innocent for what is the only right reason: because what I and Mr. Landsberg did was not criminal at all, but honourable.

"To fail to see this is, ultimately, to assume that only things such as money or power drive humans at our best. Yet that is the easy lie, a great perversion of the truth. Mr. Landsberg and I did our duty as arts students of the University of Toronto, nothing more, whereas the engineers failed to do theirs. We did not steal something, take it unlawfully. To believe that is to remain beholden, as the Crown obviously is, to the letter of the law; it is to assume that the only way we could be found innocent is through what legal technicians call 'jury nullification', wherein a law is invalidated because, though the accused is indeed guilty, he is somehow still worthy of acquittal. Instead of this, you should find me innocent because of the spirit of the law, which says what everyone with common sense knows: that Carl and I did nothing wrong. And so, ladies and gentlemen of the jury, as you deliberate over whether I deserve the noose or the light, please know that everything I have said today is true. And find me not guilty of the crime for which I have been accused."

Thus did Theo Hoshen conclude his speech. There followed a moment of silence, whereupon Justice Thomas spoke:

"Yes, well, thank you Mr. Hoshen." Then she invited the Crown to begin his own summation: "Mr. Kay."

The Crown stood up and this is what he said:

"The defendant says that what he did was honourable, and that we have lost touch with the meaning of the word. Well, I say that we know very well what it means and that what he did was not at all honourable. Who does this patronizing philosophy undergraduate think he is? He talks about honour but does he respect the rights of the engineers to their property? Does he respect the police and indeed the whole justice system when he refuses to return what he has stolen? And does he respect you, the members of this jury, when he goes on and on and on lecturing us about honour and the nature of the law? Of course not. Ladies and gentlemen, what we have here is not a responsible member of his university community, but a misguided undergrad who has gotten carried away with something he picked up from some old philosophy textbook. He says it's all about honour, but I say that it's just a fancy way for him to get attention for himself. That's why he made us go through this trial instead of simply returning the item that he and his partner unlawfully took. That's why he presents us with nothing but grandstanding and bombastic speeches. And that's why he fails to take us, not to mention the justice system, seriously.

"The defendant is right about one thing, though. He's right that I'm not calling on you to punish him for what was ultimately just a college prank gone bad. That *would* be dishonourable. Think about what he did. He got it into his head that he wanted something that wasn't his and so he went about taking it – with no regard for the many laws he would have to break or for the damage he would cause, both to property and to the reputations of some promising young students. To allow him to get away with this, particularly given that he has refused to return what he has taken, well that would send a terrible message. It would say that it is enough to invoke philosophical abstractions such as tradition, the common good, and honour to excuse oneself from having to follow the laws of this country, laws that the rest of us ordinary citizens must nevertheless respect. And we do so, by the way, in the knowledge that, whereas the law sometimes needs to be feared, it should never be mocked. The defendant, however, is mocking the law. In so doing, ladies and gentlemen, he is mocking all of us. Don't stand for it. Do the honourable thing and find him guilty of his crimes."

"Thank you, Mr. Kay," said the judge. And with that she brought the session to a close, although not before informing everyone that she wished to reconvene first thing next morning. That is when she would issue her instructions to the jury, following which they would be released to begin their deliberations.

And this is precisely what happened. When morning came, the jury was given a lecture about certain fine points of law as they related to this case and then its members were sent off to sequester themselves and begin work. That was right before lunchtime, and it was just after four o'clock of the same day that word went out that they had completed their task. They were ready to deliver their verdict. And so, once everyone had found their seats, Justice Thomas said the following:

"Members of the jury, may we have your verdict?"

Up stood the foreman, a bespectacled young man with cropped hair. "Yes, your Honour. In the case of Hoshen v. the Province of Ontario, we find the defendant, Theodore Hoshen, guilty on all charges."

"Thank you," said the judge. "Mr. Hoshen," she said, inviting him to rise. A bewildered Theo Hoshen did so and, though he held his head high, inside he was feeling the agony of humiliation. "This court has found you guilty of the crimes of theft and burglary. A sentencing hearing for both you and Mr. Landsberg will take place one week from today at nine o'clock in the morning in this courtroom. I expect the both of you to be here. Is that understood?"

"Yes," said the two in unison. "At that time," Justice Thomas continued, "you will have an opportunity to make final statements before sentencing. Oh and Mr. Hoshen, I would be remiss in not, once again, strongly suggesting that you bring a lawyer."

"No thank you, your Honour," came the young philosopher's weak but not unexpected reply.

"As you wish. This court is no longer in session." And with that, everyone was dismissed.

CHAPTER XXIX

Concerning the aftermath of Theo Hoshen's
conviction, as well as the extraordinary new
adventure undertaken by him and Carl Landsberg
at Reznikoff's Pub

A few days later and we find our two soon-to-be-sentenced convicts sitting silently together in Room 338 and about to begin work on two Landsburgers.

"You're not going to eat it like that are you?" demanded Carl.

"Like what?" said Theo Hoshen with a sigh.

"Here." Carl reached across the table. "Mustard."

"Fine," said Theo Hoshen, who promptly squeezed some onto his burger. Then the silence resumed between them. Finally, Carl spoke up again:

"Theo, you seem, I dunno, distant. You're feeling weird about being back here in the diner?"

"No, of course not."

"So what, then? You're worried about the sentencing?"

"Carl, I have already suffered the worst possible punishment that my peers could mete out."

"I understand," said Carl with a hint of scepticism.

"The worst," repeated Theo Hoshen. And the two fell silent once again.

"Theo," Carl piped up, "there's something I don't get. Remember when I told you about my run-in with ACSA?"

"Of course."

"And remember how you criticized me for not using rhetoric? You know, when during ACSA's final appeal I didn't make things easier on myself by letting everyone know I was behind the anti-apartheid motion?"

"Yes, I remember."

"Well you did the same thing. I mean, you boned-up on Aristotle's *Rhetoric* but – unless the book's really stupid, and I kinda doubt that – I can't imagine you followed it."

"Why do you say that?"

"'Cause it's almost as if you didn't *want* the jury to agree with you. Everything you said seemed designed to get at them. Maybe not at first, but as things went on that's sure how it sounded. And you know, Theo, it's not the first time I've noticed this about you. It's like, whenever you start to convince somebody of one of your ideas you get all anxious or something and start pushing all the wrong buttons on purpose. You make the idea sound even more radical, or you connect it to something you know they're just not ready for.

"I'm not saying the ideas are wrong," continued Carl. "It's just your rhetoric. It's like you've always got to make sure that, at the end of the day, whoever you're with still disagrees. I wonder if it's because that way you get to remain the contrarian ahead of his time. Anyhow, you shouldn't be surprised you lost the case – even if you were right. It's like you want to convince people, but you want to defeat them even more."

"Now that is just silly," retorted Theo Hoshen.

Silence once again.

"Theo," said Carl finally, "I'm not sure I'm up for Rezzie's tonight."

"As you wish."

"But Avigail and Simon are expecting us, eh?"

"They are indeed. And it is already quite late." In fact, it was approaching one in the morning.

"Okay," said Carl, "we should go. But I'm leaving early."

"Fine," said Theo Hoshen. The two then said not another word to each other, directing their attentions to finishing their burgers instead.

And so it was that, not long after one in the morning, they arrived at Reznikoff's Pub. As ever, the place was dark and full of drinkers and dancers. Carl and Theo Hoshen could just spy Avigail dancing unenthusiastically; Simon, it seems, had yet to arrive. So they made their way inside, ordered their beers, and sat themselves down at a table. There was nothing to do but watch the dancers on the floor.

Soon, Avigail came to them. She invited Theo Hoshen to join her on the dance floor but he refused her entreaties. So she turned to Carl, who agreed. It was not until some time later, with the pub already beginning to lose its patrons, that Simon finally arrived. Wearing a rather severe look upon his face, he took a seat beside Theo Hoshen, whereupon Carl and Avigail overheard the young philosopher ask him if he had brought "it." Simon nodded.

"Brought what?" wondered Avigail.

"Something from the lab," said Simon unhelpfully.

"Which is what?" chimed in Carl.

"Theo'll tell you," said Simon.

"So?" said both Avigail and Carl.

"A ring," replied Theo Hoshen. "A gold ring. Right, Simon?"

"Yeah," said Simon, "a ring."

"I don't get it," said Carl. "You made a ring in your lab?"

"Man," complained Simon, "do I have to explain every-thing?"

"I believe it would be wise," said Theo Hoshen.

"Yes, explain," urged Avigail. And so Simon did so. He be-gan with a brief account of the incident in the laboratory that he had related to Theo Hoshen, the one with the malfunctioning scanning electron microscope and the gold-plated insect. Then he described how, later, he went back to confirm, and confirm again, what can only be described as the strange and fantastic invisibility effect. Not that he had much understanding of its cause. Because all he knew was that, somehow, the microscope and boiling water had done something extraordinary to the gold. And even though he then put that gold through a series of tests both physical and chemical, it appeared normal in every respect – except for its temperature, that is, which always remained slightly higher than the room it was in.

"There'd been some kind of matter transmutation," Simon concluded. "Like with those cold fusion nutters back in March."

"Our modern-day alchemists," remarked Theo Hoshen disdainfully.

"Yeah, except my stuff's *already* gold," said Simon. "And the really weird thing is that, when I put some more gold in the mix, the new gold reaches the same temperature as the original. Probably some kind of electrolysis or sonic cavitation. But what's totally weird is how the original gold doesn't cool down at all. And the same thing happened to this cheap gold ring that I dropped in there."

"Like the flame of a candle," declared Theo Hoshen, "which loses nothing in lighting another."

"Wha'ever," said Simon. "So, Hoshen-boy, you want it?"

"What?" exclaimed Carl. "*That's* what you brought? The cheap gold ring?"

"That's right," said Simon. "It's in my anorak." Simon reached into the pocket of his nylon parka and removed a small, felt-lined box. Both Carl and Avigail drew back. "Don't go climbing the walls, mates," admonished Simon. "It's not radioactive or anything. I checked."

"Well why'd you bring it here?" wondered Carl.

"Ask this one," replied Simon pointing to Theo Hoshen.

"Well, to put it bluntly," Theo Hoshen explained, "I want to try it."

"Try it?" exclaimed Avigail. "What does that mean? What're you going to do?"

"Why put it on, of course," replied the young philosopher.

"That's nuts!" objected Carl.

"Sanity is in the eye of the beholder," said Theo Hoshen.

"*No*," said Avigail.

"Well, perhaps not," admitted Theo Hoshen. He nevertheless reached over and gingerly removed the little box from Simon's hand. "Still," he said, "it would be folly not to investigate the possibilities of this phenomenon."

"Here? *Now?*" demanded Avigail.

"Why not?" said Theo Hoshen. "When you're as infamous as I have become, there is little to lose. And as you can see, almost everyone has left." As indeed they had: other than the four of them, the disc jockey, a bartender, and perhaps a handful of students who were either dancing or seated at the bar, the pub was now empty. "The time has come for a new dance," declared Theo Hoshen. And with that he rose and, clasping the little box in his right hand, made his way to the dance floor. The next song, Scott Merritt's "Transistor," had just begun and, as its lilting guitar introduction increased in volume, Theo Hoshen started to dance.

"Great," was all that Carl could say.

"Simon!" exclaimed Avigail. "Are you really going to let him do this?"

"Hey, it was his idea. And anyway, I'm a scientist. I'm curious."

"This is crazy," announced Carl, who then rose and went over to Theo Hoshen. "Stop it, Theo," he shouted over the music. "It's not safe."

But it was too late. For unbeknown to Carl, Theo Hoshen had, with a good deal of grace, already removed the ring from the box and slipped it onto one of the fingers of his left hand. The deed done, he stepped forward and turned around, following which he simply stood there, motionless and with what seemed like an utterly blank look upon his face. And then, to Carl's dismay, he appeared to lose his balance and began to fall forward. In a flash, Carl reached over and grabbed his friend's bare arms, steadying him.

"You okay?" asked Carl. But as he spoke these words, he sensed that the young philosopher was not okay. In fact, neither was he. For although he felt

> fine
> the room
> was suddenly
> very strange
>
> the two sensed about
> with a new sense
> for meaning
> for music seen
> and sights heard
> for colours and shapes
> flowing vivid
> for everyone that flowed parts
> formed and connected

of a glowing stream
of living light
and liquefied walls
towards the One
as a many

like rivulets
like these words
running down the page
their meaning up

and then they sensed the speakers
the lavish colours gushing through
and the slits of   Nothing
in the liquid   melodies too
from   which would
shards   of light
burst   forth
would begin the new
flash
white flakes slicing into the water
infusing
and carrying along

and the one fluid dancer
a real improviser he
would breath in the bright bits
dissolve them in the violent run
and speed it
faster
higher
with swirls off

then
queasy
queasy
they sensed again

the walls now
the tables and the chairs
stood as flowing things
as veiled men in the twilight
promising

waiting
to yield themselves
to living meaning
and everywhere there was mission
message
know hope
know that your life can be led along
and up

a dancing couple now
whisperers
drinking in the delicious rhythms
of each other

and then theo hoshen
sensed the   Cracks
and his   friend with the face
of watery   blur
and the large   Nothing
down the   middle

then both   urned around

to be hit   by light from them
throug   Holes
in th   music that poured forth
throug   spaces
in the   Nothings
the   slits of Void
everyw   here
even i th ir   clothes
in

through which volleys
of pure white moments
would slice into the wet
through which the large   Nothing
there above   the floor
a   unnoticed
     o very big
so big   for an absence
a   privation
not   merely less good
it was   enough
to step into

of course   theo hoshen
wanted   to go
of course   carl
wished him   no
it is not your   business
to explore   this hole
but it is   reserved for me
just me
and I will   in
through   the side

said theo hoshen
reassuring his friend
for straight through
both knew
meant Destruction

and then with a single inside
out thought
he folded himself

leapt inside
and was gone

No longer touching Theo Hoshen, Carl at once perceived everything as it had been before. The world was no longer liquefied, but there appeared to be no Theo Hoshen either. Cursing the day he met him, Carl turned around to see Simon and Avigail with their mouths agape. Because of the darkness, however, no one else in the pub seemed to have noticed the slightest thing, certainly not the dancers, who were in any case at the far end of the floor. Then Carl turned back to where Theo Hoshen had been. But there was still no sign of him. It seemed as if his friend had simply disappeared. However then, just as suddenly, a hand manifested itself, floating in the air. Carl grabbed it and

  pulled
  then popped
  him out

  landing him
  on the floor
  on his face
  a cry of pain
  a splash of sound

and a new Cra   k
opened   there

carl went for the ring
while his friend covered his mouth
with his other hand
then carl reached for the small box
floating along the floor

dropped the ring inside
closed it

"Are you alright?" he said to Theo Hoshen.

"Are you alright?" echoed Avigail, who had hastily approached and was now standing above the two of them.

"I think I may have broken a tooth. Carl, can you see?" entreated Theo Hoshen as he moved his hand out of the way.

Carl peered deep into his friend's mouth. And indeed there he spied a chip on one of the young philosopher's front teeth, along with a few drops of blood from a cut lip. But then, at that very moment, before Carl could report upon what he saw, Theo Hoshen's nausea from his recent adventure began to take hold. And so did he, in one fell swoop, retch all over his friend's face, discharging, with a powerful jet, the whole of the contents of his recent meal.

"Theo's hurt!" declared Carl, obviously not comprehending what had just happened. Upon examining himself, however, he discerned from the look, smell and indeed taste of what Theo Hoshen had just dispensed upon him that it was not blood but the remains of a partly digested Landsburger that covered him. Of course this served only to accentuate his own nausea and in a flash he, too, vomited his guts all over his friend. Dismayed and disgusted, Avigail withdrew.

"Yack!" exclaimed a revolted Simon, who had just approached.

"Did it work?" demanded Theo Hoshen. "Did it?"

"Fuck yeah!" announced Simon proudly. "Couldn't see you at all! Not till you stuck your hand out. But how about you guys go clean yourselves up? You're rank, if you know wha' I mean."

So Theo Hoshen struggled to his feet and, with Carl by his side, the two made their way to the men's room where they washed up as best they could. And thus ended their strange new adventure at Reznikoff's Pub.

CHAPTER XXX

*Wherein the four members of Fahrenheit 1710
retire to the kitchen at which their society was first
established and begin a profound discussion about
the strange event that had just transpired at
Reznikoff's Pub*

"That was so wild!" exclaimed Carl.

"Yes, very exciting," concurred Theo Hoshen.

"And really weird, eh, the way everything flowed *up*?" said Carl

"Indeed."

"And the way some people were so much faster and further along than the others – like that dancer guy."

"Yes," agreed Theo Hoshen, "he was right beside me. Most of the others seemed to be just drifting along, treading water, as it were."

"Yeah," confirmed Carl, *"treaders."*

"They are the slaves of which I spoke, Carl, today's lotus-eaters. It is surely right that they take their drugs and float along rather than practice politics."

"What drugs?" asked Simon.

"Not only the obvious ones," replied Theo Hoshen, "but also television and the like. Still, clearly not everyone is adrift. The two at the bar, for example, the ones engrossed in conversation. Now they clearly were 'swimming' on ahead, albeit not as rapidly as the dancer."

"That's right," confirmed Carl.

"I haven't a clue what you guys are on about," interjected Simon, "but I gotta say: fanfuckingtastic!"

"It certainly was," agreed Theo Hoshen.

"What are you talking about?" exclaimed Avigail. "Are you nuts?"

"That's what they always say about us scientific geniuses at first," said Simon.

"I just want to know," continued Avigail, "what the hell is that damn ring? How does it work?"

"Why," replied Theo Hoshen, "it is surely a ring of Gyges."

"A ring of what?" cried Avigail.

"Of Gyges. It is an invisibility ring, you see."

"No I don't see."

"Exactly."

"What, is it some kind of trick?" Avigail demanded.

"Oh it is no trick," countered Theo Hoshen. "It is simply a ring that allows its wearer to become invisible."

"Simon," implored Avigail, "you explain."

"Well I don't know about any Gyges, but I can tell you that whatever touches the ring gets some kind of space opened up for it, and that whatever goes into that space becomes invisible. You saw Hoshen-boy disappear, right?"

"Yes, but how?" pressed Avigail.

"I haven't quite sussed that bit out yet," admitted Simon. "Okay, I got no idea."

"I do," announced Theo Hoshen.

"Sure you do, mate," said Simon. "So enlighten us."

"To begin with Gyges," said Theo Hoshen, "as Plato recounts in his *Republic* –"

"Here we go," interjected Simon.

"As I was saying," continued Theo Hoshen, "we read in the *Republic* that Gyges was a Lydian shepherd who worked for the king. One day, there was an earthquake that opened a big chasm in the ground where he had been leading his flock. In wonder, he entered. Inside, he saw a hollow bronze horse which contained the corpse of a man, naked except for a gold ring on his hand. Gyges took the ring and went out. Then, later that day, as he sat with some other shepherds, he happened to turn a band upon the ring in a certain way and the result was that he became invisible. He knew this because he could hear the others talking about him as if he had left – even though, of course, he had not. With his new discovery, Gyges decided to take a position as one of the king's messengers. Once inside the castle, he seduced the queen and, with her approval, killed the king and took over the kingdom."

"That's not how it goes," objected Carl, grateful for the opportunity to correct his friend for once. "I read it in an ancient history course I took. Gyges wasn't a shepherd but one of the king's bodyguards. And what happened was that the king, who was always going on about how beautiful his queen was, ordered Gyges to see for himself by hiding in their room and watching as she got undressed before bed. Gyges didn't want to but the king forced him and promised that nothing bad would happen to him. So he did it. But on his way out, she saw him. So the next morning, figuring that the king had put him up to it, she called Gyges in and gave him two options: either he kills the king or she'll have him killed right there. 'Course he took door number one. So that night, he went into their bedroom again and this time slit the king's throat. Then he married the queen and took over the throne. No ring, no invisibility. Guess Plato must've just made that stuff up, eh?"

"Plato does not 'make stuff up'," declared Theo Hoshen haughtily. But then Avigail shouted at them both to stop with the stories, whether fictional or non-fictional, and explain how the ring actually worked.

"Does it have a band on it that you turned?" she pressed.

"Well no," replied Theo Hoshen.

"So how does it work? What does it do?"

Theo Hoshen fell silent. Carl remained so.

"I got an idea," said Simon. "The ring, when you touch the gold, affects your perception right?"

"That's for sure," confirmed Carl. "Everything went all weird and watery."

"But you touched Theo, not the ring," Simon added. "So whatever it was must've transmitted through Hoshen-boy's skin. It's like some kind of psychedelic drug," he concluded. "What else did you see?"

"Well," said Carl, "even the music was all watery; it was like I could see it gushing out of the speakers."

"That's synaesthesia," declared Simon, "the union of the senses. It's when you taste shapes or see sound, that sort of thing. Some people always have it; others need drugs to bring it on. Cool, eh? What else?"

"Know hope," said both Carl and Theo Hoshen in unison.

"What's that?" asked Simon.

"Well," answered Carl, "it's not like we could see the words or anything, right Theo?" Theo Hoshen nodded. "It's like everything – all of the flowing water – was all beautiful and vivid and transmitting this message. Everything except for the dark cracks, that is; *they* weren't saying anything."

"Correct," confirmed Theo Hoshen. "And it was alongside one of those that I entered."

"That must've been when you turned invisible," said Simon excitedly. "Could you still see us?"

"Yes," replied Theo Hoshen, "though I am not sure that 'see' is the right word – 'sense' would be more apt. And from within, the sensation of everything was even stranger than before. I could still make out people and things, and they were still watery, but everything appeared as if it were in a painting by Picasso. On top of that, it all seemed to be happening simultaneously. Very odd."

"At least we can say," concluded Simon, "that you didn't turn transparent or anything like that – 'cause if you did then you wouldn't be able to see since there wouldn't be any refraction off your corneas. So where'd you go, exactly?"

"That is a most difficult question," said Theo Hoshen sombrely. "I had gone right inside a kind of slit on the side, in between the world and the blackness of the crack itself. I sensed that, had I gone directly into the black – well, that would not have been wise; I was somehow certain that it would cause me great harm or worse. So I just slid myself in through the in-between. From there I could have gone deeper, since there seemed to be a corridor of sorts, but instead I turned around and became aware of the whole of Reznikoff's, sensing it all in that strange Picasso-like way. Apparently none of you were aware of me, however. Moreover, though I felt as if I had been in there for the longest time, Carl says that it was but a moment."

"I got it!" announced Simon. "Somehow, by letting you see and go through those slits the ring gives access to a higher dimension. That's where you went in and it's while you were in there that we couldn't see you."

"A higher dimension?" exclaimed Avigail. "I thought you didn't go in for that woolly mystical stuff."

"No, this is real science," protested Simon. "Lots of theoretical physicists have been working on the idea of higher dimensions."

"No doubt," said Theo Hoshen with a scowl. "For the idea has all the marks of the natural sciences of our day. Because by 'higher' dimensions you mean those *in addition* to the three of space and the fourth of time, correct?"

"You got it," replied Simon.

"Typical," said Theo Hoshen in a dismissive tone. "It is no wonder science misses the world."

"Bollocks," rejoined Simon.

"Bollocks?" repeated Theo Hoshen. "Bollocks to what? I doubt you even have a clue what I mean."

"Alright then," said Simon with a roll of his eyes, "tell us." At this Theo Hoshen's face lit up, for he clearly relished the opportunity to lecture on the subject. He began:

"When, Simon, you enter the lab and put on your white coat, you may be said to look out from the world and into what you call the universe, that is, at things as they exist in nature minus human culture. You do the same when, for example, you comprehend the sounds coming out of my mouth in terms of wave frequencies instead of what the words I am saying mean. And that is what 'the world' is: a dimension of meaning of the sort that cannot be accessed by the disengaged methods of natural science because they recognize only the four spatial dimensions of length, width, depth, and time. The last is no less spatial than the first three since it is conceived in terms of a clock's ticking, which is to say as a succession of discrete moments like points in space. That is why scientists, at least since Minkowski, talk of a single field of 'spacetime' as if time is but a homogenous 'time-as-space'. Of course this is also what led Einstein to claim that the past, present and future all happen at once."

"Of course," said Simon sarcastically.

"However," Theo Hoshen went on, "this not only obscures the world, which is a cultural, organic whole, most of which cannot be spatialized, analyzed, chopped-up into bits, but it also misses the possibility of non-spatial natural dimensions."

"Anyone?" implored a dumbfounded Simon. But neither Carl nor Avigail had anything clarifying to say.

"It is quite simple," continued Theo Hoshen. "You scientists follow Galileo in making the outrageously unscientific, because a priori, assumption that the book of nature is written in but a single language, that of mathematics, with its separating out of everything into independent variables. That is why you can only ever go in one direction – up – when it comes to contemplating new dimensions because if there is a new dimension then it must be higher, capable of being added to the previous four, since like them it must be spatial, mathematically analysable. What hubris! After all, Galileo the Italian read Copernicus in Latin so he was at least bilingual, and yet he and virtually all other modern scientists assume that mother nature can be no more than monolingual. As if she were dead."

"You are *such* a git," was all that Simon could say.

"And you have insulted me enough," declared Theo Hoshen as he rose from his chair, fists clenched.

"Whoa!" said Carl, placing his hands on his friend's shoulders. "Hold on there. He doesn't mean to insult you, Theo. He's just frustrated because he doesn't get what you're saying. And frankly, Avigail and I are pretty lost ourselves. Right Avigail?" She nodded. "You see, Theo. We're just trying to understand."

"Fine," replied Theo Hoshen, who, after glaring in Simon's direction, allowed himself to be guided back to his chair. "The point I am making is not at all difficult. It is that, being so wedded to mathematics, modern scientists conceive of everything, including any new possible dimensions, as like space. That is why they miss the existence of the world, which, though bound to the natural universe like water on a shower curtain, is still distinct from it. And they miss the world even though they live their lives in it. Incredible, is it not?"

"Look, Hoshen-boy," said Simon, "the fact is everything's physical, so everything's governed by the laws of physics. If you want to believe in some crazy, mystical realm of 'the world' you go ahead; whatever gets you through the night. But to serious scientists everything's part of nature so everything's got to conform to its laws. Science gets at the roots of things, mate, at the objective mechanisms underlying them; what you're on about is just the irrational, subjective surface."

"But that," countered Theo Hoshen, "is precisely where you go astray. Not so much, again, as regards the natural universe; what escapes you is the fact that there are different kinds of reason at work in what I am calling the world, namely the productive and the prudential. They employ symbols of infinite meaning that should not be limited, chopped-up and reduced to discrete units, since they are never self-contained or atomistic like rational numbers. That is why, where mathematicians choose to call numbers that repeat or never end 'irrational', you say the same of the world of symbols."

"*And?*" challenged Simon.

"And nothing," replied Theo Hoshen. "All I am saying is that if something does not compute, if you cannot isolate it so that it may be entered into your equations, then you consider it irrational. But the kinds of reason that Aristotle distinguished from the theoretical, from what you would call the analytical, are precisely those which deal with infinites. To define their objects with sets of necessary and sufficient conditions is to distort rather than clarify, for it is to separate worldly concepts from the wholes of which they are necessarily a part."

"Well I don't know about that," said Simon, "but I'd be mighty impressed by an example of one of these so-called infinitely meaningful symbols."

"Fine," replied Theo Hoshen. "Salt."

"Salt?"

"Yes. Go ahead, I challenge you to define it with a set of necessary *and sufficient* conditions. You need the latter for it to be a self-enclosed, hence finite, concept."

"That's easy: sodium chloride."

"No, my friend, sodium chloride is a scientific entity. *That* you *can* define with necessary and sufficient conditions. But salt is different; it is a part of the world, of our culture's practices. And just like, as all those who have been adopted will tell you, real parents are not necessarily their biological ones, real salt cannot be reduced to sodium chloride."

Unpersuaded, Simon offered another definition: "Okay, how about 'white crystals used to season foods'?"

"Sugar," countered Theo Hoshen.

"Okay, 'white crystals used to season foods but not in a sweet way'."

"Fine, but not all cultures use salt to season foods."

"Alright then, 'white crystals that *Canadian wankers* use to season foods but not in a sweet way'."

"But surely the British also use salt as a spice."

"What, you want me to make a list of every bloody country that uses it on their food?"

"No, of course not. And regardless, not every British or Canadian uses salt in that way. Those with high blood pressure, for example, are forbidden from doing so by their doctors. They can, however, occasionally be seen throwing it over their shoulder for luck."

"Alright, I get it: we could go on and on with this forever. So what?"

"So, Simon, it means that the things of the world cannot be defined with closed sets, for they are parts of wholes that are always relative to context and so infinitely meaningful. And if you can miss these unquestionably real things, who is to say that there are not things in nature that you miss for the same reason? For perhaps it is not only the world that is organic, in which the whole is present in every part, but also the universe."

"*And?*" pressed Simon.

"And, my young whitecoat friend, Carl and I could not have gone into a higher spatial dimension because, as you surely know, string theorists have concluded that such dimensions must be extremely tiny and curled up – only that way can we account for why they cannot be seen in our everyday lives. So if the crack led somewhere, it must have been to a dimension that is within or alongside rather than above, which is to say part of the world."

"So why," interjected Carl, "was everything all watery?"

"That...I do not know," confessed Theo Hoshen.

"Well I know something," said Simon, "and it's that I've had enough. I'm knackered, mates; it's way past my bedtime."

"Of course," said Theo Hoshen, accompanied by nods of approval from both Carl and Avigail. Then, turning to Carl, he said: "I would be honoured if you would be my guest and take my bed for the night. I shall be comfortable on the chesterfield."

"That's okay, Theo. I'll take the couch."

"You shall not," came the young philosopher's reply. "I insist."

Judging correctly that, on this as on so many other matters, there was little chance that Theo Hoshen could be induced to change his position, Carl accepted the invitation:

"Okay, Theo. Thanks."

"My pleasure."

And with that, the four began their preparations for bed.

CHAPTER XXXI

In which the conversation, despite the extreme fatigue felt by all, continues

"Aha!" exclaimed Simon from his bedroom. This is what led to his cry:

It had become Simon's habit, now that he was a wearer of contact lenses, to remove them and place them in a solution-filled plastic case that he would then leave on the floor beside his bed just before laying himself down to sleep. As he did so on this night, first the right lens, then the left, he paused to look at the graphic of a heart that covered the container meant for the latter. In a flash an idea came to him and, after putting the lenses back in his eyes, he snatched the lens case, leapt out of bed and headed directly downstairs to Theo Hoshen's room and rapped loudly upon the door. Theo Hoshen opened it and Simon burst inside, marching to the desk in the middle of the room. Then he turned to face the young philosopher.

"Hoshen-boy," he announced, "catch!" And with that Simon tossed his lens case over towards Theo Hoshen's right. Without a moment to think, Theo Hoshen reached out to grab it – but missed.

"Aha!" Simon cried out.

"Aha what?" complained Carl from the bed. Theo Hoshen, however, said not a word; indeed, he had a most perplexed look on his face.

"You should've caught that, right?" said Simon. "It was a girlie throw." Theo Hoshen remained silent. "And now," announced Simon, who then picked up a pen from the desk, grabbed a scrap of paper from the waste bin, and held them both out for the young philosopher. "Theo, my good man," he continued in a most grandiloquent manner, "why don't you come over here and write us a little something with *this*? But no calligraphy please, I'm British."

"What's going on?" said Avigail in the doorway. "I thought we were going to bed." Avigail had rushed down from her room after hearing all of the commotion. In so doing, she had neglected to cover herself with a *négligé*, which meant that her far from excessive pyjamas, combined with luminous hair that, instead of being up in its usual pony tail, flowed down to her shoulders, made for a most beguiling sight. Indeed, it was so beguiling that not one of the three young men managed to find his tongue and answer her. "So?" she demanded. Finally, Simon spoke up:

"Hoshen-boy's got to do a little something for me. Theo?" Simon stepped forward and once again offered the young philosopher the pen and paper.

With a confused look, Theo Hoshen approached Simon and took the items from his hands. Then he bent over the desk.

"What do you want me to write?" he asked.

"Whatever you wish," said Simon mischievously.

And so Theo Hoshen began to write. But to his astonishment and chagrin he found that he had trouble even holding the pen properly. Worse, his handwriting was atrocious.

"I...I don't understand," he said. Then he became flustered: "The ring? The ring did this to me?"

"Try using your other hand," said Simon with a smirk.

"But I'm right-handed," protested Theo Hoshen.

"*Try*," ordered Simon.

And so Theo Hoshen took the pen in his left hand and began to write. And to everyone's amazement – everyone but Simon that is – the handwriting was, while not perfect, certainly much better than before.

"How?" uttered an astonished Theo Hoshen.

"You'd better sit down for this one, mate," suggested Simon. Theo Hoshen did so. "World, universe, or whatever you call it," said Simon, "the fact is, you *were* in a higher dimension tonight. And this is the proof: you've turned over."

"What do you mean 'turned over'?" demanded Avigail, who now entered the room and went directly to Theo Hoshen's side.

"Simple. In passing through to a higher dimension and then coming back down the way he did, Hoshen-boy's no longer on the same side that he was before. It makes perfect sense."

"Not to me," protested Carl. "I have no idea what you're talking about."

"I do," interjected Theo Hoshen. "I sensed something was odd since having returned from the crack, but I could not put my finger on it. I feel fine, and yet strange. Now I know why. Because at this very moment, you see, my heart is beating quite rapidly – I am not ashamed to admit that I am rather upset – and it seems that I am upset in more ways than one. For you see, my friends, and I am quite certain about this, my heart *is on the wrong side.*"

"What?" exclaimed both Carl and Avigail. Avigail looked in Theo Hoshen's eyes and then down at his chest. Sensing no objection, she put her ear against it.

"*Oh ben criss de tabarnac de calisse!*" she swore. "It's true."

And indeed it was. Just as Simon had surmised, Theo Hoshen's interdimensional trip had "reversed" him: his left side was now his right and his right was now his left.

"Cool, eh?" declared Simon. And then, in a teasing tone, he added: "Told you this one'd flip sooner or later. Lucky you didn't go inside-out, eh?" But the others were too stunned to respond.

Finally, the young philosopher spoke again: "I think I would like to lie down," he announced. And so Carl immediately escorted him to his bed.

"It's okay, buddy," said Carl. "I'll take the couch." For once, Theo Hoshen did not object.

"It's like this," explained Simon. He wrote an "R" and "L" on each side of the piece of paper on the desk and the word "front" in its centre. Then he turned it over and wrote an "R" and "L" on each side again but now with the word "back" in the centre. Turning it over again, he then slid the paper around on the surface of the desk. "You see, if I slide the sheet about in this way," he said, "I'm restricting its movement to two dimensions. But if I peel it up off the desk like this, then I'm turning it over as I lift it up into the third dimension, that of height. So when I put 'er back down again, it's back in the two dimensions of the desk surface but now it's flipped over with its left and right sides switched – just like Theo."

"Shit," said Carl. "Should we call a doctor?"

"Don't know what good that'll do," replied Simon. "Theo's flipped but he's not sick – at least not physically."

"Here I must protest," interjected Theo Hoshen from the bed, his finger raised to emphasize the point, "for I cannot claim to be feeling exceptionally well."

"That's just 'cause you've been shown up as full of shit for once," declared Simon. "But don't worry, mate, it'll do you good."

"And yet," countered Theo Hoshen, "you have still to explain how there can possibly be higher dimensions which are not so tiny that I would be unable to enter them."

"Theo!" exclaimed Avigail. "I can't believe you. Your heart's on the wrong side of your body and you still want to argue theoretical physics with Simon! For once in your life just shut up and rest a little. Please!"

"You are right, my dear. And I am sure that Simon could make good use of the time to develop an adequate response to my objection."

"Well here's one, you tosser," said Simon, inducing Theo Hoshen to both lift up his head and prick up his ears.

"Uggh!" exclaimed Avigail, who then marched directly out of the room.

"By going into the crack," Simon went on, "you were shrunk down, and that's how you got into one of the tiny higher dimensions."

"Ah, but what about when I stuck out my hand?" Theo Hoshen countered. "It was of normal size, was it not? How could it continue to be so while remaining attached to the rest of my ultra-tiny body?"

"Good point," granted Simon. "I haven't sussed that bit out yet."

"Maybe you're both right," offered Carl.

"Go on," said Theo Hoshen.

"Well, maybe Theo did go into a higher dimension, only he did so by first going around what he calls 'the world'. I was thinking about your image of the world as like water on a shower curtain. What if, just like water falls into a third dimension when it falls off the edge of a 2-D curtain, there's an extra, higher dimension that exists just off the edge of the known universe? You know, far, far away."

"And?" urged Theo Hoshen.

"And maybe the cracks are a way of somehow accessing that extra dimension, of cutting through to a far-away place that contains it."

"Yes!" cried Theo Hoshen, suddenly becoming greatly excited and lifting the rest of himself up from the bed. "And all of this is possible because the ring alters our perception – as Simon pointed out when he spoke of its synaesthetic effect. The trick is to follow Aristotle rather than those silly cognitivists for whom the mind is made up of separable components. They view synaesthesia as but the product of 'crossed-wires' whereas, in reality, it comes from our becoming conscious of the whole of sensations that we normally do not perceive since we have yet to apply the categories that distinguish its parts. In altering our perception, making everything vivid in a special way, the ring allows us to sense the cracks directly, granting us access to them. Thus may we enter an adjacent, as well as higher, off-the-curtain dimension.

"Now surely this," Theo Hoshen continued, "is what it must mean to affirm a metaphysical 'trilism' and so abandon altogether the dualisms favoured by Descartes, Kant, and quantum physicists since Schrödinger. For there are three 'domains' – shall we call them that? – of human existence: first, the concrete, practical world; second, this vivid dimension perceptible when we wear the ring; and third, nature. And just as scientists look at nature from a vantage point within the practical, we can look back at the practical from within the vivid ring dimension. Moreover, since all three interrelate in a non-additive way given the organic quality of the whole, they being contained within each other (since, just as the genetic information for the whole body can be found within each and every cell, the whole is present in each part), we can explain spooky actions at a distance within the natural, that is, the non-locality challenged by the Einstein-Poldosky-Rosen paradox. For there is no violation of special relativity's postulate that nothing can travel faster than the speed of light since an organic whole – by which, I should add, I do not mean merely the astrophysical, holographic notion of how the two-dimensions of the surface of a black hole contain all of its three-dimensional information but rather the ancient Babylonian idea of a micro-macrocosm – an organic whole means that one does not always have to travel to get around, to get from part to part. When the whole is in the parts, paired wave functions can collapse instantaneously across vast distances because, well, because *there is no distance*. That, then, is how to account for cosmic entanglement. It is also why the wise theoretical physicist should see himself as a student, not merely of quantum mechanics, but also of quantum *organics*. Amazing, is it not?

"There is more. For surely dogs do not pick up scents simply by virtue of some heightened olfactory detector; they must have another sense, one that accesses an interdimensional trail through the organic cosmos. All animals must do the same when they sense 'fearons' in others or an earthquake or tsunami long before it arrives. Of course, this also explains why reiki can be done long-distance over the phone. I could go on."

And then, ignoring the stupefied faces of his auditors, Theo Hoshen did precisely that:

"So these three domains – could they be what the great, great, great Hermes meant when he wrote of the three modes of the cosmos? – are *together*. And yet not as one, not as a unity. This is where Trismegistus, Bohm and so many others – yes, even Aristotle – went wrong (an understandable error given the monistic connotations of the terms 'cosmos' or '*uni*verse'). Because Carl and I sensed the cracks, the ones that let the light in. Perhaps there was unity once, when, during the instant of the big bang, all forces were one and so part of a virtually perfect whole. But then the universe began its rapid expansion and, as it cooled, the original superforce that held it together began to fracture, leading different forces to come apart from each other. It is just like when water freezes, transforming itself from a smooth and uniform liquid into crystals that break its original uniformity, leaving cracks and bubbles in the ice. One is also reminded of Luria's account of Genesis, in which the vessels containing the original light of creation overflowed and broke. Did you know that his 'cure' for homosexuality was to roll around naked in the snow for forty-five minutes? And how rarely it must have snowed in Safed!

"But I digress. To speak of breaks and cracks is not to deny the connection between the domains – the holism of the whole – only to highlight the spaces which serve as corridors, openings of a sort, between them. The world is still unified, as Aristotle correctly assumed; that just *must* be right. And all three of the domains are still to a degree integrated and so influence each other. Take the momentum of the world's flow – *that's* why everything was watery! So worldly time is not spatialized but like the Nazi Heidegger's ecstasis time, wherein the past flows into the present and the present into the future. This is different from natural science's empty homogenous time which, while it can certainly 'exist' cannot truly 'be' without us, since being consists of something more than bare existence, nature-in-itself. Yet it is through, or at least alongside, holes in being that we can access the natural and so every part within it. Carl, you are a genius!"

Of course all of this apparent gibberish had lost both Carl and Simon long ago.

"Uh right," muttered Carl. And, following a worried glance at Simon, he added: "Listen, Theo, maybe it's time for us to hit the sack after all, eh?"

"Certainly," came Theo Hoshen's reply. And not a few moments later, he was fast asleep. Having little choice in the matter, the others soon followed.

CHAPTER XXXII

Which finds Theo Hoshen and Carl Landsberg
having what is sometimes called a "heart to heart"

"Theo, you up?" inquired Carl from the couch, late the next morning.

"I am indeed."

"How're you feeling?"

"Fine."

"Your heart?"

"Also fine, though I believe that it is still on the right, which is to say wrong, side. Let me check." Theo Hoshen felt around his upper chest with his hand. "You know, I cannot be sure *where* it is at the moment; given that I have just awoke, it is not beating very hard. Regardless, if it is on the wrong side, it shall return to its proper place next time I use the ring."

"What? You're going to become invisible again?"

"Of course."

"What for?"

"I need to verify something."

"What?"

"I sensed something strange the last time, something that I did not mention yesterday."

"Yeah?"

"It was when I went in through the side of the big crack. There was a corridor of sorts, and I went down it for a short distance. What I sensed there was very odd. It seemed to open up into another world. Yet here is the thing: I could not sense much of it because it was blocked by two large faces. They appeared to be peering down intently upon me."

"Faces? What faces?"

"I have no idea. They looked as ours did, as everyone in Reznikoff's last night did, which is to say all watery and with those singular large cracks down the middle. The big difference, however, was that these two glowed hardly at all, and the same may be said of the world of which they were a part. But as I said, I could not sense much of it."

"So what did these faces look like?"

"Well, one was of a beautiful dark-haired freckle-faced woman. Her deep brown eyes would move slowly from left to right and then quickly to the left again.[1]

"Sensing in another direction," Theo Hoshen continued, "I became aware of the other face, this time of a handsome man with a goatee whose green eyes moved in exactly the same manner.[2] I could just make out a third face, which was much further off but, unlike the others, it glowed bright.[3] I believe there were more after that."

"What does it all mean?" wondered Carl.

"I simply do not know."

"I'm also still trying to figure out what everything I sensed was all about," added Carl. "Did you sense around Rezzie's much?"

"No, not a great deal."

"Well you know how everyone came off all watery? Each was doing different things. Some were moving through the

---

[1] Ms Yael Perets, who reached this point in the manuscript on Wednesday May 30th, 2007.

[2] Dr. Roderick Tweedy, who reached this point in the manuscript on Tuesday May 15th, 2007.

[3] Mr. Pierre Menard (the author, not the fur trader), who never really reached this point in the manuscript.

water, aiming for the turbulent parts as if they were swimming in it – like that guy the really cool dancer." Theo Hoshen nodded. "They were the ones," Carl went on, "that glowed the most. Not so much the others, remember, the treaders who just floated along as if 'caught in the waves of destiny' – you know, like in that Blue Rodeo song."

"Yes," agreed Theo Hoshen.

"Still," said Carl, "even they took in some of the shards of light that came through the cracks. It's like it energized them to swim forward a bit. Weird, eh? And did you sense how the cool dancer guy made cracks around him while the others did the opposite, you know, closed cracks or at least made them smaller?"

"No, for my attention was elsewhere."

"I wonder what it all means."

"Philosophy begins with wonder," declared Theo Hoshen.

"Then maybe I should become a philosopher." Theo Hoshen looked at Carl for the first time that morning. "Just kidding," said Carl. And then, following a pause: "Theo?"

"Yes, Carl."

"What if the sentencing goes badly? I mean, what if you have to go to jail? Does that scare you? It sure as hell scares me."

"No, Carl, I am not afraid. Not because there is nothing to fear, but because honour demands courage."

"And you just give it whatever it demands, eh?"

"I must."

"Well you know what I'd say it wants?" asked Carl rhetorically. "Responsibility. So I've got to ask you: why haven't you told your parents about your arrest, the trial, hell about any of this? Don't you think they have a right to know?"

"No, Carl, I do not."

"Why? What's happened? They live here in Toronto, right? Don't you even want them around for support? I mean, it'll make a real difference to me that mine'll be there at the sentencing."

"Carl, I know what I am doing."

"Really? It's all going according to plan, eh? You know, Theo, sometimes I really wonder about this plan of yours. Sometimes I think that our getting double-crossed by the engineers was actually a part of it. Because if even the engineers, with all their school spirit, are corrupt, then it proves that the world's as screwed up as you say, right? Is that it, Theo? Did you want to go to trial just so you could make some big speeches denouncing the system?" But before Theo Hoshen could answer, Carl continued: "And what about me, Theo? Was my having to perjure myself also part of the plan? I'm not saying it wasn't the right thing to do; what pisses me off is how, to you, I just *had* to do it, no question. Because if you ask me, there were plenty of questions. Plenty."

"Carl, what you fail to see is that there are times when one must simply stand and fight. Prudence and responsibility only go so far; in fact, sometimes they are but forms of cowardice. Could it be that you are afraid of this world, afraid of losing and being hurt within it? Or perhaps you fear winning even more, since it would mean that you must defeat someone. In that sense, Carl, you may be not only a coward but also a snob."

"*I'm* a snob?" exclaimed Carl.

"Look," said Theo Hoshen in a more conciliatory tone, "I know it was hard for you to perjure yourself. I am grateful, indeed proud, that you did so."

"Well let's find out just how grateful," said Carl. "I'll be listening for whether you show even a bit of contrition in front of the judge – if only to prove to your friends who care about you that you give a shit. Go along with me for once, Theo. Save yourself, not the world."

"But Carl, as I told you, the important thing is not merely to live but to live well, which is to say honourably and with justice. And that means never doing wrong, under any circumstances. To show contrition, to express remorse as if I had a reason to feel guilty, well that would be a lie. Therefore –"

"That's it," interrupted Carl. "That's it for once, Theo. I'm sorry but I've had enough." And with that he simply rose and exited the room. Theo Hoshen did not even have the opportunity to say goodbye.

CHAPTER XXXIII

Wherein Carl Landsberg and Theo Hoshen are sentenced for their crimes

It came to pass that, some days later, the morning of Carl and Theo Hoshen's sentencing arrived. Theo Hoshen had yet again spent the intervening period in deep preparation, for he knew that Justice Thomas would allow him to say a few words for her consideration before she handed down his sentence.

Here is how she opened the proceedings:

"Good morning, members and guests of the court. We are here today for sentencing in the cases of Ontario v. Landsberg and Ontario v. Hoshen. Mr. Landsberg pled guilty to the charges while Mr. Hoshen pled innocent, though he has been found guilty by the jury of this court. Gentlemen, before I pronounce your sentences I want to give each of you the opportunity to make whatever statements you wish and to present any information that you may have in mitigation. Mr. Landsberg, have you anything to say?"

"Only that I'm very sorry for what I've done, your Honour," said Carl.

"Tosser," muttered Simon to Avigail.

"And you, Mr. Hoshen?" said the judge.

"Yes, your Honour, I do have a few words for you."

"I'm not surprised," said the judge. "Alright then, you may say whatever you wish – even if it means you'll be going off on one of your philosophical tangents."

"Thank you, your Honour. And though, as someone once said, there is no simple explanation for anything important, I shall do my best to be brief."

"Tell me you got that," said the judge to the clerk. But Theo Hoshen simply ignored the remark and began. This is what he said:

"So, we are to be punished. There is still time, however, still a chance. The Crown is surely worried that, should Mr. Landsberg and I be seen to have committed no more than a college prank, then anything but the lightest sanction will appear draconian. So let us, then, recall Draco, the ancient Athenian who established that city's first set of written laws. Yes, they certainly were draconian – stealing a cabbage meant the death penalty, for example – but look at what they accomplished: for the very first time it was possible to see crime as something committed against the good of the whole *polis* instead of merely that of the victim. So no longer could a victim's family legitimately exact vengeance against a murderer, for instance.

"Now this idea, that the law expresses the citizenry's common good, is essential to an honourable society. It was not to last, however. During the Reformation, Luther burned the books of canon law and declared that the true Church of Christ was an invisible, apolitical, and non-legal community. The result was that the idea of the Church as a clerically ruled legal order passed on to the modern state, meaning that the laws of that state came to be identified with God – and God, as we all know, is no mere citizen since He transcends the world and so the political community. Indeed, this is what allows us to speak of *the rule* of law, for there can be no rule without a ruler, without someone or something that has the last word, and who better to fulfil this role than God, a perfect 'being' who never questions Himself? So it is that, nowadays, breaking the law means offending more than the community; even if only implicitly, it means offending God Himself.

"Now this is why our justice system has been such a failure at protecting the public and rehabilitating offenders. Because instead of restoring both victim and offender, reintegrating them into the community, the system aims to exact a divine vengeance by ignoring the victims and separating the offenders, now considered a distinct class of criminals, from society. Just look at our neighbour to the south, that shiny excuse for a country which dares to call itself 'America'. Even though, or perhaps because, Americans are a juvenile, self-obsessed people for whom everything is a game, their leaders have declared a 'war on crime' and so thrust upon their convicts the status of veritable enemy agents. Up here we do not go that far, of course, although to be convicted of a crime is still to become an outcast or, perhaps better, an 'incast', since so many convicts end up locked away in prison. There we become like caught fish: we are given good reason to cry, but our tears are redundant and our howls go unheard. Because what is prison if not a cruel and unusual punishment, a wholly mechanical process that embitters the prisoner's heart while adding, for good

measure, forgetfulness, hatred, and feelings of the most profound indifference to one's fate? How, then, do we explain
imprisonment? Are convicts comparable to the Jews of Nazi
Germany, those who, in Joseph Goebbels' words, should be
'cut out' of the community?" Of course this was too much for
Justice Thomas:

"Mr. Hoshen!" she said sternly. But the young philosopher
just continued on:

"No, of course not. So what is behind incarceration? For
the truth is that the law is not God. Even if it was, revenge
would be at the very least premature. Because surely retaliation
is warranted only when no compensation is offered. And surely
revenge is an undertaking for heroes, not the community."

At these words Theo Hoshen paused, seemingly deep in
thought. And then he paused some more. All of which led
Justice Thomas to speak up:

"Mr. Hosh —"

"So what," interrupted the young philosopher, "is the alternative? I begin by asserting that, unlike God, the law is not
One, hence no altar before which the citizenry must bow.
Rather, *we* are the law, which should thus express our common
good. This means two things. First, that we need to be well
brought up, which is to say educated to love the laws. There is
a great obstacle here for some, however, an economic barrier
that must be removed. Did you know that, by shifting merely
one percent of the first world's wealth to the third, severe
poverty could be eradicated altogether? Only one percent! Yet
we do not do so, even though every day about fifty thousand
people die of poverty-related causes. Or did you know that up
to one-fifth of Canadian children show up to school without
having had enough to eat? Clearly, the distribution of wealth
both here and abroad is far too inequitable. But even putting

economic injustice aside, what of the humiliation suffered by those on the bottom, the dishonour felt by all who must look up, up, way up to see their wealthy so-called fellow citizens, they who have achieved those riches mainly because of dumb luck? How can anyone be expected to love the laws in such a situation?

"That is why there must be both a basic minimum income for all *and* a maximum, a universal upper limit. Modern thinkers revel in criticizing the injustices of the feudal age, yet today's inequalities are far greater and just as contingent. I ask you: is the luck of being born into nobility, economically parasitic on serfs, so different from that of the free market? No need to answer that."

"Mr. Hoshen," interrupted Justice Thomas, who was only interrupted by him in turn:

"Yes, yes, your Honour, I am almost there. Now, I do not count myself among those who have suffered from economic exclusion. My case is more revealing of the second thing that must be done in order that the laws could once again express the common good: if we convicts are ever to know hope we must be *taught* to recognize our iniquities. Indeed, this is the only real, effective 'punishment'. No, I am not suggesting that we be treated by a tender, loving mother, embraced by some aloof Church looking to regenerate the fallen; I am simply asking that we be given the opportunity to display magnanimity – the one virtue that, as Aristotle taught long ago, contains all the others. We should be able to bring restitution for our crimes, to heal the damage that we have done to the community. But we cannot do this if we are sent away to prison. Only by coming to understand and so learn from what we have done can we reconcile with our victims.

"And that, your Honour, is my final request to you. I am

asking that Mr. Landsberg and myself be allowed to engage our victims in dialogue; I am asking, you could say, for the justice of Apollo instead of that of the Furies, for truth instead of retribution. Indeed, your Honour, it is all that I have ever asked. Thank you."

"And thank you, Mr. Hoshen," said Justice Thomas with a sigh. "Now, before I step out to begin my deliberations, I've two questions for you. First, do you feel any remorse for what you've done? And second, are you willing to return the Cannon?"

"Your Honour, as these proceedings have failed to demonstrate to me that what I did was wrong, I cannot in all honesty say that I feel remorse. Evidently, I would rather fail with honour than succeed with fraud. Yet I *am* open to being convinced otherwise. Perhaps I did, unintentionally of course, cause some real, unjustifiable harm; if so, then I shall certainly recognize my guilt. However, as we see in book three, chapter one of Aristotle's *Nicomachean Ethics*, this should have the effect of freeing me of legal responsibility in the matter.

"I am also open to reconsidering my decision not to return the Cannon," Theo Hoshen added. "But, once again, this requires that I be able to sit down with those from whom I took it and discuss the matter."

"I see," said Justice Thomas. "Okay then, that's it. We'll break for lunch now and reconvene at two-thirty. I suggest that Mr. Hoshen and the Crown meet now to see if they can agree on terms."

"No thank you, your Honour," said Theo Hoshen.

"I thought you'd say that. At two-thirty then."

The time passed quickly. So let us join them all again as Carl and Theo Hoshen stood together, awaiting the judge's pronouncement of their sentences. This is what she said:

"Mr. Landsberg, I am hereby awarding you an absolute discharge along with the requirement that you perform two months of community service. But as president of your student's union, I expect that you won't find the task particularly arduous, nor foreign to your nature."

"No ma'am. Thank you, your Honour," said Carl, who then looked back at the smiling faces of Simon and Avigail as well as those of his parents seated right beside them.

"As for Mr. Hoshen," said the judge in a stern voice, "it is clear to me that you have failed to treat these proceedings with the respect they deserve. What you did to end up here *was* just a college prank, but in refusing to return what you stole as well as claiming innocence when you are obviously guilty, you express contempt for this court – and to a degree that, I must say, I have not seen in quite some time. If you had been standing upon a podium somewhere and lecturing to those willing to listen to your peculiar ideas, I would have had no objection. But not here, not in my courtroom. Here we deal in justice, not politics or philosophy. Here people pay for the crimes they've committed.

"And so," she continued, "I believe that you need to be taught a lesson. Mr. Hoshen, I am hereby sentencing you to ninety days in jail." At this a gasp could be heard from the audience (it was Avigail, of course). Theo Hoshen, however, did no more than stand there. The judge then concluded: "If you had a lawyer, Mr. Hoshen, he or she would now inform you that, if you behave well during your incarceration, you can expect to do significantly less time than that. Which is why I am strongly advising you to behave, Mr. Hoshen. Alright, that's it. This case is now closed; this court is no longer in session." And with that she banged down once with her gavel.

What happened next was that the bailiff approached an expressionless Theo Hoshen, placed him in handcuffs, and escorted him out of the room. The adventurous young philosopher did not look back.

CHAPTER XXXIV

Regarding the time Theo Hoshen spent imprisoned in Toronto's notorious Don Jail

"You disrespectin' me?" Gord demanded of Wilton. The two were Theo Hoshen's cell mates. Gord was a hefty gentleman with a pony tail and a magnificent beer belly that was even more impressive for being thoroughly covered in tattoos. Wilton had little hair, no tattoos, and was much more slight. "I mean, I know you're gettin' some of the piss," Gord continued, "but what can I do, eh?" Gord was referring to the drops of his urine that splashed unavoidably from the toilet bowl and landed upon Wilton's face, Wilton's bed being so situated within that cramped, six-by-eight-foot cell that its occupant had no choice but to lay his head right next to the bowl. "And with the way yer looking at me, ya ho," said Gord, "I'd say yer disrespectin'."

"I'm not saying nothin', man," protested Wilton.

"Okay," announced Gord as he zipped his zipper closed, "time for another lesson." And with that he reached over and pulled a groggy Wilton up from his bed. Wilton had just enough time to cover his face with his arms before Gord began to pummel him with his fists, his belly moving to and fro as he swung.

"Enough!" commanded Theo Hoshen from his place on the top bunk. This came as something of a surprise to both of his cellmates, for he had said not a word to either of them from the moment he first set foot into the cell that evening.

"So the kid talks," remarked Gord.

"You, sir, are nothing but a bully!" came Theo Hoshen's reply. This was more than enough for Gord. He lurched up, grabbed Theo Hoshen by his shirt, and flung him down from the bed. And the moment the young philosopher landed, Gord began to kick him with great enthusiasm.

"Got to be respectin' me," declared Gord. Theo Hoshen could only moan in response. Then, after a few more kicks, one of which landed directly on the side of Theo Hoshen's head and left a fair-sized dent there, Gord gave out a short, satisfied grunt and returned to his bed. For a time, he watched as our hero lay prostrate upon the floor. There was a moment when Gord was surprised by what appeared to be a strange smile passing over Theo Hoshen's lips, but he soon determined that it was nothing but one of the many large cockroaches that would often scurry about the cell whenever the lights were turned off. Then Theo Hoshen began to retch, which led a satisfied Gord to conclude that his new cellmate would not be getting up anytime soon. And so did the large man simply close his eyes and drift off to sleep.

Morning came and, even though Theo Hoshen had his share of sizable lumps, since nothing was broken the guard who looked him over refused to take him for the medical attention that he requested.

"Just get yourself some breakfast, eh," said the guard. "Down to chow hall," he directed, motioning Theo Hoshen to follow his two cellmates as they made their way along the hallway.

Theo Hoshen did so and when he got there he could tell immediately that there was only one place to sit and it was right beside Wilton. Not that Wilton, who had been a guest in the jail many times before, was especially welcoming. He was an aboriginal Canadian for whom, if there had been any kindness in him once, it had been beaten out of him long ago.

"I can take care of myself," he announced as Theo Hoshen sat down. "And anyway, soon Gord and all of you won't know what hit ya." Theo Hoshen did not know what to say in response.

The diminutive Wilton wasn't expecting a reply, however. He simply continued talking, going on to inform his new cellmate all about Gord and many of the other inhabitants of their cell block, which he referred to as "the neighbourhood." Theo Hoshen could not help but feel some revulsion at what he learned about these men, though he also wondered how long he would have the luxury to experience such feelings. For he sensed that this place would change him; indeed, that it already had.

"Gord locked some asshole in the trunk of a car," explained Wilton. "He didn't like his attitude, so he just put him in there. And the guy inside decides that he just has to smoke a cig. So what happens? He ends up burnin' himself real bad. 'Course that wasn't Gord's fault." Theo Hoshen sensed that this defence of Gord was not unrelated to Wilton's suspicion that his cellmates had already joined forces in some way.

"Saw you talkin' to the badge," Wilton went on. "Don't do that, man." Theo Hoshen stared back at him quizzically. "Just don't," was all that Wilton would say.

Theo Hoshen then turned his attention to the food on the plate in front of him. It consisted of a few dry slices of white bread and crackers, two pieces of bologna (one with what appeared to be a few strands of hair clinging to it), and some tired-looking fruit. For a beverage he had a glass of skim milk. Theo Hoshen looked over at Wilton, who had begun consuming his own comparable servings with relish, and then back at his own plate. It has been said that *fabas indulcet fames*, but Theo Hoshen knew that there was no way he would be able to eat that stuff.

"So what's your bit?" Wilton asked. After inquiring about what he meant, Theo Hoshen explained that he had been convicted of theft and burglary. Wilton nodded. But then he flashed Theo Hoshen a look as sharp as a knife, for Gord had just seated himself nearby. And from that moment on, Wilton did not say another word.

The rest of the day was spent attending to what Theo Hoshen gathered would be the mindless routine that he and his fellow prisoners could expect to follow every single day. The only thing they all looked forward to was the single hour reserved for recreation, one which included twenty minutes of "yard time" spent outside – that, and their weekly visits from friends, relatives, or legal representatives. Few received such visits, however. Theo Hoshen was nevertheless certain that he would have one that day because one of the guards had told him so. Needless to say, he was awaiting it with great anticipation.

CHAPTER XXXV

*In which the imprisoned Theo Hoshen of Toronto
receives a visit from Avigail and Simon, also
(currently) of Toronto*

"Ms. Lachapelle," announced the prison officer, looking up from the list on the clipboard in front of him. Avigail, wearing a lovely dress and sporting a fetching new hairstyle, rose and approached him, followed by Simon. "You can go in now," said the guard, pointing to a steel door.

Of the many modest tables in the room, Avigail and Simon's eyes fell immediately upon one the other side of which sat none other than Theo Hoshen. They could see him because the partition which ran directly down the middle of the whole room was made of thoroughly transparent glass. So each took a chair across from him.

"*Câlisse!*" exclaimed Avigail the moment she saw his face, for both of his eyes were blackened and puffy and there was a large purplish bruise which stretched from his right temple down to the bottom of his cheek. Theo Hoshen was indeed a sorry sight.

"What the hell happened?" demanded Simon

"Why have you come so early?" was all that Theo Hoshen said in reply. In lieu of an answer his visitors simply stared back at him. Partly this was because of their shock at the injuries he had received, but it was also because, given the slumped way in which he sat there, it seemed as if something deep inside of him was absent. "No matter," he said. "I am glad you came."

"Your eyes," said Avigail with such anguish in her voice that it startled the other two.

"Yes, well," said Theo Hoshen, "let us just say that this place is not at all suited to *theoria*."

"Does it hurt?" implored Avigail.

"Of course it hurts," said Theo Hoshen with a smile. "As it should. I am here to be punished, after all."

"Stop it Theo!" urged Avigail. And so he said nothing more. It was consequently Simon's turn to speak next:

"I don't get it, mate. What happened?"

"A blow, or rather blows, to the head. But they have taught me a great deal. Time was when I would have felt the need to exact revenge without knowing it. Now I have resolved to do something grand instead."

"Who did it?" exclaimed Avigail. "Did you file a complaint?"

"Your question suggests that you do not quite appreciate the context that I and my fellow inmates find ourselves in. But no matter, Avigail, I can assure you that everything is fine."

A somewhat discomfited Simon then said:

"Alright, I'm gonna leave you two now. But I've got something to say to Hoshen-boy first. You did real great at the trial; you really let your gang out. So it didn't go your way. The point is you showed 'em that you can take it and hit back. I'm dead proud of you, mate."

"Thank you, Simon."

"Right then," said Simon. "Keep your chin up; it won't be long." Then he rose and left the way he had come.

"A good man," remarked Theo Hoshen. "For a whitecoat," he added with a wink. "And Carl? Where is he?"

"He's kind of upset," said Avigail. "He didn't want to come. But it's not like he doesn't care, Theo. I know he does. A lot."

"I see."

"Oh Theo," Avigail exclaimed, "ninety days! We've got to talk about what you're doing here."

"Why, I am doing everything that by reason appears to be the best."

"Yeah, well, about that, Theo, I want to tell you what I've been up to. You see, while you were preparing for the trial I was doing some research of my own. No, not for the thesis; in fact, I've decided to give it up."

"What? But you are so close to finishing."

"It just doesn't matter to me anymore. I don't even think coming up with a theory like I was trying to do is right."

"But what of the doctorate?"

"Exactly. I mean, even if I finished, what would I do with it? Academic life's clearly not for me."

"Why do you say that?"

"It hit me while I was at this workshop in my department. There were profs and students there, all trying to help this post-doc with a theory he was developing. What can I say, Theo? It's like they were all just snapping pieces together from some gigantic Lego set; you know, to construct some super-complex system just for the sake of it. All the jargon, the 'modules' of research imported from other disciplines, the solutions to hypothetical puzzles – they were clearly having fun but they somehow couldn't see that they were just playing around, you know, with reality's shadow. And this even though they sometimes cite Wittgenstein on language-games or Rawls on justice as fair play or Arendt on politics as a performance. As if politics was just show business for ugly people."

"True," confirmed Theo Hoshen. "It is sad how decadent philosophy has become in our time, how far it has degenerated into enjoyment. That they meet in 'workshops' is itself telling, for what is it for them to produce works if not to engage in *technê* for its own sake rather than in *theoria*? But Avigail, if you drop out now what else would you do?"

"I don't know – well, maybe a little. Theo, I want to tell you about something I read in the Talmud. It's an amazing set of books, you know, like this massive collection of inconclusive arguments. Actually, it's more than that because you get the sense that all of the arguments, from all of these different rabbis, are each in their own way right. At one point we're even told that 'Both these and those are words of the living God'. It's like, even though they contradict each other, they're all true. Somehow, the thing makes up this one big fragmented whole."

"Indeed," said Theo Hoshen in a bemused tone.

"Just listen, okay? So there's this really cool parable in which a bunch of rabbis are arguing about an oven. They're trying to decide whether it can be made spiritually unclean or not. The crux seems to be whether it should be considered a single unified thing: if so, then they all agree that it could be defiled; if not, since it was built by sticking a bunch of separate coils of clay together with sand, then it can't be defiled.

"Now one rabbi, Eliezer, says that it's not a single thing, while the others, led by rabbi Joshua, say that it is because its outer mortar coating unifies all the coils. And get this: even though at one point God Himself takes Eliezer's side, Joshua says no, that it's not up to Him and they should just go ahead and keep on arguing. So once again you get the sense that both rabbis are right."

"If I could be shown that the absolute one was many, or the absolute many one, then I would be truly amazed," said Theo Hoshen.

"I knew you'd say something like that. Anyhow, then we're told that God was asked what he thought of Joshua telling him to butt out. He just laughed and said 'My children have defeated Me! My children have defeated Me!' And as for Eliezer, the other rabbis held a vote and excommunicated him."

"That sounds rather harsh."

"Not if you see what he was doing as idolatrous, as identifying his answer with the authority of the One instead of being open to dealing with the question through exchanges with others. In fact, I think that that's the whole point of the story. 'Course you can see what the rabbis had against Greek philosophy."

"I do not follow."

"At the end of the day, the Greeks were into theory, into having a unified vision of the truth, so much so that they worshipped it, treating it like God. But to the rabbis this is idolatry; it closes you off from the inspirations from the real God above, inspirations that reach down here, between people."

"Carl, at least, would interpret the story differently. He would say that its point is that right answers can only come from *reasonable dialogue* between people, not inspirations from God."

"Well, he'd be wrong."

"Perhaps. But Avigail, I must ask: do you really believe this tale? I mean, have you become religious?"

"I don't know. I just like that the Talmud is really keen on creativity – on being open to inspirations. Whether they come from God or not I haven't figured out yet. But as I see it, the point is that you can live your life by them, you know, like an artist who channels his inspirations into actions instead of artworks. And that's what I want to do, Theo, not write up some theory for a PhD. It's like, ever since I snapped in that broom closet, I've started to really break out. So now I want to live my life in an inspired, creative way. What do you say?"

"To what?"

"C'mon, Theo, you can give me Aristotle to deconstruct – that's one way I can create, by making 'sayings' out of his 'said', as Levinas would put it. Ever been to Charlevoix? It's really beautiful this time of year – not that beauty's the point; I know that now. The point is creativity."

"Avigail, I am rather occupied at the moment."

"Oh Theo, I don't care about that. It's crazy that you're in here."

"Should one not do what one's father demands, even if you believe him mistaken?"

"What?"

"I am just saying that the law, being of the fathers – and mothers, of course – is here to be obeyed, for do we not owe everything to our parents?"

"C'mon, Theo, rules are made to be broken, right? Well, sometimes – 'cause it's only by opening them up that the light of inspiration can get in." And then, in what clearly served a radical change of subject, Avigail said: "Hey, Theo, did you know that we can have our picture taken? How about it?"

"But what of my bruises?"

"Oh don't be so vain," she chided. And then, without waiting another moment, she approached the guard, who informed her that there was a little photo room next door. It was not long before Theo Hoshen and Avigail went inside, each through separate entrances. The guard there directed them to take note of a sign posted on the wall. It looked like this:

PHOTO RULES FOR POSES

ALLOWED

SIDE BY SIDE
ONE ARM AROUND SHOULDERS OR WAIST
HOLDING HANDS

ABSOLUTELY NO

HUGGING
KISSING
KNEELING
SIGNING

Having duly read it, the two then stood beside each other and faced the camera that had been set up on a tripod at the other side of the room. Avigail placed her hand somewhat awkwardly around Theo Hoshen's waist and they both smiled. There was a click of the shutter and the flash went off. Avigail blinked at the light.

"That'll be twenty," said the guard to her, who, after rummaging through her purse, handed him a bill. "Okay," he said, "time to go." And then he began to usher them out of the room. But just before exiting Avigail turned to Theo and said the following:

"C'mon, Theo. If you don't you're gonna miss me. Fully, and completely."

As he walked along his side of the room, the young philosopher stared back at Avigail through the glass partition. She did not look back, however. And that was the moment he felt something new in the pocket of his overalls. Reaching inside, he pulled out a tiny plastic container.

Inside was a gold ring.

CHAPTER XXXVI

Wherein Carl Landsberg comes to the realization that something must be done, and that he shall have to be the one to do it

"We saw Theo yesterday," Avigail informed Carl over lunch in her kitchen.

"Uh-huh."

"It's really a travesty, isn't it?"

"Uh-huh," repeated Carl.

"It was hard to see him there. Someone beat him up, you know. Real bad. He had two black eyes and a big bruise all over the side of his face."

At this Carl fell silent, though the look on his face revealed that the news distressed him a great deal.

"So I did something," Avigail continued.

"What? What do you mean?"

Now it was her turn to be silent. Yet all it took was a few moments of scrutinizing her face for the truth to dawn on Carl.

"You didn't," he protested.

"I did."

"Jeez! Did Simon agree to this? He gave you the ring for Theo? I can't believe it."

"No, I took it myself. It was just a whim, actually. I didn't plan on giving it to him. But then, when I saw what happened, I wanted him to have it."

"And?"

"I don't know. I slipped it into his pocket and then I had to go."

"Jesus! Did he say what he was going to do?"

"Not just before I left. But earlier he said that he was going to do 'something grand'."

"Something grand? Oh God. Theo Hoshen says he's going to do something grand and you give him an invisibility ring. Are you nuts?"

"But he always talks like that," protested Avigail. "You're the one who says that he's not as bad as we think. Well Simon's come around, and so have I."

"Yeah, I gathered."

"Anyway, you had to see him. I had to do something."

"You had to, eh? Now we're really in trouble," moaned Carl. "College prank to prison break – have we ever slid right down it. You'd better tell Simon; he has a right to know. Is he in his room? We should check."

And so the two marched up the stairs to Simon's room. Once outside the door, Carl leaned against it to determine if he could hear anything inside. But there was nothing.

"Simon?" he said at the door. "You there?" More silence. So Carl knocked and, there being no answer, he tried the lock, gently turning the handle. It opened easily, following which Carl and Avigail felt the expected rush of cold air (for Simon was known to keep his room cool). "Simon?" repeated Carl into the darkness. Looking inside, he was surprised to see a tall pile of blankets and sheets on the bed. And so they both approached, whereupon they discerned that underneath it all was none other than Simon, fast asleep. "Simon," said Carl again. "What're you doing? Isn't it time to get up?" But the Englishman appeared not to hear him. So Carl repeated his entreaties, this time much louder.

At last there came a groggy reply from the bed:

"Uh," said Simon. And then, ever so slowly, he raised his heavy eyelids to spy Carl and Avigail staring down at him. "Uh," he repeated. "What time is it?"

"It's like one-thirty in the afternoon," said Carl. "Are you okay?"

"Yeah, yeah," replied Simon. "One deep fucking sleep."

"What's with all the blankets?" asked Carl. At this, Simon looked down the bed to see the massive pile on top of him. Evidently, blankets and sheets had been gathered from all of the rooms in the house. Simon was more than a little warm underneath.

"Shite!" he exclaimed and began to push the pile away. Carl and Avigail helped him to do so. Then a groggy Simon managed to sit himself up on the edge of the bed.

"Fucking hell!" he complained. "Who put all these blankets on me? I got to sleep cool or else I go so deep I can't wake up."

"Oh," said Carl weakly, for he had just guessed what had happened.

"Oh," echoed Avigail, who had done the same. Then Carl spoke again:

"Simon, you didn't put all these blankets on yourself?"

"No, why the bloody hell would I?"

"Shit," was all that Carl said in reply. Then he turned and, pushing the blankets and sheets even further along, sat on the bed beside Simon. Avigail did the same on the other side.

"What?" demanded Simon.

"I need to confess something," said Avigail.

"Yeah?" said Simon. And so Avigail admitted to having taken the ring and given it to Theo Hoshen during her visit.

"Bitchin!" exclaimed Simon. "So Hoshen-boy's out? *He* did this? I reckoned I heard someone say 'blankets time!' or something like that but I thought I was dreaming. This is so cool. Theo, mate, you here?" he called out into the open air of the room. But there was no response.

"Theo?" echoed Avigail. Still silence.

"Guess he's gone to where all the invisible escaped cons go," said Simon.

"And where's that?" asked Carl.

"How the hell would I know?" said Simon with a chuckle.

"I didn't think you'd take it this well," said Avigail. "I'm real sorry about the ring. I just didn't know what to do."

"No worries," said Simon. "This one's between you two lovebirds."

"But you don't understand," interjected Carl. "Now that he's out with the ring he could do anything. And you know him; it really could be anything. He might try to take revenge on the whole justice system, or even the planet."

"Remember him saying he was going to do something grand?" said Avigail.

"What could he mean?" wondered Carl.

"Exciting, inn'it?" was all Simon would say. "If I were him I'd be in one of those extra dimensions right now staring down on Pamela Anderson in the shower. Now that there's some wicked Canuck culture for you, eh Viggy? Then, after I'm done my business, it'd be off to a game of Mornington Crescent with Jesus."

"What?" said Carl.

"Forget it," said Simon with a wicked smile, "it's all just Silly Automatic."

"*What?*" insisted Carl. "Simon, you're not taking this at all seriously. Theo's escaped from prison and now he could be doing who knows what."

"So what do you want me to do about it?"

"Well, we've got to go after him. Convince him to stop."

"What? Into a higher dimension? And get my heart flipped over onto the wrong side of my body? No sodding way!"

"You can flip it back," protested Carl weakly.

"And no harm done, eh? You've really gone nuts if you think I'm touching one of those Gyges rings. Why don't you ask his bird here to go with you?"

"I'm not going after him," objected Avigail. "Either he comes to me or that's it."

"And if he doesn't?" challenged Carl.

"I...I don't know," replied Avigail.

"Yeah, well, wha'ever," said Simon.

"But Simon," Carl wondered, "do you even have another ring?"

"Not quite," he replied. "But I've got the original gold foil – unless Viggy took that as well. Madame Lachapelle?"

"No, just the ring."

"Right then," said Simon. "So all you gotta do is touch a gold ring to it long enough and you'll have another Gyges. Or you could just take some of the foil."

"No, it'd be easier to use a ring," said Carl. "Do either of you have one?"

"I do," said Avigail. And off she went to acquire it. She soon returned and handed it to Carl. Simon pointed him to the location of the little box containing the gold foil.

"So what do we do now?" Carl asked.

"Well," said Simon, "I'm not totally awake here but I figure that, like before, you just got to make 'em touch while they're in water and then wait for a bit."

"How long's 'a bit'?" pressed Carl.

"I dunno. An hour, maybe half. I really got no idea."

"Alright," said Carl, and so he went into the kitchen and returned with a glass of water. Then, using some tweezers, he dropped the gold foil inside and the ring on top of it.

"Where are you going to go with it?" asked Avigail.

"I don't know," said Carl. "First into one of those cracks, I guess. But after that, well, I guess I'll look around and see if I can figure out where Theo went."

"Oh good plan," said an obviously sceptical Simon. "And if you find him?"

"I'll try and get him to think twice about whatever he's planning." There seemed to be nothing more to say and so the three of them simply sat there listening to their thoughts as they waited for the gold foil to have its effect on the ring. Perhaps ten minutes passed before Carl spoke again: "Think it's ready?"

"I said I got no idea," replied Simon. "Touch it and find out." Then he handed the slightly bubbling glass of water over to Carl. "Gyges II," he declared.

Carl looked down into the glass and spied the ring sitting atop the gold foil. Then he looked back up at the other two. "Maybe this isn't such a good idea."

"You might be on to something, mate," said Simon.

"And we did just have lunch," added Avigail. "Remember what happened last time."

"But we can't just sit here and do nothing," objected Carl.

"Nothing comes o' nothing," concurred Simon.

"Alright," announced Carl. "I'm going to do it." Then he reached in, picked up the ring and slipped it on the pinkie finger of his right hand (for his ring finger was too large to take it).

"And?" inquired Simon.

Carl did not answer at first. But then, looking back at the other two, he

said it had begun
cool melting the room
his friends
his self

astonished
he sensed the know hope again
the power message

and the abstract on the wall
the lonely poster in the room
with rectangles and an inner white pasted
frame
and two purple yellow parallelograms
and a divided below
cutting white

and then he sensed
something
not   there
a   Crack
cutting   sideways
along   the middle
a Nothin   within the black
a smidgen of blu   feather touching
the   corner

the space cut   cross
but al   out
into the   river
that was the room
there were other Nothings
holed spaces
but none as inviting
simon asked if he had one
he did
mind the gap

so he folded
taking care to slide in through the side
till they said he was not there
till he called everywhere
so when he popped out his head
like a crimson word
it shocked them back

the passage goodbye
and was gone

CHAPTER XXXVII

*Concerning Theo Hoshen's thoughts while riding
a bus, reflections which lead him to undertake an
amazing adventure that begins, of all places, on the
Hill of Ares*

Theo Hoshen sat calm and alone in the back of the bus. It had not taken long before he decided to make use of the ring that Avigail had left him in order to escape from the Don Jail. So there he was now, riding a bus moving north on Bathurst Street. Why he had chosen that particular bus he himself did not know, nor did he have much idea of where he wished to go. But go he must – that much was certain.

As he sat, Theo Hoshen began to contemplate his new freedom. True, he was no longer in prison and so beyond the reach of the likes of Gord, Wilton, and the guards. But was he genuinely free? The ring was in his pocket, available for donning at any time, and yet even though this meant he could do just about anything he felt that it constituted no more than a degraded form of liberty. For it was, after all, the liberty of the individual, a merely instrumental value whose worth depended on its ability to serve the real thing: political liberty, the liberty of the citizen. Nowadays, however, the latter was available only to the very few members of a government's cabinet, and how could the ring possibly help him achieve such a post? For one thing, candidates for parliament must be visible, just as the king must be if he was not to become a tyrant to his subjects. Or so Aristotle argued.

Theo Hoshen looked about. Being addicted to reading as he was, he could not help but let his eyes wander over the various advertisements and other signage lining the inside of the bus. He quickly perceived that many of the notices were posted by the Toronto Transit Commission, or TTC, itself. For example, there was the narrow yellow sticker to be found under each of the bus' windows, the one that read "KEEP ARMS IN." And directly in front of and above him were two posters bearing the title "Our Riders Write," each of which contained excerpts from letters that the Commission had received from passengers. One was intended for all those passengers who dared to eat while riding the TTC's buses or trains: "A bus is not a dining hall," declared its writer. Another complained of the lack of manners exhibited by all those discourteous enough to put their feet upon the seats. And so on. Theo Hoshen realized that this was all but a clever way for the TTC to send patronizing messages to its customers without appearing to be responsible for them. Intrigued, he walked towards the front of the bus to see if there were any more such notices.

There were, of course. "Please move back – Thank You" announced one sticker. "Elderly and Disabled Courtesy Seating" declared another. And "Be safe and considerate" urged a third. Then, right up at the front, Theo Hoshen spied: "PASSENGERS must deposit own fare – OPERATOR forbidden to do so." And directly beside it was the elaborate: "The operator of this vehicle has been carefully selected and trained for his duties. He is required to comply with the law and to operate his vehicle with due regard to the comfort and safety of his passengers and other users of the road." Also present was: "The operator of this vehicle must have an unrestricted view at all times. Please remain behind the white line while the vehicle is in motion and move to the rear of the vehicle. Please exit by the rear doors." And under it were yet two more:

"Please exit at the Rear Doors" and "It is forbidden to converse with the driver."

They really must stop, thought Theo Hoshen to himself. All that patronising treacle, messages from the State as if the citizenry consisted of no more than children. He stormed back to his seat, turned around and, caring not a whit about whether any passengers were looking his way, reached into his pocket and slipped on the ring. Suddenly

<pre>
          he sensed them all
          treading
          the bus too

          out
          he had to get out
          so he jumped
          alongside the nearest   Nothing

          and then turned
          to take in
          the startled looks
          in a moment of perfect noise
          then around again
          to stream down
          fast
          with trailing rivulets
          until he   sensed
          a great   Hole
          that   called
          and so   dived
                          in

          then along a corridor
          till another   Crack
</pre>

with an   apotheosis
of light
streaming   through
how bright the sun shone there
on the ruins rising above
in shades of rust and dust
giving so much back
to the living river

and then a wall of tone
and a spotlight
and a sour door

but he did not enter
only went his own way
up the stairs
higher closer
to a hill above
a great beige glowing city
athens

still higher he flowed
faster
till he sensed it
the parthenon
standing sun
and shining shoulders

oh the power of the ring
perhaps one day it could help him
find the dialogues
of aristotle
the fiction

but first along a sinuous chain fence
to a symbolic sign
the acropolis

whirled
he drunk in the remnants
of the reconstruction
swished to the great one
and spotted the tourists
the girl in lily white
her mother maroon
both in an intimate afternoon
and they sang so
that he could hardly believe it

then a crowd in front
for the parthenon of immortals
who still echoed up to here
holding their place
in the river clear
as their glorious light
purled the stream

then the liquid diaphonous walls
of the erechtheion
he approached
for she would be there
amid the nebulous currents
he sensed the eddying inside
the echoing sound of her statue
and so rushed in
to stand before eight great pillars
and shoot up through two

to the strings of the fence
through the pronaos
and in

and there she was on a pedestal
echoing golden soldiers
with a chariot left and a mounted one right
he approached
athena

and sensed at the crown
with the head of the man
and the horses by his side
and the shields behind

how impelling
was the angel on her palm
and the golden serpent by the shield
and the spear

so he struggled not to kneel
and entreated as if ordered by apollo
he asked for a kindly welcome
since outside he was convicted
like one who could conquer mountains
no supplicant for purging
his hands he claimed
were clean

would she judge his plan
if he watched for her wisdom
but he saw nothing
even heard nothing

and so he was sad
and departed from that place
swished into the   Crack
between the   spear and her skirt
not her   face
whooshed   in through
the Space
to leave behind
the there
there

CHAPTER XXXVIII

*In which we follow Carl Landsberg who, with
another ring, undergoes a strange and wonderful
adventure of his own*

carl flowed
forward along a passage

then above and out
hugging the fields
fearing cutting
too far from the world

how he moved
through that endless place
the Cracks he passed
for his friend
his face

and then by mischance
they sensed him
just as he subitized them
seven little people
with duck like feet
and jointless elbows

should he flee
would they follow
he chose speech
even there

peace he said
raising his right palm out
hello hello came the reply
of reckless discernment
and indecipherable words
which then took him by the wrist
and raised the ringed hand
for two others to sense

how
he was asked
but carl grasped nothing

are you doing the true
do you real
but still carl could not hear
not all welcome the white
man
he was told
a finger pointing to the four
who stood off and away

who long ago had had enough

who are you asked carl
little folks no longer hidden
came the jolly response
from the good twin
was added incautiously
but carl grasped nothing

then he was questioned
about the principle
the one that lets you feel small from above
did he not play it

not carl
who instead would
bring angst to those who need it
and take it from those with excess

well then we have bread
and pulled out some crust
and gave it to him

who told of his search
of his friend
who could see all at once
aristotle
this startled the three
who had been taught well
beware those
who would lower the stars

still carl absorbed nothing

when with laborious determination
the four others approached
and the one who had spoke
became alarmed

CHAPTER XXXIX

*Wherein our young philosopher's adventure
continues, this time at the Kotel*

on theo hoshen went
forward along a passage
until called by the light
through another great Crack

inside now
in sharp sunlight
though the many clouds
made for great flashes on the day

it seemed an awful place
this mountain of the house
with its wall and the wailing
jerusalem

how the light streamed
through its cracks
boiling a glowing river
that gushed every which way
no wonder there was no peace here
must be something in the water

he was just above the wall now
invisible to the prayers
and the rectangled stones
as the jews in black or green with boots
retreated
from the home of the revealing
between the feeling
and the devotion

here testimony
becomes an instrument
as the pious swing and bob
and the light flashes
on
and off

here there is
no rolling along
only nature bursting through
white shirts
leading some to offer blessings
for money

here a fence cuts ishmael from joshua
as people murmur and pour
glowing notes into cracks

then suddenly a cloud
hatches a great black night
and the light becomes you
and for an instant you forget
your own name
and win some lost time

could it be that this wall
against which they wailed over their
Separation
was no liquid mending wall
but a border out of time
so unlike the other wall
of thatched golden brown metal
which stood for sex
divided him from her
and mother nature
as us from Him

then he chose another Crack
which brought him out
before a dome of eight sides
and melodious coloured arches
and grey marble columns
as hard as the cry of an electric guitar
then a woman walking
in a long roots like coat
her head under a singing scarf

and a couple with a camera
and two burly blue armoured police
who worked the bottom step of the ladder

and then he sensed it
the large   Crack
at th   entre
of the   dome
there was a   rumble and flash
as a cold   ight
burst out

slicing into the water
caressing him until
he breathed it in
to make his way
to the rock
to the dome on the top
as the light streamed through the windows

and then inside the wellspring
which leaked through the wall
as the prayers within
floated in thrall

unseen he slipped
in past the pillars
over red carpets
to the light of it all
jumped   ve   the space
and onto   the rock
the stone of all   bright
that banished the   night
upon which he lay
chin up

and breathed in
like never before

CHAPTER XL

In which Carl Landsberg finds himself amidst a mêlée of people who turn out to be not quite as hidden as he would have liked

and then came the heated argument
with carl on the sidelines
it seethed and it swirled
the waters awry

the one who spoke agreed
that it was wrong to talk
so says the principle
and his star lowerer must be
stopped

but that was not enough for the four
who then came for carlhe ran
swam
as they closed in
and he felt a terror
from beyond sin

then he noticed the Crack
and hunched up and let fly
knocking one as he came down

they had him now
not knowing what to do
it gave him a chance
a leap from outstretched arms
till he was   through

but for a final   grip on his foot
that broke with a snap

and then there he was
above a barrel
going over the falls

over and over and over
while a young man screamed inside
and light burst wide

CHAPTER XLI

*Wherein Theo Hoshen, having returned to
Toronto, makes a startling discovery in Seeker's
Bookshop on Bloor Street*

Despite his nausea, Theo Hoshen managed a smile upon feeling that his heart could once again be found on the left side of his body. It was not long, however, before he stopped smiling and took note of the cold Toronto air, for the winter sun was weak and he was without long underwear, not to mention a coat. It was time to go home and recover these and other things from his room. In the unlikely event that there were police waiting for him, Theo Hoshen figured that he had only to slip on the ring, take whatever he needed while invisible, and be off. And so he began to walk in the direction that would take him there, which is to say westward along Bloor Street.

He thought again about the ring. What was its true significance? Surely whoever possessed it was unstoppable. Did it not, as a consequence, encourage injustice by guaranteeing the fulfillment of its wearer's carnal desires? After all, Gyges himself had used it to commit adultery with his queen and assassinate his king. Then again, perhaps it would be utilized for justice. He recalled reading somewhere that most people broke laws not so much to fulfil their desires as to show others, and themselves, that they were free to do so. If true, then what point would there be in committing crimes when invisible? Perhaps, then, the all-powerful wearer of the ring would choose beneficence instead and so come to treat others as novelists tended to treat their characters, which is to say like God Himself. For there being no hidden secrets, one would see all men as they truly were.

But what if the wearer was somehow still being watched? Theo Hoshen recalled the eyes that seemed to be looking down upon him that time when he first entered a crack in Reznikoff's. Could there be others watching even now, people of whom he was completely unaware? Or were those eyes but symbols of a sort, perhaps of his own conscience? Even so, it meant that the wearer was still being watched, if only by himself. But what then of honour? For how could it power ethics in a world without privacy?

These and other such thoughts preoccupied the young philosopher's mind as he walked home. But now, having just crossed Spadina Avenue, he realized that he was far too cold to continue the trip. He recalled that the used bookstore he often frequented during trips to and from campus was only a short distance away, and so he hurried towards it.

There it was: Seeker's Books – New & Used Books Bought & Sold. Quickly, he took the stairs down and went inside.

It was warm, like the embrace of an old friend. And for once, Theo Hoshen did not mind the odour of incense that circulated perpetually about the place. He even took comfort in the cassette of classic rock that played continually in the background. Turning about, he peered at the signs in the window: Hempstop, declared one; Books, proclaimed a redundant other. There certainly were many, many books in that place. Theo Hoshen passed his eyes over the numerous signs taped to the shelves standing beside the entrance: Buddhism; I Ching; Psychedelics; Aikido/Martial Arts; Feng Shui; Taoism; Confucianism; Chinese Religions; and Chinese Medicine. Then, spying the table in front of him, he glanced at the many New Age healing books that lay upon it. He had seen them numerous times before, of course, but his recent adventures with the ring led him to look upon them now without his usual disdain. For if there was one thing he had learned, it was that there was more to the world than he had previously suspected. Not that he was going to bother opening any of these books now, however, if only because he had yet to peruse the Philosophy shelves to see if there were new arrivals. And so with a nod to the pony-tailed gentleman behind the counter, he marched directly towards them, passing Gender Studies and then Music along the way.

But at just that moment, Theo Hoshen became aware of the feeling that he was being watched. He looked about, yet he could see no one aside from the man behind the counter, and that gentleman's attention was directed at the pages of a book that he had in his hands. So there was nothing for Theo Hoshen to do but return to the Philosophy shelves and begin the task of scanning their many titles. Their order being alphabetical, his eyes soon fell upon a few of Aristotle's works, all of which he already possessed. He then thought about how, some time ago, he had changed the ordering system of his own personal library. Once it, too, had been alphabetical, but his conversion to Aristotelian philosophy led him to arrange the books according to categories instead, which is to say in keeping with their subject-matters (ethics, politics, metaphysics, and so on). He then recalled a remark of Carl's to the effect that he himself had recently also abandoned the alphabetical for ordering his books, although he chose the chronological instead. Theo Hoshen had thought nothing of it at the time, but now he made a note to ask Carl why he had done so at the next opportunity.

It then dawned on him that the bookstore he was standing in organized its books in all three of the aforementioned ways: by subject, alphabetically, and chronologically (at least when it came to the books on the shelves labelled History). Theo Hoshen began wandering about the store. Soon, he found himself amidst the many shelves containing different kinds of fiction. His eyes passed quickly over the numerous subgenres: Fantasy; Mystery; Science Fiction; Myths & Legends; Ancient Lit.; and Medieval Texts. He was somewhat surprised to find that adjacent to these were shelves labelled Psychology & Therapy, which held, among other works, the writings of Sigmund Freud.

Though he had sufficiently warmed himself by this time, Theo Hoshen was not yet ready to leave. And then he had an idea. After confirming that there was indeed no one in the store other than himself and the man behind the counter, and his eyes were still buried in a book, Theo Hoshen reached for the ring in his pocket. *No cracks,* he told himself. *Just to sense.* He slipped it on. It took

immediate effect
allowed him to sense
along the passage
then down upon himself

the bright glow
still there from his inhaling
on the rock of light
of the dome

what
would he do with it

and then
he sensed about
at all the swimming books
swirls off in their wake
so many beauties
brights
and how some did glow
the literature shelves
contained small suns
clamorous in the turbulence

it was then that he noticed
the largest division in the store
an arrangement neither
alphabetical categorical
nor chronological

for here was the fiction
glowing bright and loud
driving a violent turbulence
amidst

and there was the nonfiction
glowing faint but humming loud
swimming along the flow

strange that some among the literature
shelves were unlit
he reached for one
and found a book of criticism

strange that the freuds in psychology
shined like starbursts
so much that he had to squint

alas for the dark economics shelves
how silent he stood
economic man
of course
history glowed little
though it flowed with a strong hum
at times the harmony
tempted him to cast off in its drift

but then philosophy shocked
with its brilliant lights
so bright he had to shut his eyes

stunned
it caught his breath

he looked for his master
whose works glowed
that he could hardly see

and then
for his teacher before him
who shone even brighter
as if his works had set themselves on fire

and then down
to a mounting
flashing derrida
on
and off
on and off
with a big Crack in the middle

and then over
amidst all that light
to a dim but loudly humming
flowing warmth
sources of the self
he trembled
and reached for it
opened the preface
to hear of how those bored by history
should read nothing else

his stomach was tight now
as he turned to the final page
to read of the dilemma of mutilation
of how it could be surmounted with hope

the book was returned
and he squinted to reach up
to one by his master
glowing so that he had to jut his hand
through its raging currents
it was far too bright to open

he returned it with a defiant shout

as if that would be enough
to wed athens and jerusalem

it was then that he slid to the floor
to his knees
and cried

CHAPTER XLII

*In which two friends reunite, and a great exchange
ensues*

Theo Hoshen removed the ring from his finger. Though deeply shaken, he found to his amazement that he now had a sense of mission, as well as a question: how to realize it?

Then, as he exited the bookstore, who should he hear calling his name but Carl. His friend had just arrived by bus from Niagara Falls (indeed his clothes were still somewhat damp). He, too, was making his way home.

"Theo!" Carl yelled. "Theo!"

"Carl!" replied the young philosopher. And the two gave each other the warmest of hugs.

"I've been looking for you, buddy," said Carl. "It's good to see you, bruises and all."

"Yes," was all that Theo Hoshen could say.

"Hey, where's your coat? C'mon, let's get inside somewhere to warm up and chat. Green Room?"

"Yes," concurred Theo Hoshen. "Though I should say that it may be the last quiet talk that we shall ever have."

"What are you talking about?" wondered Carl. But Theo

Hoshen said nothing more. And so the reunited pair made their way along the nearby back alley that took them to the relatively hidden pub known as the Green Room. Once inside, they did not have to wait long before a waitress approached to take their order.

"Beer?" joked Carl as he looked at Theo Hoshen. "What, afraid you'll get drunk?" he added with a wink. And then, turning to the waitress, he declared: "He can drink a case and still be on his feet."

"Just a coffee, please," said Theo Hoshen. "Hot."

"Make that two," added Carl.

Once the waitress left, there was a moment of awkward silence. Then Carl finally spoke:

"Theo, I have to show you something."

"Okay."

Carl rose and stood beside his friend. "Give me your hand," he said, and when Theo Hoshen did so Carl took it and placed it on the right side of his chest. "Not sure if you can feel it, but trust me, it's there."

"I see," said Theo Hoshen with a smile.

"I went through. I was looking for you," explained Carl. "I'm really worried, Theo. I'm your friend, right?"

"A great friend," confirmed Theo Hoshen. "Much better than I could ever be."

"Theo, what's going on? What have you been doing?"

"It is rather hard to explain."

"Well what are you planning to do?"

"I did not know but I do now."

"What does that mean?"

"Only that while you continue before the gates, Carl, I have managed to open them."

"Well that really clears things up."

"All I mean to say is that we are on different paths."

"No kidding. Listen, Theo, I haven't been looking for you because you broke out. That's your business. I'm just afraid of what you'll do – with the ring, I mean."

"Such as what?"

"I don't know. Something bad, something dangerous. You're not planning to take revenge out on the system, are you? I'm worried that someone could get hurt."

"You have no reason to fear, Carl. For I am no longer interested in revenge. Indeed, I hereby leave all such antique gems, all honours of the good life, to you. For my aim is glory instead."

"I don't get it."

"Always trying to understand. Even though some things cannot be understood."

"C'mon, Theo."

"I can say that, after a time, I realized that I needed to do something grand. And now I think I know what that is."

"And what is it? Jeez, Theo, this conversation's like pulling teeth!"

"But it is not a conversation, is it? For that, Carl, as you once quite rightly pointed out to me, both interlocutors must be willing to listen. Yet I am not so willing – I never have been. Which only stands to reason, since glory comes strictly to those armed with grace."

Of course, Carl did not know how to respond. But then the waitress arrived with their coffees and so they both held their tongues until she left.

"Theo, I'm waiting for an explanation."

"Well I have decided to stop waiting and force power into the laws."

"What?"

"There shall be neither detections nor defections, Carl. No one will be up against the wall any longer. Nor shall there be any need for taking plates or guns."

"You've really lost me," said an exasperated Carl.

"It is really quite simple. I have learned that I am not really a lover of wisdom, of reason, after all. Not like you are, Carl. That is why she did not answer me, for she knows I follow Apollo instead."

"Who?"

"All I am saying is that, unlike you, mine was only ever a degraded form of honour. My real quest is for something higher; hence my attraction to adversity, for it is the best means of making cracks, of tearing holes in the water to invite in the light. That is why I am no longer willing to accept being ignored, Carl. But do not fear, for in empowering the world I shall be making it safe for reconcilers like you, for dialogue and honour at its best. Most either flee or fight its harshness, indeed often both; well I shall teach them, the stoners, including William, and the warriors. I shall teach them to be really free, you see. For madness to end we need more than dancing, Carl, serious dancing. But no one will be hurt since, despite the cracks between the world and the other domains, it itself remains one."

It goes without saying that Carl still had no idea what Theo Hoshen was conveying to him. Not that this was something without precedent, of course, although it was the first time, or perhaps the second, that Carl had began truly to doubt his friend's sanity.

"And to bring its unity forth," Theo Hoshen continued, "the world must see that we no longer have the luxury to make laws unloved by the citizenry. The laws must be empowered rather than enforced, Carl, and this means that the police must be made obsolete."

"The ring – you're going to use the ring for this?"

"Not as a mere tool, for that is Simon's way and, though he himself still does not know it, it would take us all directly to the wasteland. No, I shall be opening a new path. That is why I need to go on far ahead, so far that even you shall be unable to hear me. Yet is this not as it is meant to be? For real heroes never turn around. I am a friend, Carl, who if he does not kill at least wounds for life."

"Theo –"

"Nonetheless," Theo Hoshen went on, "you will be glad to hear that I shall be calling upon one of your peoples – our peoples – to lead the revolution. Yes, finally, that most self-ignorant and innocuous of nations, the Canuck nation, will be freed from itself and become chosen. Because it really is no dream – if you will it." And with that an increasingly excited Theo Hoshen shot up to his feet.

"Okay, Theo, just take it easy," entreated Carl, trying to waive his friend back down to his chair. "C'mon man," he implored, "just sit."

"No! You cannot convince me to stop; in fact, you cannot convince me of anything. All you can do is make the world a better place so that others will not choose my path out of a need to escape suffering. Just now, in the bookstore, it struck me that Tom Thomson is right: we really do need pistols rather than wisdom if there is to be a new renaissance. And so, my friend, I say goodbye to you, and God help us." And with that, Theo Hoshen turned and simply walked away.

"Theo! Theo!" shouted a desperate Carl after him. But the young man did not stop. In great haste, Carl managed to find just enough change for the coffees, whereupon he gave chase. But once outside he realized immediately that his friend had disappeared.

Theo, sighed Carl to himself. *You said God would have nothing to do with it.*

CHAPTER XLIII

Wherein Theo Hoshen sets out to perform his grand act

Removing the ring as he walked, Theo Hoshen evidently still cared not a whit about being seen. He was once again making his way along Bloor Street, albeit now much more briskly than before. For he knew precisely what needed to be done. The revelation was accompanied by no small amount of trepidation, however, because Theo Hoshen was not at all sure that what he had said to Carl was right: would fulfilling his vision really mean that no one would have to be hurt? Could he trust in the light, in the unity of the world? Yet he quickly banished these and other such worries from his mind. He had a task ahead of him, that much he knew. So on he marched, as quickly as possible.

He was now headed in the direction of the university. Having had enough of the cold, however, and having spotted a used clothing store along the way, he went inside. It was not long before he found a garment to his liking, a large cloak that resembled a philosopher's *tribon*. So he slipped on the ring

took it
the cloak
and himself

into the nearest crack
still he placed forty dollars
onto the counter
wondering
for soon there would be no point

outside again
he walked

and removed the ring right in front of a startled pedestrian. Ignoring her, he continued along until he reached St. George Street, whereupon he turned south onto the university campus. In no time at all he had reached his destination: the Stewart's Observatory Building, which was, of course, none other than the home of Carl's SAC.

He marched directly inside, passing the main lobby with its lone secretary who had no good excuse for failing to notice him. He turned right and went straight into the little office at the end of the short corridor, the one with the stairs going up. His destination was the room at the top of the tower, the one capped with the dome that the engineers' Brute Force Committee enjoyed painting with a farcical design every year. Once, Carl had taken Theo Hoshen up there when they needed to discuss something in private and, while inside, the latter had not failed to notice the numerous empty boxes strewn about the room. Some of them had surely been there for years. What an excellent hiding place he had thought to himself at the time.

Reaching those boxes now, he rummaged about for one in particular and, once located, opened it with relish to find another box inside. He had put it there himself not so long ago and it contained two important items: the Chief Attiliator's hardhat – and the Cannon. Theo Hoshen looked about again to confirm that he was indeed alone.

Outside now, with the hardhat upon his head and the box with the Cannon tucked under an arm, he made his way along Hart House Circle and then over the dangerous crossing at Queen's Park Crescent (for only by running quickly could a pedestrian be assured of making it to the other side). Then it was across the park and on to Yonge Street where, after a backward glance to ensure that he was not being followed, he began to march south.

There was one stop to make before his final destination. He came upon it soon enough: a jewellery store. Theo Hoshen then passed his eyes along the sidewalk and, the moment he determined that no one was looking his way, he slipped on the ring

> folded into
> the nearest Crack and
> unseen
> unseeable
> took the passage
> into the store
>
> then through a Crack
> came his hand
> opening the counter cabinet
> reaching inside
>
> scooping the gold rings up
> dropping them in the hardhat
> mister klancy said the customer
> marty said the lying salesman
> but neither caught a thing
> as theo hoshen filled the hardhat
> and was gone

on then
until the blow struck him

down to his knees
the second time that day

he dropped the box
as he fell
but held up the hat
as he pained
it took his breath away

he sensed up and around
at the watery figure there
and the others behind
and the next blow
that was coming

so he feinted back
and sent the swinger over the edge
down to the ground
who
how
but there was no time
if he was to lose some time
to gain some time
nor was there an escape Crack
as the others approached
so he yelled out
a merritt jewel
of how the blind find
it never too dark to travel

it did the trick
rainbowing a   Crack
just the right size

so he grabbed the box
folded in
and was away
invisible to the others
unstoppable to all

pocketing

the ring, he set out as quickly as he could for his destination,
down Yonge Street. Under one arm he held the box; with his
other he pressed the Chief Attiliator's hardhat against his chest.
There was much jingling because of the many gold rings still
inside.

He turned west upon reaching Queen Street and it was not
long before he lifted up his eyes to see that he had arrived:
Nathan Phillips Square, the plaza that forms the forecourt to
the City Hall. This was the site of many public gatherings,
including one that saw University of Toronto engineering
frosh during orientation week every September. There they
were led by their seniors and ordered to soak themselves
thoroughly by traipsing through the waters of the square's
large reflecting pool and fountain.

Theo Hoshen had not come to do any traipsing, however;
at any rate, the pool was now an ice rink. Above it spanned the
three concrete arches that had recently been named The Freedom Arches. He spotted an empty bench near the first one and
made his way to it. Then, seated, he looked over at the rink. It
was covered with a hundred or more gleeful skaters: men,
women and children, friends and family that had chosen to
spend their afternoon together on the ice. He heard a loud

engine starting up and could see the Zamboni ice resurfacer emerging from its garage. It was slowly making its way towards the rink. The skaters would soon be forced off the ice. There was little time to waste.

Quickly, he spotted a hot dog pushcart, rushed to it and purchased a bottle of water. Then he ran back to the bench and, placing his precious box to one side and the hardhat filled with rings to the other, he opened the bottle and poured its contents into the latter. Then he removed the Gyges ring from his pocket and dropped it inside with the others. It was not long before steam rose from his new batch of gold ring soup. He wondered how much time he needed to wait but, unable to do so, he stuck in a hand and

> sensed that
> yes
> they were all now
> doors to the flow
> invitations
> to never ending moments
>
> all
> gyges rings
>
> then he sensed
> the large   Crack
> above the   centre of the rink
> and he   hoped for a light
> and asked if   it was sending
> for that was the promise of unity
> was it not
>
> but nothing came of Nothing

and so he asked again

nothing
still he knew
just knew
that he would not bring
real terror

withdrawing
his hand from the hardhat of rings, he thought: *This must all be but show for those eyes, those peering faces; so it does not matter. I must conquer everything to get it back for real.*

The Zamboni was coming. And so, looking away, especially from the many children, Theo Hoshen quickly removed the Cannon from its box and placed it upon the ground. Then he took the book of matches and the container of gun powder that always travelled with it. Was he really going to act? *Yes,* he thought. *These hands, this bomb, they only seem dirty.*

So he loaded up the Cannon. First, the gun powder. Then, as many rings as he could manage to shove into the barrel. Quite a few did not make it inside but fell upon the ground instead. Theo Hoshen paid them no mind. And standing up now, he hurried to place the Cannon down on the bench facing the rink.

That was when he noticed the two security guards rapidly approaching. He hesitated. *I'm no knight of faith*, he admitted to himself, whereupon he lifted up his eyes and looked at where he had sensed the crack. "Here I am," he pleaded silently, as almost every artist had before him. Still there was nothing. Then he stretched forth his hand and lit a match – only to hesitate again.

It was then that the light struck him. He could not sense it, of course. But he just knew that it had burst forth from the crack above, that its glowing whiteness had shot directly into his lungs. *Thank God*, he thought. Exhaling in relief, he gave a loud shout and waved his arms about so that everyone on the ice would notice him. Few understood what he was up to but when he, a lit match in hand, walked around the bench and bent over the Cannon from the other side there was not a soul within view who failed to guess what would come next. Yet still no one moved, for they could not quite believe what was happening. So did Theo Hoshen, inspired by the light, begin to shout:

"C'mon everybody let's go!" As he did so he waved his free hand vigorously in front of him, motioning everyone to move well out of the way – out of the line of fire, that is. This time it did not take them long to do so. But he found that he had to light another match. And there was so little time; soon the guards would be upon him.

With a cry of "And I will create you!" Theo Hoshen managed to lower a newly lit match to the hole at the back of the barrel. There was a flash and the loudest of bangs. The Cannon shot backwards into a snow bank. The Gyges rings flew across the ice in a wide arc.

For a moment, everyone was stunned. Then Theo Hoshen yelled again:

"C'mon everybody let's go!" Many of the skaters hastened away to the benches. But others remained on the ice, attracted by the flashes of gold from the rings now scattered around the rink. When he saw them bending over gingerly to examine those rings, Theo Hoshen knew that his task was complete. For it would not be long before there were more rings, and more. So did he, not a moment before the guards managed to reach him, bend over and grab one for himself. Then he smiled the broadest of smiles, leapt into the air, and

Publisher Information

rowanvale books

Rowanvale Books provides publishing services to independent authors, writers and poets all over the globe. We deliver a personal, honest and efficient service that allows authors to see their work published, while remaining in control of the process and retaining their creativity. By making publishing services available to authors in a cost-effective and ethical way, we at Rowanvale Books hope to ensure that the local, national and international community benefits from a steady stream of good quality literature.

For more information about us, our authors or our publications, please get in touch.

www.rowanvalebooks.com
info@rowanvalebooks.com